2-80

GIDEON PLANISH

Gideon Planish

A NOVEL BY

Sinclair Lewis

RANDOM HOUSE · NEW YORK

FIRST PRINTING

No character and no organization in this story is drawn from any actual person or group of persons.

Acknowledgment is here made for permission to reprint on page 104 four lines from the song "In the Good Old Summer Time," copyright, 1902, by Howley Haviland & Dresser, copyright renewed, 1929, by Edward B. Marks Music Co.

To

MARCELLA POWERS

*who explained Carrie
Planish and her friends
to me*

GIDEON PLANISH

1

THE URGENT WHISTLE of the Manhattan Flyer woke the boy, and his square face moved with smiling as in half-dreams he was certain that some day he would take that train and be welcomed in lofty rooms by millionaires and poets and actresses. He would be one of them, and much admired.

His present state, at the age of ten, in 1902, was well enough. His father was not only a veterinarian but a taxidermist, a man who had not done so badly in a city like this—for Vulcan, with its population of 38,000, was the seventh city in the great State of Winnemac. The Planishes' red-brick house, too, was one of the most decorated in that whole row on Sycamore Terrace, and they had a telephone and a leather-bound set of the *Encyclopedia Americana*. A cultured and enterprising household, altogether. But as the small Gideon Planish heard the enticing train, he was certain that he was going far beyond eagle-stuffing and the treatment of water-spaniels' indigestion.

He would be a senator or a popular minister, something rotund and oratorical, and he would make audiences of two and three hundred people listen while he shot off red-hot adjectives about Liberty and Plymouth Rock.

But even as the boy was smiling, the last whistle of the

train, coming across the swamps and outlying factory yards, was so lost and lonely that he fell back into his habitual doubt of himself and of his rhetorical genius; and that small square face tightened now, with the anxiety and compromise of the prophet who wants both divine sanction and a diet much spicier than locusts and wild honey.

Gid already felt a little dizzy on the path that mounted high above his father's business of embalming hoot-owls. He could feel a forecast of regret that life was going to yank him up to greatness and mountain-sickness.

Into the office of the dean of Adelbert College hastened a chunky young man with hair like a tortoise-shell cat. He glared down at the astonished dean, upraised a sturdy arm like a traffic officer, and bellowed:

" 'If they dare to come out in the open field and defend the gold standard as a good thing, we will fight them to the uttermost!' Huh?"

"Yes, yes," the dean said, soothingly. He was an aging man and a careful scholar, for Adelbert was a respectable small Presbyterian college. And he was used to freshmen. But Gid Planish was furiously going on:

" 'Having behind us the producing masses of this nation and the world, supported by the industrial interests——' "

The dean interrupted, "It's 'commercial interests,' not 'industrial interests.' If you must quote William Jennings Bryan, do be accurate, my young friend."

Gid looked pained. Through all of his long and ambitious life—he was now eighteen—he had been oppressed by just such cynical misunderstanding. But he knew the

[4]

Bryan speech clear to the end, and he was a natural public leader, who never wasted any information that he possessed. He roared on:

" '——supported by the commercial interests, the laboring interests, and the toilers everywhere, we will answer their demand for a gold standard by saying to them: "You shall not press down upon the brow of labor this crown of thorns, you shall not crucify mankind upon a cross of gold," ' and look, Dean, I got to take Forensics and Extempore Speaking, I got to, that's what I came to Adelbert for, and I asked the prof——"

"The professor."

"Yuh, I asked the prof, and he said freshmen can't take Forensics, but I got to take it."

"Don't you think that Freshman Rhetoric and a nice course of Freshman English, Wordsworth and the daffodils, would satisfy you?"

"No, sir. I guess maybe it sounds highfalutin, but I got a kind of Message to deliver."

"And what is your message?"

Gid looked out at the waiting-room. No one was there but the dean's secretary. He insisted, mounting on his own eloquence:

"It seems to me, what this country needs is young men in politics that have higher standards of honesty and more profound knowledge of history and, uh, well, of civics than the politicians of today, and who will advance the unfinished work lying before us of leading this country to, uh, higher standards of Freedom, Liberty, Equality,

Fraternity, Freedom, and—well, I mean higher standards of——"

"Of Democracy."

"That's it. Of Democracy. So you see I *got* to take Forensics."

"How do you spell Forensics, young man?"

"I guess it's f-o-r-e-n-s-i-k-s. Can I take it?"

"No."

"What did you say, sir?"

"I said 'no'."

"You mean I can't take Forensics?"

"No."

Gid felt confused. This business of preparing to lead the masses seemed to be going around in circles. And he was aware that a fellow freshman, but a thin, tall, un-idealistic and devilish kind of freshman, had entered the waiting-room, and was listening. Gid urged, more softly:

"I was the star on the debating team at Lincoln High, in Vulcan, and that's the fifth biggest high school in the State."

"No. It is a rule. Public Speaking is reserved for upper-classmen."

"And we debated with the Webster High team from Monarch on 'Resolved: Flying-machines will never be useful in war,' and we won."

"My young friend, your fervor is admirable, and so——"

"I can take it? Forensics? Bully!"

"You can not! Please—go—away."

Gid went away, a little bewildered, as later in life he

was so often to be bewildered by the world's inappreciation of people who want to help it.

The thin devil of a classmate leered at him as he crossed the waiting-room.

At Doc's Bar-B-Q Lunch, Gid was taking refreshment, this late afternoon of his second day at Adelbert College. To his disillusionment was added the stress of choosing between two fraternities, the Philamathean Club and Tiger Head. Meantime he lived at Mrs. Jones's and endangered the nice fresh digestion that the son of a veterinarian ought to have by dining at Doc's on hamburger sandwiches and pickles.

Next to the broad-armed chair which was also his dining-table he found the lean devil whom he had seen in the dean's office.

"How you makin' out?" said the devil.

"Oh, all right, I guess."

"Did you get in on the public-speaking course?"

"No, damn it."

"Why don't you try for the debating team?"

"Gosh, I've tried to try already. I went and saw the captain, and he told me you can't get on the team till you're a sophomore. Gosh, I guess they don't *want* freshmen to be intellectual and idealistic here! But I don't suppose you care a darn about that."

"What makes you think so?"

"You look so—— Say, what do they call you?"

"Hatch Hewitt, my name is."

"Gideon Planish, mine is."

"Pleasedmeecha."

"Pleasedmeecha."

"What makes you think, do I care can freshmen be idealistic in this dump, Mr. Planish?"

"Well, I'll tell you, Mr. Hewitt; it's because you look like you'd make fun of sentimentalists."

"Maybe I would, at that, Mr. Planish. But that's because I *am* an idealist."

"Is that a fact, Hatch! Well, well, is that a fact! Say, I'm tickled to death! It would knock you for a row of small cottages if you knew how few idealists I had to discuss things with, in a factory town like Vulcan."

"That's how it is even in Chicago."

"Chi-cago?" Gid was reverent. "Do you come from Chicago?"

"Um-huh."

"Gosh! What do you want with a half-sized place like this, then?"

"Low tuition."

"Wouldn't I like to see Chicago! Holy mackerel! I hear where there's an auditorium there that seats six thousand people. Imagine seeing a gang like that stretching out before you! And I hear where there's a big women's suffrage organization. That's a very fine cause. Women had ought to have the vote, don't you think so? Don't you think we had ought to have women for their moral effect in the purification of politics?"

"That isn't exactly my idea of what I want 'em for."

"I thought you said you were an idealist, Hatch!"

[8]

"I guess maybe I'm an idealist *against*. I hate all this fakery. I hate these rich women bossing clerks in department stores, and these fat boys with cigars in the corner of their mouths, like elongated warts, and I hate books like this Mrs. Barclay's *The Rosary*, that they say is selling by the hundred thousand. See how I mean?"

"Me, I don't hate things so much—only it does kind of make me mad when I hear about little kids working in cotton mills. But I'm on the positive side, you might say. I want to kind of, you might say, rouse people to the idea this nation, under God, shall have a new birth of freedom. I s'pose you think that's sentimental!"

"No—no! Only, I just wish people wouldn't quote Lincoln or the Bible, or hang out the flag or the cross, to cover up something that belongs more to the bank-book and the three golden balls. But I envy you. I wish I could trust human enthusiasm. But I come from across the tracks. My dad was an awful smart drayman and he could sing Harry Lauder songs and he was a good union man, but my God, did he lap up the licker! I went to work as a Western Union messenger at twelve—one Christmas Eve I worked at the joyous Noel business till four A.M.—and I wound up in the South Chicago bureau of the *Chronicle*."

"Gosh! A re-porter?"

"Yuh. But I'm a lot older than you are. God, I'm twenty-one!"

They both sighed at that senility, and Hatch went on:

"I got what education I could reading at the branch library. I don't think so much of colleges, but maybe I can learn some economics here, and some vocabulary besides 'holocaust' and 'suspended sentence'."

"Maybe you and I can do something in politics together, some time."

Gid felt exultantly that perhaps he had, for the first time in his life, a Friend.

He was a tail-wagging pup, and in high school he had always been member of some respectable gang, but it had been only of baseball, fudge, dances and swimming that he had been able to talk, while deeply he desired a Real Friend, to whom he could confide his intentions toward eloquence and justice and How to Get into the Legislature. He was jarred now when Hatch Hewitt shook his head, and droned:

"No politics—no spieling. I'm a reporter. I do like Swinburne, though—nice, smooth, slippery, marble words."

"My ideal is Bryan. But I guess maybe you think Bryan does a lot of spouting."

"He loves dogs and mothers."

"What's the matter with loving dogs and mothers?"

"I don't know. I never had either. Probably I'm just jealous of you, Gid. Maybe I wish I could hypnotize audiences too. Go to it! Sock em! I'll write a speech for you, now and then."

"You bet, Hatch! We'll do that!"

So he did have the friend. But he did not intend to let even a Hatch Hewitt write his speeches. Himself, he might not be so doggone poetic, but he didn't guess even a big journalist like Hatch could turn out anything better than his own salutatory in Vulcan:

[10]

"The fruits of the seven seas and the fruits of our broad fields from the legendary East to the broad-bosomed West have been garnered together by our illustrious princes of transportation and who have lent themselves to enlightened barter not to merely expand their own princely fortunes, so helpful, however, in benefactions to colleges and hospitals, but first and foremost to fill the hungry mouths of the clamoring multitude."

Beat *that?*

Hatch hinted, "Let's get out of here. C'mon over to my room. I got an idea, and I don't want all these dopes listening."

Indeed the small lunchroom, with its faded green tin ceiling, its faded blue plaster walls, its gallery of posters advertising gum, was filling with young men yelping, "Hey, Bill!" and "Say, is this History of Art stuff a gut course?" and the place smelled now of ham and cabbage and fried onions. As Gid wandered out with Hatch Hewitt, he resembled a plump spaniel trotting beside a wolf hound. Yet it was Gid, the comparatively prosperous, who was fashionably sloppy and collegiate, in shaggy blue woolen sweater and corduroys and thick brogans; Hatch who was fussily neat in the cheap gray suit, the plain white shirt, the cautious blue bow tie, that he was to wear for four years to come.

Hatch's room was a stable, Gid romantically found; an old small stable built for a team of inconsiderable horses, leaning and shaky, with hayseed caked about the windows. But it was as orderly as a widow's tea-room: a cot-bed in one stall, and in the other an old wood-stove and a wooden table with a dozen exactly arranged books.

"I do my own cooking here and just go to Doc's barbecue for a cup of coffee and company. With what I've saved, and a syndicate of papers for college news that I'm working up, I'll get through," said Hatch. "But this dump must look pretty messy."

"It's grand! It's Bohemian! Vie de Bohemia!"

"I hate Bohemians."

"Oh!"

"I like order and precision."

"Oh, you do!" Gid was not too meek about it.

"You—I suppose you have a handsome apartment, with a fumed-oak Morris chair."

"I have not! I just got a stuffy room in a boarding-house till I find out which frat I'll choose."

"So you're going to be a Greek—to join a select young gentlemen's social club."

"Why not?" Gid was admirably angry now; he was not much afraid of other people, only of himself. "I'm a social young gent myself. Just too bad you don't like it!"

"Oh, I didn't mean——"

"You have such a hell of a time admiring yourself as a hater, and I'm expected to sit at your feet——"

"No, no, Gid! I guess I just have mental sour stomach. You're okay. You're not content with this dumb world, the way it is, either—you're not mediocre. I don't think you are. Forgive me."

So did Gid find his first friend, and they sat at the table drinking Hatch's privately brewed coffee—very thin and bitter—while Hatch glanced up at the small high window of the stable to make sure the Secret Service wasn't listening, and admitted his perilous secret.

"Gid, if you can't get into the debating club, why don't you—— I'm going to start a Socialist Society."

"What? But socialism is against the home and marriage!"

"What of it?"

"Of course there's Gene Debs."

"Exactly."

"I hear he's a grand guy."

"Exactly. And we'll have a lot of debates, and you can be in 'em. Maybe we'll challenge the entire college to a debate."

"That would be swell. I'd like to show up those galoots that wouldn't take me in! I sure would! When do you start your society?"

"It's just started this minute. It only takes two fearless guys like me and you to unsettle one little college."

"Let's go!"

That was the entire struggle involved in the conversion of Gideon Planish to socialism. His deconversion was to take longer, a little longer.

A train was whistling, and Gideon Planish was lying awake.

He remembered that he had a friend now, not just a companion to go walking with. Between his brains and Hatch Hewitt's imagination, there was nothing they might not do. Probably he would never really be President of the United States, but if he ever were, it would be a pleasure to appoint Hatch Secretary of State—or anyway, postmaster at Zenith.

But of course they must think first not of such glories but of the good they could do.

Before the train had ceased its piping, he had built a glass and marble hospital in every village in America, he had Christianized China, he had stopped all wars forever by courts of arbitration, he had given the vote to women —and they had been very grateful. He remembered the co-ed in the tight blouse whom he had noticed in front of the Library, and he forgot his imperial benignity.

2

THE FIRST MEETING of the Adelbert College Socialist League, with all five members present, was held in Hatch's stable home. It was felt that it would be dangerous to meet in the libidinous atmosphere of Tiger Head fraternity, where Gid Planish, as a newly elected member, had a bed, a bureau, two chairs and a portrait of Longfellow.

College had been coursing on its wild hunt of culture for two weeks, and it was now September 20, 1910. In those days, Adelbert opened during the first week in September, and how innocent and medieval the whole system was may be seen in the fact that students came by train instead of in their private automobiles.

The five Socialists, in their awe at saving the world, gave up clogging and all the kittenishness that was then considered proper to freshmen. They sat about Hatch's table on two chairs and three boxes: Hatch, Gid, young Francis Tyne, who was going to study for the ministry, an iron-faced older man who had once been a labor organizer, and David Traub, a handsome, precise lad from New York, forerunner of the eager and rather heroic caravan who were later to escape from too much racial discussion in New York, and emigrate like their fathers.

Francis Tyne was a thin, earnest youth with a biggish head and fine colorless hair. He suggested their calling one another "Comrade," but it didn't go. Gid and Hatch were still too close to the horrors of being called "Brother" by loud evangelical pastors.

Gid looked them all over like a born chairman. Back in Limbo, before he was born, he must have presided over committees of the Young Cherubim's Anti-Birth-Control Association. He said merrily, "We don't seem to have any girls with us. We certainly ought to, these days."

"Rot!" said the ex-labor organizer. He was a solid man, named Lou Klock.

"Why?" demanded Francis.

Klock growled, "Women are useful in all left-wing movements—addressing factory rallies and addressing envelopes—but give 'em a chance on the strategy and they'll have you wearing red neckties and dancing on the green, instead of pounding the bosses for higher wages."

"Wait now!" beamed Gid, with the conciliatory good-fellowship of the professional presider. "This ain't 1890, Lou. No! This is 1910! The revolution has been won, except for a few details. War is finished, except as an instrument of protest, and women are recognized by all thinkers as our equals—practically."

"Rot," said Lou.

"Well, let that pass, for the moment. Frank Tyne, Comrade Tyne here, has an outline of what he thinks we ought to do, and I vote we hear from him."

Hatch Hewitt suggested, "By the way, don't you suppose it might be a good idea if we elected a chairman?"

Gid felt pained and ill-used, for it had not occurred to him that anybody save Gideon Planish could be chairman. His hard-won glory was already being questioned, and that by the one man whom he had these many years trusted as his friend and partisan. Somebody snickered—probably Lou Klock—and all his life, however brave and impassioned before an audience that hated him gravely, Gid would always feel watery in the backs of his knees when anybody jeered.

David Traub snapped, "Don't be silly, Hewitt. Of course Planish is our chairman. Or do *you* want to be?"

"Oh, no, no!"

"Then he's the goat."

Gid blossomed with glory. He commanded, "Go to it, Frank. Let's hear your plan."

Francis Tyne produced a pack of small filing cards, dark with tiny notations. It was his moment. For years, in his Sunday-school classes, in a village where it was not kosher to admit any doctrine more subversive than that women might with decency become rural mail-carriers, he had pictured just this hour, when he should be banded with desperate but talented comrades. He looked up from his notes with the eyes of a cocker spaniel, and Gid's tender heart was touched and he was ready to go right off and build a barricade with Francis, provided it should be finished in time for supper.

"Well, it's really awfully simple and reasonable, but I suppose there will be objection to my program in privileged classes," said Francis. "First, of course, the Government has to take over the ownership of all mines, water-power, agricultural land, and all industries employing more than a hundred people."

None of them looked worried, and the newly converted collectivist, Gid Planish, definitely glowed.

"But I don't think that's enough, Comrades. There's a lot of these foreign and European Socialists who go that far," said Francis. "What would make a peculiarly American socialism would be to have a state church."

"What?" shouted the others, while David Traub proposed, "How about the Jewish faith?"

Francis protested, "No, no, Comrade Traub. You don't understand these things. Our Savior started an entirely new dispensation. But about the set-up of a true revolutionary church: of course the Catholic Church and Christian Science and the Mormons are out, and the Baptists are pretty doggone super—supererogatory with their immersion, and it's against Scripture to have bishops, like in the Methodist and Episcopal, and the Congregationalists come awful close to verging on heresy and wishy-washiness, and so it seems to me the true American model is the Presbyterian Church—which happens to be my own, but merely by coincidence."

"Say, what is all this wordage about?" said Klock.

"God knows—maybe," said Hewitt.

"Now wait! I never thought of it in that light, but he's absolutely sound. I'm a Presbyterian, too!" said Gid.

All of them were young—even Lou Klock was but twenty-six—and in the ardent next two hours it was variously stated that:

[18]

Christianity is exhausted and a failure.

Christianity has never yet been given a chance.

The church is the trap wherein the Capitalist class nabs the workers.

The church is the one union wherein all workers can defy the heathenism of the Capitalists.

The Russians will have socialism first.

The Russians are lazy; they drink tea and read novels, and never will have socialism.

Adelbert College is in a class with Abraham Lincoln, science, football and the Packard car.

Adelbert College is snobbish and hasn't had a new idea since 1882.

With each of these opinions, Gid voluptuously agreed. He felt that they were having a fine, free, enlightening time, but at last he pounded the table, with Hatch's dollar watch, and announced, "We're beginning to see light in this discussion. It's a sure-enough round table, all right. But before we try and go any further, it's time to organize. We got to decide on just who will map out each department of our activities."

"That makes sense," said Hatch.

Francis begged, "Oh, not yet! Let's spend a month or so searching each other's minds and sort of inspiring each other."

As a professional, Gid was horrified. "You mean go on chewing the rag about all these mighty topics without *or*-gan-iz-ing?"

"Why, yes. The natural form of organization must grow out of what we think and then decide to do."

Gid explained, with great sweetness and reasonable-ness:

"Never! The kind of organization you set up, and who's on the committees, decide what you can do, and what you do determines what you think. Honest, that's the straight goods; that's modern psychology. I know by ex-perience. You bet." The veteran nodded sagely. "That's the way I've seen it work, for many years now—ever since the Sixth Grade. We started in to collect litter on the school grounds, but do you know, we had such an active organization that we improved the whole basic idea, and turned it into a co-operative revolving fund to buy mo-lasses popcorn. Yessir! And how can we raise money unless we have the right organization—fearless but flexi-ble?"

"What do we want to raise money for?" they protested.

"So we can send out letters and do publicity and get more members."

Hatch suggested, "Then when we get more members, we can raise more money so we can get still more mem-bers?"

"Why, certainly! And then when we get a *lot* of money, we can put on a real campaign and get a whole *lot* of members! That's what organization is. That's how you progress, in *this* ole world!"

David Traub complained, "I don't see that. If you want to promote some reform, and not get all tangled up in jealousy and politics, you want to avoid organizing for the sake of organizing."

"Oh, I agree with you, heartily," said Gid.

Some time during the evening there was an election of officers. Gid had assumed that he would be president.

He was president. Not only that, but, without the least hesitation, he made an inaugural address:

However much they might disagree upon minor details, such as the value of Christianity and of women, they stood shoulder to shoulder, through fire and obloquy, an army small but determined, invincible in their loyalty as in their enfranchised intellects and their common determination to throw off their chains, a force to make the blind monster of Capitalism look up from its prey in terror, denouncing unsparingly the capitalistic tyranny of Compulsory Latin and demanding lower prices on tennis balls at the Co-op.

He, their leader, would retire for meditation and consolidate his plans. They must not Breathe a Word. It would take some time to win over the entire student body and, though on principle he was opposed to Fabian tactics, it might be better to enlist the undergrads before lining up the faculty and the president—and particularly that damn dean—and giving them the choice of joining the revolution or resigning. As to immediate strategy, they must decide whether their next step should be a mass meeting in the college chapel, or the publication of a weekly magazine, illustrated, and including articles by Eugene V. Debs and George Bernard Shaw. He himself would be willing to write to Comrades Debs and Shaw and instruct them to shoot along the articles, quick. But whatever they did, they might now say that socialism had already triumphed at good ole Adelbert!

After this springing verbiage, Comrades Traub, Klock and Tyne filed out, looking dazed.

Gid fretted, "Hatch, do you suppose we can trust those dubs to keep our plot absolutely dark till we're ready to spring socialism on the world?"

"Gid, do you think that pikers like me ought to have even a vote? Does your sea-green radicalism go that far?"

"Oh, yes."

"What's your real plan? To turn this thing into a rival of the orthodox Debating Society?"

Gid brought out a smile that Hatch could not withstand. "I haven't any idea! What do you think we ought to pull, Hatch? Anyway, we got to get rid of Frank Tyne. Why, that goat would actually like to overthrow the Republican Party! But you're the brains in this gang. What shall we do with the League?"

"I'll think about it," said Hatch, in subjugation to a man whom he liked and envied and despised.

3

THE DEAN OF Adelbert College said feebly, "You again?" Gid's expression declared that they were old and helpful friends; that he was fond of this aged pal, and glad to give him new vigor and ideas.

"Yes, sir. I thought you ought to know that I have founded a secret Socialist club."

"Well?"

"I just thought, if it was forbidden to have revolutionary clubs, I'd better report it, so it would be okay. Gosh, I guess it must be awful unusual to have secret juntas in Adelbert!"

"No, not unusual; a little annoying, perhaps, but not unusual. Some years we have an anarchist club, and frequently a nihilist club or an atheist club, and once we had a nudist club—I really had to speak to the inaugurator of that one, a very nice young fellow who is now assistant rector of St. Dimity's, in Philadelphia. But with most subversive organizations, we don't do anything unless they parade in nightshirts or trample the shrubbery. But it is somewhat rare for the chief instigator to come in and inform us."

"Would you like me to wind up the club, Dean? I'd be glad to, if you'd let me in on the course in Forensics.

And in the circumstances, I guess I'd have to be taken into the debating society, too."

"Please—go—away!"

"Well, sir, you'll remember I warned you."

"Just let me know well beforehand any particularly destructive sabotage or direct action that you may plan. I wouldn't foresee them—my curious learnings are rather along theological and ichthyological lines. You'll let me know, won't you?"

"Oh, I couldn't do that, Dean. I have to be loyal to my gang. But I think I may say I have a lot of influence, and I'll see they don't perpetrate anything too dangerous. And if you'll just think over that Forensics course——"

"Please—go—away!"

Upon Gid's suggestion, the Socialist League challenged the college debating society to a discussion of the government ownership of railroads, and that official body accepted, with the notion of having a practice match before the classic annual contest with the great University of Winnemac.

Hatch Hewitt, who didn't really believe in government ownership of anything except congressional spittoons, and whose idea of socialism was that under it an enlightened young man could tell the city editor to go to the devil; Gid, who hadn't believed in government ownership until today; and Francis Tyne, who always had, sat together in the college library, garnering statistics about socialized railroads in Germany. In 1910 that country, under the enlightened and scholarly leadership of Kaiser William, was universally known to be the brightest nation in the world.

As he was often to do in his later career as a professional promoter of ideas, Gid nearly convinced himself of the truth of his own crusade. He was deciding to go out and nationalize all rails, he was beginning to believe he had invented collectivism, when the catastrophe struck them.

On October 2nd, they had the news that the plant of the Los Angeles *Times*, which had been warring with union labor, had been blown up, with nineteen deaths. And the Adelbert Socialist League blew up with it.

The League now had nine members. Most of them would have preferred to meet dramatically at Hatch's stable, in conspiratorial darkness, but they were up against reality. They weren't merely defying God and the House of Morgan now; they were in danger of getting demerits from the dean. The executive committee gathered in a corner of the Y.M.C.A. lounge at three o'clock on a bright afternoon.

Gid panted, "Meancometorder. Lissen, Comrades, I think we better get the hell out of this Socialist club, or turn it into a literary society."

"You're going to lay down and take it? You mean you don't dare to face the ruling class and defy 'em when there's something to defy 'em about?" demanded Hatch.

"Not at all! We'll call our literary society the Walt Whitman League. That's defiant enough for anybody!

[25]

Whitman never went to college!" explained Gid. "There's nobody wants to hammer tyranny more than I do, but this isn't the time for it."

All the rest of his life, in crises, Gideon Planish was to say, "But this isn't the time for it." It is the slogan of discreet Liberalism, as profound as St. Francis's "The beasts are my brothers," or Governor Alfred E. Smith's war-cry, "Slice it where you will, it's still baloney."

Hatch Hewitt was demanding, "Why isn't it the time for it?"

"Because there may be a chance that these labor agitators, the McNamara brothers, *did* blow up the *Times*."

"Impossible!" protested Hatch, while Lou Klock challenged, "And suppose they did? Wouldn't you guys still support them? Do you know what *war* is?" Unanswered, he walked out of the room, out of the Socialist League and, in a few weeks, out of Adelbert College.

Hatch reflected, "I don't agree with Lou—yet. But I see his idea. Now, Gid, you run to the dean again and tell him we've ducked for cover!" And he followed Lou out of the Y.M.C.A., while Gid wailed after him, "Me? Run to the dean? *Me?*"

That was the death of the Adelbert Socialist League, and for the funeral there were no hymns, no flowers, and only such exhibits of Christian resignation as were provided by Francis Tyne.

For a month Hatch looked at Gid with bleakness, and there were no intellectual gallops in his stableyard. But Hatch Hewitt was a lonely young man; he loved people

[26]

too much and he despised them too much to have long and casual friendships. When Lou Klock had gone and Dave Traub had wandered on to the University of Chicago, Hatch was left companionless, and by the end of their freshman year there had been restored between him and Gid a flinching amiability. They sneaked over to a neighboring city and drank beer and discussed the danger of war with Mexico.

"I don't think a country as big as what we are had ought to pick on a neighboring state," said Gid, the old Liberal.

"Is that a fact?" marveled Hatch.

On the day after the decease of the Socialist League, Gid sought out the secretary of the college debating society, reminded him that it had been announced on all bulletin boards that the society would debate with the Socialists, who had blown up the *Times* personally, and suggested that the only way out of such a perilous connection would be for the debating society to elect Gid a member. Then, he might possibly think about killing off and generally disowning the League.

The debating society met, in haste, changed its constitution so that freshmen might be admitted, elected Gid, and thanked him for something—they weren't quite sure what—that he had done to save Adelbertan oratory from shame. Late in the spring he was actually on the debating team which invaded and conquered Erasmus College; and the fame of Gideon Planish promised to be as firmly established in the glorious annals of the college as that of Old Pug, for eleven years the baseball mascot.

Erasmus College was in Eastern Ohio, and Gid had never been so far East—almost into New York State!

With his associate debaters, including a very large junior who sang grand opera in Dakotan, he traveled on a day coach to Erasmus. They had large stickers, "Adelbert Champion Debaters," on their suitcases, and they talked in enormous voices about taxation, to improve the minds of their fellow passengers.

They were met by a cheering crowd of nine, and put up at a fine hotel: twenty-two rooms, twenty-two pitchers, and twenty-two bowls. Gid had never before stayed at a hotel, except with his fussy father and mother, who kept telling him about the fire-escape. He had a room of his own, and he proudly raised the shade, felt the bed, as he had seen his mother do, demanded a luggage rack of the cynical bellboy, and unpacked the two shirts, the chemistry textbook and the shoeshine rag.

They were all dressing for the debate, in dark-blue suits —practically in evening clothes, felt Gid. He sat down to his debate notes, not very nervously. He might not be a William Jennings Bryan, but he had worked hard, he was full of earnestness, he had a great message for the student audience of Erasmus, and there was no reason to suppose that God wasn't enthusiastically with him.

They were entertained at dinner in the college, and when the Adelbert heroes came into the Erasmus Commons, very modestly, just one of them carrying a small banner lettered

Will in

the student body clapped their hands, all six hundred hands, and some of them threw bread in an affectionate way, while Gideon Planish tasted the fiery brandy of public greatness and just acclaim.

At the debate, in the college chapel, there wasn't as large a crowd as he had hoped; in fact, there were less than a hundred—in fact, there were less than seventy-five. The hosts explained that it just happened that there was also a basketball game tonight. But as Gid spoke, the crowd seemed to stretch out endless, and they were all his, all looking at him, all listening to him, and his power was on them.

For a moment he found it amusing that what he had to say was the opposite of what he would have said for the Socialist League. Then it was the truth, and the only truth, and he had invented it. He maintained that the government ownership of railroads was not only inefficient but naughty. He played on figures as on cello strings, and wound up his Message like a Beethoven finale:

"I think we have shown by the statistics of railroad operation in New Kamchatka how wasteful is the political control of transportation. But there is another aspect that is even more important: the spiritual side of this economic crime against suffering mankind.

"How would you like it if you were one of our fine, honest toilers, say, like a conductor on your own K Line here, a man who has supported his family and paid his debts and his charities and his lodge dues, and been loyal to his State, his country, his God, and his company, and he finds that some apparently innocent passenger is nothing but a snooper, a Government spy, put there on the train by inimical politicians and bosses to see how many cash fares the conductor knocks down? Do you think any man could carry on, like the fine, honest workmen ought to in our land of liberty, in that atmosphere of political intrigue and distrust? Oh, to ask that question is to answer it! And so, finally, do you know what that kind of stuff is? It is nothing less than that menacing, that subversive, that most European doctrine—SOCIALISM!"

And Gid and God and the Adelbert team won the debate.

He came down the Erasmus Hotel corridor, broad, confident, shining with youth and victory.

The night maid was a German woman of thirty, unmarried but not very virginal, just from the farm, and lonely for her Otto. She had a radiant skin, and a smile for returning heroes.

"Well, you been out," she said.

"Yes! I won a debate!"

"A debate? Well!"

It was the first time that he had ever encountered a person who was completely worldly-wise. Marta had the sophistication that came from seeing a mortgage foreclosed, a father killed by falling on a scythe, a thousand animals bred and a hundred suitors smirking. He was overwhelmed, and he said, by her volition more than by his, "Don't I get a kiss after winning the debate?"

"Yuh—maybe."

Her lips were as sweet as fresh-made johnnycake with honey. He unbuttoned her bodice, kissed her again and shakily unlocked the door of his room. She followed him in, cheerfully, and much later she told him he was a fine young man—just like her Otto.

But as Gid went to sleep, quite happily, to the urgent whistle of an express flying through town, he was thinking not of the dark blind chasm of Marta's love, but of how the applause had marched across his audience, and he muttered:

"Now, nothing can stop me! United States Senator—why, I got it cinched!"

4

ALL THAT SUMMER after his freshman year, Gid went to sea and met hairy men who had known fog and shipwreck. He talked with passengers who could toss you off a Capetown hotel or a Viennese countess or a Saskatchewan fishing trip as easily as you could toss off a game of checkers.

He was a waiter on a Great Lakes steamer, running from Buffalo to Duluth, and he learned something about navigation and more about beer and the surprising varieties of cheese. He had time to think of girls and religion and making money and all the things he could do in the way of organizing the loose high spirits and good nature of his fellow students. Standing in darkness on the lowest of the four sprawling open decks, he listened to the lake water singing past him, and made two romantic vows.

He would be a Good Man, a bringer of Messages to the poor old longing world—Messages about brotherhood and democracy and the regular use of green (including yellow) vegetables. He'd show 'em that there was nothing to all this predatory vice. He'd inform them that the waiters and deck-hands who gambled and got drunk had no bank accounts nor even much jollity to show for it.

Otherhand, he perceived that most of the Good Men, such as his college instructors, had little to show for their virtue. The trouble, he decided, was that they fooled their time away, without direction.

He selected virtue as his lot, but virtue had to be organized.

There were but few born organizers; few that had his gifted combination of imagination, power and accuracy. He wasn't sure but that he was an even greater organizer than orator. Among Good Men, he would be the Most Good Man, and their chairman.

In some slight awe he perceived that this was probably Destiny speaking, and not just his humble willingness to serve mankind.

As for girls, God, scenery, also family life and physical fitness, he was glad to find that he considered them all very nice things. He hoped that he would never refer to any of them in any speech without saying, "God bless 'em!" But for a devoted artist like himself, he felt, they were important only as they could be organized and so made available to mankind.

He returned to college with some acclaim. The dean was almost polite to him, and the debaters assured him that if he would be patient, they would elect him their captain in another year. The football captain asked his advice as to whether there really was anything to all this Reading that he kept hearing about in his classes, and the leading bootlegger in the village gave Gid a box of thirty Turkish cigarettes.

[33]

Diligently harkening to the voice of the Lord, the first Great Organizer, Gid started on his new plans.

The pants-pressing situation in Adelbert was deplorable. Pressing was carried on, without co-ordination, by the village tailor shop, by the janitor of a fraternity house, and by two students; the elapsed-time factor was variable; and the prices ran anywhere from fifteen cents to half a dollar, with collections, Gid estimated, not over 67%.

He disliked the tailor shop—he had had words about his bill—so he eliminated it from the blessed society of justifiable pants pressers. He called the janitor and the two student pants craftsmen together; he smothered them with words, and set them all up in the janitor's basement room, as The Adelbert Snappy Dressers' Pantorium— Terms Cash. He increased their joint business by persuading the football captain to come out for pressedness instead of manly sloppiness, he got sixteen co-eds to sign a vow not to be "dated" by unpressed males, he coaxed the editor of the *Weekly Delbertan* to run an article, written by Gid, stating that visitors from Yale and Harvard were shocked by the normal state of the Adelbert trouser, and he even tried to remember not to throw his own clothes on the floor when he went to bed.

He spent joyful hours in the basement pressing shop, sniffing the pleasant steaminess, watching the tailors' geese—or gooses—turn wrinkled cloth into smooth elegance, and going over the account book, looking like the founding Rothschild. And the Pantorium prospered and the rival tailor shop went gratifyingly bankrupt. Gid collected twenty-five per cent of the Pantorium profits. And so, by April of his sophomore year, he was so busy and so expanded that he was two hundred dollars in debt, and likely to be suspended from college.

To set up the business, he had had to provide better irons and a quicker furnace, to advance rent on the basement and, particularly, to pay for the dodgers which communicated his first printed messages to a surprised public. It is doubtful if ever in his life he was to be more forceful than in the hot rhetoric of "Hey, fellows, do you want to look like college men or town muckers? The garment oft bespeaks the man. Don't go around bespeaking that you don't belong to the bon ton. Co-eds' suits also pressed scientifically. Welcome, girls. YE OLDE PANTORIUM. Terms cash."

For this enterprise, which was in the true American tradition of Jim Hill, the Rockefellers and Jesse James, Gid had borrowed three hundred dollars from an aunt who read nothing but the *Boston Cook Book* and who was deaf and pious, though she lived in the great city of Zenith. He had promised to repay her within a month.

But his student patrons interpreted the phrase "terms cash" just as Gid himself would have interpreted it: as somewhere between a poor joke and a threat of horrid tyranny. In five months, Gid was able to pay back only one hundred dollars, and his doting aunt stopped doting. She wrote to his father on the same day on which the Adelbert Sportshop reported to the dean that Gid owed them seventy-two dollars.

Gid's father arrived, a melancholy veterinary insignificance with a thin gray mustache, and while the dean listened with small smiling, Gid's father explained to him that the worst of all sins, excepting treason and the neglect of sickness among domestic animals, was being in debt. At the end of it all, Gideon cried out, as Gideon Planish was so often to cry out, "It just seems like people don't appreciate it when you try to do things for them."

He really got more credit for other enterprises which did not require half the boldness involved in the Pantorium and which may have brightened up the college public far less than a year of well-pressed trousers. He organized the first Sophomore Prom ever known in Adelbert. It is true that this Prom never did come off, but there were weeks of splendid committee meetings, and, after them, Gid was elected president of the class. He then combined the warring Student Volunteers and the Society for the Study of Missions into one body, and he got the Zenith Electric Lighting Company to invite the Social Conditions class to go up to the city and inspect the plant, with free transportation and lemonade.

He seemed to have won back the friendship of Hatch Hewitt, who said to him something which Gid never quite made out, but which he felt to be complimentary: "If I just stick around with you, I'll understand all of American education and American benevolence."

Gid was glad to hear that, because one of the intelligentsia had been complaining that though he was useful at starting great cultural movements, like the evening class in Great Women of the Bible, he was no true executive, and incapable of keeping his crusades alive.

Well, by gosh, Gid reflected, if he could hold onto the worship of an ole bandit like Hatch, he certainly was a better executive than *most* people, by gosh!

And so he flashed on into junior year and senior year, as class president, assistant chairman of the Junior Prom, business manager of the baseball team, vice-president of the Y.M.C.A., vice-fourflush of the Four Aces and Growler Association, and as a scholar whose A's in Rhetoric and Forensics made up for his C's in everything else. He was a senior, and it was time for him and Hatch to decide which of the rewards in the world outside college they would prefer to pluck.

Gid's professor in the speech department had hinted that if he would "settle down to work and quit trying to uphold the arms of Moses and teach everybody on the campus how to go to the bathroom," he might become a fairly good teacher. But Gid saw himself and a whole armament of Messages in a larger arena.

"I suppose you still intend to go back to newspaper work," said Gid.

"Sure. And what mode of gracious living have *you* picked on this morning?" said Hatch Hewitt.

"Say, I wish you wouldn't always try to kid me."

"I admire you, Gid. I think you're cockeyed when you look in the mirror and talk about 'doing something for humanity'—which usually means giving 'em another excuse for getting into war. But after four beers, you have virtue. What are you really going to apply it to?"

"I'm still more tempted by politics than by anything

else. I tell you, politics needs men with intellectual training. I could be a doctor, but I don't like sick people. Or
a lawyer, but I hate sticking in an office. Or a clergyman.
Yes, I been a lot tempted by the ministry. But I do like
a glass of beer now and then, and anyway, I don't know
as I could work up the real feeling of instant communion
with God that I'd like to, if I was going to go around
doing a lot of public praying. So, you see, I do really feel
a call to politics.

"Gosh, what I could put over! Old-age pensions for
every man, woman and child, and scientific measures of
free trade, and adequate defense, which would be the
surest guaranty of world peace and——"

"Sure, sure, I know. Which party do you feel yourself
called upon to revive?"

"I don't care a damn which it is, as long as it isn't the
Socialist. Yuh, I got to hand both the major parties something. I'm all for Jefferson, but then I think very highly
of Lincoln, too."

"Really?"

"Yes, I certainly do."

"Look, Gid. The State Legislature is in session. Why
don't we get a day off and go up and visit it? I've been
thinking about going into political reporting myself."

(Years later, Gid explained to his wife that by taking
Hatch to the State capital, Galop de Vache, he had started
him off as a newspaperman.)

The dean gave them leave, and this time he said almost
nothing about beer. He had come to feel that young
Planish was a really useful member of the college, and

that, no matter what the psychology professor said about the boy's "bumbling busyness," he did have a fine, earnest interest in Christian missions.

The dean was growing old.

Galop de Vache was a smallish town surrounding a State capitol building, and the capitol was a jungle of marble corridors and onyx pillars and cases of Civil War flags and marble ex-governors in frock coats, together with eight or ten rooms in which the State business was done. The gaudiest of these was the senate chamber, and when Gid, with Hatch, teetered down the steep stairs in the visitors' gallery, he was impressed.

The chamber was lined with mahogany, save for the front wall, which, in one vast mosaic splashed with rose and gilt and scarlet, recalled the history of the State: pioneers beside their ox-teams, tall river-boats with buckskin huntsmen, and Stephen A. Douglas addressing a crowd, women in bright calico and men with beaver hats, on this same spot where the capitol stood. In front of the mural was the Lieutenant-Governor's desk, upraised on yellow-and-black marble, and over the chamber the vast skylight was jeweled with the arms of every State in the Union.

Here was glory, here was high politics, here was marble, and Gid wanted to be standing upon this lofty and burning stone.

But he noticed, as he settled down and looked for flaws —a college senior has to be practical—that the thirty-six seats for senators were nothing but mahogany school-desks. And how sick he was of schoolrooms and desks!

He had hoped for high oratory, about flags and eagles and the brawny arm of labor, but a bald fat man was on his feet and, while nobody seemed to listen, while one senator ate a sandwich and another snapped spit balls, was mumbling:

"This bill—this 179—I know there's been some opposition to it—the gentleman from Grolier County has been kicking about it—but it's been pretty well talked over in committee and I guess it's a sound bill, I don't know much about it—it's about muzzling dogs in the southern tier of counties."

Gid groaned, "Good God! So that's how senators trifle around when we elect 'em to preserve our liberties!"

Down on the floor, a silver-haired man with schoolmaster spectacles rose, yawned, handed a peanut to the senator who was speaking, walked to the back of the chamber, and stood yawning again.

"That old fellow seems as much bored as we are," approved Gid.

"Yes, and I know who he is—he really is something—that's Senator Kurtshaw, the minority leader," said Hatch.

The man on the throne, presumably the Lieutenant-Governor, said something rapid and entirely incomprehensible about the dog-muzzle bill, there was a growl from the caged senators, and the measure seemed incredibly to have passed. It wouldn't have if *he* had been a senator, Gid asserted. But he was to hear still more abysmal legislation slide through, presented in the reading clerk's furry mumble——

[40]

"To amend the markets law in relation to the definition of 'limburg cheese'."

"To amend the education law in relation to school camps for children."

"To revive and extend the corporate existence of The Highlife Brewing Company of Monarch."

It was on this last that the silvery Senator Kurtshaw yawned most destructively, and walked out of the chamber.

"Now there's one representative of the people that seems to have an idea what it's all about!" said Gid. "Gosh, I wish I had a chance to talk with him and ask him if we can ever really do anything with this castiron political machine."

"Why don't we just butt in and do it?"

Gid appreciated the gall and ingenuity of his journalistic friend. Some day he might give Hatch a newspaper of his own.

A doorman suggested that they might find Senator Kurtshaw in the Financial Committee Room. Unaware that senators themselves slip up and down in small smelly elevators, the two young seekers descended the Napoleonic flight of the Grand Staircase—the first persons ever to do so except scrubwomen, sparrows and General Lew Wallace. Gid was declaiming, "Certainly a swell lot of legislative junk our guardians of liberty are fussing over, while widows starve and the myrmidons, or whatever you call 'em, beat up protesting wage-slaves! 'An act to tax the State for red paint for the noses of brewery salesmen, to enchant, I guess it's enhance, the sales of Old Dog Rover ales and lager.' Now I know I *got* to go into politics and clean up the mess!"

The Financial Committee Room was a bareness of plaster and steel filing cabinets. Senator Kurtshaw was at the end of a ponderous table, reading the Zenith *Advocate-Times*—the sports page.

"How do you do, Senator?" said Gid.

"Huh?"

"We're a couple of college men, from Adelbert."

"Well?"

"I could see how amused you were by that Highlife Brewery Bill."

"What d' you mean, amused? Very necessary bill. What do you want?"

"Well, to be frank, I wanted to talk about entering politics."

"Go ahead. There's nothing to prevent you, if you're a citizen, and twenty-one. Why talk to me about it?"

"I thought I might find it a little complicated, as a college man in politics."

"What about it? I'm a college man in politics. In fact, I once taught in the university law school, and I suppose I was a conceited damn skinny nuisance, just as you're a damn fat nuisance."

"I am not fat!"

"You will be. Now what do you expect to do in politics, with your especial knowledge of Cro-Magnon tribal lore?"

Gid was becoming decently angry. "I'd speak up for the people, that's what I'd do, and get 'em shorter hours and longer wages, more wages, I mean—but I mean, of course, without allowing any of this tyranny of union labor. I'd denounce all these consolidations of predatory interests that——"

"What predatory interests you mean? The farm-bloc or the Medical Association or the Methodist Church or your Adelbert Athletic Association?"

"You know what I mean! Anyway, I'd do something about justice and education and, well, I mean the Larger Issues, and not waste the public time on a lot of tripe about dog-muzzles and limburger cheese!"

"And just who do you think *is* hired by the people to see they get good limburger cheese, to see that we have food inspectors who know cheese from Euclid? Do you think these things get themselves done by prayer and reading the Gettysburg Address and listening to lectures by Emma Goldman? If you get gypped on a street-car fare, or your mayor appoints a chief of police that steals your shirt, or your eggs are rotten, or your car breaks a spring on a bad road, then who do you blame? The State Legislature! And then you don't re-elect us. We're not a bunch of actors playing *Julius Caesar*. We're business men, and badly paid ones, trying to carry out what the citizens want, or think they want, or some boy orator from the River Platte, like you, tells 'em they want. If you'd like to get into politics—all right. Go to your county committee, where they know how good you are, and tell 'em you're fixing to step out and save the country. I'm sure they'll cry with delight—but don't come and tell *me!* I didn't walk out on the session upstairs because I was bored or 'amused'. I had a toothache. And it's getting worse every minute!"

For ten miles, on the train to Adelbert, Gid was silent with a silent Hatch. Then he broke up:

"Say it! I know. He was right. I'm just another college amateur. *And* fat! I don't know one doggone thing about how a government is carried on. That senator has certainly knocked all the ambition out of me! And I haven't got any deep philosophy. Why, this question I noticed in the Zenith paper—if there was a fire and you had to decide between saving the Mona Lisa and a two-year-old child—I don't know which I'd save."

"Neither did the joker that wrote it."

"But it shows me I'm not so gosh-awful profound. I guess I better just get into the teaching game and hand out the correct-speech guff, like my prof thinks I had ought to." Then Gid became cheerful. "Maybe some day I'll be a college president and get the alumni really lined up on contributions, and double the college attendance. I could do *that*, don't you think?"

"I'm sure of it," said Hatch.

5

HE HAD A rich brown small beard, a good thick beard for a man of twenty-nine. He had grown it to give a more interesting look to a certain commonplace squatness, and he had cultivated a trick of glancing sharply at people who spoke to him, then casually looking away, as though he had already learned everything about them. He wore brown tweeds and a bright-blue shirt and a loose purple bow-tie. He hoped that all the respectable people on the Pullman chair-car would be puzzled and excited, and wonder whether he was a college professor or the kind of Englishman you read about in H. G. Wells, the kind who was intellectual but who rockgardened in front of an artistic converted mill in Surrey.

And at twenty-nine, in 1921, he really was a college professor. He was Professor Gideon Planish, Dr. Planish, Ph.D. of the University of Ohio, Professor of Rhetoric and Speech in Kinnikinick College, Iowa.

That was a small college with beautiful elm trees, a faint Episcopal flavor—esthetic but responsible—and a pleasant feeling that scholarship and piety were good old historical principles but shouldn't be overdone. The college was attended by the sons and daughters of manu-facturers and physicians in Iowa, Minnesota and the

Dakotas, and it had football, but not too much, music, but not too much, and co-educational flirtation, but not too public.

Professor Planish was well esteemed, in Kinnikinick. He looked at the athletes, he looked at girl students who came to beg him prettily to raise their marks from C Minus to C, he looked at the trustees and the new president, new since last Christmas, as though he was on to all their charming little dodges, but was amused by them and didn't mind.

He also did some teaching, in a fair routine way.

He did well at lectures to the women's clubs in Central Iowa, for which he was often paid twenty-five dollars and expenses, with attendance for tea at the banker's house obligatory. The clubwomen admired him, admired his beard, admired his merry eyes, admired his trick of becoming moistly ecstatic as he recited W. B. Yeats, then chuckling at himself and at them for their emotion.

Yet he was not quite happy. He was, he felt, too young and strong to go on sitting in classrooms. He was a bachelor, and the girls bothered him, their legs bothered him, their knees mocked him, and he was obsessed and extremely annoyed by their sailor blouses. He was afraid that he wanted, even more than crowds and glory, to be holding one of these sweet, collapsible little flappers in his arms. It seemed, he groaned, to be the Lord's incomprehensible purpose that a pure and studious young man who took cold showers regularly and played tennis and was willing to serve the people as a United States Senator should keep having Evil Thoughts about the flashy way in which these young women crossed their legs as they sat in front of him.

Of course the way out, and the Biblical way at that, as suggested by that wise old Y.M.C.A. man, St. Paul, was to be married. But Professor Planish had never yet found a young woman who combined the three imperative elements: that she should be young and curving; that she should appreciate his humanitarianism and his gift for high hot wordings; and that she should have the bland social talent that would help him to go higher. He had not found her as yet, but meantime he was able to control himself by his early Christian training and by the constant availability of his mistress.

She was Teckla Schaum, and she was really a good soul, with money of her own.

He had spent the summer of 1921 in the Yale Library, being snubbed by such professors as were not up in Vermont being snubbed by the farmers or over in England being snubbed by the professors at Oxford. He believed that he had been trying to write a book on what he called *The Genius of American Orators:* Webster, Lincoln, Calhoun, Bryan, Ignatius Donnelly and all persons named Roosevelt. He had done only two chapters of the book. Years afterward, he found them in a trunk, and turned them into a singularly useful pamphlet which showed that True Americanism was synonymous with extensive giving to uplift organizations. But he had had good luck with the daughter of his landlady, out on Orange Street, and he had learned to appreciate lobsters, salt water and dancing cheek to cheek. He had spent a week in New York, and he could find his way from the Grand Central Station to the Public Library to Billy's speakeasy in Greenwich Village.

He was ready to take his place in the world of the Eastern Seaboard, but those damned snobs of Columbia and Harvard and Princeton and Yale, those high-voiced academic Pharisees, did not encourage him. Perhaps what he needed was a loving girl who would, like a domesticated Joan of Arc, show him the path.

Professor Planish decided that the passengers on the chair-car from Chicago to Kinnikinick hadn't even noticed him. He looked gloomily at his new tan-leather kit bag, with the grand gold letters GP. It didn't seem worth while to have paid so much for it.

He sighed, shook his head at the porter's "Brush you off, sir?" and carried his own bag to the vestibule.

Kinnikinick was now galloping past the train: two fat-bellied oil tanks, a yard littered with shattered old automobiles, two gangling grain-elevators, one exclamatory in red and the other of gray galvanized iron, standing raw against the faded prairie. It all seemed cluttered and flimsy to Professor Planish, after the shaded security of New Haven, but he was comforted when, as he hitched down the train steps, carrying the big bag, he was greeted by the station agent with a hearty "Welcome back, Prof!"

He was home. On the plank platform, by the small red frame station, a pretty girl junior was evidently pointing him out to a garland of still prettier freshmen—pointing

[48]

at him and whispering, while the girls all looked at him gravely, without giggling. He was home, and he was important, and the driver of the flivver taxicab was calling, "Back again, Prof? Can I drive you up to the house?"

It was the custom at that time and place for the young men to paint their ancient and derivative automobiles with such texts as "Pike's Peak or Bust—Busted" or "How about it, Babe?" None of these amateur exhibits was so florid as this taxi, this open Ford touring car, which was labeled "Kinnikinick's Komical Kommon Karrier," and decorated with a mural of young men in white evening ties and ladies in indiscreet evening gowns attending a rural picnic at which was served nothing but bananas and hard-boiled eggs. Professor Planish felt humiliated at having to come back from the elms of Hillhouse Avenue to such frippery, and he sat in the flivver glaring, his stout little beard straight out.

It all seemed better when they came to the campus. On the bluffs of the Kinnikinick River, which curved like a question mark, the half-dozen gray Tudor buildings enclosed a quadrangle shady with oak and maple, a place for contemplation. Looking at it, young Professor Planish exulted, "Not as big as Yale, maybe, but a lot purer architecture and sounder scholarship—and a damn sight more human!"

The flivver left him at his residence, a bedroom and a study in the square white house of Mrs. Hilp, a widow woman whom no one ever noticed and nobody has ever described. She stood on the wide screened porch, crying "Welcome home, Professor!" and heating up his sense of his own importance. He unpacked by throwing his clothes on the bed and leaving them for Mrs. Hilp. He was not a particularly tidy man.

It was still warm enough for him to show off the new linen suit he had bought in New Haven, and in that pale angelic glory he started out on his errands—a man who was again wanted and needed. He looked into his private office, a grim and slate-floored coop in the basement of the Administration Building, and looked at his secretary, a lady who adored him but who was stringy and virginal. She had answered all his mail, and he hadn't a thing for her to do, so he patted her on the shoulder, to show that he was friendly but also keeping his sharp eye on everything.

He went through the memorial gateway, ornamented with the shields of nine New England colleges, and walked down Wallace Avenue to the Kollege Klothes Korner, where he bought a bright green tie that he didn't need, and to the Smokes & Book Co-op, where he bought a red rubber eraser that he didn't like. Thus he was able to receive from the clerks, "Well, well, we missed you, Professor. Glad you're back with us."

He had planned his call upon Mr. W. C. Pridmore, president of the Drovers' National Bank and Chairman of the Board of Trustees of Kinnikinick College, for half-past three, when the bank would be closed to the public —a caste to which he still referred as "the hoi polloi." At five he would call on the new president of the college. This expert schedule of weighty conferences would give him, in between, three-quarters of an hour for the demands of love, which just now concerned the slim person of Dr. Miss Edith Minton.

Mr. W. C. Pridmore sat near the entrance to the bank, in a compartment railed with golden oak and of the general size of a pigpen. But neater, much neater. He was a gentle, anxious man, with a stubby mustache, and he was always sorry when he had to foreclose a mortgage. And as he thought that Professor Planish was going to marry his widowed daughter, Teckla, and as he considered Professor Planish to be the most book-read and eloquent young man that he knew, yet with sound principles about the Republican Party and with a decent salary, he rose from his steel desk—the look of which gave money-borrowers a headache—he held out his shaky hand, and cried, "Well, well! Teckla and I missed you, Gideon. You're a sight for sore eyes!"

Professor Planish wondered if it really would take as much as ten years for him to become president of the college.

He told Mr. Pridmore that there were fine bank buildings and large factories in New Haven, also some scattered college buildings, but as for him, he was mighty glad to be back among friends.

At five minutes to four, Professor Planish was at Lambda Lambda Lambda House, slightly nervous, to call upon Dr. Edith Minton, proctor of the House and instructor in English. All summer he had been thinking about her, remembering her as a quartz crystal, as a doe with large eyes and tiny elegant hoofs. What a mistake he had made, this past school year, not to have seen more of her!

He had to wait in the Lambda reception-room, an apartment with Maxfield Parrish prints, and throne chairs so straight and stiff and hard that they caused you to wonder whether it was really the heads of the crown-wearers that got so uneasy.

Edith Minton slipped in, and his bounding heart told him that here was his true love wending; that Edith would be a credit to him and adorn his dinner parties, no matter how great a magnifico he might become. He was a little touched by his own cleverness in having recalled her so accurately: pale, reedy, erect, and undoubtedly very soft and pleasing under that armor of gray suit and crisp lace jabot. He thought about trying to kiss her, but the Infinite shot a warning to him. He shook her hand, her thin strong hand, and waved her to a chair—in her own house.

"You're looking fine, Edith. Have a good summer?"

"Not bad. I spent two weeks at a Wisconsin lake, but mostly I stayed in Chicago and worked on Chaucer."

"Oh, I forgot to thank you for your card. I enjoyed hearing from you. Well . . . You're looking fine. You look as if you'd had a good summer."

"Yes."

"Well, back to the mine."

"What do you mean?"

"Back to work."

She thought this over. "Yes, that's so. Back to work now."

"Yup. On the job now."

"I suppose you liked New Haven better than here."

"I did not! They want to see your passport and a certificate signed by three respectable clergymen that you attended Hotchkiss, before they'll say good morning. No!"

"And yet you aren't content to be here, either!"

"A man has to keep on advancing, doesn't he? But why am I being jumped on, my dear?"

"Oh, I'm sorry, Gideon. I forget you're my superior officer, don't I!"

"Nonsense—nonsense—nonsense! Academic democracy —all on the same level—even undergraduates—in some respects. But why so grouchy?"

"Oh, I've just had an afternoon of girl freshmen who couldn't make up their minds whether they wanted to be scholars or women or have careers. I get a little cranky."

"You'll get over it!" He arose in a superior sort of way and patted her shoulder as chastely as he had that of his secretary. "Now get a good rest. See you soon."

"She doesn't think so doggone much of me. She'd never be one to appreciate me and help advance my career. God but she's bloodless and sexless and conceited! . . . No, she's all right. Maybe she sees through me! Maybe there isn't so much in me to appreciate, except punchful words. I'll have to realize that and profit by it—study and do a lot of hard, quiet thinking," meditated young Professor Planish.

He was clumping back to Administration Hall, his beard bright in the September sun. With his self-confidence and his determination to make an impression on the new regime flowing back into him, he walked boldly into the green-carpeted, portrait-fretted anteroom to the president's office.

He was a full professor; he was kept waiting only five minutes and admitted to the fervid cordiality of the Rev. Dr. T. Austin Bull, the new president of Kinnikinick.

There are rambling and rustic fellows, beanpoles with long noses and disordered hair, who prove to be suave Men About Town in New York or London, polo players or editors of gossip magazines, up to the latest thing in music and morals. By contrary, there are sleek, slender, quick-moving men, curly-headed and neat-featured, who wear their clothes like popular actors, who are as quick as cavalry captains and poised as infantry majors, but who prove to be studious pastors, doctors of divinity, or teachers of manual training.

Of these deceptive elegants was T. Austin Bull who, after a Methodist boyhood, a decade as an eloquent and money-raising Episcopal minister, and a couple of years as secretary of an elephantine university, had, at forty-four, come to Kinnikinick as president.

The business was under new management; the sales and advertising departments were being reorganized; and the highest standards of American business, piety, learning and manhood were to be advanced. Dr. Bull was against sloth, debt, the teaching of Greek except in graduate schools and the seduction of co-eds.

His handshake was virile, small though he was, and he greeted Professor Planish in the best of glee-club tenors:

"Thank you for coming to call so early, Professor, but I'm not sure but that I should have called on you. I'm so new to this job that I imagine I'll have to lean heavily on your experience.

"Let's see now: three years you've been at old Kinni-kinick. I can't tell you what splendid reports I get of your splendid teaching and your, uh, your splendid effect on the morale of the students. Oh, everywhere. But—— There is one thing, one small detail, that I should like to take up with you—oh, more in a spirit of asking advice than of giving it, perhaps.

"Will you have a cigar, Professor? Of course as an ex-parson, I don't smoke much, but I find that a really good cigar at once cheers the heart and clears the head, pro-vided it's a really good cigar, I mean, not a five-cent one —and light, I mean. Good! Now settle back in your chair, all comfy, and try and have the patience to hear me out.

"What I've ventured to think about, in a very tentative way, is: I'm sure you make every effort to shelter our dar-ling girl undergraduates just as much from yourself as from any other man, but have you ever given thought to the somewhat disturbing position of a strong, young, un-married man among so many lovely girls?"

"Oh, yes, I've given thought to it!"

"I imagined perhaps you had. And may I, in the most impersonal way, ask if you have any plans for getting married?"

"I can't say anything definite just at this moment—only rash fools tempt the gods by prophecy, you know."

"How true that is!"

"But I hope before long to have something very inter-esting to tell you."

"That's fine, that's fine. I'm very pleased, Professor."

To himself Professor Planish grunted, "Yeh, it *would* be interesting to know who the dickens this is that I'm going to marry! And it would be interesting to Prexy if he shadowed me for the next few hours and found out why I'm not likely to be a menace to the cute co-eds!"

So he tramped to the little gray widow's-house where lived Teckla Schaum.

He knocked, instead of bursting in as he usually did. It would be a pleasure to see her tremblingly peeping out, in hope. She'd be at home, all right; hadn't he telephoned her that he was back! She would never spoil the perfect art of his return.

He knocked and rang the bell, and with perfect timing, as rehearsed in his mind, there she was, edging the door open, then throwing it wide as she whimpered, "Oh, Gid, you're here!"

"Me? No! I'm in New Haven. You know—in Connecticut."

He closed the door behind him, to shut off the censorious eyes of Kinnikinick, and kissed her profoundly, holding her small frail figure close to him, conscious of her fine springy back.

"I've missed you so," she was sighing.

"Missed you, too. Nobody I could talk to."

"But you must have met some wonderful people in New Haven."

"Sure. Some swell English scholars—some real word-painters—make Beowulf sit up and beg. And boy! What buildings and old New England churches, and a very fine old town, Guilford, quite convenient on the trolley, but—Jesus, Teckla darling, how I did miss talking to you! You know—natural."

He was relieved to find that he could, without straining, tell her the truth. He reflected that for all his talent, maybe genius, he was a simple fellow who hated talking through pink gauze to Edith Minton or President Bull. He wondered if he might not actually be a little in love with Teckla. There was only one thing against the theory—he didn't like her very much.

Teckla Pridmore Schaum, daughter of the head of the college trustees, was four years older than Professor Planish. For two years she had been married to a promising young townsman, head of the Power and Light Company, who had been killed when an automobile turned over. She was incessantly hungry for the smell of a man's pipe, the horizon thunder of his grumbling. All the past winter she had been going to bed with Professor Planish, but she didn't know much about him. She thought he was a simple and friendly young man who wanted to help his students. She was four years older, and thin, and she hadn't much of a complexion, nothing very interesting in the way of hair or a nose or wit; nothing at all but a rigid passion for him and an unquestioning joy when she could comfort him and assure him that he was a superior man. She knew that he was not in love with her, but she went on convincing herself that some day the darling boy would see the gold she gave him.

"That's the sweetest new linen suit!" she adored.

"Like it? From the East! God-awful expensive!"

"It's so smart."

"Huh! I bet you think President Bull dresses better than I do. I just saw him. He wore a double-breasted gray suit with the waist cut in like a chorus man, and damned if he wasn't wearing a red carnation—the curly-headed dude! Don't you think so?"

"Father and I always thought he was such a good scholar. But now you speak of it, I guess he is a little dandified. You're so deep and discerning about people."

"No, I just get around a lot."

"Dear, why don't you take your coat off? It's terribly hot, for September."

"That's not such a bad idea, at that."

"And I know you'd like a highball."

"That proposition certainly has a lot of merit in it."

With such delightful love talk and academic interchange of ideas, they played along.

There was no Prohibition-era drinking at Kinnikinick, which was moral though Episcopal. There were no saloons in town; Holy Communion was drunk in grape-juice; and at large public dinners, the bishop and the football team were toasted in Coca-Cola. The students carried abstinence so far that they never drank in the dormitories, except in the evening, and perhaps afternoons. The president had to be known as a teetotaler, and it was only in the houses of the professors who had married money that there were any very large private cellars.

Not having had a drink since he had left his rooms at

Mrs. Hilp's, the Professor chummily helped Teckla crack the ice, open the White Rock bottle, and look over her Prohibition stock: four bottles of Bourbon whisky, two of Scotch, twenty-seven gin, and a bottle of rock-and-rye like an anatomical specimen in a museum.

Teckla had no servant, but her kitchen was nearly automatic, and brutally handsome. The electric stove resembled a mahogany hope chest; the sink was of stainless steel; the cupboard of steel enameled a pale blue; and off the kitchen was the "breakfast nook," a pair of cherry-red settees facing each other across a blue metal-topped table, with wallpaper flourishing strawberries and bluebirds.

In this metallic lovers' bower, where the rosebuds were pink electric bulbs, Professor Planish and his Aspasia grew happily drunk. Before that, the Professor gloated, "You haven't asked about my present for you."

"You don't mean you brought *me* a present?"

"Ha, ha, who else would I bring a present to!"

He curvetted back into the living-room, which was in blue and silver with an Arthur Rackham print, and from his coat pocket he took a jewelry-box of the most elegant pasteboard, icy to the fingers outside, with the most luxurious honey-colored satin lining. His left hand on her shoulder, leaning over her, he flashed the bright costume-jewelry bracelet which he had anxiously bought on Madison Avenue, in New York ($11.99 cash).

"Oh, darling, it's lovely, just lovely! It shines so—like diamonds! You shouldn't of!"

He kissed her, and for some seconds he was almost certain that he loved her. But he was thirsty, and the ice and amber of his drink lured him back to the settee across from her.

"Gideon, I think I've done something really useful for you this summer."

"What's that?"

"I've been reading Trollope for you."

"Oh, yes—uh—Trollope."

"You know: *Barchester Towers.*"

"Oh, I remember. I tackled that guy once, but he was pretty strong going. Not even a shooting. Too slow for me."

"Well, you know in your Rhetoric lectures, where you say an author can have humor and excitement without falling into bad taste and immorality, like all these young writers, Trollope would be a dandy illustration. I made some notes for you on his plots and moral principles."

"Oh, swell! Fellow busy as I am, trying to ram art and eloquence down a lot of boneheads, to say nothing of all the work I do on committees, he don't get time to do all the reading he'd like. It's a great sorrow to me, sometimes, Teckla. What I always say is, there's no friend like a great book."

"Oh, I know how it is. Gideon! There's a hero in Trollope that's so much like you—the same combination of learning and virility. He's a clergyman, but he has a beard just like yours."

"Do you think I ought to go on wearing a beard? I thought President Bull looked at it kind of funny."

"Don't you ever dare take it off! It makes you so distinguished. Like that minister in the book."

[60]

"You know, I've worried a good deal, off and on, whether I hadn't ought to gone into the ministry, instead of teaching. Of course what I always say is, a man can do as much good by training these young minds in oratory as in purity, but I guess I'm kind of a perfectionist—I'm funny that way—I can't seem to be satisfied unless I follow the highest and noblest and no compromise, yes, sir, and no matter how practical we are, still we had ought to imitate the lives of the saints and sacrifice our all to humanity without flinching and HOORAY, I feel wonderful!"

He had a quick one, without ice or soda. Was he—he pinched his mind, to see if it hurt—was he getting lit? Oh, what the devil! He had to celebrate his homecoming, didn't he? And Teckla looked at him with such admiration and surrender. Pity she was so much older than he.

She was breathing, "Oh, I know how you want to help and lift up this poor bewildered world. But I honestly don't see how you could do any more good in a church than in your wonderful work of teaching your students to write and orate so beautifully, and then those of them that get a call to go out and influence mankind will be just that much more gifted."

"Anyway, I'm not sure I've got the right kind of a voice for a clergyman."

"Do you know the kind of voice you ought to have?"

"What?"

"Just the kind you got now, dear!"

"Oh . . . But do you think it's deep enough?"

"It doesn't sound like a rainbarrel, if that's what you mean—thank Heaven! But listen, darling: you haven't told me one word about New Haven. Of course I understood perfectly that you were working so hard you didn't have time for much letter-writing. But now tell me about it. Did they offer you a position there?"

"I've got a more interesting idea than New Haven." He rose. "Come!"

Mutely she followed him into the living-room, sat on his lap, fondly rubbed her cheek against his chest, while he stroked her knee.

The Professor sighed to himself, "She's a good woman. She's one person that does appreciate what I am. It's a darn shame that she's so small-town and ordinary. It wouldn't be fair to her to take her off to New York and Washington and face those snobs and intriguers."

She said, as though the words meant something quite different, "Getting hungry? I've got the nicest little steak for you."

"Don't you think that can wait a while, sweetheart?"

"Yes, maybe it can," she whispered.

6

PROFESSOR GIDEON PLANISH was not satisfied with the workings of Providence, at the beginning of this college year of 1921–22. He was not satisfied with Teckla Schaum. Oh, she admired him, in her shallow womanly way, but she did not understand the complications of a statesman's career, did not even understand the problem of his beard —how he looked rustic if he had one, and yet if he took it off now, everybody would laugh.

She couldn't tell him how to jump from college to the Senate chamber without going through a lot of sticky handshaking. She actually thought he might go on teaching, and yet she didn't see how embarrassing it was for him to have, as rival star in his department, a new English professor who had taken the advantage of actually being English.

No, he was alone with his high dreams, no one to help him, no one to hold his hand while he followed the road to the stars.

Damn it, he wasn't even quite sure that he ought to go on being Teckla's lover. Maybe it wasn't altogether moral.

One of his most prickly grievances was that in this small college, with only thirty-one on the faculty, he had to take the huge required freshman class in Introductory

Rhetoric and Composition. He was happy enough in his small seminars in inspirational subjects like Argumentative Composition, Oral Interpretation of the Drama, Persuasion, and Speech Psychology, but to process this knotty raw material of almost a hundred freshmen of every state of sex and unenlightenment was to pant and strain at an intellectual assembly-line. Yet all that Teckla said about it was, "You ought to feel that it's a privilege to stir up all these young minds."

So it was with a shaky feeling of having been unjustly used that he began his first lecture to the class in Freshman Rhetoric.

He came through the R. U. E. entrance into Atkinson Amphitheater, carrying only a thin notebook. He was proud that he was too well organized to need the green bag or the pile of shaggy brown books with which the old troupers among the faculty messed up their unstylized entrances.

With stilled and waiting power he looked at the huge class—ninety-seven of them, all green. With most of them he hadn't even had consultations. Ninety-seven children from supercilious but provincial households, all busy with apples, chocolate, tennis rackets, newspapers, and with one another, boy drawn to girl already, in the first week of college, in a jungle of young life that was uninterested in professors—even those with rich beards. If he did manage to stand there, looking a little amused, a symbol of cold dominant wisdom, it was entirely an act and he an actor. Inside, he felt lonely and, at best, he hoped they wouldn't find him very funny or intolerably dull.

He gravely laid down his notebook, rapped his desk, and croaked:

"Young ladies and gentlemen, let us start this consortium, in which we are compelled to be associated for the next nine months, nine long long months [he did get a smile on that line], by firmly understanding certain fundamental principles. Doubtless some of you are Shakespeares, piping your native woodnotes wild, but for most of us, the magic art of Rhetoric is rules, rules, rules, and yet more rules.

"It is discipline. It is a humble and willing subjection to the great formulae worked out for us long ago by the Masters. We are not here to show off or to think we are smart enough to do everything in new ways. I shall tell you, and I shall expect acute attention when I tell you, what the Masters have decided, in all such supreme mysteries as style, beauty, conciseness, aspirations toward the Divine, the correct ratio, in fiction, of analysis and narrative and description to dialogue, scientific paragraphing, appeal to the nobler emotions such as love and patriotism, the accepted punctuation and gosh——"

The last word had not been said aloud.

He couldn't be sure that her name did begin with an A or B, the girl at the right end of the center section of the front row, for the ushers had not yet assorted the class alphabetically. Maybe she was sitting there so close to him because she wanted to listen to him. But whether she began with an A or a B or a C or a Z, she was his true love forever.

It was true that her shoulders, like his own, were menaced by plumpness, but her legs were sleek, her ankles fairly thin, and if her little paws, twisted together on the writing tablet of her chair as she listened to him, were not so delicate, they were white and sweet and shapely. And her face was as amusing as a monkey's, round and pert. She had wise and lively eyes, astonishingly wise and determined for a girl who couldn't be over nineteen, and her friendly lips, not tight nor thin, kept moving with excitement. Her high pride was her brown hair, shining like polished walnut and, unusual here and now, not bobbed but flauntingly feminine.

He was already telling her, under the campus maples by moonlight, that she must be careful with her diet and not get fat—lovely child like her—while his outer voice was rolling on:

"—and take, for instance, the case of a novelist less known than Dickens or Thackeray or Harriet Beecher Stowe, yet always to me one of the lords of language, Andrew—ah, Jupiter nods, I mean of course Anthony—Anthony Trollope. Did a tremendous writer like Trollope think the proper stunt was to go and live with a lot of Bohemians and Frenchmen in an attic and try to invent a lot of new rules? He did not! He was the soul of discipline. While constantly traveling as a—as a school inspector in a—in a number of parts of England, he made himself sit down every day and write—and write—and write, and all according to the accepted RULES!"

His girl in the front row nodded. There was a serious-minded and helpful young woman. He could imagine her being witty at a soda-fountain or bouncing in her seat at a high-ranking basketball game—full of fun, a jolly companion, but with a heart that would appreciate idealism and ambition.

He was explaining to the class that elegant language was useful not only to preachers and editorial writers but also to businessmen. Which, he put it to them, would sell a vacuum cleaner better: a rich, full, mellifluous address (and he strikingly illustrated it, playing both the salesman and a pleased housewife), or a mess of crude language, as used by persons who didn't go to Kinnikinick and love their Rhetoric class?

The girl's eyes forcefully agreed with him.

And for such of them as planned to enter politics—what was it that elected Woodrow Wilson? His titanic knowledge of history? No, never! It was the discriminating way in which he laid words end to end according to the rules.

The end of Professor Planish's discourse was somewhat in the style of the courtroom scene in *The Merchant of Venice*. He stopped dead, he fixed them with the eye, he raised the hand, he gave with the voice: "Let me conclude in the words of Alexander Pope's immortal translation from Horace." He glanced at a slip filled with the handwriting of Teckla Schaum.

> "Sages and chiefs long since had birth
> Ere Caesar was or Newton named;
> These raised new empires o'er the earth,
> And those, new heavens and systems framed.
> In vain they schemed, in vain they bled!
> They had no poet, and are dead!"

He wondered if, after all, he shouldn't have been a leading actor instead of a senator or a college president. Wouldn't his girl down there have appreciated him even more? He calculated that she was near to weeping. He looked at her knowingly, eye understanding eye, heart snatched out of his body and joined to hers. When all the others had gone, after only half a hundred fool questions about hours and assignments and at what sort of an establishment did one accomplish the abnormal feat of buying a book, he saw that she was still waiting, at one side of the room.

She came up to his platform-table. Who said her shoulders were too plump? Why, they were lustrous and soft for a man to lay his head——

Professor Planish caught himself. After all, he wasn't a mooncalf any longer. This was a jolly-looking young woman, but she was no Theda Bara. Seated with the table safely between them, she standing humbly below, he looked at her like a judge.

"May I bother you a moment, Professor?"

"What is it?"

(These were, definitely, the first words between the celebrated Romeo and Juliet of Kinnikinick.)

"I want to see if you'll let me take Oral Interpretation of the Drama."

"That's an upper-class subject."

"I know. I just want to take it as an auditor, without credit."

"Isn't your schedule full?"

"I'll say!" She shuddered.

"Then why do you want to take it?"

"Oh, I think maybe I might be an actress and——"

"Yes?"

"And I'd like to have another class with you!"

She was delicately shameless, and he stiffened with interest. He marveled, "But why?"

"Oh, it was so stimulating today, and the other day I listened to you in the hall—I was waiting for a vaccination appointment, in front of C7, and I heard you talking to Professor Eakins. He was so sort of dry and cranky—they all are, all but you—and I've snooped into a lot of classes and listened—they just grind out a lot of information—gee, Professor, I guess maybe I'm being fresh, but I'll bet you a billion dollars the rest of the faculty think you're too dramatic, too exciting to listen to."

"My dear young lady——" Then his flatulent academic tone changed into a boyish demand: "What's your name?"

"Peony Jackson. From Faribault, Minnesota. I was on the platform when you got off the train."

He got back the professorial manner. The self-protective superiority. The armor against the mirth of young women.

"Well, Miss Peony Jackson, from Faribault, Minnesota, I'm sure you mean to be complimentary, but the fact is, the members of the faculty, however much they may differ——"

Never again, in private, did he speak to her with this stage burlesque of himself—not to Peony. Raw and boyish again, remembering that he was only ten years older than she, he cried, "Let's sit in the front row—all these dumb

[69]

freshmen gone now—come on!" They laughed; they sat side by side. Probably to the eye even of President T. Austin Bull they would have seemed decorous enough, but Professor Planish felt as though he were holding her hand.

"Peony—Miss Jackson—you don't want to take that Oral Interpretation junk. It's a lot of stupid analysis."

"Well, I came here to get educated, didn't I?"

He felt a tiny chill. "Did you?"

"That's what they claim!"

"Don't give it a thought."

"I won't!" They laughed, like freshmen, or very aged professors. "Honestly, Professor, I just love the way you treat your students—tell 'em they're a bunch of lil Socrateses one minute and then jump right down their throats the next. That would make even a dumb bunny like me get busy and learn something—learn K-A-T, the cat, sat on the M-A-T-T, mat. I betcha I learn enough here so's the court will let me get married."

"And who may this be that you are going to marry?" Very coldly.

"I haven't got the slightest idea."

Was it possible that she was looking at him with appraisal?

"Look, Miss Jackson—Peony. I've got the idea. Forget the Oral Interp. Did you know that it's part of my job here to coach a play, four times a year?"

"Swell."

"We'll have try-out for the first one, *Poor Papa's Prize*, in just a few days now."

"Swell."

"And will you read for it?"

"Sw—— You mean, try and see if I can act one of the parts?"

"Professionally, we call it 'read for a part'."

"I'll be glad to." Her wrist-watch, he noted, was rather expensive. "Gee, I got to be skipping along now."

"Don't go yet!"

"I got a date."

"With some boy, I suppose!"

"Uh-huh."

He was writhing. He was sick. These blab-mouth freshmen boys! Not human yet!

"Well, look, Peony, I'd like to have more chance—I mean now, at the beginning of the year, when we're sort of making plans—I mean, for the year—and I'm very interested—I mean in your reactions to the different—you know, different styles and modes of instruction—and it's so interesting to get your reactions and——"

"Aw, Professor, you don't want any reactions from a Problem Child."

"Give me some, and see if I don't!"

"Swell!"

"Where are you living?"

"At Lambda House."

"Um! Well, look. I'll be in Postum's drug store at exactly ten o'clock tonight, buying a soda." He remembered that he had an engagement which might be expected to last all evening, but he kicked out the thought. He could not wait for forty-eight hours to see Peony again. "Exactly ten. Suppose you happened to be there, and had a soda with me?"

"I thought the co-edibles weren't supposed to have dates with the faculty."

"They aren't. But if you just happened to be dropping in there to buy some talcum powder——"

"I got some talcum powder!"

"Are you going to be there or are you not?"

"Maybe so. We'll see. G' bye!"

He was nervous. Had he given one of his natural enemies, an undergraduate, a hold over him?

He was jealous. Peony was off to meet some brash and unknown boy, who had the worst of intentions, while he himself had nothing but an innocent engagement with Mrs. Teckla Schaum.

Teckla's father, the banker and trustee, owned a one-room cottage with a cook-stove and a two-story bunk, six miles out of town, on Lake Elizabeth, to be reached by a sandy trail, on foot or with horse and buggy. The Pridmores had given him a key and told him to call the shack his own; here he had worked undisturbed on his book about the American Orators—it was, in fact, an excellent place for catching up on sleep. And here, this evening, while the early autumn was still warm, he was to picnic with Teckla.

The road to the lake was deep in scrub oak and hazelnut and sumac; flies gyrated in a backward dream of summer; and the aged Pridmore horse moved unambitiously.

The time should have been full of contentment, but Professor Planish, driving, his shoulder bundled against Teckla's, felt that he was wasting his talent. He was impatient even with the glimpses of the lake through networks of brush, for he wanted to be undisturbed in his thoughts of Peony Jackson. Yet Teckla took this touchy time to chatter, looking at him as though she owned him, as though she were his mother, his true sweetheart.

"Did the Freshman Rhetoric go well, Gideon? Was it a terrible ordeal?"

"What do you mean, 'ordeal'?"

"You always say the freshmen are so stupid——"

"I never said anything of the sort! I said some of 'em are. But some of 'em are mighty bright. *Mighty* bright! Keen, unspoiled minds. They're eager, not blasé or fussy, like a lot of older people."

"I suppose that's so—— Did you use my stuff about Trollope?"

"No, I didn't!"

"Oh."

"Well, I used part of it. And I had to go to the dentist's, this noon."

"Oh, you poor darling! Did he hurt you?"

"No, he didn't!"

"You sound so tired and cross, dear."

"Me? I'm not tired! *Or* cross!"

A vast silence, fringed with the tiny barbaric music of the flies and the thump of reluctant hoofs.

Professor Planish was not a cruel man; at least, he had

no definite pleasure in giving pain, not even to those he loved. He said repentantly, "I'm sorry if I sound touchy. I'm just worried—about the students."

"About what are you worried about about them?"

"About their morals! Freshmen girls making dates with unknown, immature boys! Very dangerous!"

"Is it?"

"Certainly it is! And then I've got to make out a whole lot of notes for—— In fact I have to be back in town by 9:30 sharp tonight."

"Oh, I'm sorry. It's such lovely soft fall weather. I was hoping we might stay at the shack all night."

"I'd like that fine—nothing I'd like better—but tonight I just can't make it. Have to be back by 9:30 at the latest."

Silence.

She said slowly, "I wonder how long it'll be before some sweet young thing that's lots younger than I am will take you away from me."

He started to forswear himself, then felt honest. He not infrequently did. He spoke affectionately—to the little mother:

"I don't know. Maybe some time. Not for a long time, let's hope. But if that ever does happen, no girl can be half as tolerant of me and all my fool talk about fool ambitions as you are."

"No, she won't be. Kiss me!"

The Pridmore shack, unpainted but clean and trim, was of the same autumnal golden-gray as the long rough grass upon the bluff above the lake, which slept in a stilly haze.

[74]

Peace came upon the Professor, and for seconds at a time he forgot Peony Jackson and his need of her. Stripped to trousers and thin ribbed undershirt and looking, with his brown beard, like a Manet portrait of an artist picnicking on the Seine, he ran along the pebbly edge of the lake, and skimmed stones across the tender-colored water, savagely breaking its pliant surface. Teckla was happy because his fretfulness seemed to be over, and happily she spread their supper on a black-and-red tablecloth in front of the shack. The lake was half copper, half rose, now, and the western horizon exclamatory.

When she called him to supper, he felt young and gay. But she was looking at him with such possessiveness. And she was always doing things for him—oh, he liked to have things done for him, but he certainly didn't like to have people think that he ought to think that they were doing things for him.

She had brought out for him a canvas reclining chair, but she herself squatted on the grass.

He raged to himself: that was how she'd try to hold him—by pretending to be so thoughtful that he would try not to hurt her feelings. And she was so settled and routine. He wanted adventure. "I'm going places," he vowed. Yet he was surprised to hear himself bawling at her, "Oh God, not hard-boiled eggs again!"

He would have thrown himself pettishly into the canvas chair, but it just wasn't the kind of chair you threw yourself into—not pettishly. He lowered himself into it, as he went on, "You're always kind to me, Teckla, but you haven't got one bit of imagination."

Was this nice, to be hurting her like this? No, maybe not; but he'd better get it over, for keeps. "Can't you ever think of anything new? You're in a rut, just like Kinnikinick College. Wake up!"

She mutely turned her eyes away from his scolding. She sat limp and wordless, then crept up into his lap, softly kissing his cheek, forgiveness-begging for whatever terrible thing it was that she must have done.

He thought, gosh, this chair will collapse with the two of us, but how can I tell her to get the hell off my lap, the poor darling, the damn sentimentalist?

He thought, she's so hot and sticky, her hand feels sticky as fly-paper, and it beats all get-out how heavy she is for such a thin woman.

He thought, this Peony Jackson is so fresh and jolly and *cool*. Even if she is a little plump. And so brainy. Wouldn't have to keep explaining and apologizing to *her* all the time.

He said aloud, "Forgive me for being such an old sorehead today. I always am, the beginning of the school year. Well, we better get busy with the chow, or the cold eggs will get cold!"

He was at Postum's drug store at 9:56.

Miss Peony Jackson wiggled in at 9:59. Without looking at him she went to the cosmetics counter and said, "Have you a small box of rice powder?" She was even fresher and softer and more miraculously special than he had remembered.

As she turned around, he said, "Oh, good evening, Miss Jackson."

She said, "Oh, good evening, Professor."

"Can I buy you a soda?"

"A soda?"

"Why, yes."

"Oh, a soda. I'm afraid it's very late, Professor."

"No, do sit down and have a soda. Or a sundae. I want to ask your opinion about—weekly themes."

"Well——" Her voice was plain, but as she sat down her eyes seduced him.

7

FOR A GENTLEMAN PROFESSOR in Kinnikinick College to look upon a maiden student as a human being was poorly thought of, and to meet her over a dish of marshmallow, ground nuts, caramel and two kinds of ice cream was as dangerous morally as it was dietetically. Now that he had once run that danger, he did not dare try to see her except across the footlights in his Rhetoric class.

She was, by alphabetical arrangement, half-way back in the room now, and when he started his second lecture, he looked about for her flutteringly, and was reassured by her smile that said, "Yes, here I am!" Through his discourse, her attention told him that he was good—but afterward she treacherously slipped away with the rest of the class, and he was in a terror of uncertain love.

He knew that for the first time he was really in love. In all his life he would have only four or five people who would completely know him and accept him. Certainly Teckla Schaum did not. For all his warnings that he would be stepping out into glory, she thought that he was really a born progenitor and mower of lawns, who would settle blissfully into domesticity if she was but loving and patient. Of these four or five connoisseurs of Gideon Planish,

Peony would be the only seducible girl, and he no more intended to lose her than to lose his life.

His chance to talk with her came at the Freshman Reception, held in the gymnasium, which was decorated with red and green paper streamers and an enormous sign "Welcome Class o' 1925."

The male costumes at the reception ranged from President Bull's white tie and tails to old Professor Eakins's eccentric white flannel suit and red bow, with Professor Planish soundly middle-road in a dinner jacket. The hundred freshmen, in the ancient religious ceremony of the Reception Line, filed before the president, the dean of men and the dean of women, and all the full professors, complete with wives, fetishistically shaking hands as though they really enjoyed the rite and from the magic touch gained heroic strength. The preceptorial priests themselves were hypnotized and stood mystically flapping their arms and croaking "Spleasure." The only one who kept awake was Professor Planish, and he only till after he had felt the firm warmth of Peony's young paw.

Yet during the reception he was apparently devoted to Mrs. Bull, the wife of the new president. She was ten years older than Professor Planish, but she looked sparkling; she wore a Chicago dinner-gown and a Cedar Rapids hair-wave, and she liked young professors.

Professor Planish felt that he might need influence at court very soon, and he danced with Mrs. Bull twice, stepping high and wiggling his plump behind and thrusting out his beard in an ecstasy of social elegance, and telling her that on the entire Atlantic Seaboard he had not found a lady with so light a foot and such vital ideas about teaching domestic science. In return, she gave out everything about her son Eddie, aged eleven.

Just once he danced with Peony, and that far more sedately than with Mrs. Bull. But he had been watching her, in her cheery yellow silk frock with a golden girdle, kicking up hoydenish heels with unspeakable brutes of young freshmen.

Now he was talking to Peony; he was talking to a woman, not to a social obligation:

"Why didn't you come up after class, last time?"

"I didn't want people talking about me."

"You mean about *us!*"

"Why, Professor Planish!"

"I'm not Professor Planish, and you know it. I'm Gid."

"Gid!" mockingly.

"I've got to see you."

"It's so hard. I'd like to, but people watch you. You're too popular, Gid!"

"Nonsense. I'm just unmarried. Listen! You know that little park across the tracks from the station? Nobody from the college ever goes there."

Mocking again: "I suppose that's where you always have your dates with co-eds!"

"I've never had a date with a girl there and you know it."

"How would I know it?"

"Because I just told you so, and I never lie—to you. Can't you feel that's true? Don't you know it?"

"Maybe—yes!"

"Then be there in the park at ten tomorrow evening."

"I'll try."

"Do you like me, Miss Jackson?"

"I can't tell yet, Professor Planish. I don't know how sound you are on the gold standard."

They laughed. That laugh was the only possible betrayal in a tabby-looking conversation, and Professor Planish looked hastily to see if Teckla and President and Mrs. Bull were observing. No, he was still safe.

With Teckla he danced only once. She had been frozen in with the chaperones, the faculty wives, who all had a fixed and smiling look of intense distaste.

"Having a good time, Teckla?" he glowed.

"All right, but it's not much fun for me to sit back like a Mother in Zion."

"I'll dance with you again, and I'll see you home, and now I'll bring you a bottle of strawberry pop. I know how you like strawberry pop."

He did not dance with her again, but he did bring her a bottle of that horrible drink, and he did "see her home." He had always been afraid of scandal for himself—he had sometimes gone so far as to fear it for Teckla—and he rarely was to be seen entering her house later than suppertime. When she said, "Come on in for a while," he gurgled, "I don't really think I'd better. Got to think of your reputation, you know!"

Brightly. Like a professor.

She snapped at him, "Oh, come *in!*"

In the house, she held him with her hands on his shoulders. "Is there something wrong tonight, Gideon?"

"Course not!"

"Because if there is—— Gideon, you never once looked at me. When I was dancing with you, I was dancing with a stranger—a stranger that didn't like me very much. Darling, it's awfully hard to see a man that you know so well suddenly turn into a stranger right in your arms, with the muscles and the way he moves all different. I knew something was distracting you—I really felt frightened."

"Oh, you just imagined——"

"Why do you ever lie to me? I always catch you, you know. Even college professors or preachers oughtn't to lie unless they can get away with it—— So you fell pretty hard for her! Didn't you!"

He was aghast.

"Oh, I could see it. Gideon, she must be ten years older than you are. At least."

"R?"

"I know she's handsome, but after all, Gideon, Mrs. Bull *is* the president's wife——"

He hooted with noisy joy; he kissed her with fond brotherliness. But his relief was not merely in being safe; it was equally in being free from Teckla's understanding. "She doesn't really know me then. She's never got through to me. There's only one girl that can, that ever will," he rejoiced to himself, as he palavered aloud, "Mrs. Bull? I don't even know she exists. You don't know how funny your jealousy is, Teck! Matter of fact, my crime is much worse than being after a married woman—my crime is that I was making up to her in order to stand in with the president, and that *is* pretty low!"

"Yes, it is, you bad thing!" She was delighted; she believed him. "Do sit down, and I'll make you a cup of coffee."

"No, I got to be moving."

"Why? It's not late. And you won't do any more work this evening."

"No, I just——"

"Gideon, I do love you so. God knows why, but I do. But you don't have to make love to me, if you stay. If you'll just go on being a friend—— You'll never have any idea what it can mean to a widow, a young widow, who was so happily married, not to have a man around the house to turn to and have him close the shutters and open the bottles and be bossy. It's terrible not to have anybody care enough for you to boss you and—— Oh, sorry I'm sentimental. But don't neglect me again the way you have at the reception all evening."

(He was thinking, "Oh, all women are annoying—except one. They poison the very instincts that ought to lead a man on and up to a clearer light. Why don't I be honest with this female? Go on, Dr. Planish—can you ever be honest? By God, I will!")

"Teck! You've saved my life, out here in Kinnikinick," he flowered.

"And I do give you coffee."

"Very fine coffee! But now I'm going to be very serious, and this may sound like a funny question, but do you think I'll have a chance to be a leader of the United States Senate some day and maybe even go higher—say a post in the Cabinet?"

"How can I——"

"Do you?"

"No! Frankly, I don't. I think you are a good teacher—you have a sort of zest that makes up for what you lack in scholarship——"

"So I lack in scholarship!"

"——but I don't think you'd ever have the patience or the ideas to become a political leader."

"Darling Teckla! Oh, I don't mind. But you don't really believe in me."

"I think I love you—some!"

"That's sorta beside the point. You're tired. You lack the enthusiasm of youth. I shall certainly try to keep from it, but I'm afraid that, as you yourself hinted recently, some day I'll fall in love with some girl that's—oh, call it credulous, if you want to."

"Have you fallen for one yet?"

"No, of course not!" (He congratulated himself, "That's the only lie I've had to tell her!") "But I might. And if I ever did, I know that she and I would both turn to you as the wisest and kindest woman living, as a woman——"

"Hey now, wait! I'm only thirty-three, you know, not seventy-three. Oh, yes, I suppose I'd be kind and sensible —damn it!"

He had, then, to get through not over six minutes of farewells.

He felt, on his way home, that he had won a triumph,

though he was not quite sure what it was. But it must have something to do with keeping him free to advance the welfare of mankind. He put on his own halo, and it stuck there till he was asleep—a child in Vulcan, hearing a distant train.

On that evening of early October there was neither harvest moon nor the wine stains of afterglow, but only dusty air and an uneasy brilliance from the arc light on the station platform. Professor Planish was wriggling on a bench in the sick little park, feeling vaguely foolish yet trembling with the coming glory. He tried to look at a line of flat-looking flatcars, at a bumptious little caboose, but he could really see nothing till, miraculously, Peony was crossing the tracks, carefully stepping over the rails. He knew that it was she, but he couldn't believe it, for she was grown-up and rich and courtly in a white-flannel cape with a gold-braided military collar.

She said in a small voice, "Hello."

He slipped his arm under her coat, he whispered, "My girl—my girl!" and he kissed her lips. "Do you know that I'm in love with you?"

She said comfortably, "Oh, you couldn't be."

"Well, darn it, I am!"

"That's good."

"Are you in love with me at all?"

"Sure. I have been for almost a year. Oh, yes. I came down from Faribault with Daddy, to see about my entrance, and we sneaked into your Rhetoric class. Dad said you were a great spellbinder."

"And what did *you* think?"

"I thought you were cute. Oh, all right, all right, don't look so cross. I thought you were wonderful."

"You know, all this is extraordinary. What are we going to do?"

"Do, Professor? Why, as I seem to have led you captive already—with practically no expense for lipstick—we might get married."

"Oh, yes. Married."

"You've heard of it?"

"I certainly have, and we're going to be married, at the proper time, but I want you to finish at least two years of college."

"Why?"

"Oh, to be prepared to take a great place in the world. I'm not going to stay in a dump like Kinnikinick all my life."

"I should hope not! But why can't I be married and still go to school?"

"Against the college rules here for an undergraduate to get married."

"Why, the old meanies! Anyway, there's no rule against being engaged. Will I do some ring-flaunting! (I know where we can borrow a dandy ring, if you're busted.) Will I sit in class and stare at you and embarrass you! 'Folks, meet Pee Jackson, the fiancée of that charming Professor Planish, the poor dope!' Poor Professor! Darling Professor! Do I call you Gideon or Gid?"

"Gid, I guess. But darling, look here——"

It had come to him that if Teckla heard of his being

engaged, she would be annoyed, and that her father was chairman of the Kinnikinick Board of Trustees, who could make the place itchy for a professor, contract or no. He picked up Peony's hand and kissed it and put it carefully back, and told her the whole story of himself and Teckla—or enough of it for daily use. It had never been so nearly easy for him to be so nearly honest. He asserted that Teckla was a good and helpful soul, and Peony did nothing more than snarl, "I don't trust *any* woman!" and, at the end, demand, "But now you're not even going to have tea, call it tea, with that woman any more, are you!"

Certainly he wasn't. How could she think of such a thing?

"Gideon! If her father and the trustees are likely to cut up—maybe get us scandalized—why do we need to stay here? Maybe it's time for you to beat it, on and upward. Excelsior!"

"Maybe it is, at that. I'd like to have a job in Columbia University."

"But I see you doing something more active than teaching, Gideon. You're still so young——"

"Do I seem young to you?"

"A baby! What you could do! You're the kind could buck the business world, say, like a banker or running a fifty-thousand-acre farm. And you're so eloquent I just love it, but why didn't you take up economics instead of rhetoric? Some day maybe you'll be governor or a senator."

"Now isn't that strange, your speaking about that! I've

[87]

always had a hunch I could do something big in politics—get to the top—and of course do a lot of good for people."

"Yes—sure—do a lot for people."

"You really think I could?"

"Sure you could! I know it! Oh, Gideon, isn't it wonderful! And do you think I could help you? I bet at dinner at the Governor's Mansion, I could get all the old bags talking and laughing like a son of a gun, don't you think so?"

"Sure you could! I know it! And it would make all the difference, your believing in me, so I'd have self-confidence and be geared for success. That's what wins—being geared for success, don't you see?"

"Yes, I can see that now."

"Not be willing to take anything but the best—in fame and financial rewards and power—and the ability to do good—and be friendly with all the big men, like the Rockefellers. Have your machine tooled for top-notch success and refuse to go on with poky little jobs in places like Kinnikinick. That's the formula!"

"Oh, yes!"

"And with you, I'll do it! Darling!"

She kissed him to exhaustion.

"We are engaged then," he said. "But can you keep it secret?"

"I'm the best Mata Hari in college—but of course a good Mata Hari."

He scarcely dared to, but it was a critical question, and he whispered, "How good?"

She whispered back, "That depends. Not too good."

Then, loudly and brashly, sounding like a freshman, she yelped, "Gracious! It's late! I've got to skip."

She was gone before he could grasp her flying white cape, and he didn't know when he was to see her again.

For weeks he agitatedly never did know when he was going to see her again, except at Rhetoric class, where she looked up at him like an amiable monkey.

8

Two weeks gone; they were in October, and he had a birthday and was thirty years old. Teckla gave a birthday party just for the two of them, with cake and ice cream, and a bottle of Iowa corn whisky for a present. Still he could not tell Teckla, except by a cagy flinching which told her too well, that his love had left her and flown off to the wars.

Yet he was less afraid of Teckla than of Dr. Edith Minton. It was distinctly out of his way to pass Lambda House, where Dr. Minton dragoned it and Peony lived in horrid security from seduction, but he passed it, twice a day. He tried to look like a real professor, bustling along in strict devotion to paragraphing and suffixes, but he could not help peering hungrily at the yellow wooden Ionic of Lambda House. It did seem reasonable that just once, at least, he might see Peony up there in her room, shining in a chemise, but what he more often saw was the eyeglasses of Dr. Minton.

She would probably rush out some day and grab him and haul him off to President Bull. Oh, he was a most harassed young professor!

He hated Dr. Edith Minton, he hated President Bull, he was afraid of Teckla Schaum and her father, and he was done with college—place of twittering and of marks. He wanted to be out on the broad highway, skipping hand in hand with Peony, and he was willing now to take any highway—even an insurance agency. He had written to a dozen colleges about a brighter job, but his letters conveyed no huge confidence in his own ability to go on tenderly leading Youth amid the orchards of knowledge.

He who had often told his students, "An inspired business letter can pull the heart-strings of the prospect just as well as the best love lyrics by Shelley or James Whitcomb Riley"—he himself could think of nothing more forceful to write than, Please, he would like a new job.

He hadn't enough Boosters or Contacts, he decided. He had no one but President Bull to recommend him. The authorities at Adelbert College and the University of Ohio did not, he guessed, feel strongly about him; in fact, they had distinctly stopped feeling about him at all. Somebody had said that Hatch Hewitt, his sardonic classmate, was already a powerful newspaper reporter in New York, but just where was he?

Professor Planish sighed, and wrote in his notebook, "In future career shd cultivate hold onto friends more esp ones w influence, big bankers, journalists, must be sure to do this, memo: ask P what she thinks, she has so much sense."

He mustn't let himself get lost in the thicket of academic life, he warned, and in a fury of contemporary research he read almost entirely through a copy of the Nation—until he realized, from the fact that it com-

[91]

mented not too affectionately on Mr. Harding's campaign, that it was a year old.

Professor Planish persuaded himself that he studied current events as carefully as an undertaker. But this autumn of Peony, he noticed nothing except that Mr. Harding was a handsome, confidence-showering man, and that, after Wilson's demands, it was "fine to be back to Normalcy." He stated this often at party dinners full of the two kinds of faculty wives: those who sighed and were shabby and talked about diapers, and those who were hard and flirtatious and shiny, and talked about the latest shows in New York. Of the two sorts, the latter was the more provincial and more likely to send him off yelling for Peony.

The casting and direction of the college play, to which he had looked forward as an orgy of unacademic art and a much better ground than classrooms for getting thick with the pretty girls, proved, entirely on account of Peony, to be an embarrassing game of hide and seek.

The play this time was a nasty little work called *Poor Papa's Prize*, one of those farces (1 set, inter., 3 acts, 6 f. 5 m.) jammed with references to Hoboken and mothers-in-law, which in 1921 were still the delight of provincial colleges that twenty years later would be haughty with Saroyan and Sherwood and Maxwell Anderson. It was the idea in such colleges then, and often much later, that the position of Professor of Speech and Rhetoric automatically equipped the holder with a tricky and veteran art in such matters as lights, make-up and stealing lumber for scenery, and that a Professor Gideon Planish ranked with Belasco and Lincoln J. Carter.

He agreed, and he considered *Poor Papa's Prize* as on the same level with Aristophanes. He thought it was a very funny scene when Papa's prize turned out to be ten thousand plugs of tobacco, not dollars. He felt masterful about stage business and gestures, but with all this wizardry he was overthrown by the fact that, even with the grossest nepotism, there was no way of wedging Peony Jackson into the cast.

She came faithfully to the try-outs, happy and handsome in the best green sweater that ever came out of Faribault, Minnesota. She read in turn for the parts of the ingénue, the mother, the comic great-aunt and the comic Swedish maid, and she read them all with the same pleased smile, the same accent, and the same complete lack of meaning. Sitting back in the unlighted auditorium, his hat over his eyes and his legs thrust way out, like a professional director, Professor Planish pitied her and loved her for her lack of talent.

She stopped, looked down into the dark pit, smiled in unspoken agreement, and said, "My, I am rotten, ain't I! Do you suppose I could do the props, Professor Planish?"

"You can! You shall!" he shouted.

But before working the properties, she had first to acquire them, which was a combination process of theft and brazen borrowing, and though his one dream had been of snuggling beside her in the darkness, she was rarely there at rehearsals. He was cross about it. He scolded the actors, and they hated him; and all this time the letters he was getting from other colleges in answer to his petitions indicated that they thought he had too big a job already.

At last Professor Planish knew every one of the fine and racking sorrows that glorify young lovers.

She was there for a moment after rehearsals, painting a pine box which was going to impersonate a grandfather's-clock, and he gave her the first of all his gifts. In the window at Postum's College Pharmacy he had seen a "Novelty Gift Make-up Kit" that had tickled everything that was young and fanciful in him: a pink, leather-covered box containing nail polish and drying cream and all the feminine idiocies that seemed to him strange and luxurious; with a mirror, inside the lid, that was shaped somewhat like a shield and somewhat like a diamond and a good deal like the map of Africa. It cost $5.65, which was, except in the case of Teckla's bracelet, $2.65 more than, on any grounds, even those of extreme passion, he had hitherto ever been willing to pay as love's tribute. He bought it, but he had them wrap it in plain white paper. Full-Professor Planish did not wish to be seen going about with Novelty Gift Kits.

After rehearsal, back-stage, he was able to slip the package covertly into Peony's hands. She yanked off the wrapping, let the paper slide to the floor—he picked it up —and opened the box.

"Oh!" she squealed, with an ecstasy that delighted and rewarded him. She would have made an excellent monkey to have around and smile at, if her face had been thinner and less fair. She picked out each of the charming bottles, she studied them with pleasure, she pinched them, she smelled them, and then she kissed him in the double rapture of love and cosmetics.

Every night, without ever having quite agreed upon it, they headed for that same dim bower behind a prop fireplace—every night until, just as he scrambled over a sawbuck and a pile of flats to reach her, he saw Dr. Edith Minton watching him from the shadows beside the switchboard.

His talent for swift intrigue was considerable. With no especial stress he called, "Uh, Miss—Miss Jackson—when can you help Miss Smidley with the gelatines? Good gracious, I wish I could make you children understand the importance of lights!"

Peony had an even richer natural intrigue. She could actually see nothing more menacing than a roll of canvas and the beard of Professor Planish, but she replied loudly, in the naked tone of a scared freshman, "Oh, I am trying to get to it, Professor, but I've been studying so hard." (Followed in her miniscule silvery murmuring that could not carry beyond him, "You little sweet thing. Who is it? Go bite hell out of him.")

He turned his back on her, turned his back on everything that was joyful and fresh and living, and not too elaborately he then proceeded to discover Dr. Minton, off R. "Why, hel-lo, Edith!"

("The blasted iceberg! I suppose she wants to bawl me out for something. I ain't going to take it. I'm her boss.")

But Dr. Minton was smiling in a puzzling, diffident

way, and as he wabbled up to her she hesitated, "I've been listening from the back of the auditorium. I think you're doing wonderfully with the rehearsals, Gideon. Have you finished for tonight? You don't happen to be walking my way, do you?"

"Fine! Let's go!"

Professor Count Cagliostro pranced away with the princess. There were times when he wished that he were not a charlatan, not even a charlatan of genius, but the ear for applause, the taste for spiced meats, always dragged him on.

Dr. Minton was saying, as they cantered respectably to Lambda House, "I was admiring the way you taught that stupid boy his Irish accent for the play. Do you know, Gid—I've never confessed this to any one at Kinni-kinick—when I was a girl, I wanted to be an actress."

"No!"

"I had a lot of eagerness and maybe some ability. But I had to take care of mother, and I got into graduate work, and my thesis was so demanding, and there never happened to be any chance and—— Oh, I guess it's better the way it is—— Gideon!"

He jumped. "Yes, Edith?"

"You haven't been at Lambda House for quite a while now. Do drop in, won't you?"

"Oh, yes—yes, sure."

"And Gideon!"

"Ye-es, Edith?"

"Let me know if any of my girls in the play are ever

[96]

lazy or impertinent, and I'll take their heads off. It does seem to me that this year they're the most undisciplined gang of young female rowdies I've ever had to deal with. You're lucky you don't know any of them outside the classroom, as I have to."

"Ee—that's so."

"It's this Post-War Generation, and Prohibition. But I know how to handle 'em. Don't let them waste your time. Good night. Such a pleasant walk!"

He was aghast. "She likes me a lot better than I thought. There's a volcano under that ice-cap. How come both Teckla and Edith like me? Oh, I suppose there isn't much for 'em here—nothing but undergraduates, and all married men on the faculty except me and one pansy and one drunk.

"Nothing but undergraduates—but that's what Peony will be falling for—some hairy-chested young clown of a football player, as soon as she gets over the novelty of my being crazy about her. Oh God, I'm sure to lose her!

"But Edith Minton—she is good-looking, too, in that Diana sort of way. I might of had a chance, if I'd gone right after her—no, no, I mustn't think about such things. I'm absolutely faithful to Peony, absolutely, the damn Cheshire cat, the way she grins at me, she's absolutely onto me and yet she still likes me—— But for her sake, I ought to give her up entirely. After all, she is a freshman. Not twenty yet. Just a baby, the darling. If Edith, the vixen, ever thought a faculty-member had so much as patted Peony's hand, out she'd go—they'd send her home, with a scandal tied to her, nobody would know exactly what it was, but it would get worse year after year.

"If I could marry her now—— No, she ought to finish her college course. A college course is absolutely necessary, nowadays. I suppose colleges have some value. Hell, of course, they must have! Didn't I do time breaking rocks for three whole years so I could get a Ph.D.? Then after she graduated, I could marry her, if she wanted me, but I'd be too old and she'd of met so many boys—— Oh God!"

Out of all his babbling as he walked home, as he clumped about his white plaster bedroom, nothing came out clearly except that for Peony's dear sake, he ought honestly to give her up.

And for her sake he did honestly give her up; he did incredibly force himself to something he did not want to do.

Until the opening of the play, which had a successful run of two nights, it was not difficult to avoid her. He did not go back-stage when he felt, as he always did feel, that she was there. His dread was that she would come up after his Rhetoric class and demand to know why he was neglecting her. All through each class, he was enormously busy not looking at her, and thinking of the coming horror of her reproach.

The real horror was that she went placidly out with the other students, not glancing at him at all. So! he gasped. She wanted to break it off, too.

That made it harder.

The opening night of the play should have been his compensation. The college auditorium was full, with sixteen people standing; President and Mrs. Bull and Mr. Pridmore and a man from Buffalo, New York, were there; and sixteen newspapers were represented, in the persons of two student correspondents.

But except for Teckla Schaum, Edith Minton and Mrs. Bull, nobody congratulated Professor Planish, the director. In fact, most of the mob did not know there was such a thing as a director, and it was the actors and the student orchestra whom the groundlings applauded. When the comic Irish hired man tried to be Irish and comic, this supposedly cultured audience (the Professor noted bitterly) clapped and whistled as though it hadn't been the director who had hammered every ringing "Shure an' Oi will" into that stiff Pottawattamie County larynx.

The hall was rich in college flags and fragrant bundles of kinnikinick; the light caressed the actors capering up there in the magic frame of the stage picture; and even old Professor Eakins leaned forward with a refined leer. But no one looked gratefully at Professor Planish; no one knew.

He had to force himself to go back between acts and congratulate his cast. They scarcely heard him, for they knew how good they were, even if they blissfully didn't know how good they weren't. He made much of ignoring Peony, but as she was helping shift scenery, she did not notice. He left by the stage entrance and walked half-way around the building to the lobby, chilled in the darkness of an early November night, more chilled in the wind

[99]

of man's ingratitude and woman's greed. In the lobby, he posed a little, not too conspicuously, but it did no good. President Bull said only, "I think they are doing very well."

They!

Mrs. Bull, Teckla and Edith Minton did recognize him as somebody they had seen somewhere, but the rest of the herd did not look at him—they were right there at the Battle of Waterloo, and Wellington was riding past them, and all they talked about was the costumes of the lesser drummer-boys.

After the play he went home, with the curtest of congratulations to the cast and the stage crew. And Peony had had the nerve to smile at him as if everything were all right!

He was extremely angry with Peony. And it scarcely seemed worth while now to have attended two real stage plays in New York and one in New Haven in order to equip himself as a professional director.

He sat in his room, and earnestly kept from telephoning to Peony at Lambda House. She might have known, mightn't she, that he was doing this, and have telephoned to him instead? Mightn't she?

For the first time in his life, Professor Planish had insomnia, which to him had been merely a silly word, like prolegomenon. He had sometimes lain awake for five minutes, but then his face, tucked deep into the pillow, would turn peaceful and childish and still. Now, he went to bed tired and drowsy, but there was no sleep. It simply was not there. He was as astonished as though he should put down his hand and find his familiar legs missing.

This was all nonsense. He'd lie still and quit thinking about Peony and Teckla and Edith; he'd relax. He did relax, so elaborately that he was frantic with the tension of keeping himself limp.

All right then; hell with it. He just wouldn't do anything. He'd trick himself. He'd pretend not to notice himself, and drift off into sleep.

None of this strategy worked, and he kept on being very noticeable indeed to himself. He was sleepy and there was no sleep. The machine, always as dependable as light or air, was not working.

It was with surprise, and some pride in finding himself so complex a person, that he realized that this was insomnia—the sort of thing that Mrs. Bull boasted of having. Well, he *was* a case! Insomnia! Hopeless love and self-sacrifice and a theatrical opening and insomnia all on the same day!

He became bored even by his singularity. It was interesting to have spiritual distress up to the point of insomnia, but he wanted to get some sleep along with it. He was becoming distinctly tireder, but ever more resolutely awake. Well, why not give up the insomnia for the present, and try it tomorrow night? Just now, he needed a little sleep, to be fresh for his Oral Persuasion class in the morning.

The insomnia would not be given up. It calmly stayed on, and Professor Planish was annoyed.

Well, he was a man of the world and a psychologist.

He'd rise and smoke a cigarette and relax and lie down again. Certainly. He was one who could always turn the current of his thoughts.

He smoked the cigarette and lay down again, and instantly he was as awake and quietly frantic as ever.

He seemed to be in an unfamiliar and unwelcoming world, with its own cold tone and every sensation different from the secure world of daytime. Nothing could be identified. There was a rattle that might be far off, on the campus, and might be fearfully near him, in the house —something like the rattle of a milk wagon or a lame man walking or clicks from a revolver. The half-drawn window shade quivered with but little breeze, and its half glow seemed to change, as though some one were passing between it and the street lamp down below. The night sounds were woven together, defying his vulgar daytime ears to identify them.

He had been seeing images of Peony, her young breast and her smile of friendly irony, but now he was not thinking at all, nor feeling. He floated in a sublimated current in which no thought was definite, no emotion quite real.

The urgent whistle of the Chicago Special, hastening to the East and all its glories, awoke him, and his square face moved with smiling as in half-dreams he was certain that some day he would take that train and be welcomed in lofty rooms by millionaires and poets and actresses. But he wanted to know them so that he might take their friendship and glory to Peony, he thought in his descending sleep.

9

FOR THREE NIGHTS the insomnia returned, with its mockery. For three nights he told himself that he was protecting Peony and her reputation; for three nights he retorted that he was really afraid only for his own job, which he would lose if it should be known that he was a tamperer with virgins. It seemed to him that his rooms, with their suggestions of a professorial life, their piles of *The Annals of the Northern and Midwestern Society for Semantics*, brought on his illness. If he could go off to a fresh rude place, then he could sleep.

After the third night of torture, on an edged late afternoon of November he tramped out to the Pridmore shack, by the rustic shore of Lake Elizabeth. He had told no one but his landlady. He was not in a mood to have Teckla come mothering him.

The six-mile walk, the first two miles a panting discomfort but the rest a vigorous swing, deep-breathing through the dusk, with the smell of leaf mold and fresh lake water and cornstalks about him, restored his life. He carried a professorial briefcase, but he swung it buoyantly.

He had his own key to the shack. Whistling, he opened the door, groped in the one rough room, lighted a lantern, lighted a fire in the small stove. The room smelled pleasantly of fresh-cut wood and burning resin, and in it there was healing and woodland peace. From his respectable briefcase, of unscarred and glossy tan leather with GP stamped on it in sleek gold, he took out one large pork chop.

He dropped it into the frying pan, and the sizzle was cheerful and somehow manly. Sure. He was an outdoor man as well as a deep scholar, and some day he was going to cut down a tree. Maybe not too big a one, for a start.

He gnawed at the pork chop when it was practically cooked and, more daintily, he ate a chocolate bar, and humped over in a chair beside the stove, his arms hanging between his knees and, without quite remembering what it was, he hummed a lyric of his boyhood:

> You hold her hand and she holds yours,
> And that's a ve-ry good sign
> That she's your tootsy-wootsy
> In the GOOD old SUM-mer TIME.

Yes. Everything would come out all right, in the providence of God and President T. Austin Bull and the courageous Professor Planish. He laughed, he opened the stove door and spat into it as gallantly as a lumberjack. And then he yawned. . . . He'd loaf a moment before basking in the pages of *The Americanization of Edward Bok*, which was in his briefcase, just slightly spotted with pork.

Still dressed, and purring, he lay meditatively on the

lower bunk. Just how everything would come out all right, he was not quite sure, but he'd do something clever— he'd count on Mrs. Bull—count on Peony, who was smarter than any of the faculty—good old summer time and that's a very good sign—summer time, summer meadows, deep meadows with Peony——

The wooden latch of the cottage was creaking. A thousand years later, the door was closing and whole armies were blundering across the room with thunderous efforts to be mice. If he just kept hidden in that deep soft dark well of sleeping, they would go away and not torture him.

A whole history after that, he had a witch-led illusion that he had heard Peony's giggle. Giggle—chuckle—low laugh—what would he call it? Illusion, all illusion. But revolving aeons after that, he came sharp awake as some one sat on the edge of his bunk. Bewildered, defenseless, he heaved up his ponderous head—and, by God, it was Peony Jackson sitting there.

"Hello," said Peony.

"What in the—— How did you——"

"Why, I walked, same as you did, great one. My gracious, that's a long dark walk through all those woods, even if I did borrow Mrs. Hilp's electric torch. Twice I got lost, and I've looked into more darn shacks that *weren't* yours—you'd be surprised if you knew how many shacks on this ole lake aren't this one, even after you prowl around 'em and burgle 'em——"

"But how in——"

"Your landlady said she thought you'd come out here. Of course I knew in a general sort of way. When we had the Lambda picnic out here on the lake, all the girls pointed out the Secret Love Nest of the Widow Schaum and Professor Planish."

"R!"

"But it's simply classic how different it looks in the dark, with all the cunning ole tree roots reaching out to trip you up."

"LOVE NEST! Now what do you mean by——"

"Oh, yes. That's one of the reasons why you'll have to marry me. Professor Planish, how could you! The other reason is that it's now seven minutes past midnight——"

"What?"

"You heard me, dearest. So I'll have to stay all night, now—— Cheer up, poor lamb. You don't really have to marry me, you know. I don't care a hoot." She bent, to kiss him lightly. "I want you to quit worrying about that poor lil freshman gal, Jackson. 'Professor, my feeling is that a girl like her, with her upbringing and her father the best wholesale grocer in Southeastern Minnesota, a girl that would do a thing like that, absolutely pursuing that poor man out to the shack where he'd fled to hide from her after he'd been so careful and not even said a word to her after the college show, why, she deserves all she gets, because she must 've known what she was doing.' And did she know?"

Peony was off the bunk, swiftly crossing to his sacred briefcase, while he was still rubbing sleep out of his hair and eyes. "Of course she did, the little devil!" said Peony.

Busy and monkeylike as always, brimming and gay with monkeyism, she was pawing into his briefcase and bringing out his chaste bachelor possessions. "Hm. Silver-mounted hair brush. Pretty choice ... Squibb's toothpaste. You don't keep the tube rolled up tightly enough. I see where I'll have to educate you ... A book? Now what do you need a book for? Don't you *know*? ... And pajamas. Aw, the sweet lil baby-blue pajamas! Aw, Gid-eon! They're too sweet for words! With his lil monogram embroidered on his lil pocket! I'll look lovely in them!"

He was shocked now out of his immense lassitude and he was on his feet, weaving over to her.

"Baby, you've got to go home. I'll take you home."

"Do you think it would be any better for my reputation to have people see me walking into Kinnikinick with you at two o'clock in the morning?"

"Why——"

"Besides, I'm in Davenport. Staying overnight with my aunt. As I explained to Dr. Minton. Golly, I'll have to do some work on that aunt. How old do you think she'd be? Gideon, I'm going to stay. You know I'm always right. I always have been, all these years with you, haven't I!"

He rather thought that she always had been right, all these years, and anyway, with this particular young woman, how did you persuade her to let you be gallant if she didn't see anything in gallantry? With a prodigious effort, Professor Planish rose above the middle-class chivalry which he believed himself to have exemplified all these years. He kissed her, very close to her, and, hastily getting away from that, he commanded—only it sounded more as though he was petitioning—"All right. Probably it would be safer for you not to show up till tomorrow. You crawl in that lower bunk the way you are, and go to sleep, and I'll take the upper one. And I'll be good."

"Of course you'll be good, Professor Planish. You'd always be good to a poor freshman, wouldn't you?"

"Oh, shut up! You better take your shoes off."

"Do you honestly think that would be safe? To take my shoes off?"

"Oh, please shut up, darling! Good night."

With dignity he hoisted himself to the upper bunk. She had turned down the lantern but she had not blown it out. As in a Pullman berth, he wriggled out of his coat and vest and tie, tried to hang them on the edge of the bunk, then in fury threw them into the air, to flop on the floor.

Lying rigid, he realized that the room was rustling with the soft sound of buttons, of a zipper, of garters being unhooked, of the tiny plump of silk on the table. He looked over the edge and he could see his own pajamas being fantastically flapped in the air as she put them on. He lay back, sternly, and heard her blowing out the lantern; heard then, in the lake-whispering darkness, small bare feet crossing the floor, and the creak of the lower bunk.

In twenty seconds he went through a million light-years of sensations which he supposed to be thoughts. He had lost his fear of her and of her encroachment. He knew that it was not that she "trusted him," but that, for some imponderable reason, she cared enough for this poor

[108]

thing, himself, not to care whether he was to be "trusted" or not. He knew that he was now married, in the most old-fashioned and undivorceable monogamy.

Then, terrifyingly, she was sobbing, down there below him. He was out of his bunk like an alarm rocket, sitting by her and begging, "What is it, what is it, sweet?"

"I feel so shamed!"

"Oh, no!"

"Shamed and scared and lonely. It did seem like such a bright idea, back in town. I thought, 'Maybe he's lonely for me.' I thought, 'Maybe he wants me, dreadfully.' And I was so busy rushing out here, stumbling and getting sand in my shoes and losing my way and laughing—I thought it was fun—I never really thought till now, maybe you don't want me here. It's hard to realize, maybe to you I'm just another fool girl——"

He as nearly came of age then as Gideon Planish ever could. He grunted, "Move over." He patted her head down on his shoulder, and as her whimper died away and she was trustfully sleeping, moving her head only to burrow closer into his shoulder, he lay awake with no insomnia but with happiness and security.

They laughed as she dressed in the morning—she was approximately modest about it, but not a fanatic. They breakfasted on the end of the chocolate bar and pure cold water. They tramped, arms about each other while he swung his briefcase high, two miles to a farmhouse, where he hired a Ford. In town, while she sat on the floor of the car, out of sight, he recovered from the station the suitcase with which she had ostensibly been traveling, then drove her to Aloosia, and put her and the suitcase on the train there, so that she could return from Davenport in all decorum.

By this time they had been married, had honeymooned in Europe for a half year, had produced a family—four sons, and seen United States Senator Planish into his second term in Washington, and they thought extremely well of it all.

He called on Teckla Schaum that morning at 11:30, which for her was early. Widowhood had made of her a late lier, an avoider of all the problems of boredom which daylight brought to a lone woman.

He was shocked that it meant so little to him now to see Teckla in negligee, while to encounter Peony thus meant so much. He was, in fact, sorry for himself that he should have to feel so sorry for Teckla, but Peony's valor was with him, and he plunged:

"Honey, I guess the kindest way would be for me to come right out and——"

She wailed, "The kindest way for you would be to wait till I've had some coffee before you do whatever unpleasantness you refer to as 'the kindest thing.' Would you like a drink?"

"So early? No indeed!"

"Well, don't be so virtuous about it. Sit down and read the paper and I'll be with you in a minute."

He felt that Teckla was being pretty frivolous. Frivolity was all right for a girl like Peony, but Mrs. Schaum was supposed to be tragedy in a black veil—— Oh, let the poor thing cling to her fool's paradise for a few minutes more, the poor thing.

She was back in the room, dressed in rosy gingham, before he had finished sneering at the morning editorials. She said calmly, "Gid, I imagine you've come to tell me that you've finally managed to fall for some girl. Is that it?"

"Something like that, I'm afraid. But listen, dear: it's because I was a lonely scholar and you accustomed me to a woman's tender care that I ever began looking around——"

He was wondering whether he could get away with it. He was wondering why he was always honest—within reason—with Peony, yet capable of such acrobatics with other women.

She ignored his craft. "Gid, I suppose you wouldn't understand it, would you, if I said that I used to be so fierce and proud and pure that no one ever dared to try and use me; that if I've ever humbled myself to you, it's because Max's death broke me; and that I'm still at least proud enough not to hate you? I don't want to know about your girl, and I shan't snoop. Go with my blessing, if you still care for it."

"I do care for it, and I do need it, Teckla. I won't try to be proud——"

"Is that a crack?"

"No, honest to God it isn't! I mean, I can't afford to be proud, because if your father, as a trustee, got a down on me, it would probably ruin me, whereas if he thought it was you that—— Don't you see?"

[111]

"I suppose that's fair. He might think you'd been trifling with the poor widow-woman. I suppose he's so strong himself, in a queer, lonely, rustic way, that it wouldn't ever occur to him that, far from being too strong and vicious, you were so weak that you were perfectly willing to be my house cat. I'll have to tell him I threw you out——"

He told her that he'd see her in hell first. He was for a moment willing to give up Peony and the mild honor of wearing a professorial white collar rather than endure her sneering. Then she kissed him, as fondly as she ever had, and speculated, "Maybe you will grow up. Maybe I'm fond enough of you to want you to. Maybe that girl, whoever she is—oh, blast her!—can do it. I never could. So run along, and I'll take care of Father Pridmore—— Oh, Gid, be true to that poor girl, won't you? Women need loyalty so much; they're so bewildered when they don't get it, no matter who they are, young or old or famous or humble."

"I will!" said Professor Planish.

He had always been a good hand at Seeing the Proper People. He was calling upon the president's wife at five o'clock; he was drinking tea, with no especial distaste, and being eloquent.

Mrs. Bull was the first of many influential women whom he was to call "dear lady."

Dear lady, he explained, he was throwing himself upon her mercy; he was turning to her as the only human being who would understand. He was in love. (But purely.) Believe it or not (only she'd better believe it if she didn't want to mangle his heart), the first thing that had attracted him to this girl (no, wait, he'd tell her the name later) was that she was so much like Mrs. Bull; the same aristocratic manner, the same womanly sympathy, the same gimlet of intelligence and, if he might be so brash, the same agate eyes.

But, and here were the old accustomed woes, and Abelard and Heloise, and Rutherford B. Hayes and the postmistress, his girl was an undergraduate, here in Kinnikinick, and according to college regulations, and possibly the Bible and the State Constitution of Iowa, if they were married, she would have to drop out of college and less agile minds might even hint that there had been goings-on inconceivable in a rhetoric professor. And what would a lofty Puritan like President T. Austin Bull think about a teacher who confessed himself more enthralled by all women who reminded him of Mrs. T. Austin Bull than he was by the use of the semi-colon?

"You just leave that man Austy to me!" beamed Mrs. Bull. "Now what is your girl's name?"

At Christmas Holiday he was, for the first time, part of an authentic home.

There had been little of home in the thin brick house of his father in Vulcan—only a resentful contest between parents and children, between brother and brother. Professor Planish did have two brothers and a sister, but since he had left home they had existed for him only as a theory.

[113]

This Christmas, Peony masterfully carried him up to her family, to Whipple Jackson, vestryman and wholesale grocer, in Faribault. The place was bursting with brothers, sisters, aunts, sets of Walter Scott and Washington Irving, fudge, plum pudding, mandolin-playing, rum punch and family prayers immediately followed by family laughter; a wide white house that had thrown off wings and porches as a fountain throws off spray, up on the bluff near the Immaculate Conception church, looking across the noble Cannon River Valley to the towers of a whole tribe of preparatory schools.

President Bull had forgiven Peony and Professor Planish; he even seemed to think the marriage an excellent escape. He and the aged dean would permit Peony to take all the courses she wanted, as a special student, and they would manage to break the laws legally and give her a degree.

Teckla had had Peony to tea, and advised her about buying cuts of beef. But Dr. Edith Minton had looked at Professor Planish with astonishment and a certain fear in her eyes. That was the only thing he had to brush off in order to be riotous at Christmas. He did brush it off, very satisfactorily.

His welcome in the Jackson mansion was as warm as the forgiveness at Kinnikinick. Whipple Jackson was a rangy, nervous, good-tempered man, with ideas. "Gideon, my boy," he said, "Peony tells me you have a hankering to get into politics."

"I don't know, but anyway, I don't want to be stuck at teaching all my life."

"Well, if you ever want to start in here, let me know and I'll give you a job and introduce you to all the Boys. You'll like Faribault—best prep schools in the country, and did you know Faribault is the peony capital of the world? That's how I happened to name my girl. But if you're going in for politics—— Belong to a church, Gid?"

"Presbyterian."

"That's not so bad. The voters sure do like a man to be liberal in morals and illiberal in theology. But what about a lodge? Do you belong to the Masons? Odd-fellows? Elks? Modern Woodmen? Knights of Pythias? No? Better join 'em all; fine bunch of friends and they'll all vote for you, and speaking both as a patriotic citizen and a good churchman, there's only one thing a politician ought to bother about—the votes. Heh?"

"That's right, all right," said Professor Planish fervently, rejoicing at having a family to back and guide him.

They were married, Peony and he, in Easter vacation, 1922, with the Bishop starring. But if Peony played nothing more than ingénue at the wedding, it was she who took the lead when they returned to Kinnikinick, and she who chose a gold-and-scarlet cabinet to brighten up their cottage, and Professor Planish was so proudly in love that he liked it.

10

THE DEAN OF Kinnikinick College, Dean Gideon Planish—he was a new dean; in the fall of 1926, he had been so exalted for only a year—had almost finished the annual plague of straightening out undergraduate schedules. He was looking amiably at a thin girl with curly hair and troubled eyes, and he was chuckling.

"This won't do, Miss Janes. Your schedule is badly unbalanced. Three courses in literature! I never heard of such a thing! 'Advanced English Poetry' and 'The History of the Novel' and 'Chaucer and Spenser.' What do you plan to do? Teach?"

"I don't think so."

"What, then? Newspaper work? Write yarns?"

"I'm engaged to be married after I graduate."

"Then, good Lord, what do you want to take all this books-and-reading for? They're no good for running a household. What is the idea, anyway?"

"I don't think I have any. I just like to read."

"Well, I don't suppose there's any real objection to your taking a lot of literature and stuff if you *enjoy* it!"

As she went out and left him in peace, in his handsome new office with its partitions of oak and clouded glass, its portraits of Professor Edward Lee Thorndike and President Coolidge, he congratulated himself on having been so generous and so suave with her. Yet, even after his summer vacation on Gull Lake, he was a little tired of this unending persecution by smart-aleck students who acted as if they knew more than he did.

Dean Gideon Planish thought pretty well of literature. He was an expert in all its branches, and though he preferred the bright hard rocks of Oratory in the literary landscape, he could pinch-hit any time for the regular instructors in metaphysical poetry or commercial correspondence or the rules of play-construction, and he had a fascinating theory that Shakespeare was written by Queen Elizabeth. He knew all about teaching literature in both of its aspects—as an incentive to morality and as an aid to earning a living. He had figures to prove that he could increase the vocabularies of freshmen 39.73% in nine months.

But, as he told the Kinnikinick Rotary Club, the teaching of literature must be as manly and practical as the teaching of physics or football. He had mastered that doctrine even as far back as 1918 when, after his three months' service in an army camp in Illinois, he had started teaching, with his caste-mark of Ph.D. freshly painted on his forehead. At that time there was a universal expectation that literature would modestly take its place, along with advertising and preaching the Gospel, as a glad assistant to the expansion of American prosperity.

But now, in 1926, even after more than six years of the National Prohibition which ought to have produced universal efficiency and patriotism, there were everywhere hints of subversive ideas, probably introduced into America by such Bolsheviks as Emma Goldman, H. L. Mencken and Clarence Darrow, who, a year ago, had practically murdered the Dean's hero, William Jennings Bryan. And unless literature set its face like a flint against all such feeble-minded infidelity, he, for one, would actually prefer th' unlettered hind (or farmer), said Dean Planish.

As dean and as the readiest speaker in Kinnikinick, he had constantly to enlighten the public on such problems as the recent Women's Suffrage Amendment, the Sacco-Vanzetti trial, the progress of the Weimar Republic, the heroic heart of the martyred president, Mr. Harding, the Florida Land Boom (in which the Dean had lost a hundred dollars that he badly needed for payments on Peony's new piano), the pedagogical significance of the fact that Bryn Mawr was permitting students to smoke within the college, and, always, the crisis of Flaming Youth: gin flasks and giggling from automobiles parked in darkness and such dancing as had not been seen since the Serpent and Mother Eve.

Dean Planish was, as his proprietor, President Bull, frequently told the press, a philosopher and a leader of humanitarianism. The Dean said right out that regrettable though the Flaming and the Petting and the Bootlegging were, there was less danger in yielding to them than in talking about them or in writing about them. He hated to encounter students who jeered at all that was sturdy and helpful in literature, and called their cultural murders "experiments." He sometimes said that he would rather see his daughter lying dead at his feet than reading callous innovators like Dreiser and Sherwood Anderson, and as his daughter was only three years old now, it may be seen that he felt pretty strongly on the subject.

He smiled to himself at his desk. Yes, he could fairly be called "the fighting philosopher." But what was he doing here in Kinnikinick, wasting his time listening over and over to the same dreary bleatings from successive flocks of students, when he ought to be out in the world, battling for civic righteousness? That's what his wife Peony kept asking, and, reflected the Dean, she was dead right.

He was interrupted then by one of the Flaming Youth in person. As she slammed in, she might have been a particularly skinny boy; she might have been a plucked chicken wrapped in a dish-towel; she might have been almost anything except a flame. Her hair was clipped short, her sleeves were short, her bosom was at once exposed and non-existent, and her rolled stockings advertised her knees, which could have done with a little washing. She was both an invitation and a denial. She was a college senior in grade, a babe in intellect and a Hecate in guile.

When he had been a mere young instructor, the Dean might have been aroused, but Peony took care of all that now, and Peony was not skinny. He merely growled, "What do you want, Gwynn?"

She grinned in an excess of dry youthfulness.

"What have you been up to, young woman? Drinking too much? Roadhouse?"

[119]

She giggled, and made the preposterous remark, "I think you're gorgeous!"

"Young woman, is that any way to talk to the dean?"

"Oh, I knew you years before you were a dean!"

"You did not! Only two years before. And even in that brief period, you've been the cause of the gray hairs in my beard."

"There isn't a gray hair in it. It's just as brown as ever. I think it's gorgeous!"

"You have five other adjectives that you haven't used yet: dandy, slick, swell, cute and lousy. You aren't losing any of 'em, are you? Gwynn, seriously, we're old friends, and I hate to see you graduate from this institution next spring with only a hundred and seven words in your vocabulary. Can't you make it a hundred and ten?"

He reflected how different, under his influence, Peony had become from this brat. Why, Peony must have a hundred and twenty words.

"Honestly, Dean, I didn't get sent in to get hell. I want to change my course. I want to major in art and architecture and geography, this year, and cut out the physical training and Platonaristotle."

"Heh?"

"You know that Chinese boy in my class—Li?"

"Huh?"

"Well, him and me—he and me—you know what I mean —we were at the same lake this summer. Li says China and India are going to have a big renaissance—that's what he calls it—and I thought I'd like to go out to Asia and be an architect."

"You mean as a sort of Christian missionary? Teach the little Oriental brother?"

"Oh, no. According to what he says, when China and India join up, they'll be teaching us. They're the oldest and the smartest nations in the world, Li says, and they've decided to chase out all the carpet-baggers, and I'd be lucky if I was allowed there. What do you think, Dean?"

"What do I think? I'll tell you what I think! I think that I can stand it when you Lost Generation jazz-babies, you unspeakable drug-store cowboys and hot mamas, act like tarts and bootleggers. I have the faith to believe that by the end of these barbaric 1920's, you will all have come to your senses. That is, if—*if*, I say—vou retain your essential philosophy.

"And part of that philosophy is that the white races, America and Britain and France and Spain and Italy—yes, and Germany, now that the Germans have seen their folly and given up warfare as an instrument of progress—that we of the superior race are, by some compulsion whose divine origin and sanction must remain a mystery to us, destined to rule, tenderly but firmly, all the yellow, brown and black hordes, and that they can never be anything but clever children—especially including your slick friend, Mr. Li—who imitate our civilization to perfection but——

"No, you can't take architecture! And I want to see you behave yourself this year, Gwynn, or even though we are old friends, I'll bounce you right out on your ear, and as I told you, I want to see if you can't develop some elegance in speaking and the normal vocabulary of a six-

[121]

year-old child and—and you know damn well that as dean I'm not too hard on a little drinking or petting, and I trust I'm a Modern Thinker and a Consistent Liberal, and I think you must admit I'm up to date if not a little ahead of it, but when it comes to a point of degeneracy where you consider subject peoples, whose brain sutures close up quicker than ours do, as just as good as we are, and you're willing to see the whole destined world-structure bust up in—— NO!"

So at last the Dean could scamper home to his sympathetic wife.

The Planishes' rented house was the first of the charming small white houses, cheerful and clean and realistic, with wide clapboards and built-in garage and automatic oil heat, that had been erected in Kinnikinick. Later, they were to brighten the whole Middlewest.

The weary Dean came up to it, admiring the small sleek lawn—mowed by Peony before breakfast; inspired by the crazy-pattern of the walk—the stones had been picked out by Peony; impressed by the white-painted solid oak door—Peony had repainted it after the workmen had made a botch. He edged the door open and remarked, "Oo-hoo!"

His wife answered, "Oo-hoo!"

"How's the baby?"

"Oh, she's just dandy—she's swell—she's just slick—she's so cute. Want to see her? But first——"

Peony led him by hand through the small living-room.

She stopped in front of their major treasure, the Chinese Chippendale cabinet, a splendor of gold and scarlet and carved mandarins, which they had bought in Chicago on their honeymoon, and which had cost approximately ten times what they could afford. As always, she breathed, "Isn't it slick! It's the swellest cabinet I ever saw!" and as always, he agreed, "Certainly is; it lights up the room like a house afire."

She led him on into their bedroom, with its wallpaper of silver sailboats on a green sea, and its twin beds, of which one was more hollowed than the other. She led him to the farthest corner, as though it were a secret niche, and kissed him convulsively. There was in their young and parochial love something dark and hidden and fierce, dissolving him to water.

She led him to the second bedroom. It had been planned as a guest-room—here, Father and Mother Jackson would often be staying. But Father and Mother Jackson had, after a surprisingly short period, been compelled to stay at the Kinnikinick Inn, for this had become the place sacred to the baby.

At the age of three, Carrie Planish was cheerful and active, a genuine grocers'-calendar baby, of whom it could be said, of whom it frequently was said, "I declare, that baby's got the sunniest disposition I ever saw in all my born days."

Carrie was likely to be darker than either of her parents, and more slender.

She rose from her business interests—nine leaden soldiers, a decayed doll, and a water-color portrait of the family cat—she sprinted across the floor and yelled, "Daddy!"

"That's a darn smart baby, Carrie is," the Dean said, as they returned to the living-room. "She'll be a dean of women, some day."

"She will like hell! She'll be a contented wife and mother. Like me."

"What's the plans for supper? You didn't tell me to bring anything home."

"Nope. It's the hired girl's night out, and we're going batting. I've got Mrs. Hilp coming, to take care of Baby. We're going to drive down to Mabel Grove and eat at the Appleton House."

"That's swell—fine and dandy," said the purist.

Their car was a powerful new Maxwell, with a maximum speed of not much less than forty-eight miles an hour. The Dean was behind on his payments on the car, but only a month or two.

They swung south into the rolling cornland.

It was the Dean's happy belief that, despite his own eloquence, force and tact, it was really Peony who had made him dean, with a salary of two hundred dollars a year more than a full professor's, with more control over the students, and with less necessity of pretending that he had read the latest works of Mrs. Wharton and Miss Cather and this new fellow, Hemingway.

Following their marriage, Peony had called on Teckla Schaum and after being snubbed more than usual, had become Teckla's closest friend, and been asked to dine with Teckla's father. She had also, entirely against the college etiquette of waiting for the president's wife to call first, popped in on Mrs. Bull and, after being kissed and petted more than usual, had become Mrs. Bull's closest friend. She had then called on Dr. Edith Minton and, after meeting a blankness which she could never quite understand, had become Dr. Minton's one frank enemy, and as nobody liked Dr. Minton very much, that attitude on the part of Young Mrs. Professor Planish was considered pretty deep.

Peony had urged her husband to offer himself to President Bull for every style of committee work, and within a year it was expected that whenever a Visiting Celebrity was to be introduced in Assembly, or a program made for combining the organic chemistry and salad-making courses, it would be Professor Planish who would take on the ordeal. When the old dean died, in harness though also in liquor, the choice of Planish for the deanship was inescapable, and his child-wife considered not unworthy of the purple.

She was an earnest young matron as they drove into the county seat, Mabel Grove (pop., 11,569). One who knew her high position would have supposed that she was thinking of racial problems or social hygiene, but she was saying to the Dean:

"I think we can sneak in a glass of beer at the Appleton House without getting caught. But first I got something to show you: the most fool extravagance you ever heard of, and God knows how I want it! Do I get it, Gideon?"

"What are you asking *me* for?" he said fondly.

She bade him stop at an old brown house with the modest sign, "T Shop & Antiques." She looked nervous as they went up the walk; she yanked the door open as if to get it over; she pointed at an object, and tightly held his arm. The object was a huge Chinese rug, blue as a June lake, with a border of dragons and fuzzy-headed lions, saffron and sage-green and yellow.

"Isn't it the most beautiful thing you ever saw?" gurgled Peony.

"Mm."

"That'll be something for us to have when you're Senator from Iowa."

"Sweetie, I guess maybe we better wait till I *am* Senator."

"It's a thousand years old—well, a hundred years old, I guess—and it used to cost fifteen hundred dollars, but we can get it for three hundred."

"Sweetie, I swear to God we haven't got three hundred dollars in the world, and we must be over two hundred in debt—I don't really know—I kind of hate to add up the bills."

"But you can get it for twenty-five dollars down, and it's worth five hundred. The woman here told me so! That rug—it's got class! Don't you want it?"

"Oh, yes, I like it fine, but it's utterly impossible——"

They drove up to the Appleton House for dinner with the Chinese rug in the back of the car.

In celebration they drank not beer but old-fashioned cocktails, and at dinner, looking in a pleased way at all the luxuries, pickled melon rind and ripe olives and nut bread, everything that spelled richness and worldliness and delicacy of taste, Peony said, "Don't forget Dad is a crank about debts. We can count on him to pay up to a thousand, if we get sunk badly enough, and by the time that's all dished out, maybe you'll be earning more dough. Oh, and I got another surprise, just as big as the Chinese rug, bless its blue soul!"

The Dean squeaked, in terror, "I hope it won't cost another three hundred!"

"It won't set you back a cent, my boy. Honest it won't. I know how you feel. I hate to spend money, and I hate to be in debt—I just hate it. It's simply that I like to *have* things, don't you see?"

"Yes," said the Dean, and "Well——"

They both looked relieved.

"Here's the new stunt, Gideon. We've been talking so much about your getting on and taking your proper place in the world, and now it's time to really start doing something. The chairman of the County Censorship Board has just resigned, and they're looking for a new one. And has that board got power! I don't suppose it has any legal position at all, but every movie house and library board in the county listens to it. So tonight we're going to call on Mrs. William Basswood, and then watch my little man become chairman of the board!"

"Mrs. William——?"

"She's the widow of a dental supply house—lives here in Mabel Grove. Looks just like a sweet little ivory statue, but is she hell on wheels! She's so doggone moral she thinks pussy cats ought to wear step-ins. You be good now. Try to look like the Y.M.C.A. was named after you."

Mabel Grove had, as happens in the Middlewest, leaped from crossroad hamlet to small city without ever having had the leisure to stop and be merely a pleasant village. It had concrete paving, a seven-story office-building belonging to a bank, and a dozen rather squashed apartment houses. By 1940 it would also have a radio station, a chromium cocktail bar, a public swimming pool, and a much-mentioned unmentionable scandal about a male high-school teacher. It showed that in eighty years the prairies can go as far as Europe in eight hundred.

By nature Mrs. Basswood should have lived in a lilac-shaded cottage, but she was found in a compressed flat with an electric log, and portraits of Mary Baker Eddy, Tennessee Claflin and Mrs. Hetty Green. She had a radio, which was pretty modern in 1926, but her torso, covered with jet to take away the curse of sex, still creaked in the old-fashioned way.

"Oh, I think it's wonderful that you're interested in our little fight for godliness, Dr. Planish, and your dear wife, and you must meet Mr. Pederson, the Reverend Chauncey Pederson of the Lutheran Church, but it's affiliated with the English Lutherans now, I mean it doesn't call itself a Norwegian Church any more—I mean, of course, the Norwegians are a fine, upstanding, God-fearing people but—and—oh yes, I'll telephone Mr. Pederson right now."

This was Mrs. Basswood speaking. She continued speaking as they awaited the Reverend. She always continued speaking.

Mr. Pederson was a wide, middle-sized man, weighing about 190 in his stocking feet, and he seemed to be entirely free of vice and practically free of everything else. He privately grew sugar corn and asparagus, but he was without guile. He welcomed the Dean to their censorship board; he explained that the Dean's name was supposed to be voted upon by the other members of the board, but as those two dogs weren't even very good Protestants, the Dean could consider himself elected right now; in fact— and here Mrs. Basswood and he exchanged some small language of nods and winks and pious smiling—he might almost say that Dean Planish was already chairman of the board!

"I know he'll be proud to help you and the cause of Purity, though he is so dreadfully busy and so much in demand for meetings everywhere, but I'm sure he'll accept!" cried Peony, before Mrs. Basswood should hesitate, or the Dean put his foot in it.

Mr. Pederson shouted, "That's fine! That's, if I may say so, dandy. I want to tell you, Dean, we're all of us mighty proud to associate with a man of your scholarly attainments and vast reputation. Now, Dean, I want to ask you a question. Don't you feel, as Mrs. Basswood and I do, that there is no force or factor which is a stronger factor in producing the dreadful vice that we see rampant about us at this moment, a condition that would bring a blush of shame to the cheek of Nero or any of those notorious high-rollers of history, with King Alcohol ruling his rowdy crew on all sides of us now, and women, even young women, pursuing the males" (here Peony looked pious)

[129]

"and doing things and acts that I could not describe in the presence of ladies, and don't you think that there is no factor that more grievously tends to produce these awful conditions than the so-called popular and best-selling novels, with their shameless word-painting of naked women" (he smacked his lips, Mrs. Basswood looked hungry, and the Dean blushed, while only Peony remained innocent) "and the at once bold justification, in these novels, of the lowest vice, and malicious sneering at the dauntless defenders of purity in the church and home? Scandalous!"

The Dean said he thought there was a lot to that.

Before the first meeting of the censorship board with the Dean in the chair, Peony prompted him, "I've got something for you to go after—novel published a couple of years ago—*The Tattooed Countess,* by Carl Van Vechten. Why don't you get busy and censor hell out of it?"

"You can't! I understand Mr. Van Vechten was born here in Iowa. He's a Native Son!" The Dean referred to Native Son as though it had a close relationship to the Nativity.

"That's why I picked it. All the guys in the State that knew-him-when, or claim they knew-him-when, will be jealous of him because he went off to New York."

"But is it immoral enough to get folks interested?"

"I haven't read it. I tell you, with all I got to do, I just don't seem to have time to read novels. But I hear there's a woman and a young fellow interested in each other in the book, without being married! And it's all laid in Iowa—the setting, I mean."

"I see."

"And then it's kind of highbrow and kind of humorous, and that makes immorality a lot worse."

"We'll see what we can do to it."

The rest of the committee, when the meeting was held at Mabel Grove, were pleased to censor a refugee Iowan, and they set forth with verbal flaming torches to drive the Tattooed Countess clean out of Garfield County. But in the entire county, though in cities like Dubuque and Des Moines it was rumored to be plentiful, they could discover the book only in the homes of a newspaper owner, a doctor, two lawyers and seven clergymen. There were listed in the county five book shops, of which three actually sold books, at Christmastime, but none of these had a copy.

Peony was not satisfied. "There *must* be some on sale. This is a bright, educated county—Yankees and Scandinavians. There must be some people here who're cultured enough to read immoral books." Ranging by automobile, she went into every stand that sold magazines or toys, and right there in Mabel Grove, not ten blocks from the grotto of Mrs. William Basswood, she found two copies of *The Tattooed Countess* on sale in the cigar store of one Mr. Rood.

The five members of the censorship board, attended by two admiring wives, waited upon Mr. Rood in his shop. He looked thin, amiable and dangerous. No, he hadn't read *The Countess*. In fact, he never read anything but Chic Sales and sometimes Louisa May Alcott. No, he didn't know how he happened to have two copies of *The Countess;* they probably came in with a job-lot of magazines, book-ends and Easter cards. No—truly no—he wouldn't promise not to sell *The Countess.* He was running his business to suit himself, not a bunch of bottle-nosed preachers and—he looked at Peony—dumb bunnies. All right, why *didn't* they arrest him? There was just as much dividends in going to jail as in running a cigar-store.

The Dean remarked, "We'll see about this!" and with all the dignity of his short beard and gold-rimmed eyeglasses, he led his crusaders out of the den of vice.

On suggestion of the Reverend Mr. Pederson, they consulted Mr. Bill Peniston, chairman of the commissioners of Garfield County.

Mr. Peniston reported, "You got no legal right to do anything, but I don't see why us Republicans shouldn't have a fit of morality once in a while, as well as the Democrats. I'll get the Mabel Grove police to let you hold a meeting in Hawkeye Park, and you can lambast Brother Rood to a fare-you-well. Say, tell me, Dean: Is this *Tattooed Countess* pretty hot stuff? I must get me a copy before Rood sells out."

"I haven't had time to read it—I mean, read it all, yet," the Dean explained.

Dean Planish was a dignified man, an educator and a student of statesmanship. It would be very fine indeed to address a teeming throng, provided it teemed in a regularly rented hall, with the sanctities of a Bible, a flag, ice water and cane-seated chairs. But to stand in a park, bawling like a street evangelist—he confessed to Peony that he was "scared stiff."

"But sweet Gideon, the newspapers expect you! There'll be reporters from Kinnikinick and Mabel Grove and maybe even from Waterloo and Cedar Rapids."

"No foolin'?" marveled the Dean, in a delicious commingling of pride and terror.

"I'm practically sure of it."

Peony might well be practically sure of it. She had telephoned to the newspapers herself.

"But do you think President Bull and the trustees will like these monkeyshines?"

"They're sure to think it's a fine campaign."

Again she had reason, for she had told these dignitaries that Kinnikinick needed a little hot moral publicity, and they had sighed, "Well, mebby so."

When the five censors appeared on the bandstand in Hawkeye Park, not more than fifty persons had gathered to listen, and most of them muttered, "What are they? Mormons or Seventh Day Advents?"

In a hasty prologue lasting seventeen minutes, the Reverend Mr. Pederson introduced Dean Planish.

The Dean was in a deplorable state. It seemed to him that all of the twenty-three auditors who were still remaining were snickering.

"My—my friends," he groaned, and somebody down there laughed. He struggled, he tried to think of something better, and came out with a thunderous "My FRIENDS!"

But Peony was looking up at him with eyes that promised that if he walloped them good, she would be very sweet to him tonight. Without effort or any apparent control of it, he heard his voice suddenly start flowing, strong and steady, full of morality and adjectives and grammar. Five minutes later he was trumpeting:

"If you will permit a teacher to use such a phrase, maybe we better quit kidding ourselves into the belief that it's Wall Street and Paris and Hollywood that start all this vice. Here's an Ioway boy, Carl Van Vechten, and here's Al Rood, a neighbor whom you all know, conniving to flood us with a masterpiece of such insinuation, immorality and wicked brilliance that we are all tempted to thoughts entirely different from those proper to the Middlewest. And what are we going to do about them?"

He never did answer his question, but wound up with Martha Washington and the Coast of Maine.

Afterward, Bill Peniston shook his hand, and exclaimed, "First-rate spiel, Doc. You ought to think about getting into politics. Come see me about it."

As they left Hawkeye Park, the Dean sighed, "Poor Rood! I'm sure he's not a bad fellow at heart. It's kind of a shame to ruin his business."

As he was driving past Rood's Cigar Store, he stopped. Standing on a box in front of the shop was Mr. Rood, a pile of a hundred books on a box beside him, and he was shouting, "Step right up, folks, and get your copy of *The Tattooed Countess*—all about the French countess and the sheik, in the Arabian desert—wild doings by moonlight on the banks of the Congo—the book that's being advertised right now by the president of Kinnikinick College, at the meeting in the park, as the hottest yarn since the Song of Solomon."

They were buying.

Peony urged, "Oh, Gideon, I want to get a couple of copies. President Bull said he'd love to read it, and I think I might send one to Daddy for his birthday."

Like mightier men before him, actors and murderers and generals and pugilists, the Dean nervously prepared for the worst and had the shock of not having any worst or best. The State newspapers mentioned the crusade, variously giving the title of the book as *At Tattoo, The Tattooed Count*, and *The Stewed Countess*, and the author's name as Carl Van Doren, Marie Van Vorst, Hendrik Van Loon and Upton Sinclair, but reporting nothing more sensational about Dean Planish than that he "also spoke."

The Des Moines *Register* did have a small editorial, suggesting that if the Dean had stayed home, he might have learned that on the same evening certain of his own students had broken nine street lamps, and placed a goat in the office of the Professor of Biblical Literature. This editorial was mailed to the Dean by twenty-seven old friends, most of whom he had not seen since graduation from college. But with this orgy of friendliness, the incident dropped.

Bright balm descended upon him, then, in a letter from the Governor of a neighboring State. His Excellency stated

[135]

that he was always glad when any of the teachers in institutions of higher learning showed that they could leave the cloistered life and bring the benefit of their learning to the Man in the Street. Dean Planish galloped over to show this wreath to President Bull, who said, "Now that's fine—that makes me feel better about the whole business." He galloped home to show it to Peony, who said, "Oh, slick! Tell the Gov we'll call on him and Mrs. Gov some day and look over his mansion and see which bedroom we'll give Carrie when we move in there."

"Meaning I'm going to be the governor of some state?"

"I don't know about that, but meaning I'm going to be the governor's wife of some state—— Aw, the poor little man, I didn't mean it. He *shall* be a gov!"

Bill Peniston came over to the Planishes' for dinner, and Bill Peniston said:

"Dean, if you want to get in on politics, you better get acquainted with the voters. You might have a chance at a seat in the Iowa House, two years from now. We're going to have a Republican County Harvest-Home Festival at the armory at Mabel, next Friday evening. You and your girl come—bring some pickles and a banana layer-cake—I'll introduce you to everybody that counts."

The Dean told Peony afterward that they might just as well go down now and reserve their compartment to Washington. Peony said no, better make it a drawing-room—it only cost a little more, and after all, thev'd have Carrie along, wouldn't they?

He gloated, "You watch me be chummy with the Garfield County peasantry, next Friday. I'll kiss all the babies, in Swede, Plattdeutsch and Czech, and I'll admire all the old ladies' elderberry wine receipts, and listen to every old hound that wants to tell me about whitewashing his corncrib. Seriously, they'll be lucky to have a man with my knowledge and experience in their political horse-trading. Come kiss Senator Planish, sweetie."

For reasons unknown, the baby Carrie started yelling in the next room.

The National Guard Armory was decorated, as the derivatively urban Planishes had expected, with strings of pumpkins, garlands of summer squash, gonfalons of sumac, and a mural made of kernels of corn, yellow, red and purple, depicting Indians on horseback. The long pine tables were, as in the Dean's evangelical boyhood, brave with seven kinds of pie, nine kinds of cake and three kinds of meat loaf. The Planishes were a little disappointed that the farmers were so well dressed, in mail-order blue suits and brown silk dresses, but their necks were as brown as cigars, creased like eroded hills, and the Dean felt superior again.

Bill Peniston did not, as expected, have them shake hundreds of hands and be delightfully sympathetic about babies. He said, "I'm going to have you two set with the county committee, and you can size 'em up—and vice versa." The Planishes were mandated to a table with a dozen people who were uncomfortably lacking in awe: a doctor, a superintendent of schools, a lady milliner, an auctioneer who was a state representative, and a stock farmer who was a state senator.

The Dean tried to think of a Message to hand out, but what could you talk about to such a calm-eyed jury as this? Certainly not about paragraph formation, and probably not even Flaming Youth. While he was trying to tack together something in regard to the recently martyred William Jennings Bryan, he listened to these backfield politicians.

They talked of taxes. Dean Planish hadn't known there were so many kinds of taxes: federal and state and county and city, road and improvement and amusement, licenses to sell tobacco and to sell pop. They talked of the congressional candidates for this fall, and they talked of caucuses. The Dean had always assumed that he knew what a caucus was, just as he assumed that he knew what an aardvark was, but suddenly he wasn't sure that he knew how either of them looked.

They talked of road commissioners and warehouse commissioners and the state railway board, all mysteries to the Dean. They even talked, and approvingly, of young Henry Agard Wallace, editor of *Wallaces' Farmer*.

"You seem to think well of him," suggested the Dean.

"Sure we do!" said the state senator.

"But I thought he was friendly with the Democrats."

"Well, I'll tell you: way we feel, an Iowa Republican is smarter than an Iowa Democrat, but an Iowa Democrat is smarter than an Illinois Republican."

"Oh, I see," said Dean Planish.

As they drove back to Kinnikinick, the Dean was forceful.

"It's too late for me to get started in politics. Those party leaders—they kept talking about some fellow here in the county named George, like he runs everything, and I didn't even dare ask what George's last name is. George Washington, probably."

"I thought he was dead," said Peony.

"And that's just typical. There's too much I don't understand. Caucuses. Now why caucuses? Who starts caucuses? Who does what to who? *Damn* caucuses! I'm too old to start in acting like I knew all about caucuses. It's a shame, too, because—— Did I ever tell you how Senator Kurtshaw begged me to join him in the party, when I was in college?"

"Sometimes."

"Yes—well—no. I could be a governor. Those fellows don't have to know anything; they got guys they can ask. But to be a local politician in Garfield County, you got to know too many mere *facts*. Darn it, I suppose I'll go on the rest of my life, telling a lot of college children that we don't hold classes just to be mean. It's a shame, too. When I think of what I could bring to politics—freedom and democracy and normalcy! High strategy; not a lot of bayonet practice. Warehouse commissions! Huh!"

"Gideon, sweetie, you shall have your lil ole high strategy!"

"Whom do you think you are? George?"

"We'll find out how you can get one of the big political appointments—not these snide elective jobs. You'd make a wonderful Secretary of the Treasury—you're so cute the way you add up my bills and almost always get the same total. Or Governor General of the Philippines. Gee, I'd love to live in the Governor General's palace—all palms and parrots and parades!"

"Wouldn't mind that myself," said the Dean, gratefully.

The Dean discovered that his career as dean was interfered with by his business as dean. He was tired of having a new crew of freshmen bring up a lot of silly questions every year that he had settled for all time a year ago. But his position did enable him to do one or two things that were lovely with careerism.

Peony, who played at Chopin perhaps twice a month, had revealed to him a thing called Music. He saw that this fad promised to go a long way in America, and therefore needed to be organized, and he burstingly called a meeting and created the Kinnikinick Music Guild.

Its members were to compose symphonies and mammy songs, to found an orchestra, and to tour around advertising the college. He was proud of the Guild, and he continued to be so for weeks after it had, without his knowing, broken up in a riot about whether an accordion-player could have as pure a talent as a violinist.

11

It was Peony who suggested that, since they were so very much in debt, they must economize all that next summer and fall. Peony was always being spectacular.

She said, "I love to blow money in, and I'd give my virtue for the Chinese rug and the Chippendale cabinet, but I can save, too—I can save like a son of a gun." During vacation she found for them a three-room cottage in Northern Minnesota, and she cooked, swept, scrubbed, amused Carrie. She would let the Dean help her only with the dishes; she had him reading economics, anthropology, history, and they both felt very advanced and improved. Neither of them saw any difference between Lothrop Stoddard and William Graham Sumner. Any book was good and very useful if it said anything about head-measurements, the training of youth for democracy, or the increased production of gas-stoves.

With advisory aid from an Episcopal clergyman who smoked a pipe and was frank and helpful about Sex and was therefore called "Father," Peony had the Dean inducted into the Episcopal Church. She felt that if he ever got to be a leader of progressive thought in New York or Washington, he couldn't very well be a Presbyterian; he had to be either an Episcopalian or an atheist, and for an employee of an Episcopal college, the former seemed a lot more thoughtful. Later, he was to know that this was a mistake, and to see that if he was to be either a great Liberal or a staunch Illiberal, and if he was to raise money extensively, he ought to be a Methodist, a Baptist, a Congregationalist, a Quaker or a Russian prince.

The Planishes came back to the campus in the autumn with many new ideas, first-rate tans and only two hundred dollars in debts.

The Garfield County Censorship Board had gone on attacking and advertising good books, and Mr. Rood had, with amazement at himself, taken to reading, and had established the first adequate book shop in the county. The name of Chairman Planish, "a scholar who isn't afraid to get out into the dust of the streets" (Waterloo *Courier*), had been advertised almost as loudly as the books. Through the whole State there began to slide a feeling that he was a very sound man, though nobody except Peony was sure what he was sound at, and he was appointed a member of the Legislative Advisory Electrification and Creative Planning Committee.

Suddenly he was dashing to Ottumwa, to Mason City, to Sioux City, to Muscatine, over a period of two months; his name was in the newspapers daily—on page 7; he took Peony to public dinners of more than three hundred persons, with sixteen speeches; and at the end of the meritorious crusade, the Planishes were four hundred dollars in debt, and Whipple Jackson sent a check to cover half the amount, and with it Peony bought a rock-crystal lamp and five hundred shares in a diamond mine.

Dean Planish had been honored by his first invitation to become a "national director" of a great organization with its office in New York: The Sympathizers with the Pacifistic Purposes of the New Democratic Turkey. He was assured that they desired only the use of his distinguished name, and he need give no time nor money unless he was eager to.

He wasn't.

Afterward he was often to have the experience, as warming to the stomach as hot toddy, of seeing his name on organizational stationery. But this was his first drink. He viewed the Turkish Sympathizers' letter, lavishly signed by a Dartmouth professor, as a symbol of cultural advance and the international low-down. Centered at the top was the head of a fezless Turkish workman, with the mystic letters S.P.P.N.D.T. circling him like a necktie blown in the wind.

To a resident of Kinnikinick, the address was inspiring: Fifth Avenue and 43d Street, New York City.

In the upper right-hand corner of the letter were the National Officers, who included three prominent clergymen, a Chicago corporation lawyer, and a treasurer who was the fourteenth vice president of the Sixteenth National Bank of Manhattan. The Dean did not know that all proper national organizations, including many that pass away after a run of six nights, have New York bankers for treasurers.

Beneath the list of officers was the item, "Constantine Kelly, Executive Director," in letters so modest that the Planishes, amateurs in the organizational world, did not notice it. They were interested in the left-hand side of the stationery where, among the forty-eight directors, appeared:

> *Iowa*
> Gideon Planish, Ph.D.
> Dean, Kinnikinick Cge.

The Dean and Peony looked at each other, and looked at Carrie, and all three of them sighed—the elders with radiant joy, Carrie with boredom and possibly wind.

The news of this honor appeared in the Iowa newspapers, and the Dean received invitations to become a director of two other national organizations, and to contribute to sixty-three of them. He accepted the first two.

His duties in the S.P.P.N.D.T. did not tax him. After having appointed him, that body seemed to have forgotten him, except for breezy monthly letters, theoretically signed by the Dartmouth professor, explaining why no one in Europe or Asia would ever go to war again, and suggesting that he get more people in his State to contribute. It would be all right with the S.P.P.N.D.T. if he held meetings and shipped them the collections.

His many honors had now started the Dean on a meaty career of oratory and public enlightenment. As the Kinnikinick *Record* said, "This gentleman is always in great demand as the speaker at alumni banquets, high-school commencements, conventions, annual Rotary and Kiwanis jollifications, and other occasions where there is a demand for wit and culture, in this and neighboring counties, and there is no hand we are prouder to shake than that of Dean 'Giddy'."

The invitations to speak were coming in, two a day, three a day, and Peony took charge.

"Gideon, honey, you've been doing all this spieling free, and it's a chance to cash in. We'll pay up that ole five-hundred-dollar debt in jig time, and I can get me a real evening dress that tinkles. You let me answer these bids. I'm going to stick 'em twenty-five and fifty bucks apiece, and up to seventy-five, with traveling expenses, and there's no reason why they shouldn't pay for a chair car, even if you don't feel like taking one."

The Dean meditated, "I do get a lot of spiritual satisfaction out of stimulating their intellects, but I swear, people that want free oratory are the naggingest beggars there are, especially the women that run committees. They got no mercy. If I let 'em, they'd have me making addresses twenty-four hours a day, and look pained if I stopped to blow my nose. Sure. Go ahead and soak 'em. I just never had the nerve."

"Nerve? Why the man never even had the nerve to seduce me, and Heaven knows, that wouldn't have been hard."

"H?"

"Listen. I might pick out a regular topic for you and advertise it a little—mention it in all my letters."

[145]

"Ausgezeichnet! Peony! Which do you think would draw more—a lecture maintaining that the Post-War Generation are okay, and will get over it, or just the opposite —a message that they're a gang of cockeyed hellions and harlots? This is very important. A lecturer has got to get his message straight, and more or less know what he's really talking about, even if he isn't so eloquent."

"Oh, give 'em the young-generation-gone-to-hell number. Nobody wants to pay their good dough to hear that the kids are simply human beings. What's the use of a forum, if you only tell folks to act natural and try to have some common sense? Besides! I got a wonderful name for the kids that *are* tough: singe cats! Isn't that beautiful?"

"Wow! You're the poet of this household, Peony! That ought to drag 'em in. 'Don't Be a Singe Cat.' Okay! Let's go!"

This was the real origin of the term "singe cat," which spread over the United States and became one of the permanent treasures of American fancy.

The suggestion that vulgar money might be involved lessened the number of invitations to toss the torches, but eight or ten times a month, now, Dean Planish was called out of town, sometimes a hundred and fifty miles from home, and the family debt was reduced to three hundred dollars, and Peony did buy an evening dress that tinkled, and one, very soft and feminine, which unfortunately made her look maternal.

President Bull was crosser and crosser as he saw his dean, whose job was really to run the college and let the president go out and sell it, both neglecting his duty and getting the pretty orange checks that should have gone to T. Austin Bull.

Dean Planish was to speak this evening at the joint dinner of the Daughters of Pilgrims, and the Upsala Bach Society, at New Ipswich, sixty miles from Kinnikinick. He would drive there. The roads were snowy but passable, and he had bought new chains for the Maxwell. He came home at four-thirty in the afternoon, kissed his wife, spanked her slightly, kissed the baby and put on dinner clothes.

He decided that the dress shirt would do one more time, but he'd better change the collar. It had a spot on it from the quick one he had grabbed in the men's-room at the Hotel Grampion in Des Moines, last Tuesday, when he had addressed the Hawkeye Association of Agronomists. That had been a sixty-dollar fee, but worth more, because he had had to make up an entirely new lecture, something about the History of Agriculture, of which he knew nothing whatever.

He ate a tuna-fish sandwich, hastily sucked in a straight rye, and put on a dogskin coat, a plush cap and coonskin gauntlets, which utterly disguised the scholar and philosopher. The visible remnants of him, the brown short beard and the brown cheerful eyes and the ruddy nose, looked somehow like a horse doctor's.

Peony bade her warrior, "Be a good boy. Have you got your key? Keep your muffler tight around your neck. Don't go bringing any blondes home with you, or I'll gouge their eyes out. Oh, where's that ten dollars you were going to leave me? I have a feeling I'm going to buy me some silver slippers before the store closes. Oh, nemmine, don't unbutton your coat just to get it. I'll charge 'em. I love to charge things, anyway. Oh, darling, do slow down on the curves, and remember to call your typical singe cat 'Mamie,' not 'Meggie'—don't forget what a hell of a time you had with that real Meggie at Clinton. Goodbye, lover."

As he lighted a cigar and eased his car into gear, Dean Planish reflected, "That's the best little wife any man's had since——" He balked. Since Caesar? Since Alfred Lord Tennyson? Since U. S. Grant?

"The best little wife any man ever had," he finished it.

He went buzzing, steady as a train, through a gray, steady wind over the prairie. His car was a small fast bug, lost in that immensity. He thought about the young men who had come to his office today, about the luscious girls —but none of them could touch Peony—about his salary, about how pleasant it would be to live in New York and not drive his own car, about Professor Eakins's statement that he had heard of an explorer who got $750 a lecture, about giving Peony some day an ivory-colored bed with carved and gilded cupids, and, briefly, about his coming lecture.

Tonight he was, in a craftsmanlike way, going to combine his spicy revelations about Youth's naughtiness with a denial that they were even naughty, and he was calling the talk "It's up to the Parents."

Ten billion acres of flat grayness slipped by as the cozy philosopher brooded:

"Must remember not bring the term singe cat in till after the tourist camp story—oh, must be careful to tell that tactfully, so nobody will realize I'm referring to contraceptives. Then introduce the phrase with a rising inflection: singe—*cat*. Like that.

"Damn that farmer! What's he think he's trying to do? Crowd me over into the ditch?

"She's not a bit fat. Just a good figure.

"Yes, in New York, have our bedroom like *she'd* like it: carved bed and a great big dressing-table, mirror big's a barn, and every kind of soap and rouge and cream in the world—fun to arrange it and then take her in there and surprise her. . . . Don't kid yourself now, Doc! Fat chance your ever having a say about furnishing any room. Well, now, shut up! That's the way it ought to be. I'm the scholar and a crank for high-tone talk and accuracy, but she's got the punch and the genius. I wish I were kissing her right now.

"Hm. Missouri license, eh? Wonder what he's doing up here, this time of year. Nice job. La Salle, I guess. Gracious, is he going fast!

"Explain that it isn't the surface appearance of vice that matters, but are the kids, no matter if they do tumble into the Slew—what is it? slew, slau, sluff?—of Despond, still, are they trying to march on toward intellectual solidarity with the leaders? (Like me.) Better bring this in dramatically: youth with banners—mud on their robes may merely show the fact that they been in the what-d'yuh-call-it of Despond, fighting. Plenty dramatic.

"This will make a hundred and ten bucks extra this week. Wow! Well, I'm worth it. They don't get many lecturers that hand 'em thoughts the way I do. 'There's Dr. Planish—he's read just about everything, and he's completely honest. I'll bet he's satisfied with the part he's playing in the march to moral victory!' I don't care if she gets *three* pairs of silver slippers, bless her!

"By golly, here we are in the outskirts right now. That wasn't so bad. I'm certainly a good driver. These kids, these students, that think they can speed so! It's skill and steadiness like mine that covers the distance.

"I wonder if any of these undergraduates *do* do the things I tell about in the lecture."

New Ipswich, Iowa, was exactly like Chicago, except that it was only one two-hundred-and-fiftieth as large, and the March of Empire Hotel, in New Ipswich, was exactly like the nobler Chicago hotels, except that it had only one-tenth as many rooms. It had four stories of red brick trimmed with gray limestone, and in the lobby was a mural depicting Richelieu selling the glories of New France to Louis XIII.

The Bach-Pilgrims dinner was held in the Royal Bourbon Banquet and Ball Room, on the mezzanine floor, with its own Pompadour Coatroom. But Dean Planish could not venture up on that gala floor looking like a farmer. At the main coatroom, downstairs, he took off his dogskin coat and plush cap, tipped up his imitation silver pocket flask, combed his hair and beard with a small baby-blue pocket comb, and put on his harness of gold-rimmed eyeglasses with a broad black silk ribbon. Their lenses were of plain window-glass.

As he ambled up to the mezzanine, he looked the perfect Maestro, unafraid of ideologies or chicken croquettes.

He could without an introduction tell who his chairwoman was. She would be the sharp-nosed and prosperous but slender lady who looked sick with anxiety. The Dean sailed down on her, as she stood with her program-flapping gang by the double door to the Banquet Hall; he held out his hand, and purred in his deepest tomcat voice, "Mrs. Wiggleman? Mr. Planish."

By all union rules, his job was done now, except for the mere eating and lecturing; he was there, he was on time, he was sober, he was in dinner clothes, and he had not forgotten his necktie.

He was not one of your nervous lecturers who poke at their apple-pineapple-peach-creamcheese salad, who shakily fill up on coffee, and look glassily at the ladies to left and right, who answer "Ladies and gentlemen" when anybody asks if it is cold enough for them, and wonder how many cigarettes they can get in without being considered libidinous. Dean Planish ate stolidly, and he thought very well of the Surprise Ice Cream, while to Mrs. Wiggleman, the chairwoman, on his right, he was saying, Yes, he did think the movies were a pernicious influence on the young. After that he said to the lady on his left that Yes, he did think the movies stimulated the imaginations and slicked up the manners of the young.

All this he did with one lobe of his brain tied behind him.

He was not jumpy even when Mrs. Wiggleman introduced him. She had neither of the virtues that a lecturer longs for in an introducer: to keep it down to forty seconds, and to get the lecturer's name right. Mrs. Wiggleman kicked up her palsied heels for two minutes and forty-three seconds, by the Dean's wrist-watch, and she called him "Professor" instead of "Dean." Yet when she had collapsed and sat shrieking to herself in a whisper, he rose, put on his fraudulent eyeglasses with a flourish, and sailed his plane steadily into the tradewinds of intellectuality:

"Madame Chairman, Right Reverend Sir, ladies and friends, it is altogether fitting and proper and a happy portent for the future that the descendants of the Yankees, my own stern but noble forbears, and the sons and daughters of the great Swedish race should thus have met together, and that I should endeavor to address you on the ever-burning topic of Today's Youth, for in what have these titan races better united than in their emphasis on the scrupulous rearing of our children?"

He pushed his crumpled napkin away from him on the tired and geographical-looking tablecloth behind which he was standing, and really took flight. That he could soar at all while standing on a level with the customers showed his skill, for normally the wisdom and stimulation that will be tolerated from a lecturer are in ratio to the number of feet he is elevated above the audience.

Sixty-two minutes later, he made his landing, a little dazed now, and they yelled and hammered the tables. He enjoyed that, but it did not keep him from getting down to the real climax.

The first rule of all professional lecturers, whether inspirational, comic or travel, is to get your check before you leave the hall, for otherwise, in the spell of your wizardry, they might forget to send it on to you. So after he had shaken hands with forty-seven ladies and five men, he turned merrily to Mrs. Wiggleman and said, as though it were just a little joke between them, "I think I can save your committee a whole postage stamp if I take my check along with me!"

Mrs. Wiggleman looked shocked, but before he went down to shrug himself into his dogskin overcoat, he had the check tucked into his billfold.

He was weary now. He drove back to Kinnikinick in so still a paralysis that he noted only that it had started to snow, and that he must see if he couldn't find a not too expensive snakeskin belt for Peony.

She was asleep on the new chintz-covered chaise longue when he came in, but she jumped up and kissed him.

"Were you wonderful? I got some hot beef-tea waiting for you. Did you get your check?" she said.

12

Mr. A. J. Joslin had been a country school teacher, a country banker, a country editor. He now owned an excellent printing plant in Des Moines, and he was publishing a bi-monthly magazine called *Rural Adult Education,* which had a reputation that extended into Saskatchewan but a circulation that didn't reach much beyond Osceola.

Mr. Joslin had twice heard the inspirational service furnished by Dean Planish, and during January, 1927, he wrote begging the Dean for a few articles. He would pay two cents a word. The suggestion came just when the Dean and Peony were looking over the Christmas bills. It was Peony who had had the courage to add them up, and she was grunting, "Believe it or not—I guess it's witchcraft —we seem to be seven hundred dollars in debt."

They looked at Mr. Joslin's letter, they looked at each other, and Peony took him by the lapel, led him to the corner of the living-room which they called his "study," pointed to his portable typewriter, and went out to mix him a drink—and to telephone to the furniture dealer that he could send up that leather floor-cushion after all.

Within three hours, the Dean had written an article on the consolidated country high school as a means of preparation for college. Mr. Joslin accepted it and sent a check for $52.60; the Dean made the check over to Peony; and she went out and bought an imitation French imitation porcelain mantel clock. Two weeks later, he wrote some spirited advice to college girls about teaching district school; he received $63.44, and Peony paid a dry-cleaning bill and bought a lovely thing in the way of a picture map of Iowa, depicting Jack of the Beanstalk climbing a forty-foot stalk of corn, and Neptune and attendant dolphins frisking in the Des Moines River.

The Dean was cheered thus into doing a rather larger essay on the important books of the day (for his material he had to read clear through the advertisements in a New York Sunday *Herald-Times*) and on the use of college libraries by rural communities. This check, for $93.88, Peony banked, unlooted. They both felt wonderful over the way in which they were tackling their debts, and in this mood the Dean dashed off a fantasy on farm boys earning their way through college.

This check was for only $25.94. Peony took it and went out and ordered a new motor car, a Buick, and paid down part of the price, and this time, when she added up their debts, they came to $1,687.79.

"I just don't know how it happened!" she wailed.

"I'm afraid you'll have to stop buying things—for a little while, I mean," fretted the Dean.

"Oh, lover, don't be cross and beat me!"

"No, I won't do that. But we both got to restrain ourselves."

"And just when I've gone and written a letter ordering

that English picnic basket with the silver fittings. I suppose I can tear up the letter."

"No, no, sweetie, don't do that. It would go so beautifully with the new automobile. But after that, we simply got to do without things."

"Gideon! Why don't you write an article for *Rural Adult* about how folks can economize on the farm?"

"I've never hardly been on a farm. . . . But I'll write it."

"Oh, goody! That solves everything! And it was my idea, wasn't it!"

Before the end of March, when the faculty appointments for the next school year in Kinnikinick were made definite, Mr. A. J. Joslin wrote to the Dean that he was discharging the editor of *Rural Adult*, who was a very poor public speaker, and would the Dean like to give up his present job and take the editorship? The emolument (a word used among the loftier teachers and the more amateur editors, and meaning "wages," just as the wages of lecturers are called the "honorarium") would be $4,200 a year.

As dean, he had been receiving $3,800 a year and, despite a five-hundred-dollar check—and an irritated letter —from his father-in-law, he now seemed to be $1,200 in debt. He fluttered home to Peony; they talked for half an hour; the Dean accepted the editorship by long-distance telephone; then ceremoniously called upon President Bull, to ask whether he ought to accept the editorship.

The locks of T. Austin Bull were still theatrically curly, but they were gray; and, with executive scheming, his face had grown more folded. "Poor old devil, he must be over fifty now," thought the Dean. Feeling tolerant of this hedge schoolmaster who would never get invited to go and be a big man in Des Moines, the Dean finished his speech:

"Of course it's a great honor to be offered the editorship, and I'm not sure but that I can do even more good there than I can here—reaching thousands with the message of education, instead of just a few hundred. But I always feel that a man's first duty is to be loyal, and if you can persuade the college Board of Trustees to raise my stipend from thirty-eight hundred to forty-five hundred a year, I'll see if I can't stay with you."

The President was a little abrupt:

"Dean, I'm glad you came in. I'd been thinking of asking you to drop in before we confirm the next year's appointments. And the fact is, I think you better take this editorship."

"Eh?"

"The fact is, I'm afraid you've outlived your usefulness as an educator."

"Eh?"

"You're a good speaker, and you're popular with the students, and you've started some interesting novelties—the course in Russian and the Music Guild and the abolition of hazing. But you've seen the Russian and the Guild fade and die, and you haven't done a thing about it. You're not really an executive—you're a promoter—and the activities that you promote aren't very sound. You just dream 'em and let 'em float off in smoke. And you've been increasingly neglectful of plodding day-by-day details. You haven't even been here very much. So I guess both sides are perfectly satisfied, and we can say farewell with the best of good feelings."

President Bull arose and stuck out his manicured hand, with his popular actor's smile, his smile of a popular ex-clergyman, but the Dean, that trained practitioner of scholarly good-fellowship, could not smile in answer.

Peony said, "I knew it all along. It's because he's been jealous of your speeches, and wanted all those lil fifties and twenty-fives for himself. I'm glad we're going, and I hope we never see this dump again. I hate Bull and Mrs. Bull and Teckla and her stuffy father and everybody except Edie Minton—she never liked me and never pretended to. On avong! Lez go!"

So Gideon Planish firmly set his plump foot upon the upward path that would lead through the miasma of lecturing and the bleak wind of editing to the glory of cloud-cuckoo-land, yes, even unto the world of committees and conferences and organizations and leagues, of implementing ideals and crystallizing public opinion and molding public opinion and producing informed public opinion and finding the greatest common denominator in all shades of opinion——

Of grass roots and liberal thinking and blue prints for democracy and the system of free enterprise and far-flung armies and far-flung empires and far-flung money-raising campaigns, together with far-flung night-letter-telegrams about the imminence of the crisis and far-flung petitions to Congress about the state of politics in Chile or Iran, and ideologies and ideological warfare and in general the use of the word "ideology" as meaning everything except Far-Flung and Coca-Cola, and the longing to serve and the need of discussion and constitutional measures and challenges and rallying-points and crises, lots of crises, practically daily crises, and basic appeals and spiritual ideals and the protection of the home, and directives, and the sickness in our civilization——

Of firm beliefs and doing the job without further discussion and outstanding events and outstanding personalities and the logic of events and catching history at the tide, high tide or low tide or neap tide, and resisting pressure groups and also the formation of pressure groups to exert influence, and upholding morals and reaffirming principles and agreeing in principle and getting the average voter's reactions, and educational campaigns——

Of prospectuses and money-raising letters and three-color-job circulars that were folded in a funny way and if you opened the little pasteboard door you would find out what the message was, and testimonial dinners and organizational dinners and round tables and speakers' tables up on daises and microphones and P.A. systems and lousy acoustics and dead spots in the hall——

Of constructive philanthropy and the appeal to the heart and the privilege of giving and the spiritual values inherent in giving and the pressing necessity of giving at once and the higher levels of giving and planned giving and systematic giving and the allocation of gifts and subscription cards, sign on the second line, and generous responses and unparalleled responses to this appeal and the joy of giving and the duty of giving and giving till it hurts the giver and non-giving till it hurts the hired hands at the organization——

And Conditions and Situations, Conditions and Situations in the Chancelleries of Mitteleuropa, Conditions and Situations in Washington and the A.F. of L. and the C.I.O., and inside information and the low-down—always the low-down on Conditions and Situations, to be discussed by little groups of authorities on foreign affairs, from 8 P.M. till 1:30 A.M., Conditions and Situations discussed over and over and over and over and——

Of organizators and philanthrobbers and propheteers and directors and executive secretaries and executive directors and managing directors and the honorary chairmen and the sponsors and the trustees and the board of advisers and national headquarters and Chicago headquarters and local units and appeals to the press to give publicity to the unexampled needs of this great cause and you ought to be able to get this picture of Miss Viv de Vere, in bathing suit and holding a coin box, into the rotogravure sections and maybe get five minutes on Station WSOB and photographs and Dr. Geschwighorst addressing the students' forums or fora at all the far-flung colleges on imperative giving and Conditions and Situations——

Up into this earthly paradise was trudging a new Intellectual Leader whose fresh and eager voice would inspire the philanthrobbers to give till it hurt them, but enable him to provide his wife Peony with sandal shoes and symphony season-tickets and five-pound boxes of Fanny Farmer candy and his undiminishing love.

Though he had lost the Christian name Dean, still he was Dr. Planish, always Dr. Planish—that was his first name: Dr.; and as such, along with every Colonel, every Reverend Doctor, every M.D., every Monsignor, every Rabbi, every Herr Geheimrat, every Judge, every Lord, every Governor, he was so highly exalted that he was not merely a man, but a title.

13

"WHEN WE GET TO Des Moines, we'll rent a flat. I've always wanted to live in a flat. It's so citified," said Peony.

"Aw, don't you think it would be better to take a nice little house, so Carrie can play in the yard?" urged Dr. Planish. "Sure! We'll take a house."

They took a flat.

The flat was, crowed Peony, the most tremendous bargain: only fifty dollars a month, provided they did all the repairs; and their Kinnikinick furniture would fit it perfectly. The blue Chinese rug, the Chinese Chippendale cabinet, the French porcelain clock, and the leather pouf, she pointed out, looked as if they had been made for this bright little flat, with its balcony sun-room and its electric fireplace and only two flights to climb. All they had to pay for was papering the flat, in soft yellow, scraping and painting the floors, white-enameling the woodwork, replacing a few warped window-frames, and buying a new electric refrigerator, which was, Peony impersonally reported, the dearest little jewel she had ever seen.

So, though rather grumblingly, her father sent them another check.

They were welcomed to Des Moines in July with a

party given by Mr. A. J. Joslin, a small and nervous man who had bright eyes but a mouth that was always slightly open. The party was operated in a private dining-room at the Count Frontenac Hotel, with Iowa vodka and Mississippi River caviar, and they met a society editor, a congressman, and the chief agent for the whole Middlewest of a great tractor company, who sang "Here's to Giddy, he's true blue; he's a drunkard through and through."

Mr. Joslin stated that under the inspired genius, lofty humanitarianism and practical hustle of the new editor, he expected to see *Rural Adult Education* on every parlor table from Kalispell to Paducah.

Then he called Dr. Planish aside and explained that he had left his wallet home, and could the Doctor let him have fifty dollars till tomorrow? (But on the morrow, he did not seem to remember it.)

So the Planishes were launched on a metropolitan stream of elegance, excitement and fame.

"At heart you're a complete rustic. I believe you'd rather have a house than our ducky flat. You'd like to mow the lawn and shovel the walks. You *like* the soil, even when it sticks to you. Maybe you were born in a bigger town than I was, but it's me that's got the zip. But I'm going to make a city slicker out of you yet," said Peony—but fondly—but seriously.

And in the city, free from the spying of students, master of his own office hours, among people whom Peony pronounced "fit to meet"—men with three cars, women who

[163]

were just as used to Le Grand Pension des Deux Mondes et de Tooting, t.c.m., in Cannes, as they were to Charley's Eats, Counter Service—he did enjoy the sea-change of becoming urbanized. At least, he enjoyed Peony's becoming urbanized. . . . Though they never did seem to meet any of the people with the three cars and private Baedekers. But matter of time when they would be frisking in swimming pools with the richest and most public-spirited. And from the first they had what the Doctor called Urban Opportunities.

They could go, any evening, to a choice of a dozen movies, a dozen restaurants—one of them with real Parisian red-leather wall-seats. At any time, night or day, they could hear motor horns, radios, ticklish lovers and riveting. They could adventure in department stores so large that they never found what they wanted. They could read in the social columns that right there in the city, not twenty blocks from them, a bona-fide artist was promoting a studio party, that Madame Fitzinger, of New York and Stuttgart, was conducting a children's class in the ballet, and the Z. Edward Matzes were giving a whole series of parties to celebrate the engagement of their daughter—in fact, the Matzes seemed pretty relieved about it.

So Dr. and Mrs. Planish were Successes in Life, according to the best American tradition: they resided in a larger city than before, and they knew many more people much less well, if you counted in all the street-car conductors whom they met professionally, and they had a somewhat larger income and very much larger expenses. So Peony sang oftener, and next winter Carrie had a new snow-suit of white imitation fur, and only Dr. Planish was slightly bewildered.

His job as editor of *Rural Adult* was not working out as he had dreamed. He had expected to spend his time in reading entertaining manuscripts and being interviewed by the newspapers regarding his opinions on politics and the American woman and, instead of having to talk with boorish college students, being witty in a large leather chair with sparkling but grateful authors.

But he found that authors were stammering in speech, vicious in their demand for quick payment, reluctant to give anecdotes out of which to make publicity notes, and yet insistent on getting the publicity. In a hurt and jumpy way, he found that they were very vain, poisonously jealous, and usually musty of aspect.

For usable conversation, the printers and stenographers were much better.

He had to learn painfully, from his own assistant—an aged party who would himself have been the editor if he had not been a periodic drunk—a whole tiresome technique of getting out the magazine: how to read manuscripts by smell, without wearing out the eyes; how to get a thousand-word article into an eight-hundred-word space; how to choose the lead article and, with a stern printer waiting, rewrite its title; and, most of all, how to obtain photographs for illustrations. He usually telephoned to the press agent for a railroad or a factory and promised him a credit which would undoubtedly sell ten threshing engines or 10,000 passenger-miles.

Particularly, he had to learn taboos and libel laws. He must invariably speak reverently of mothers, duck-hunting, the Y.M.C.A., the Salvation Army, the Catholic Church, Rabbi Wise, the American flag, cornbread, Robert E. Lee, carburetors and children up to the age of eleven.

All these mysteries the Doctor could learn and did learn. What troubled him was that he was getting only half of his handsome salary.

Mr. Joslin explained that this wasn't his fault; that he was, conservatively, ten times as anxious to pay up as Dr. Planish was to be paid up or Mrs. Planish to get the check. It was the fault of the printers, who insisted on getting their wages every week; it was the advertisers, always so slow to meet their bills; it was the paper manufacturers, always so intolerant about credit; it was the dead-beat subscribers; it was everything except the publisher himself.

When he did pay, Mr. Joslin handed the Doctor a job-lot of wrinkled bank notes, hotel due-bills given in exchange for advertising, due-bills for school blackboards, and an occasional precious silver dollar.

Jittery now for the first time since their marriage, the Planishes had their landlord dunning them for the fifty dollars a month, the corner grocer refusing to charge it, and the maid becoming so impudent that they had to pawn Peony's wrist-watch. The Doctor was terrified. The warmth and faith of Peony were even more important to him than the good steak dinners which he was not getting and of which he thought all through the hungry days. And it bothered him even more that Peony was not getting the brown juicy steak either. But she did not nag.

She scoffed, "Well, look at us! The hometown boy and girl that went to the city and made good! One bottle of milk in the house, and that belongs to that yelping young sparrow, Carrie. Oh, honey-sweet, I think maybe it was all my fault. I was too greedy!"

She sobbed against his shoulder, she sobbed and looked up at him with the face of a little girl who has been naughty. He kissed her, and her sobs dwindled to a tired little whimpering.

Her fault? he thought. *Her* greedy? Why, she was the one person in the world who didn't know how to be greedy. By God, she'd have a palace on Long Island and a marble swimming-pool before he was through!

This time it was the Doctor who wrote to Whipple Jackson, and he enclosed a promissory note, and they had steak again, and dry martinis.

Though he did receive only half his pay, it was not easy for the Doctor to quit *Rural Adult Education.* He enjoyed the small distinction of being a real editor and he, the one time Dean and Professor, had little value on the labor market now.

President T. Austin Bull would not give him any ardent recommendation, and, anyway, not till late winter would the slave philosophers be standing in that labor market while the trustees and presidents of the several colleges looked at their teeth and wind and conservatism.

[167]

So the Doctor again took up the traveling-salesman's routine of the itinerant lecturer.

This time, he went at it professionally. Instead of having Peony book his engagements in her chatty pink notes to the committees, he submitted himself, inspiration and beard and all, to a minor lady lecture-agent who was not superior to dates at the Kosciusko High School Lyceum or the Kiwanis Ladies' Night. She liked cross-word puzzles, and in the trade she was known as "The Dragon."

Under her skilled hand, the Doctor scheduled a whole repertory of shows from which the local committees could pick:

W. J. Bryan: Soldier-Saint
Don't Be a Singe Cat
Trust in Youth
The Dangerous Age
Home Learning for Grownups
How to Keep the Young Generation at Home
Is College Worth While?
Should Girls Go to College?
What's the Best School for Your Children?

The answer to the last query was "the nearest one." This discourse was described by the Dragon as "sixty-one minutes of fun, learning, bright anecdote and sound advice, by a great professional educator." These topics, with a half-tone of Dr. Planish smiling sidewise at the cord on his eyeglasses, were emblazoned in a leaflet sent out to all customers interested in cultural wares. When the leaflet was shown to Carrie, aged four, she laughed so much that her parents looked at her suspiciously.

For two weeks out of every six, that winter, Dr. Planish pounded the pebbly trail of the small-time lecturer.

He arrived in Washout at 5 A.M., caught the connecting train at 5:45, rode two hours in the red dust of a day coach, and arrived at Napoleon at 7:37. He felt dusty, his eyes felt glued, and his hope for the young generation was that they would quit it and grow up.

He was met by the Committee, three women and a husband, and asked to wait just a minute, because the reporter and the photographer had got mixed up and gone to the C.B.&Q. depot instead of the Union Station. He sat on a wooden bench for forty minutes, wanting coffee but talking about education, while the husband looked at the Doctor's beard and loathed it.

At 8:17, they gave up the Press, and the husband drove the Doctor to his hotel. Barking with weariness, the Doctor telephoned down for coffee, stripped off all his disguise except a gray flannel union suit—and the beard —gulped the coffee, stuck the tray out in the hall so that he would not be disturbed by the return of the room-waiter, drowsily forgot to lock the door and cut off the telephone, fell on the bed, looked cynically at the hotel picture of Marquises Horsing Around with Pages, and was asleep at 8:58.

At 9:16, the reporter and the photographer walked in, without knocking, and laughed very much at the union suit. The Doctor could scarcely see his clothes as he wallowed back into them. He sat in an armchair with his forefinger to his temple, and when the photographer's flashlight went off, he hoped that the hotel had caught fire and that this would end it all.

In answer to the reporter's questions, Dr. Planish stated that he considered Napoleon the most beautiful city in the State—though they must also permit him to say a word for the cities in his own beloved State of Iowa; that he thought women had a perfect right to study chiropractic or parachute-jumping but doubted if in these arts they would be as happy as in bringing up a nice little family; that there were many, many college girls who did not get seduced; and that President Hoover was an even greater man than Coolidge.

At 9:41, after having locked the door, Dr. Planish was asleep again. At 9:52, the telephone exploded.

"Yesh," said the Doctor, blurrily.

"I bet you can't guess who this is."

"Well, I'm afraid you're right."

"How is the old rooster?"

"Fine—fine. Who is this?"

"You don't sound so fine. You sound cockeyed to me."

"Well, I'm not! Who is this?"

"Can't you guess?"

"I'm sorry, but somehow I don't seem to recognize the voice. I didn't remember I knew anybody in Napoleon."

"So you're giving people the big Des Moines runaround now, are you!"

"Not a bit of it, but—who is this?"

"Well, who do you think it is?"

"I haven't any idea."

"Well, you old lobster, this is Bert!"

"Oh—— Bert."

"You heard me!"

"Which Bert?"

"Well, for God's sake! Your cousin!"

"I'm terribly sorry, but——"

"Bert Twitching, your second cousin! From Akron!"

"Oh—— Say, did we ever meet?"

"Why, of course we did! What's the matter—losing your memory from so much chasing? You ought to watch that! You remember—Dad and I stopped by your house about twenty-five years ago—you were ten-eleven years old. And we didn't get such a hell of a friendly reception either, as I recall it. But I'm the kind of a guy can always forgive and forget. Well, well, well, well, what you waiting for? I can't loaf around all day like you gab-artists! Get busy— put your bonnet on and come down to the office and I'll buy you a drink."

"I'm afraid I can't, just now. There's a lot of people here. What's your telephone number, and I'll call you up. Or say—will you be at my lecture tonight?"

"Of course I won't be at your lecture tonight! Don't you think I got anything more important to do with my evenings?"

He told the hotel exchange not to put through any more calls; he slept almost till noon, and bathed, and cursed with a small impotent cursing that sounded more like weeping, and wrote his *Rural Adult* editorial on his portable typewriter. He had had the telephone connected again, and during his period of inspiration he answered

[171]

calls from an insurance man who wanted to know whether he had ever given any thought to his wife and little family of sons, from three several girl reporters on the same high-school magazine, from an unknown lady who wished to submit to his magazine song lyrics upholding Prohibition, and from another lady who wished to know whether he was Joseph F. Snyder and, irately, why not?

The chambermaid came in, slapped his pillows once, and wanted his autograph for her little lame son. He happily asked her how she had found out who he was. She hadn't. She had no clear ideas about him beyond the facts that he was a Doctor and had a beard and therefore probably was a goat-gland specialist.

At 12:49, the silent and anonymous husband who had met him at the train came in and took him to a luncheon of the Wholesale Stocking Dealers' convention, at which he had to speak (gratis). This first husband was relieved after the luncheon by a second and equally unwilling husband, who drove him out to Maplewood Park and to the seventh Pioneer Log Cabin (replica) that he had inspected in twelve days.

From 3:30 till 8, the hour of his lecture, he blessedly had all his time to himself, except for being interviewed by the three high-school girls, each of whom asked the Doctor what he thought about education, eighteen telephone calls, a tea, at which he had to stand up beside the signed photograph of Hugh Walpole and speak for five minutes, dressing for the lecture, and a dinner of forty people—at a private house and yet no cocktails—during which he had to explain the philosophy of Plotinus, whom he had never read, to his hostess, who hadn't either.

His lecture was under the auspices of the Ladies' Current Events Club of the Percival Boulevard Methodist Church, and it was held in the church auditorium, which meant that he could not have a cigarette just before speaking, that he could not say damn during the lecture nor refer to abortions or garters nor tell his one prize story about the drunken Deacon, and that he had to be hopeful about the Future of America—regarding which, in view of sixteen more days of lecturing, he actually felt very black.

He was met at the stage entrance to the church by his lady chairwoman and the pastor, the Reverend Dr. Bowery, who pressed his hand, and whistled, "It's a great privilege for us to have you with us tonight. Let's see; I believe you were dean of old Kinnikinick. Did you ever know Professor Epop of Bowdoin College, Maine, Doctor?"

"I'm afraid I don't, Doctor."

"You don't, Doctor?"

Dr. Planish had a distinct feeling that he'd better, or get thrown out. "Oh, I know him by reputation, of course." The Reverend Bowery still looked suspicious. "Know him *very* well, by reputation. A fine scholar and gentleman."

"He's a stinker. He drinks liquor," said Dr. Bowery, and sniffed at Dr. Planish's breath.

The local newspaper photographer came in to do another bombardment, not because the paper or anybody else wanted a picture of Dr. Planish, but because no committee considers a lecturer fit to go to work unless, just before the show, he has been fed to a state of coma,

[173]

talked-out at a large dinner, and finally blinded by flash-lights.

Meanwhile the chairwoman was going crazy trying to remember her introductory speech. She was circling round and round the vestry like a Mexican bean, muttering "One who—than whom—one whom—than who." Dr. Planish grasped her shoulder, shook her, and snapped, "Stop it, will you, young woman! Don't worry about the audience. Those boneheads are lucky to have a superior gal like you say *anything* to them!"

She looked at him with surprised adoration, and from then on it was his day, his night, and he was tolerably happy in the skilled performance of his grisly professional duties. At 9:17 P.M., grasping the edges of the pulpit, looking serenely out on all those rouge-patches and red hats and blunt mustaches, feeling how all their attention poured in on him, and loving it, he ended, "And so, my friends, I leave with you the thought that it is not by asking advice or expecting a miracle that we shall bring security to our children and solidarity to our families, but by patiently doing what we know is right."

He got through the question-period afterward with only one nasty moment—the inevitable heckling by the ubiquitous Communist. After that, he had only to get his check in hand, and the gay funeral was over.

Sometimes there was a party after the show. Sometimes unremarkable-looking people, whom he hadn't even noticed down in the audience, came up and asked him if he didn't want a drink, and he was taken to a real home, with a private bar and sufficient ash-trays and good ribald conversation, and thus recovered from the sickness of fluency before he had to take another train. But there was no such oasis tonight, not in the Percival Boulevard Church, and in his hotel room his only joys were the check, which he took out of his wallet and lightly kissed, and his nightly long-distance call to Peony, at eleven; a joy which he never denied himself unless at that hour he was on the train. If that happened, he called her whenever he got to the new town—1 A.M., 3 A.M., it did not matter. She always awoke quickly and sweetly, and spoke as though his voice was the greatest surprise she had ever had.

Tonight——

"Hello, baby!"

"Oh, Gid-e-on! Lover! Where are you?"

"Napoleon."

"Now stop it! What would you be doing in a place like that for?"

"For eighty-five bucks, minus twenty per cent to the Dragon."

"You can consider it already spent, toy-man. Oh, Gideon, I do miss you so, every minute. Even with Carrie yellin' her crazy head off, this flat seems so empty, with no big bear bumbling around. I was just thinking tonight, if you were here, we'd go chasing all over town, laughing like fools, and have a drink and go to a movie and hold hands. Tell me, lover, how are you?"

"Oh, fine. My throat is holding out fine. That's better than I can say for the behind, on the seats in all these trains every day."

"Why, Gid-e-on!"

"And you're all right, dear?"

"Just dandy."

"And Carrie?"

"Oh, she's swell."

"Well, I got to hang up now. Take care of yourself."

"You take care of *your*self."

"I will, pet, you bet I will. Kiss Carrie for me. And be sure and take care of yourself and—and—— God, I wish I were there with you, right now! Good-bye, my dear—so long."

His train did not go till 12:30, and it was too late for the second movie houses. Till 12 he sat bolt up, keeping himself awake by reading a *True Confessions* magazine, the financial page of the Napoleon evening paper, and, several times, the interview with himself in the same. It was pleasant when at last he could close his bag and call for a bellboy to take it down.

As he sat in his Pullman berth, fumblingly undressing, he wished that he were back in Kinnikinick, going to bed in the honorable cottage of the dean. The picture of the placid campus reached out before him as he was shaken to sleep—and then the porter was twitching his pillow, and it was time to get up and do it all over again, and he knew that at the depot, waiting, was another cultural posse of three nice but resolute women and an anonymous husband, and maybe the Reverend Dr. Bowery, swanking under another name, with girl high-school reporters lurking behind every baggage truck, and all of them expecting these damn quips.

He came home, to his wife's embraces and to Des Moines' surprise that he had ever been away, with a handful of checks which he threw into the air before Peony, so that they fell about her in a flashing storm. He had five clear weeks before he had to go out on tour again, and they planned to put in practically every moment of it making love, playing with Carrie, shopping, drinking martinis and doing enough editing to keep from being fired.

Before the next summer, they had eleven hundred dollars in the bank, the new car and the newest piano had been paid for—nearly—and they had cautiously put up a little money on margin with a conservative firm of stockbrokers. For this was in the late 1920's, and with their reading in economics, their unusual clarity and imagination, Dr. and Mrs. Planish could foresee a rise in prosperity which might make them millionaires in another ten years.

"What if that ole meanie, A.J., don't pay your salary very often," crowed Peony. "We're going to have the marble swimming-pool without him!"

After their financial recovery, the Planishes were able to step up on a fairly high plane of society: investment counselors and general managers of packing plants and high-school principals and lawyers and dealers in music, with wives who had most of them been born middle-aged. They looked on Dr. Planish as their proprietary Intellectual, and he now first had the pleasure of being taken out to play golf, clad in the short, baggy, Persian-looking trousers then called "plus fours."

"We're going ahead again!" Peony crowed. "These people ain't so hot, but wait 'll we get to New York! We'll be chumming up with the Rockefellers and Mary Pickford and Nicholas Murray Butler!"

One of their warmer friends at this time was a gasoline dealer who owned a new radio station. He invited Dr. Planish to make a regular Saturday-morning fifteen-minute address for three weeks, and even paid him ten dollars per augury.

No longer was Dr. Planish an old-fashioned schoolmaster at a meager desk in a stale classroom which might just as well have been in the 1820's instead of the 1920's. He was a master of modern machinery, a lord of the airways, as spiritual and up to date as a safety razor. He could reach and influence thousands now—indeed, far-flung thousands, and pretty soon it would be far-flung millions—instead of dubious hundreds uncomfortable in lecture halls. He was coming into his own, he was putting on the robes of prophecy, and he had always known that they would fit him.

So, on the miraculous radio waves, carrying his message at 186,000 miles a second, the streamlined philosopher told the far-flungs that they ought to read the Bible, that wealth did not ensure happiness, that just the other day he had talked, personally, with the Governor of a populous State, and that all conscientious citizens ought to vote—a virtuous act that Dr. Gideon Planish had never yet performed.

14

BACK IN 1924 there appeared a book which, like *Das Kapital* or Shakespeare or the Koran, inspired a generation and enriched an age. It was *The Man Nobody Knows,* by Mr. Bruce Barton, a treatise which proved that Christ Jesus was not a rebel or a peasant, but a society gent, a real sport, a press agent and the founder of modern business.

This Epistle to the Babbitts had upon Dr. Planish such an effect as cannot be comprehended by the wild children of an age which is more concerned with Hitler and Expressionism. They miss the quivering zest with which Dr. Planish said, "I learned a whale of a lot more about the writing racket from Mr. Barton than I ever did from Walter Pater."

He proved it in what became the most beloved feature of *Rural Adult Education:* his witty column called "Cornpone and Popcorn." In this appeared his essay "Mental Elbow Grease," and this little masterpiece was to be more quoted than any other foam from his pen. It began:

"As the Swede fellow says, the saws and chisels in your tool chest von't yump up into your hand. And the books on your shelves aren't going to crawl down and get inside your brain. It isn't the number of books that counts in your mental development, but how you read and re-read them. Books don't give up their inner secrets to the man who snubs them and isn't friendly with them and doesn't try to coax out their confidence. The proverbial old-time country doctor's library, just Shakespeare and the Bible and Gray's *Anatomy*, contained plenty for the man who dug out every word as though it were a golden nugget."

This pasticcio was reprinted by little treadmill magazines and trade journals all over the country, and from these lifted as a filler by some hundreds of newspapers. Occasionally they even gave credit to Dr. Planish, and he began to receive letters about it addressed to him in care of everything from the Salt Lake City *Manna* to the Alabama Department of Education.

One of the warmest letters was from the Reverend James Severance Kitto, S.T.D., pastor of the Abner Jones Christian Church of Evanston, Illinois, and president of the famous Heskett Rural School Foundation of Chicago.

Dr. Planish knew him by mail, though he had never yet looked into his red and friendly Scottish face. Dr. Kitto had contributed to *Rural Adult* a small panegyric on a handsome new illustrated edition of *Ben Hur*, a classic which, as he wrote, lives on with the Bible and Wentworth's Algebra. He had written to *Rural Adult* that he was not sure that he ought to keep their generous payment of $7.44. He did not, however, return the check.

A. J. Joslin had lunched with Dr. Kitto in Chicago, and reported that he was a learned but hearty fellow, who felt that the Kremlin was plotting against rural church work in Nebraska, Missouri, and portions of Southern

Illinois. But this interested Dr. Planish less than Joslin's tip that the paid executives of the Heskett Rural School Foundation—known to all professional good-doers as the H.R.S.F.—weren't cashing in adequately on the large funds of the Foundation. Dr. Kitto had taken Mr. Joslin to the Foundation offices, and they had found no one there except the managing secretary, a spinster named Bernardine Nimrock, and two stenographers, who weren't so much as sending out red and green circulars to supply the far-flung wastebaskets of our broad land with information about the beauties of rural education and with the plea that unless the wastebasket send in a generous contribution at once, the little red schoolhouses and the big gray consolidated schoolhouses would all be turned into speak-easies.

It appeared that old Heskett, the gents' furnishings chain-store king, had left three million dollars to the H.R.S.F., but it was not using half the interest. It did occasionally publish a report fly-specked with statistics, it did give grants-in-aid to a few worthy schools, but never, said Mr. Joslin, did the officers perform these deeds with enough ballyhoo. They were regular bushel-hiders.

Dr. Kitto who, as president, was unpaid, was too busy with other idealistic jobs to think up new ways of spending the Foundation's income, and the salaried Bernardine Nimrock too timid, and both of them, marveled Mr. Joslin, too lazy or conceivably too honest to take the opportunity of giving their nephews, sisters-in-law, ex-lovers and classmates such suitable jobs with the Foundation as knitting, copying poetry, telephoning and drinking tea.

"I'd like to have my hands on that show. I'd make it take care of the proper people—— Oh, by the way, Doc, I'm going to be able to pay you that two hundred smackers I owe you by the end of the month, positively," said Mr. Joslin.

All this Dr. Planish recalled when there came from Dr. James Severance Kitto the letter praising his essay, and inviting him to accept a National Directorship in the H.R.S.F. and to attend its Annual Midsummer Conference. (Conference, not Convention, because Convention means strip-tease shows and illicit liquor and the singing of "Happy birthday, dear Henry Hargett Huisenkamp, happy birthday to you," while Conference indicates only mental stripping.)

Dr. Planish accepted, and had his own Conference, with Peony.

Her father made a dozen trips a year to Chicago, and on the next one he looked up certain things, and wrote to the Doctor:

"I went in the Heskett place and got acquainted, and I even took the virtuous Bunny Nimrock, the secy, out to lunch. I didn't know I was so much of a beau, your father-in-law, the little devil, I had her quite flustered.

"I think you ought to let her alone, the poor gal thinks she is doing a good job and getting city folks to take country schools seriously and trying to do a little amateur lobbying with State Legislatures, but if you want her job, go to it, she does not look so hot and I imagine you could expand it into a pretty well-paying proposition. I found, as you asked, that the fellow to honey up to, be-

sides Reverend Kitto, is another preacher, Reverend
Christian Stern of New York City, a slick politician who
is in all the uplift rackets and will certainly be in Chi for
the conference.

"I also went out to the North Shore and sponged supper
off my cousin Lucy and got to meet Reverend Kitto himself by accident on purpose and what shd we get to talking about but you, and I told him you were a national
director of this New Turk outfit and a trustee of this
Standard English society, whatever its name is, and cd
have been president of Kinnikinick if you'd wanted to.
Got Kitto so het up he is ready to give you the keys of the
city, if you want to go there, I don't know why, personally wd much prefer Faribault or even Northfield or
Winona.

"The Nimrock woman gets only $2,200 but sure that
cd be jacked up to $4,500 by the right second-story
worker. Don't be too hard on Bunny Nimrock, try and get
her a pension, she is OK, likes checkers and cats same as
I do.

"Yr. afft father,
"W. Jackson."

It has never been quite clear whether it was Peony or
Dr. Planish who originally decided that because he loved
country schools so much, right down to the tin wash-
basins, he ought to take over the Rural School Foundation. Certainly it was Peony who, on her own impulse,
skipped up to Kinnikinick for a week-end. She came back
cooing.

[183]

"Lover, you'll be interested to know that old Prexy Bull is going to interrupt his summer vacation and attend the Heskett Conference in Chicago, and Teckla Schaum is still in love with you, and she and her pappy have become Sustaining Members of Heskett."

"What's all this?"

"I told Bull that even if you *are* so popular among the alumni, you're opposed to this new movement to make you president of Kinnikinick——"

"*What* movement?"

"——instead of him, and just as I suspected, he is a member of the Heskett Foundation, and he's promised to be there with bells on and support this project to make you managing secretary of it. And I told Teckla that, frankly, I wasn't sure but that she'd of been a much better wife for you than I am, and that I suspected you thought so too, and—— You don't, do you, Gideon? I'd murder you, if you did! Say you don't! Okay. Now go down and tell Joslin that if he doesn't show up in Chicago and support you with Kitto and Doc Stern, you'll sue him for the salary he owes you. I mean it. Now skip, hero."

He skipped.

Before the annual conference of the Heskett Foundation, Dr. Planish had learned everything about it except why it existed at all.

The two mysteries regarding any organization for philanthropy are who really owns it and what, if anything, it actually does, besides create a pretty letterhead and provide a warm office for the chief executive to take naps in.

In the business, the term "Foundation" usually means an institution which is entirely supported by a trust fund established by a philanthropist (meaning a man with more money than he can spend on houses and pearls) and which does not solicit donations, but somewhat coldly picks out worthy persons or enterprises to which it does the giving. Occasionally, organizations call themselves Foundations without the benefit of large enough or oily enough trust funds, and send out begging letters like any League or Committee.

But the Heskett Foundation was mixed. It had the trust fund, but it also urged the pious or the guilty of mind to become Sustaining Members at $100 a year, or even Founding Members, at $1000 flat.

But more mixed were its accomplishments. Neither Dr. Kitto, the president, nor Dr. Christian Stern, the chairman of the board, got anything more than carfare and glory, and that was all right with Dr. Planish, but he was sorry to find that the Foundation was not more devoted to guaranteeing a worthy living for the managing secretary, who was a regular employee.

It published speeches about rural education by Kitto and Stern and by one H. Sanderson Sanderson-Smith, Esq., in flat little gray pamphlets, but no country teacher seemed ever to have received them. They were sent to managing editors, who turned them over to the drama editors, who threw them into the wastebasket, along with Hollywood releases about Miss Sylvia Silva's goat farm.

The Foundation had been known to give blackboards to a school in Kansas, two motion-picture films to a teachers' college in Dakota, and a collection of Turkish stamps to a Hawaiian institute for pineapple growers, but the pattern for these benefactions seemed to exist only in the head of Miss Bernardine Nimrock. Dr. Planish studied the Foundation reports, he talked to rural contributors to his magazine, but he found nothing more.

Well, he said to his wife Peony, he'd change all that. Under his direction, the Foundation might not make more gifts, but they'd be brighter and a lot more talked-about.

On the hot evening before they set off for Chicago, the Planishes sat late in their flat, the Doctor in saffron pajamas open on his chubby chest, Peony in mules and a wisp of nightgown.

"Well, looks as if we're going to take a shot at something new," he said.

"Aren't you excited, Gidjums?"

"Oh, I guess so, but—— Same time. We don't always want to go on shifting and changing. I've got pretty fond of Des Moines and the bunch here—I don't even mind playing golf—and I get kind of homesick for Kinnikinick sometimes. I liked our little white house. We ought to have a dog for Carrie to play with——"

"Big tiny, I know how you feel. I want to be settled down, too. But first we got to make New York. You'll be boss of the Boy Scouts or the Red Cross or some really big philanthropy in another five-ten years, and then we'll get a house out in some lovely suburb, with elm trees and a stone wall around it—and yes, we'll *get* a dog for her.

We can't stop now, with that ahead of us, *can* we! It—wouldn't be fair to young Carrie!"

"Maybe not—maybe not."

"And wait till you see the new red velvet opera cape I got today. It'll knock Chicago's eyes out!"

"But won't it be kind of warm, this weather, on the poor girl's little shoulders?" he protested fondly, and kissed her shoulder by way of illustration.

15

THE HESKETT FOUNDATION CONFERENCE did not assemble in a hotel, with thunderous celluloid badges, sales managers boosting quotas by awarding to the best go-getter a golden calf, and a procession of delegates trotting damply to the bar and their wives to the Powder Room. It convened at the Foundation Building, and there were only a hundred delegates.

Dr. and Mrs. Planish, a little rustic with suitcases and a paper parcel, went to the fabulous Golden Strand Hotel, on the north side of Chicago—naturally they went there, and naturally they took a suite, for the Foundation was paying the expenses of delegates.

A little muted and impressed, Peony looked at the lilac-colored couch with silver-brocade pillows, in front of it a carved teak coffee table covered with glass, at one end of it a super-heterodyne radio in a Sheraton cabinet, and at the other a Russian brass table holding a Swiss smoking-set made in Japan, while behind it stood a Japanese screen made in Switzerland—she looked at all this richness, and sighed, "This is what I like! This is by golly what we're going to have all the time, from now on. I tell you, most people don't understand will-power, if you choose to use it, isn't that so?"

He agreed.

The Heskett Foundation Building, when they found it, was less than magnificent: a barracks made by throwing two brownstone houses together. The lower floor was all in offices lathered with enlarged photographs of unhappy country schoolchildren, and the second leaked pamphlets, but the third floor an auditorium which, packing them close, would hold three hundred people, especially educative people, who are not very well fed. "This hall is fancied up real nice, with those silk curtains," admired Peony. There were two murals, showing a teacher leading her flock from dark pigpens up to a lighted mountain peak—nobody ever did say how it would have been if the pigpens had been lighted and the peak in darkness —and of Madame Montessori chatting with William Penn, Socrates and Bronson Alcott.

Peony giggled. "That ole girl's got some awful stuffy boy-friends," she said.

"Sweet one, you mustn't sneer. All earnest effort is commendable," the Doctor gently instructed.

"Oh, I know. I'm sorry, lover," she whimpered.

"And I'll bet they laid out not less than ten thousand bucks on those murials," admired the Doctor.

"Well I'll be damned!" his wife said fondly.

Then, at the secretarial and registrative desk of Miss Bernardine Nimrock, they met their first leaders of the organizational world. They had not experienced such handshaking, such a counterpoint of congratulatory voices, since their last Freshman Reception at Kinnikinick.

Dr. James Severance Kitto shook hands with them as

though he enjoyed it. He had a broad soft red face and a broad soft white hand, and his voice was wonderful: molasses basso with a stick of Scotch in it.

"I feel that you and I can do great things together, Dr. Kitto, and I want you to meet my wife," said Dr. Planish.

Dr. Kitto held Peony's ardent paw almost permanently; he looked at her and then he looked at Dr. Planish, and he boomed, "Right you are! GREAT things!"

More satisfying, even, was the meeting with the Reverend Dr. Christian Stern, of New York, chairman of the executive board. He was a sandy-looking man in his late thirties, dry, thin and galvanic. He said that he was fond of Tolstoy and canoeing, and his sandy hair was parted in the middle, but his handshake was powerful.

Dr. Planish bubbled, "It's most annoying, Doctor. I keep hearing such praise of you from everybody that goes to New York. We all get very jealous!"

"Well, well, Doctor! Is that true!" said Dr. Stern.

A crew of others, less brisk about Heskett Foundation politics yet actually more famous in the banquet world in general, made as though they were delighted to have the Planishes introduced to them. There was Maude Jewkins, M.D., who said, humorously but pretty often, that women were better doctors than men because they weren't so poetic. There was Mrs. Natalia Hochberg, of New York, who was now trying to settle a horde of violently unwilling sweatshop workers on the wholesome farm land.

There was Mr. H. Sanderson Sanderson-Smith, born in

New England but a graduate of Columbia and therefore refined, and now resident in the hobohemian hinterland of California; book-reviewer and editor of Little Magazines and founder of leagues for nudism, Thomism, cricket and the black mass. He had red whiskers and pale eyes and a merry smile, and he had once been taken for a son of Bernard Shaw. He kept on saying that he did not believe in Democracy, but he said it with such gentleness that you thought he didn't mean a word of it—that's what you thought. He remarked to the Planishes, "I dare say I am the only person in this rapturous assembly who is at once a Nietzschean and a cabalist." They weren't sure what that meant, and they didn't like him very much.

All this happened at tea—the Heskett Foundation and Miss Bernardine Nimrock sprang to tea and raisin cakes as readily as a policeman springs for pretzels.

"Didn't I *tell* you so?" whispered Peony. "Some day we'll be meeting John D. Rockefeller and Bishop Manning and the Prince of Wales!"

Then they saw President T. Austin Bull of Kinnikinick, standing alone, like a solitary birch tree on the Iowa prairie. "My, how we've missed you and Mrs. Bull!" caroled Dr. Planish, and the President yelled, "And how we've missed you dear people!"

But the Planishes met their one real treasure in Professor George Riot.

They had heard about Professor Riot, so young and yet so brilliant and so deep. At only thirty-one, he was Professor of the Philosophy of Education in Wisteria College for Women, and author of *Don't Be Afreud*. He had had a little trouble, which made the Planishes only the more sympathetic with him; the sensational newspapers said that in a lecture he had asserted that, by Federal law, no girl ought to be allowed to remain a virgin after twenty-six. For two years now the poor fellow had had to go all over the country explaining (at $150 per denial) that he hadn't meant that at all, but merely something that sounded the same.

He looked like an English Guardsman, on the tall thin side.

The Planishes and he instantly drew toward each other, since they were so much younger than the other uplifters: Dr. Planish, thirty-seven, Riot, thirty-one, and Peony but twenty-seven. She whispered to her two men, "Let's shake this bunch of old dodoes and sneak out and have a cocktail."

"Splendid!" said Professor Riot.

At cocktails, Dr. Planish anxiously watched Peony watch Professor Riot. At last she turned to her husband and nodded, and he went into his act:

"Dr. Riot, my girl and I don't hardly know a soul here, except President Bull, and I hope we three can play around together. Without handing ourselves too much, I feel maybe we three have a slightly more man-of-the-world attitude toward education than antiques like Bull and Kitto—but not cynical, you understand, Doctor!"

"I know just how you mean, Doctor," said Dr. Riot.

"Perhaps more sophisticated, Doctor."

"Yes, I think that might be the word—more urbane and realistic, Doctor."

"That's what I mean, Doctor."

"You boys have another drink," said Peony.

The three musketeers, after an evening in the Heskett Auditorium devoted to enduring it through addresses on Religion in Education by Reverend Kitto and Education in Religion by Reverend Stern, hastened to the Planishes' suite, and they parted at 3 A.M.

They were calling one another George and Gid and Peony by then. The Planishes did not merely consider Riot useful now; they really liked him, which in the philanthropic realm was extraordinary.

Dr. Planish had explained that he would be willing to become managing secretary of the Heskett Foundation. There were wonderful things he wanted to do for the country schools, and after his experience on *Rural Adult Education*——

"Right-oh! I'll put it over," said George Riot. "You and I could work out some plans together. Besides, I don't see why Kitto and Stern should go on hogging the whole three million. But have you got acquainted with Hamilton Frisby?"

"With who?"

"Little sawed-off lawyer—an uh'er—he says, 'I, uh, I feel that, uh, we should, uh——' "

"I think I ran into him. What is he?"

"The real works behind the Foundation. He's trustee for the whole Heskett estate—the heirs are all imbeciles or painters or both; they live in Italy or the Berkshires and leave everything to Frisby."

"F-R-I-S-B-Y." Peony was writing it down. "He's in the bag already, George. Hey! Put more soda in."

Next noon, the Planishes had lunch with President Bull, and Dr. Planish was full of ideas about What Could Be Done. That afternoon, he read before the Conference a paper that proved you can't have spirituality in a school without sewerage. Late that afternoon, the Planishes had tea with Dr. Christian Stern, and cocktails with Mr. Hamilton Frisby, who liked the Doctor's ideas about golf. Before this, Dr. Planish had said lavishly to the Reverend Dr. Kitto, "I know how busy you must be, Doctor, with this Conference as well as your tremendous regular clerical duties, so how about our having breakfast together, tomorrow?"

That evening, the Planishes were the dinner hosts to Mrs. Hochberg, Mr. Sanderson-Smith, Dr. and Mrs. Stern, Professor Riot, Mr. Hamilton Frisby—and Miss Bernardine Nimrock, whom Peony encouraged to talk her heart out.

She didn't seem to have much to talk out.

The others left at ten, busily but courteously, as great humanitarians and the whole tribe of Celebrities usually do, and the Planishes and George were left to themselves.

"That Sanderson-Smooch is a cross between a cobra and a pussy cat," yelled Riot.

"Mrs. Hochberg keeps on being so rich, Bull tells me, because she never gives anything to her own charities," shouted Dr. Planish.

"That poor Nimrock woman had on the damnedest hat I ever saw!" screamed Peony.

"Oh, by the way, speaking of that, and I do hope I won't be infringing on your good nature," said George, "but will you go shopping with me tomorrow afternoon, Peony, and help me buy some pajamas for my wife? Gracious, she certainly would've come along if she'd known I was going to meet you folks instead of a lot of windbags like Chris Stern."

Sure she would.

They had another drink, and said they were having *such* a good time. They had still another drink, and became cultural.

"The trouble with a lot of these muffs like Stern and Kitto and your poker-faced President Bull is that they haven't any sense of the artistic," said Professor Riot.

"That's so. Like music," mused Dr. Planish. "You bet. I certainly am fond of music. I wish I had time to hear some now and then."

"So do I. I certainly do like to hear Beethoven. And Rimsky-Korsakoff," cried Professor Riot.

"You bet! And Rosa Bonheur," said Dr. Planish.

"I don't think she was a composer. Wasn't she a shark about radio or radium or something?" worried Peony.

"Oh, that's so, of course she was." Dr. Planish laughed heartily. "Just for the moment I got her balled up with that French woman composer. *You* know, George."

"Of course I do, Gid. Know her name 's well as I do my own, but just for the moment it slips my tongue. Claudette? No, that's not right. But anyway—— Don't you play the piano, Peony?"

Dr. Planish said, weeping, "George, do you know that, for my sake, Peony gave up a career which would have made her the greatest woman pianist? . . . Sweetie pie, how long is it since you've touched the piano?"

"What of it?" explained Peony.

"You see? Gave it all up for our sake—no, for sake of cause of—— What's our cause, George?"

"Idolism—i—idealism."

"No it ain't! It's cause popular education and honesty politics, strickly honest!"

"Same thing. Hurray f'r idealism! This dumb country—lot of farmers, pot-wallopers. Where'd it be if wasn't for us, Gid?"

"Hurray for us!" said Dr. Planish.

"Oh, boys," wailed Peony, "I think I'm getting a little tight!"

They both kissed her tenderly.

The Executive Board of the Heskett Foundation met at 10:30 next morning. They decided to buy a new carpet for the auditorium, to appoint a committee to elect a chairman to authorize the secretary to draw up a resolution to inform Professor John Dewey that they agreed with him in principle, to publish a symposium on spreading democracy by saluting the flag in all schools, and to elect Dr. Gideon Planish as managing secretary of the Foundation, at $3,900 a year.

Professor Riot went to see if he would accept.

"Gid, I'm sorry as hell I couldn't jack 'em up higher than thirty-nine hundred, but that's all the tightwads would stand for. And you getting forty-two hundred already! Still, I do think this slow-poke institution might lead the way to nobler and much better publicized organizations. How about it, Gid?"

Dr. Planish said bravely, "Yes, it may be a step into a wider and more useful field. I'll take it, George. By the way, I hope they're pensioning off Bernardine Nimrock."

"Yes—eleven hundred a year."

"Oh, fine! I certainly would hate to think I was doing that poor old hen out of a job. A fellow's got to be chivalrous, George, no matter what."

Peony fondly protested, "Now I won't hear a word about either of you boys ever being anything but chivalrous!"

"That's sweet of you, baby," admired Professor Riot. "You're a real Hypatia—if that was her name. So I'll tell 'em the thirty-nine hundred bucks is okay, Gid?"

"Yes, you may tell them so. I think I may honestly consider myself non-commercial," said Dr. Planish.

He had already decided that since he never actually got more than twenty-eight hundred out of Joslin, he would take the new job even at three thousand. He continued:

"But they must understand what a sacrifice I'm making."

"I've already explained that to them. You bet I have!" said Professor Riot.

"The first quality an organization executive has to have is willingness to sacrifice."

"That's so," sighed Professor Riot. "I wish the public who bellyache over their privilege of giving a little to philanthropy out of their great treasury would appreciate that fact."

The telephone rang.

Dr. Planish answered it. He stuttered, "I g-guess you better let her come up." He turned to his guerrilla forces with a terrified "It's Bernardine Nimrock!"

Peony seized Riot's arm and melodramatically muttered, "Let's skip in the bedroom! Giddy can get rid of her quicker without us!"

Three minutes later, Miss Nimrock crept into the living-room, a dusty moth of a woman, fluttering, and Dr. Planish backed away from her. This was not going to be fun. He felt that it was very unjust of Peony and his old friend George Riot and the Reverends Kitto and Stern to put this upon him. Her mouth was working queerly. Was she crazy? Sometimes frail women picked up things like that Bourbon bottle and killed powerful men.

"Dr. Planish, I've just heard that the Foundation plans to fire me, after ten years' service, and give you my job, and you don't need it—you don't need it—you're a man and you've been a college professor and you could always get some kind of job. But I'm supporting my mother, and Dr. Kitto promised I should have the job always, and if I never have accomplished much as managing secretary, and I know I haven't, it's because I've had to submit everything to Dr. Kitto for his okay, and I'd never get it—I'd wait and wait and telephone and never get it. It'll kill me and kill my mother if you just amuse yourself by coming in and taking this job away from me —I've got to have it—oh, you're not a hypocrite like Dr. Kitto, or cruel like Mr. Frisby, are you? You'll stop and think about this, won't you? You'll try and see if there isn't something else you can find to do, won't you? I've never been a beggar like this before. I thought I was a decent independent woman and I worked so hard. You are a man of honor, aren't you? You won't kill us, just to get ahead?"

He had backed clear to the windows; he stood with his hands behind him, twitching at the net curtains. He had to say something.

"Well, this is all news to me—practically. I've just heard rumors. Certainly the last thing in the world I'd want to do would be to injure you two ladies. Yes, I'll look into this——"

Miss Nimrock was looking at him with sunny, adoring eyes. She seemed almost young and pretty. This was what he could do for women, the poor things! He went on, "Certainly look into this right away, and see if we can't——"

Then Peony walked in.

She charged on Miss Nimrock like St. Catherine, or Mrs. Calvin routing a witch, and this time it was Miss Nimrock who backed up, as Peony chanted, "Oh, I didn't know you were here. Isn't this dandy! I did want a chance to congratulate you on getting that lovely eleven-hundred-a-year pension, so you can have that and still get a second job if you want to, any job you want, say like teaching, my, you'll be making so much money you won't know what to do with it, and personally I should think you'd be glad to get away from Kitto, the ole stuffed shirt——"

She had Miss Nimrock through the door into the corridor, she closed the door while the adversary was trying to speak, and she cried to Dr. Planish and the now cautiously emergent George Riot:

"My, I do think women are the worst sports! Imagine her trying to welsh like that! I did hate to be so mean to her, poor thing, but I thought it would be kindest to just be brutal, really, and get it over. Poor Gideon, I was so sorry for you, and for you, too, George, and I guess that calls for a drink. Let's make it a quickie, because I got to go out shopping with George and get some pajamas for his little wife, I swear, I'm so jealous of that girl of yours, I could bust, George, and me promising I wouldn't do one ounce of shopping all the time I was in Chicago, and save and scrimp and economize and—there you are, boys."

Where, glowed Dr. Planish, was there another wife like that?

16

THEY WERE DRESSING for the great annual Heskett Foundation dinner, final ensemble of the Conference, at which
his appointment as managing secretary would be announced.

"You always look so distinguished in your tuxedo,
Giddy," she said.

"Oh, not so much. Well, go on. You haven't told me anything yet about shopping with George."

"I think most men do look better, dressed for dinner,
but especially a man with a beard. That's where the English are so smart, dressing for dinner. My, that must be a
grand city, London—and neither of us ever seen it yet!
England's a so much more civilized country—as the English themselves so often tell us. Will we go and live in
London some time, when we're rich, sweetheart?"

"Go on. Tell me. What've you been up to?"

"Gideon! I did promise not to throw money around this
time, didn't I!"

"It was a voluntary promise. I never asked you to make it."

"I know you didn't. So don't you see?"

"See what?"

"Well, after we found George his pajamas—my gracious,
now that's a slip, isn't it, you better page Dr. Freud, I guess

—and anyway, after we found the pajamas for his wife— and George and that giggling hyena of a saleswoman did make me kind of sore, even though they were just joking, his putting his arm around me like that and pretending to show her his wife's bust measurements with me for model. I told George I had a good mind to slap his ears off. But anyway, I certainly did pick her out some lovely pajamas, my, I'd like to have 'em myself, all silk, in peach color with green piping and——

"But anyway, as I was saying, George insisted we might as well look over the department store while we had the chance, and we went up and down on the escalators, gee, that was fun, and the things I wanted to buy, heavens and earth, you have no idea how strong-minded I was—a white bearskin rug that would be so delicious on my toes on a winter morning, and a portrait of President Andy Jackson —Daddy says we're related to him somehow, way far back —and an electric drink-mixer—it would really be economical, it would save so much time, but I was firm, and oh, Gid-e-on, a real Finnish hand-carved wooden salad bowl!

"They'd all be so useful, but I was adamant, absolutely ada*mant*. Maybe it just shows us that pride goeth before the most God-awful fall, because George and I stopped at the antique jewelry counter and oh, honeybun, you'll probably murder me, but it did look cheap, and so darling, oh, the loveliest thing I ever saw, and it didn't seem expensive and—— Let's get it over. Look at it."

She had sneaked out from the dressing-table drawer a ring with a sparkling oval center.

"God! Not diamonds?" he grunted.

[202]

"No, don't you see? It's steel points, antique. But it was expensive, I'm afraid."

"How much?"

"Eighty-nine dollars."

He winced. But he was quickly on another track.

"I'm glad George Riot didn't give it to you."

"The funny thing is, he offered to."

"Oh, he did, did he!"

"Prob'ly not seriously. Not on a professor's salary!"

"So he offers you rings! He pretends to be buying pajamas, and feels you up! Damn him, I'll show him!"

"Why, Gideon Planish! Do you mean to say you're jealous?"

"Huh?"

"Are you?"

"M-maybe, a little."

"I'm tickled to death! Seems like you haven't been jealous for a long time, lover. But you don't think I fell for him, do you? . . . Do you?"

"No, I guess you and I are about as loyal as any couple living. That's *one* thing where we aren't phony humanitarians."

"Why, Gideon Plan-ish! What do you mean? To dare and say a thing like that, when we're giving up such a lovely job as editor and dean and all, and just sacrificing and sacrificing and *sacrificing,* and not even buying the white-bear rug or the salad bowl or anything. What a thing to say about yourself just when you're starting this wonderful new path of service!"

"I know. We really are beginning to dedicate ourselves

[203]

to mankind. I don't know what made me say that. And you're sure you still love me?"

"Shall I show you?"

"No, no—this is the only clean dress-shirt I got along. But do you love me better than George Riot?"

"Manny darling, you aren't going to get a grouch on George, I mean and show it, are you?"

"No, no, course not. He's helping me to get planted in the organizational field more than anybody else, isn't he? Oh, no, no, no, no, sweetheart, you mustn't misunderstand me about old George. They don't make 'em any better than old George."

"So now, you see, everything's fine, isn't it, hero! You don't suppose I could afford an orchid tonight, do you? Or do you feel like *giving* me one?"

The dinner guests clapped profusely when Dr. Kitto announced the appointment of Dr. Planish as managing secretary.

Dr. Planish lubricatingly told them of his practically rural birth and rearing.

Miss Bernardine Nimrock was not present.

They gave her a rising vote of thanks.

That night, Dr. Planish turned and turned in bed.

"What is it, faun? I know something's bothering you. It isn't my new ring, is it?"

"Good Lord, no!" (That is what Peony sensibly expected him to say.) "I just can't get that Nimrock woman's face out of my mind—this afternoon—so scared, and all blubbered up with crying."

"Silly! Dear silly! Progress has to go on, doesn't it? We know as students of biology that certain lower forms of life are bound to suffer. Indeed, if they didn't suffer and get themselves eliminated, they would block all true progress, wouldn't they? But do you know what I'm proudest of you for? For being so sensitive to the feelings of others. I suppose that's what has made you a humanitarian and a sort of prophet instead of just an ole college professor. So proud!"

"Well——" said Dr. Planish.

They had the Chinese Chippendale cabinet, the Chinese rug, and the porcelain clock crated and sent on to Chicago in early August. They left behind them the leather pouf. "It looks kind of hick to me now. Goodness gracious! How one's taste does get improved by traveling!" said Peony.

They drove by automobile from Des Moines to Chicago, with an overnight stop at Davenport, three hundred miles in the brilliant heat; and Dr. Planish said, over and over, that it was the most enjoyable trip he had ever made, and that little Carrie was proving to be a True Gipsy, like her parents.

Now that they were practically started for New York and London, and she was therefore no longer bound to debts and worry, Peony was a foamy cataract of ideas dashing around and over any vulgar rocks of fact. Her ideas all entailed the Doctor's doing a lot of work and magicking a lot of important people, but she looked sidewise at him, at the wheel, with such wide admiration that he had to accept them. (He was still doing most of their driving at this time; it would not be for five more years that she alone would be trusted with the car.)

He was to be a senator, after all, but from Chicago or New York, where he wouldn't have to pretend about country road-taxes. After that, he was to consolidate a string of small colleges, be president of the lot of them, run them like chain-stores, and give them such sprightly advertising —and profits—as no university in history (since the U. of Al-Azhar, Cairo, f. 970, colors: green) has ever enjoyed.

He was to combine the foreign missions of all Protestant churches, and take personal charge of them. (She would simply love traveling with him through India, and seeing palm trees and natives.) And as the start of all these glories, he was to get rid of Dr. Kitto and Mr. Hamilton Frisby and control all the funds of the Heskett Foundation, and she rather thought she would like to have one room of their house in Paris all in scarlet and black.

As Peony chattered, as she read the map and navigated, as she slipped down from the car to take Carrie to a "rest room," Dr. Planish loved her each moment with a more wistful amazement at being with his own particular girl, who would always be there, and give him a purpose for living and laboring. He marveled at her swift evolution. She was so smart, in her black and mustard suit, her black cloche hat. How had she done it? He was almost forty, and he had seen the world, had spent an entire week in New York, but it seemed to him that his country chick was as old and worldly wise as he himself, that she knew everything there was to know—except possibly the exact time of day, the amount of her bank balance, and how to spell Cincinnati—and that there was nothing that a trudger like himself, learned, rock-steady and fanatically honest though he was, could better do than to follow her divine intuitions in everything.

Peony was the best of traveling companions, interested equally in a meadow lark or a special-job Cadillac, uncomplaining of cold or heat or hunger. Only once did she worry him.

The first day, the car had run too easily, and at each restaurant they had said, "Oh, we'll find a better place farther on." Toward three, they were passing a converted village store-building with a shaky home-painted sign announcing EATS. At this suggestive word, Carrie howled.

They stopped.

The interior was gaunt and long and skinny, with three round tables, a gas stove, a lunch counter behind which were shelves of cigarettes and horrible candy bars, and a sign "Not respble for hats coats."

While Peony and Carrie were in the washroom, the lone waitress, a frightened-looking woman in a red sweater and lilac slacks, dropped on the wet surface of the table in front of Dr. Planish a hand-written menu presenting "Ham and eggs, Steak, Hamdburger sandwich, Hot Dog sandwich, cofee, coke."

"Uh—what kind of steak you got?"

"We're just out of steak."

"Let's, uh, let's have three orders of ham and eggs."

She went to a mysterious back door and yelled. As she came back, she looked at him wearily, and suddenly he knew all about her; he was one with her in the devastating struggle to keep on living. He greeted her as a fellow human being with a cheerful, "Business not so hot just now, I guess."

"Mister, there ain't any business. God, I don't know what my old man and me are going to do. I hear where there's a big stock-market boom. I guess that's where all the money's going then, stock market. Yours's the first order that's come in here today."

"That's a shame. I certainly hope you and your husband catch on soon."

Peony reappeared, and he looked at her in a dazzle of admiration. This released and Chicago-bound Peony was a new woman to him. She was so solid on her two feet, yet her fresh cheeks and reckless eyes were as adorably young as when she had first sat in front of him, a baby student.

"What do we draw?" she said amiably, as she tucked Carrie into a chair.

"Hamneggs."

"That's fine."

But that was the last cheerful thing she said at EATS. She pointed out that they had had to ask for water three times, that the table was damp, that there were no napkins in sight and no sugar, that cigarette butts covered the floor, and that the eggs were sour, the ham was salty.

"A woman that serves the public as badly as this ought to be arrested for slow murder," muttered Peony.

"Oh, the poor thing's hard-up and untrained."

"You're *sorry* for her?"

"Yes, I am!"

"I'm not, one bit. The slut!"

Their daughter Carrie spoke: "Mama, what's a slut?"

"You shut up now, sweetest honey-pie, and eat your nice ham."

"You said it wasn't nice ham."

"Now don't interrupt, little mocking bird. Mama and Papa are discussing philosophy."

"Why?" said Carrie.

Dr. Planish went on, "After all, that's going to be our job now, to encourage rural rehabilitation for just such poor victims of environment as this woman. We got to educate them."

"Wh——" Carrie had started, but she found an enchanting fly.

"Oh, pooh!" said Peony. "You can't educate animals like that. I'm terribly glad you're dedicating yourself to uplifting the soggy masses, big one, but don't wear yourself out getting sentimental about them. They're hopeless. You devote yourself a little to your wife."

"Don't I?"

"Course you do! Me just cwoss. But just the same, don't waste your time trying to help a lot of unemployables. You can't get around it: people with good taste don't decorate restaurants with fly-specks. Yes, my Hari-Carrie, Papa and Mama are going to get started now, and off for the pretty Chicago we go, all of the jingle bells gay in the snow."

"Why?" objected Carrie.

Their overnight halting-place in Davenport was the first

large hotel in which Carrie had ever slept. She was not at all frightened by the crowd in the lobby, nor by the near-marble pillars. When the clerk leaned across the desk and chirped at her, "And is this little lady staying with us, too?" she looked at him and gravely nodded.

After dinner, Carrie was put to bed in a tiny single room, and Peony urged, "Will my darling be awful scared if Papa and Mama slip off to the early movie, and get back by nine?"

"No," said Carrie.

"This sweet, old-fashioned, maply bedroom—doesn't my babykins think it's the sweetest little room she ever saw?"

"No," said Carrie.

"What, my pretty?"

"I'm sorry, Mama, but I don't."

"And pray why not?"

"I think the wallpaper is silly—all those flowers like pink worms."

Peony looked at her husband adoringly. "Will you listen to that now, will you? For six years old, isn't she the grown-uppedest thing you ever saw!"

"N-yes—oh, yes," said Dr. Planish.

For three days Peony shopped through Chicago for a flat, and in the evenings she cried against Gideon's shoulder. Doubtfully they leased an apartment in an oldish building on the South Side, decent enough but depressingly inferior to their green and silver cottage in Kinnikinick, their canary-yellow flat in Des Moines. She shuddered, "I wonder if we really are going ahead so fast? I never realized how hard it is to make a dent in a place like Chicago."

Their flat was all in brown, a clean but sullen brown; all long and tiresome lines, all tightness and a smell of respectable resignation; and it looked across the street to the brownstone front of a house wearily resigned to dullness.

"We won't stay in this dump long," vowed Peony. "You'll shake a bigger salary out of Hamilton Frisby—looks like he's the one that guards the Foundation cash. Pretty soon we'll have a modernistic apartment, right on the lake."

He felt guilty.

Within two days, Peony was caroling that the Chinese rug, the cabinet, the airy French clock "brightened up the flat something wonderful." But, naturally, she had to buy a few other things—"gay and civilized junk that you can live with," she called them: a chromium and black-glass portable bar, a pale birch radio cabinet, a sage-green Chinese lamp imitating jade, and a Gauguin print.

By laying out only $362.75 for these adornments, Peony concealed the in-soaked brownness of the place phenomenally. The only slip was that they were again two hundred dollars in debt.

"Why?" asked Dr. Planish, but Peony kissed him.

He was busy now at the Heskett Foundation offices, finding out what Miss Bernardine Nimrock had done, and hemming, and telling the stenographers to go right on doing it—only more so.

17

It must not be thought that Dr. Planish did nothing at all as managing secretary of the Heskett Foundation. He took part in conferences, almost weekly conferences, promoted by colleges, libraries, municipal forums, state educational associations, and he unflinchingly told these conferences that rural education was a fine idea. He sat on committees, and if the sitting was not actual and physical, at least he had his name on the rosters of committees, scores of them. He benevolently allowed students to use the pedagogical library which Miss Nimrock had collected, and he supervised the publication of three pamphlets prepared by university instructors who had concluded, after examining all the figures issued by the state governments, that teachers could be better paid and better heated. This was called Research.

He was fond of these pamphlets, because whenever his accounts looked a little confused, he could always put down "printing and promotion" as an item of expense.

The publication of the Foundation that he really pushed was that more popular and chatty volume *New Light in the Red Schoolhouse,* published two years before (clothbound, illus. & map, $1.65, discount in quants.). By the happiest of coincidences, it had been written by Mr. Hamilton Frisby, trustee of the Heskett estate, and contained his signed portrait as frontispiece. The use of this book enabled village-born philanthropists to benefit their native states and get proper credit for generosity (and perhaps show up their old boyhood friends who had stayed home). If they purchased it in lots of one hundred, their names, as donors, would be stamped on the cover in purest gold, and the books sent to any list they desired, along with a beautiful form letter, with the Heskett Rural School Foundation heading and signed by Dr. Planish—or anyway, by Dr. Planish's secretary—or anyway, signed—stating that Mr. M (or N) was a fine gentleman, nationally known for his large heart, great wealth and intellect, and now weren't they sorry they'd laughed at him when he was a boy!

This official letter was Dr. Planish's addition to the soulless routine which Miss Nimrock had used in selling *New Light in the Red Schoolhouse,* and it doubled the output of this spiritual item in six months.

It was indeed chiefly as a literary man that Dr. Planish markedly improved upon Miss Nimrock. He gave no larger financial grants for school-garden contests, but he increased fourfold the number of letters of advice sent out monthly to rural educators: advice on whether blackboards should be greenboards or blueboards, advice on reading poetry, advice on the established code for school janitors. He sat dictating oracles all day long, stopping only to steal his information from the publications of Columbia University, the Carnegie Foundation and the Association for Adult Education.

He was spectacular in giving interviews, in what he called "the application of modern high-pressure publicity technique to the ancient causes of learning and righteousness." Weekly he sent out to the press Human Interest Stories about six students in Wyoming, average age 11.7, banding to study atonal harmony, or an Oxford graduate, frequently sober, teaching in the mountains, or Lafayette Heskett's one-man knitting show, or Mr. Hamilton Frisby breeding Hereford cattle, or Mrs. Hamilton Frisby purchasing the pearls of the Grand Duchess Tilly, or Master Hamilton Frisby, Jr., inventing a glider.

As a literary man, Dr. Planish also composed the Heskett Foundation's first aggressive series of fund-soliciting letters. Mr. Frisby insisted that the Foundation had enough funds so that it was not worth the bother "to circularize a lot of fourflushers that you couldn't pry a sawbuck loose from with dynamite," but Dr. Planish saw it more professionally, with the eye of vision and of the Future.

The Biblical virtue of philanthropy was in this era turning into something far nobler than the impulsive handing out of a quarter. It was no longer emotion and friendliness, but Social Engineering, Planned Giving, with a purpose and a technique; it was Big Business, as big and busy as General Motors, but with God for executive vice-president. Dr. Planish saw that today the Good Samaritan wouldn't do anything so silly and unsanitary as to pick up a man who had fallen among hit-run drivers. According to every rule of First Aid, the silly suburbanite might have killed the poor fellow by moving him. Today, the Samaritan would telephone to the nearest hospital and say, "Take care of him, and when I come again, I shall increase my subscription to your nationwide chain of hospitals, now headed by that great Organization Executive, Dr. Gideon Planish."

Thus dreamed the Doctor, tender heart and powerful brain running strong and true, as he took his daily nap among the steel filing cabinets in his office.

All this colonization of hospitals was as yet merely in his prophetic vision. Not for some time yet would Organized Philanthropy rank eighth among the major industries of the United States. But already Dr. Planish could foresee a wedding of generosity and efficiency which would make the Crusades look like a bonus march, and perceive that it was going to be valuable for a scholar with a wife and child to be stationed close to this waxing flood of gold.

He saw himself dedicated now to the new life of service; in labors more abundant, in conferences above measure, on committees more frequent, in journeyings often, in long-distance telephoning often, in hunger and thirst at unpalatable public dinners, in cold audiences and nakedness of meaning—and he was not afraid, and gloried of the things that concerned his infirmities.

Despite Frisby's doubting, Dr. Planish prepared a new letter of solicitation for the H.R.S.F.

HESKETT RURAL SCHOOL FOUNDATION

11872 Royal George Avenue

C H I C A G O

J. T. Niminy, Esq.,
3756 Wynadotte Ave.,
Marquette, Ind.

Dear Friend of Education:

This letter isn't for you. We know from our huge files that you are sound on the subject of rural education; you realize that unless our country schools are just as well staffed and supplied as the snootiest city private school, there is no hope for our beloved America in its race against world anarchy.

But you have a friend who believes just as you and I do, but doesn't know about the HESKETT RURAL SCHOOL FOUNDATION. He doesn't realize that if he will take a mere $10.00 a year from his cigar money, he can make that sum do $1000 worth of imperative national good -- and make him a proud Contributing Member of the H.R.S.F.

He'll get all our publications free, with the privilege of attending our Conferences and hearing the biggest men of the nation explain the solution of all rural problems. And you, dear Defender of Education, will be doing the greatest good to the country by telephoning to that Unknown Friend of Ours and giving him our address and greetings.

We can't locate your friend -- YOU CAN! While you're reading this, why not lift the receiver and call his number and tell him -- RIGHT THIS MINUTE! -- we want to send him, FREE, the four-color booklet "OUR SECRET SHAME."

Cordially yours,

Gideon Planish, Ph.D.

Managing Secretary.

This letter was sent not only to all members of the Foundation, but to all persons who had promisingly inquired about its work, and later sent to a general list. Dr. Kitto thought it a rather shocking letter, and Mr. Frisby thought it funny. But, in the technical term, it "pulled." With the passion for exactitude and flapping charts which is part of the New Scientific Philanthropy, Dr. Planish calculated that it cost ten cents to send out the letter, including stationery, postage, mimeographing, filling in, the booklet, overhead, and purchasing lists of persons known to have been philanthropic—which were rather coarsely known as "sucker lists," and which were sold commercially, like fly-paper. As the professional saviors put it, "If one per cent of the prospects on the sucker list kick through, the cost of the campaign is covered."

To the gratification of the Doctor's love for beautiful letters, 1.37% of his prospects did "kick through," and showed their devotion to education by taking out Foundation memberships.

Even Mr. Frisby was impressed. Dr. Planish had been truly ordained as a priest of Scientific Philanthropy.

And as for the pamphlet *Our Secret Shame* which was sent out to prospects—that was Bernardine Nimrock's old tract, *Statistics on Salaries and Attendance in District Schools*, with a new cover on it.

18

It was not the success of his circular so much as his genius in foreseeing the stock-market crash of October, 1929, that brought Dr. Planish to the acute personal attention of Mr. Hamilton Frisby.

All that summer and early fall, America had been speculating on a soaring market. Kitchen girls had made five thousand dollars, managing editors of newspapers had made a million—all on paper, which meant that they left their supposititious profits to double, triple, increase a hundredfold.

But the Planishes, the gamblers with life, for once were not gambling. It was Peony's doing. She had pinned the Doctor in a corner and given an order: "You're not to buy one share of stock, on margin or any other way. We're more broke than ever. If we invested, we'd have to borrow some more money, and we mustn't do that. Never. It's a matter of principle—— Besides, there's nobody we can borrow from. Dad turned me down!"

This was a new Peony, much firmer than any he had known. She was a little frightened by the stretching, paw-curling indifference of the great cat, Chicago. And they had not met any of the magnificos with whom she had expected to dine and dance. They knew only a couple of dentists, a couple of liberal pastors, an insurance broker, an instructor from Northwestern, some minor philanthropists and a graduate student in the University of Chicago. Peony was in a constant frenzy of being calm and economical, and she announced to the Doctor, though pleasantly, that she wasn't interested in one thing except the price of onions and the fact that Carrie, in public-school kindergarten, had an Italian "boy friend," aged seven, who gave her green lollipops.

The Doctor dared not deceive her and make investments secretly, though his obedience was grievous to him, because he was certain, after looking glassily at the stock-market pages of the papers every day, that he could easily make a million. Indeed one day he made, on two sheets of quite inexpensive yellow scratch-paper, $7,880 clear, though hypothetical. He was keeping up his brief lecture tours, but Peony made him turn over every check, and she banked it, with no more extravagances than a weekly bottle of vodka.

Now in that day and among the people he knew, you had either to invest frantically, throwing in the laundry money and Aunty Emma's $100 legacy, or be willful and prophesy disaster. If you did the latter, it was believed that you lacked faith in the Pilgrim Fathers, and were either a drug-user or a dog-poisoner. But Dr. Planish was trained to dazzle audiences with words that sounded bold, no matter what they meant, and he brazened out his unpatriotic shame.

The Reverend James Severance Kitto, S.T.D., said to him, "Doctor, as you know, I entirely disapprove of gam-

[219]

bling, but the present Wave of Prosperity shouldn't be called gambling; it's more a rising tide of democracy, and I rather think anybody who doesn't take advantage of it is failing to show his trust in American Institutions. I'm two hundred thousand ahead of the game—at least on paper—and I can give you a straight tip on a wallboard stock that will double in the next month."

"I'm sorry, Doctor, but I think the market is going to crash," said Dr. Planish.

Dr. Kitto looked at him as at one who had slapped the baby.

Mr. Hamilton Frisby said, "Planish, I've got a tip on a radio stock for you. Quadruple in a week."

"I'm sorry, Mr. Frisby, but there's something phony about this bull market."

"Oh, you think so, do you! Well, let me tell you that I'm two million bucks ahead right now—on paper, but I could cash in tomorrow. And I'm a director of two banks, and supposed to be able to find my way down State Street without a Seeing-Eye Dog!"

Early in November, when all the paper that those profits had been on blew up the chimney, blazing, both Dr. Kitto and Mr. Frisby telephoned to him, in the tones of men just out of the hospital, and timidly asked how he had known the disaster was coming. For weeks afterward, he found himself everywhere revered as a wizard in finance, the one art that transcended theology and music, as really meaning something. His acquaintances begged, "Give us the lowdown, Doctor. When the next big bull market comes, say couple months from now, I don't want to make the same mistakes I must 've made this last time."

The world got progressively more suicidal, and many supporters of national organizations went bankrupt. But the Heskett Fund could still support Dr. Planish's good works, and he was out of debt, and felt superior as an Angora cat.

In December he was invited by Hamilton Frisby to go down to a shooting-box in Louisiana.

His fellow guests were Frisby's old intimates, Dr. Alwyn Wilcox, the surgeon, and Jesse Veith, the investment counselor, who had so brilliantly guided his clients through the boom and the crash that he himself had not gone bankrupt. Frisby had taken two drawing-rooms on the southern train for them. Dr. Planish happily noted that he was apparently not expected to spend any money, and he liked this touch of high life.

In one of the drawing-rooms, they opened up on him as soon as the train had started and they had poured out the first of the illicit drinks.

"Planish, now there's just us girls here and we've all taken our hair down, tell us: what inside dope did you have on the stock market?" said Frisby, with the awful geniality of a detective being chummy with a murder suspect.

The other men bent toward the Doctor like two older and tougher detectives.

"I didn't really know anything special. I just figured it out, as a mathematician would."

"You a mathematician, Doc?" said Jesse Veith.

"It's one of the branches I specialized in—sort of," beamed Dr. Planish.

"Tell me how much the cotangent of the ellipse of the cube root of seven is."

"Oh, shut up!" Frisby remarked to Veith. Dr. Wilcox did not look much amused.

Then Dr. Planish knew where he was, realized what memory it was that he had been trying to tag. "I certainly have been here before!" he shuddered. These three rich men were the bulky, silent, sardonic football players who used to terrify him in freshman year at college, squatting around him with this same placid and beefy intention of taking him to pieces to find out why he was so earnest and funny.

Frisby was purring on, "What did Marduc tell you?"

"Marduc?" Dr. Planish was puzzled.

"You mean to pretend you don't know him?"

"I don't believe I do."

"Colonel Charles B. Marduc, the big New York advertising man and publisher—Marduc & Syco?"

"Oh, yes. I think he's sent us a sizable contribution. But I've never met him. What would he know?"

"That man's a buddy of all the billionaires, and somebody has told me that you saw him when he was in Chicago, a couple months ago."

"No, I didn't. Never met him."

Veith snorted at Frisby, "I told you so. This Planish guy hasn't got any more of the lowdown than——"

"Than an investment counselor!" suggested Dr. Wilcox.

"Oh, shut up. Let's play a little bridge," said Veith.

Mr. Frisby brought out the cards, very silently.

For all of that horrible week-end, during which they did three hours of card-playing and drinking to one hour of hunting, Dr. Planish felt that he was endured only because they had to have a fourth at bridge. When he pumped up something neat to say, they ignored it. Over against their pretentious laced boots and plaid Mackinaws, in his old gray suit and khaki shirt he felt over-refined and over-fussy.

During every hour of this rich-man's vacation, he longed to take the money and power away from this gang of bullies, and give it to Peony.

On the train back to Chicago, Frisby led Dr. Planish aside, looking as though he must have met him before some place.

"Doc, you seem to me a very confused person," said Frisby.

"How's that?"

"Maybe I ought to tell you the facts of life about the Heskett Foundation, and most other philanthropic foundations—not all of them, but a good share. You're supposed to be a professional organizator——"

"A what?"

"Fellow that makes his living by running an uplift organization; a professional at begging for money to use in publicizing the statement that when the world becomes civilized, two plus two will equal four. An organizator. He's the fellow that starts a society first, and then looks around for a purpose for the society afterward. And the rich suckers that give him the money, either to soften their own consciences or to climb socially by associating with Vanderbilts on committees, or to show off, or once in a while even because they think that a social club chartered to befriend Liberia may really help the Liberians—these come-ons I always call the *philanthrobbers*.

"But Old Man Heskett was no philanthrobber, and neither were quite a few of the other moguls that set up Foundations. Here's their idea: With the increase in taxes, especially this damn income tax and supertax, a man can't afford to have too much income. And yet he wants to keep control of the big corporations in which he owns a majority of stock. So he places a big block of it in a Philanthropic Institution, in a trust fund—he doesn't get the interest, but he doesn't have to pay any pyramiding taxes, and he or his agents—that's me, for the Hesketts—hold the voting proxies on the donated stock, and control the corporation as much as before.

"They don't care what the Foundation income is spent for, as long as their name gets whitened—and how many coats of whitewash it does take, sometimes! A man that slashed a billion acres of timber buys the reputation for loving the trees and birdies. And Heskett was a pretty typical case. He made his dough by bankrupting small businesses through lowering competitive prices, and he got so rich that he had to turn philanthropic—that's a lot showier sign of great wealth than any nonsense like buying yachts or titles. Then he had a second reason for protecting his financial controls. His children and his nieces and his nephews are idiots—all of 'em. One sculps and one married a Communist and one lives on an island called Lesbos. Heskett hated 'em all, and he put his boodle into two trust funds, of which the Heskett Foundation is one, and made me trustee of both, because I am, somewhat to my own surprise, comparatively honest.

"Now I advise you, as a simple-hearted organizator, to blow in as much of the Foundation income as you want to. Even with this stock-market crash, there's twice as much as you've been spending. Go ahead—do anything that will advertise the grand old pioneer name of Heskett. Only don't forget that I still audit the books."

Dr. Planish felt shy but desperate. "Then how about raising my own salary? I could use it."

"Certainly not. It's much more likely to get lowered, if this depression gets bad enough. You have some reputation—not much, but you have been dean of a hayloft college, and a lecturer—but how would it adorn the sacred Family Name to pay you more than rock-bottom wages? You talk about economics, Planish. Be realistic!"

Dr. Planish sat and hated him.

Peony cried, as he came in, "Did you have a lovely time, Gidjums?"

"Oh, yes, sure—you know—hunting. And bridge."

"Do you think I'd like Dr. Wilcox and Mr. Veith?"

"I'm sure you wouldn't! Listen, Peony, let's not make any special effort to work up a circle of friends here in Chicago. I have a hunch we'll be able to hit New York before *too* long."

"Swell!" said Peony.

Dr. Planish was sitting in his office on the Friday before Christmas, filing his nails and thinking that it would be nice to write a book—maybe about the use of radio in schools—and hating Hamilton Frisby.

His secretary brought in the card of the Midwestern representative of a new schoolbook factory, one Mrs. Eaglestopper, a shiny woman. She said, in coloratura, "Dr. Planish, you mentioned our series of school readers once, at a teachers' convention."

"I'm afraid they're not very good."

"Oh, now, *you!*" She looked coy. "That's because you haven't examined them closely enough. I want you to take a real good look at them, and at our new series of geographies—they're written by such a fine university scholar who's also a champion swimmer! I'm going to send you all of them."

"I'm afraid I'm pretty busy——"

"Why, Dr. Planish!" She was prettily shocked. "We wouldn't *dream* of asking you to bother with them, we know what demands there are on your time, without compensating you. Here's a—nice Christmas present!"

He peeped into the envelope she had handed to him. He lost his presence of organizational mind. "Are you trying to bribe me?" he snorted.

She rose. "My dear man, I most certainly am not! We just want you to appraise the books, and we know there's no scholar in America whose time is worth more. If you do like them—you're the judge—then you might care to mention them in your Foundation literature and your lectures. Otherwise, distinctly not—dis*tinct*ly! Good-bye and merry Christmas, and give my love to your wife. I hear she's the sweetest and smartest woman in Chicago. Let me know anything I can do."

Out of the envelope he fished two hundred-dollar certificates. They looked as different from dull-green five-dollar notes as blessed light from dubious darkness. The fat ciphers did go on and on so cheerfully after the digits. He took them home, to discuss with Peony the legitimacy of accepting them.

"Anything you can put over on that bullfrog Frisby is proper," she said; and, "This just about fixes up my Christmas problem. Now I can get you something that I've been longing all week to give you—a cedar blanket-chest, bound with the loveliest ornamental brasswork that you ever laid an eye on, going for a hundred dollars—just giving it away. It would just *make* this hallway, don't you think so? Or am I being a teeny mite extravagant?"

"Anything you do is always all right with me," he said.

Carrie trotted in. Peony knelt beside her and gurgled, "Oh, baby, Mammy's going to get the loveliest new cedar chest!"

"Why?" said Carrie.

19

In any national organization, the persons whose names are listed down the lefthand side of the stationery, the persons who are supposed to love the organization and guarantee it and work daily for it—these old friends are sometimes labeled the Directors, sometimes the Trustees, the Sponsors, the Advisory Board, the State Chairmen, the Honorary Vice-Chairmen, the National Committee, the General Committee or the Central Committee.

In the T.A.F.A.R.P., these apostles were called the Trustees, and in January, 1930, Dr. Planish was elected a trustee of that association—the True American Federation to Attack Racial Prejudice. With the suspiciousness of one who has now lost his philanthropic innocence, he skimmed over the names of his fellow trustees and even that of the treasurer—the president of an insurance company—knowing that they would all be the familiar bunch of Signers, and he looked sharply at the name of the executive secretary (or, technically, the Works). He approved. The Works was Professor Goetz Buchwald, of the psychology department of Erasmus College, on leave of absence—a leave that had now lasted for seven years.

Buchwald really was an honest and earnest man. He had read all the books, and he hated the oppressors of the Chinese, the Negroes, the Slovenes, as much as he hated the oppressors of the Jews. He spoke vigorously, but he was equally vigorous with scissors and typewriter. He nudged the press about hundreds of small incidents of tyranny or prejudice. A good man and a good organization, felt Dr. Planish. There were only two things wrong about it: Buchwald would keep on calling himself Professor, letting his staff and the newspapers call him Professor, being introduced at public meetings as Professor, though he had stopped professoring years ago.

No, felt Dr. Planish. In a democratic world like this, where we rebel against all such artificial distinctions as titles, a man ought simply to be called Doctor.

The other flaw in the True Americans was that they had never yet been able to convince anybody who was not already convinced. But that, argued Dr. Planish, with the greatest fairness, was scarcely their fault, since it was also true of ninety-seven per cent of all national organizations—practically all of them except his own. And maybe it overlapped the work of a few dozen other bodies, but then, insisted Dr. Planish—but *then!*

He respected the officers of the True Americans: Natalia Hochberg, the general secretary; Bishop Albertus Pindyck, of the Catholic or more acrobatic wing of the Episcopal Church; Dr. Christian Stern; Monsignor Nicodemus Lowell Fish, Ph.D., known as "the apostle to the Yankees"; and Rabbi Emile Lichtenselig. When he was invited to attend the annual conference of the T.A.F.A.R.P. in New York, in April, he was delighted. He felt that here he would be stimulated, and meet the better minds.

[229]

Besides, Peony wanted to see the Empire State Building.

She did, and she smelled the ocean and the roast chestnuts. She moaned, "Oh, lover, it looks—it looks like New York!"

There is a particular flavor to Celebrities, to people who have their names in the papers and who expect to be recognized on the street. Most of them will, within a year or two, slide back into the pit of anonymity whence they scrambled, and that will either make them human again or, in their resentment, destroy them utterly, for a Celebrity who has lost celebrity is the emptiest of God's curios. But a few of them will remain notorious till the hour when respectful ears reach for their unintelligible dying words, and the majority of these regulars will cease entirely to be human beings. They will be overly cordial or preposterously peeved; they will be irritable when reporters bother them at the train-gates and hysterical when no reporters show up at all; they will shake the hand, chirp the good morning, willingly give the autograph, leeringly pose the picture, and say a few nice words about soy beans or the football team.

There are also adhesive persons who are unlikely to become Celebrities themselves, but who relish the stir and smell and incessantly clattering noise of the rotogravure Olympus, just as merchants may enjoy being volunteer firemen, or elderly ladies like watching dog fights.

Of all Celebrity fans none was livelier than Peony Planish, and when the delegates to the convocation of the

True American Federation to Attack Racial Prejudice met in the elegant lobby of Terpsichore Hall, in New York City, she could enjoy her mania at its highest. On view were Bishop Pindyck, Msgr. Fish, Dr. Christian Stern, Professor Buchwald, United States Senator Felix Bultitude, General Gong, who was not only a general but an army general, not a real-estate or newspaper general, Captain Heth Gishorn, the distinguished explorer, Dr. Procopus, who was so famous a psychiatrist that the Freudians took time out to hate him, Judge Vandewart, Henry Caslon Kevern, rated at twenty million, and a genuine but social-minded actress—Ramona Tundra, the movie star. Not only that, but there was a title of nobility, the first that Peony or Dr. Planish had ever tasted, the Principessa Ca' D'Oro, a real princess though she just happened to have been born a Miss Togg of Arkansas.

She wrote social columns.

But, nobler than nobility, bluer of jaw than the principessa was blue of blood, was Colonel Charles B. Marduc, deity among advertising agents, owner of a dozen magazines, major on the Western Front in World War I and now colonel in the National Guard; a man of fifty, sleek as a greyhound but burly as a mastiff, with a planned graying mustache against a cherry face.

Dr. Planish quivered, "That's Marduc, the fellow Ham Frisby admires so much," and Peony answered, "And could I go for him! I'm going to wriggle over and talk to him."

But Colonel Marduc, after shaking only the whitest and plumpest of the assembled hands, slipped away, and the

[231]

Planishes forgot him, for coming toward them, hands out, was their friend Professor George Riot.

"One drink and one drink and one drink makes sixteen drinks, hurray," said Professor Riot, a little later.

Dr. Planish wanted to know how these authentic Top Men talked, that he might do likewise.

He was sorry to find (he reported to Peony and George Riot) that they didn't seem to talk much about saving mankind. Chiefly, they all said, with slightly different vocabularies, that they had lost their shirts in the crash.

But Dr. Planish did see that only in New York could you adequately keep a national philanthropic organization. Where else could you count on generals and principessas and stars and Marducs and bishops of every brand from Roman Catholic through Methodist to Pentecostal Abyssinian?

He devoted himself to the Reverend Dr. Christian Stern; he even attended services at the reverend's Universalist Byzantine basilica—the first time he had gone to church, except twice at Dr. Kitto's, in a year. He got himself and Peony invited to the parsonage for tea, and told Dr. Stern that it was a shame the Heskett Foundation was not situate in New York, in proximity to Dr. Stern's spiritual guidance, to give pious publicity to him instead of to those selfish and violent men, Kitto and Frisby.

Dr. Stern agreed with an enthusiasm that was good to see in such a busy man of affairs. His imagination trembled. Yes! If they had the Foundation here, he'd be willing, as chairman of its executive board, to have an office in its quarters, and to combine its work with his other activities, to the greater glory of God and the little red schoolhouse. Yes! If Dr. Planish would circulate around and find other Heskett directors of like mind, he would be glad to talk to them at the annual conference in Chicago, next summer.

So Dr. Planish informed Peony that she could get ready to move, that the Heskett Foundation would be established in one of the taller and more gaudy midtown sky-scrapers in New York, that he would undoubtedly be getting a salary of ten thousand a year, and that the way he saw it in his new position, if she and George Riot didn't quit horsing around Greenwich Village joints and drinking rotgut, he'd—he'd get uninhibited.

To all of this the Doctor's wife murmured, "That's just lovely, Pan."

She was so absorbed in New York that it seemed to her but natural that they should be moving here. She spent hours at the windows of Fifth Avenue jewelers and per-fumers and furriers, which, trying to deny that their better customers were now ruined, were brilliant as they never had been, with jet and crystal and gold and cocky little signs in French.

But this time she had not gone shopping-mad. She had not bought one dress, one footstool for their flat—one steel-point ring. No, she had merely found a basement lingerie shop conducted by the most beautiful Hungarian countess, who had had misfortunes and had smuggled her silks and laces through without paying duty. They were so cheap that they did not constitute shopping but really an investment, and——

Anyway, Dr. Planish paid for them perfectly easily by merely omitting the next few installments on the radio and on most of their other possessions.

With a thoroughness that one was surprised to find in her young and smiling head, Peony examined New York like a housewife buying melons. She saw the Episcopal cathedral, the Catholic cathedral, the Rockefeller up-town cathedral, a burlesque show, a Chinese restaurant, a Roumanian restaurant, a Hindoo restaurant, an Oletime Sunny South restaurant, one gallery of the Metropolitan Museum of Art, and George Jean Nathan. It was her one purpose now to conquer New York and make it recognize her and her husband and her baby.

If she could make this spiritual triumph, she said, she would for all time be willing to put up with a maximum spending-reservoir of forty thousand dollars a year.

In the quality of the entertainment given to the T.A.F. A.R.P. delegates as much as in the solemnity of their discussion panels, the more shining life was demonstrated. The final public dinner, at the Waldorf-Astoria, had a much larger percentage of tail-coats and of necklaces rising and falling on the tide of plump powdered bosoms than the Planishes had ever seen in Chicago, and the chief speaker was no clergyman nor professor, but Colonel Charles B. Marduc himself.

The Planishes and George Riot, way over at Table

D 17, could only look from afar upon his glory. Standing up there at the speakers' table on the dais, his graying brown mustache a handsome streak across his beefy cheeks, the Colonel looked like God arising from His throne and twirling His eyeglasses.

He began, "Friends and Honored Chairman and Your Right Reverence, I cannot speak to you as a profound scholar, like my friend Professor Buchwald, but only as a blunt soldier and merchant."

Off among the second-string Celebrities, among the Intellectuals whose lecture fee was not over two hundred dollars, Peony whispered to George Riot, "I'll bet he's just as darn profound a scholar as anybody in the room, at that. All those ads his agency gets out about glands and refrigerators."

Dr. Planish inquired, "How big *is* his agency?"

Dr. Riot said reverently, "Well, Marduc & Syco is one of the Big Four. The Colonel is supposed to have something like five million tucked away."

Dr. Planish sighed, "He looks like a fellow it would be nice to know!"

"Hush, you boys! I want to hear what the Colonel said to Pershing," commanded Peony.

Besides the dinner, the delegates received, in the most luxurious and Manhattan manner, a reception at the apartment of Dr. Procopus, on Park Avenue, and Peony knew finally that New York is not so much a city as a state of bliss.

They never did understand the role of Dr. Procopus.

[235]

He was called a psychiatrist; he was supposed to teach women how to endure rich husbands; but beyond this, he seemed to be the midwife for every intellectual movement in town. He was always introducing authors to radio executives, and politicians to managing editors, and Austrian bankers to American bankers, and pretty wives to doctors who knew somebody who knew the address of an abortionist. His apartment had twelve rooms, each as large as the Planishes' cottage in Kinnikinick, and all of them splashed with the signed photographs of opera singers.

It was here that Peony conceived an innocent passion for Captain Heth Gishorn, the explorer. He was English and trim and monocled and he had been in Celebes, which impressed Peony, though she never could remember whether that was an island or a state of matrimony. He kissed her hand and brought her a pink cocktail.

"You boys never will have the *savoir-faire* of that monkey," said Peony to George Riot.

"Nonsense! He's a powder-puff!" protested George. "If you fall for anybody, you fall for either Gid or me."

"Yes, and you can go farther than that, Peony—you can fall for just half that number!" raged Dr. Planish. He glared, then remembered that George was his only friend in this staggering world of twelve-room apartments and explorers and colonels who were millionaires.

He longed to be sitting with his classmate Hatch Hewitt in a beer saloon. . . . Peony, Hatch, George Riot, his daughter Carrie—had he anybody else in the world to rest with? . . . He was dimly glad that Peony and

George would probably never go farther than a finger-tip of flirtation.

Behind all this intellectual shimmer, Dr. Planish was busy mustering directors of the Heskett Foundation to support him in the plan to move the Foundation to New York. He got promises of backing from George Riot, Mrs. Hochberg, and a newly elected director, a fine, manly New York clergyman named Dr. Elmer Gantry.

Dr. Gantry was perhaps the best known of Manhattan radio pastors. It was said that he had studied at Harvard and in Germany, but there was a folksy quality about his regular daily broadcast, "Love Is the Morning Star," that won him a million far-flung auditors, particularly shut-ins, and had brought him no less a sponsor than Phosphorated Chewing Gum. He had an audience, too, in his church, but the experts noted that there was something about Dr. Gantry that exactly suited the radio.

But even with this encouragement from the more powerful directors, Dr. Planish kept from tackling Hamilton Frisby about the hegira till May, two weeks after his return to Chicago. Before the scene, he studied all the possible interpretations of his role: the tender and sensitive, the manly and courageous, the aloof and slightly amused, then decided upon the brusque man of business. In that mood he played to Frisby:

"Been making a lot of investigation and looking into things pretty sharply. We mustn't be prejudiced or sentimental. Much though I like Chicago, for the sake of usefulness it's about time to move the Foundation headquarters to the Atlantic Seaboard. Like the proverbial homing pigeon!"

Frisby looked at him a long time. "Yes, I've been hearing from Chris Stern. So Chris and you think you can take this racket away from me! Planish, you're fired!"

"W—w——"

"Illegal? Of course it's illegal. But the directors eventually do what I tell 'em. You won't be re-elected at the annual meeting. So you have from now till summer to find a new job—if any, Planish, if any."

He stormed at the Reverend Dr. James Severance Kitto. He said that if Dr. Kitto took orders from that poker-faced hijacker, Mr. Frisby, then he was a slave and a hypocrite.

Dr. Kitto said it was a shame, it was indeed a—a—in fact, a shame.

And that was all that Dr. Kitto did say, there in his handsome pastoral study with its portraits of Alexander Campbell and Calvin and Cotton Mather.

His parsonage was a bulging, brick-fronted, semi-detached dwelling on a respectable old residence street in Evanston. Dr. Planish looked at it as he went back down the street. He stared at the window of Dr. Kitto's study. The curtain was up a few inches, and he could see Dr. Kitto thoughtfully scratch his chin, yawn, pick up the fresh evening paper, open it, and with untroubled placidity begin to read the day's pleasant toll of murders, traffic deaths, divorces and starvation. Dr. Kitto did not even raise his eyes in reflection.

Dr. Planish stood looking up, and he knew then how dead men feel.

20

THE TWO OF THEM sat down to dinner with Peony—the compulsory self that told him he must speak up and get it over, let her know that he was discharged, and the physical self that was so tired and timid it could scarcely lift this burden of confession. Peony and the half-handed maid had prepared a particularly elegant salad of avocado and hard-boiled egg and cherries and a few other trifles that must have been Peony's own idea, and the ridiculous salad became to him, brooding upon it, a tender symbol of her, like a glove still bearing the warmth and heart line of her hand.

When he spoke he dodged up a dozen alleys. He told her that he had gone out to Evanston, and that Dr. Kitto certainly wore a toupee. While she was giggling, "Let's throw him out of the Foundation," he was sharply calculating that he had no notion whatever about a new job, that he must be about $850 in debt, with some $375 in assets (he felt in his pocket and concluded that maybe he could add another dollar), and that his father-in-law had been pretty nasty about that last touch.

He said that the lawns in Evanston were full of daffodils, and she said: that reminded her, they really must get busy and decide now where they would go for summer vacation—Northern Michigan, Vermont, Battle Lake in Minnesota?—and couldn't he take a couple of months off instead of one?—it was a shame the way those old dodoes Kitto and Frisby bossed him—couldn't he get rid of them?

The serenity in her voice relieved his hesitation.

He ended his confession with, "I guess I ought to be boiled in oil for endangering you and the baby this way."

Just then Peony could have played the perfect American wife, could have been sorry for herself and asked what good he was, if he couldn't take better care of her than that. For a moment she sat with the volubility of her smile checked. Then she laughed.

"It's a joke on me. Oh, toy-man, it's all my fault, being so extravagant. Otherwise we could tell Frisby to go to hell and start off for New York without worrying. Come slap baby's fingers for being such a bad baby." He kissed her, in a rush of returning faith, and she cried, "Listen, darling, I want you to write George Riot. He'll dig up something temporary for you. And maybe this is the time when I ought to tell you there's nothing between George and me."

"M?"

"You looked in New York like you thought there was something. But I love you too much. My vice is more along the line of wanting to get ahead and be Somebody. And we will. You watch us. This is just another break in the market—prosperity is just around the corner for us—with bells on! We'll hit New York so *hard!*"

"Wouldn't it maybe be better to ask Austy Bull for some kind of a temporary college appointment while I try to make connections in New York?"

"No, no! I couldn't stand even a month in Kinnikinick. Nobody there that could even stand up to the top people, like Colonel Marduc and Senator Bultitude. I despise Kinnikinick. The people are so provincial. Whatever you can say about your bad little wife, you can't say she's provincial, now can you!"

Apparently he couldn't.

"I'll tell you what. I'll make up for the financial hole I got you into. We'll store the furniture, and I'll go back and live on Mr. Whipple K. Jackson, Esquire, till you get a really swell position with a high-class salary."

"I'd worry so about——"

"Don't you worry about my worrying! I know when I got a good thing. Say, I'll bet if you'd been a preacher, you could have prayed circles around Jim Kitto and Chris Stern—you'd have had God tuned in on you all the time. And do *good*—why, say, I'll bet you've already done rural education more good than William Jennings Bryan put together!"

It was mid-August, and the movers were lugging their furniture down to the storage company van. Dr. Planish's eyes and throat bothered him as he stood with his arm about Peony, watching the bumpy departure to prison of their treasures: the adored new cedar chest, the gold and scarlet Chinese Chippendale cabinet, the Chinese rug that they had bought at Mabel Grove—they had been so

[241]

young then!—the faded little porcelain clock, the jade lamp, the friendly birch cabinet of the radio, to whose music they had sometimes danced, they two alone, after midnight, triumphant in new success.

And the black and silvery portable bar.

"Oh, do be careful of that!" quaked Peony to the movers. He could feel her breast heaving under his fingertips. He thought that for the first time she was afraid. Men who had had desks and office titles a year ago were huddled on street corners now, selling apples. In what hot slums or stripped and mortgaged homes were their wives and babies panting, he wondered.

"I do hate to see that bar go into hock. We had some good times here, and—— No, sir!" Peony stoutly interrupted herself. "When we get ready to unveil that ole bar again, in New York, it'll be Bishop Pindyck and Senator Bultitude that'll be lapping up my martinis, and not just these Chicago profs and docs!"

For their last night in the flat, they had only their suitcases, a cot-bed borrowed from the janitor for Carrie, and for themselves, a mattress on the floor. The flat seemed by dusk not only empty but menacingly large, as though nobody could ever fill its spaces again, and they felt that they would never furnish out any dwelling again, never sit softly and eat true meals and talk with friends. They were city Okies.

They fled to a cafeteria for a late supper and then, with Carrie, aged seven now, to a movie, to see the lovely Joan Crawford. They three walked through the gasping summer streets—a respectable family, in some sense a holy family, trudging and round and stuffed with food, permanent-looking as the brownstone porticoes. But Dr. Planish stared at a brick mansion turned boarding-house. Its curtains were torn and filthy, and on the hot stoop was a man who might once have been a professor, a doctor; a bent man with a beard much like his own, but hacked and dirty. Dr. Planish shuddered.

As they marched, Carrie babbled, "Why are you going to New York, Papa—why?"

"Hush, pimpernel," remarked Peony. "Papa has to go there on business."

"Why?"

"I said, on business."

"I wish he'd come home to Faribault with us. I hate the city," pondered Carrie, and Peony said:

"Why?"

"It's got too many street cars and too many people."

"Don't you like people, babykins?"

"No, I don't think I like 'em. They talk so much. I like dandelions and sailboats better."

With Carrie luxuriously asleep in the borrowed cot, Dr. Planish and Peony sat low on the edge of their mattress, in the abandoned flat, which was lit with one unshaded bulb. He blurted something that had been forming in his mind all through the motion picture:

"I guess we're supposed to be good Christians, aren't we?"

"Sure-you-bet. Good Episcopolopians, anyway."

"Then I wonder if we couldn't turn to our religion for

[243]

comfort. The clergy insist that people do still turn to it. Let's—uh—let's think about the Lord."

"Okay."

"He's, uh—— Hell, I wish we'd kept a Bible. We still got a Bible, haven't we?"

"Sure you-bet. I saw it when I was packing the books and blankets."

"There's something in the Bible about—now what the devil is it——"

"Honestly, hero, I don't think you ought to say 'what the devil' when you're talking about religion and God."

Dr. Planish looked at her with admiration for her good taste, and fretted, "Maybe you're right. Anyway, this stuff—this verse, I mean—in the Bible, I mean—it was in Proverbs—something about 'all was vanity and there was no profit anywhere'."

"No, it's from Ecclesiastes. And I bet I can quote it."

"Really?" He looked with new admiration at this re- markable young woman.

"You bet your life I can. I was a Sunday-school teacher in Faribault, and I was a corker, too, before I went to col- lege and ran into all that irreverence, and all the menaces to a girl's morals. Lessee. I almost got it. Something like this:

" 'I was great and I increased more than anybody that came before me in Jerusalem, and also my wisdom did increase—no, remained with me. And whatever mine eyes desired I did not keep from them, nor my heart from any joy, and I looked upon all the works that my hands had

[244]

done and behold, all was vanity and—and vexation of spirit and there was no profit under the sun.'

"Gee whiz, that doesn't sound so good for my side," Peony reflected. "Looks like God was telling us, 'What's all this business about going to New York? Go on back to Kinnikinick and stay there—blackmail the Prexy and make him give you back a job.' Oh, no, He wouldn't tell us that, would He, lover? He wouldn't, would He? Not *stay!* Tell me He wouldn't!"

"Of course He wouldn't. You're His own best lamb."

"Well, I do think He might be a little more careful about His lamb and her husband always being so broke all the time. I just can't understand it."

"Yes, yes, sweetie, there may be something to that, but you must be more serious if we're going to try out religion properly, and God knows, we need religion or *something!*"

She whispered.

"Now, Peony, that's absolutely shocking!"

"Okay, I'll be a serious little God's little lamb. Why don't you try praying?"

"How?"

"Christians *do* pray, don't they?"

"Well, of course, Peony, in church and so on, but I mean to say——"

"Why not take a shot at it?"

"Very well, if you want me to. After all, I suppose I *am* a true believer—everybody must be that devotes himself to the service of mankind, as I do, and so—so——"

He looked upward, longing to feel the veritable presence of God, to experience a merciful omnipotence that would protect his beloved wife and his surprising daughter and his own fading ambition to possess power and glory.

But he could see nothing and feel nothing above him save the one spotty electric bulb.

"O Lord, our God——"

The words were empty to him and without destination. He blurted, "I can't do it. I don't believe that God, if there is one, is listening to me. And I don't believe Kitto or Chris Stern really thinks God is listening when they spout, so glib and intimate. I believe they'd be scared to death if He actually spoke up and answered. Oh, baby, no way out. You and I just got to depend on each other, against everything."

"Well, that's enough, isn't it? We're lucky!" she said blithely.

He was on the train to New York, and for the first time in his life he was sitting up in a day-coach all night. Dinner would have cost a dollar or more on the diner, so he had been picking at two chocolate almond-bars for hours now, and he was pleased to find a couple of tin-foil-covered crumbs in his pocket.

His seat-mate, a shifty-looking man, hinted, "How 'bout gettin' up a game of poker?"

"No—no thanks—don't play."

"What's your racket, Brother? Schoolteaching or book agent?"

"Book agent."

"How 'bout me for a prospect?"

"No—no," drearily. "I'm off duty just now."

Mr. Planish, Mr. Gideon Planish, a jobless vagrant, had no desire to sell books, to communicate ideas about rural education, or to abuse the public for their lack of freedom, generosity in contributing to philanthropy, and the far-flung greatest common denominator in the implementing of ideological blue-prints for crises among the grass roots.

He wanted to be let alone, he wanted to sleep, and he wanted to contemplate blowing in an entire quarter for coffee and eggs at breakfast in New York tomorrow morning.

21

HE FOUND THE Reverend Dr. Christian Stern of New York amiable but jumpy.

"Too bad the power that that vile man Frisby has in the Heskett Foundation. I wish you'd been a little more cautious in jumping the gun on him, but still, I know how he is. Now about another organizational connection. Of course with the Depression on, things couldn't possibly be worse. I know what sterling ideals and executive competence you have, Dr. Planish. And oratory. But our best benefactors have been hit. All jumping out of windows. Really touching. But I'll see what I can do."

Captain Heth Gishorn, the distinguished young explorer, was by birth an Englishman but, like most of the English, he did not look very English. He was smooth and solid and square, with a thick white skin which never looked tanned, and he carried a monocle but used his spectacles.

His voice was caressing and unpleasant. He was given to double-breasted blue jackets, which looked pressed even when they were wrinkled. And for a man of action, who was presumably always leading caravans somewhere with camels, he was surprisingly business-like, being the president, executive secretary, and sole beneficiary of the Association to Promote Eskimo Culture, Inc., New York City.

"Dr. Stern tells me that you are experienced in organizational activities," Captain Gishorn said civilly, in his office.

"Oh, yes—yes." Dr. Planish put his finger tips together and tried to look even more efficient than he was hungry. "Getting out circular letters, both appeals for funds and morale-boosting; teaching the staff to be cagy on the phone about whether the director is in or not, and to distinguish, among callers, between mere cranks who just want to ask questions, and real sympathizers that might come across with some money; scholarly research on all subjects—there's always college instructors with big families that are willing to work cheap and grub out the facts at the library, and write acceptable articles for the director to sign, or executive secretary, as the case may be; addressing assemblies, especially of women, both in the drawing-room and in hotel ballroom meetings; getting actors and pianists to make free appearances at large rallies, and coaching the ushers to pass the pledge blanks at the right signal; making the speakers, if politicians, pipe down at the proper time; getting concessions and a fair price from hotel banquet managers—I needn't tell you that if you charge the guests five dollars for a philanthropic dinner, you don't know your business if you actually pay the hotel one cent more than a dollar sixty-five, including dinner, tips, hall and light, and that a really skilled man ought to get it for one thirty-five, including after-dinner peppermints; going to lunch with bankers and listening to whatever they have to say about a new bull market; attending committee meetings and moving a vote of thanks and keeping all speeches about the call to immediate action down to three minutes; keeping lists of prospects right up to date as regards both changed addresses, present financial standing, and susceptibility to emotional appeal; how to address important people on the telephone; wangling publicity in the newspapers and on the radio; making all organization literature and interviews a nice mixture of optimism and warnings about the menace to the American Way of Life——

"Yes, I think I may honestly say I know the whole routine of scientific philanthropy, educational propaganda, the skilled encouragement of the virtue of generosity, and the publicizing of all noble causes—such as your promotion of culture and, I have no doubt, music among the Eskimos. Yes."

Captain Gishorn shook his head. "Then, my dear fellow, I'm afraid you're not the man I'm looking for."

"Oh?" said Dr. Planish, and thought about fried chicken, golden dripping fried chicken, with giblets and candied sweet potatoes and corn fritters.

"You're evidently a real leader in intellectual advancement, but in this Eskimo racket, I do most of the oratory and committees myself. All I need is a good man to answer important telephone calls and lunch with the lesser donors and keep the circularization going. And I can pay only thirty-five dollars a week."

"Make it forty. I'm broke."

"Sold!" said Captain Gishorn, who was very clever

about languages, and could speak American just as well as he could Persian or Swahili.

Dr. Planish went out to telegraph Peony that he had a job, that he loved her and Carrie, and that he hoped to send for them before Christmas.

He did not tell her about his present salary, and he tried not to remember that he was now getting only forty a week, as against seventy-five at the Heskett Foundation plus tokens of gratitude from school-supply firms. (He doubted if he could count on Eskimos to do much with tokens of gratitude, no matter how he cultured them.)

He found, before October, that Captain Gishorn had not done by him as one likes to be done in philanthropic circles. Actually, Dr. Planish had to use all of the professional accomplishments that he had outlined, for the Captain went off to explore Hollywood and Santa Barbara, and for months he showed no interest in Eskimo Promotion except to receive the weekly financial report and to draw out all moneys above office expenses and salaries.

Oh, he was thoroughly gentlemanly about it; in his letters he never complained of anything—just encouraged the Doctor to send out more letters of solicitation and hold more small meetings of evangelization and get more money out of all persons who could be encouraged to "recognize, with head and heart, the plight of our Brothers to the North in being as yet entirely divorced from the stream of international comity."

Dr. Planish sometimes thought this was rather hard on the Scandinavian missionaries in Greenland; he sometimes felt that he himself could do with less comity and more cash.

He was not very comfortable, that autumn and winter of 1930—his triumphal invasion of New York. He lived in a dollar-a-day hotel room in the theatrical district, a room with an iron bed, two straight chairs, a Gideon Bible, a cockroach splash on the wall, and the bathroom seven doors down the hall.

His Eskimo Promotion office was not much more entertaining. It consisted of an inner room with one shredded oak desk for himself and one handsome green steel one for Captain Gishorn, letter files, prospect files, abandoned overshoes and, on a shelf, a specially bound and extra-illustrated seven-volume set of *The Mistresses of French Monarchs and English Dukes.* There was also a window-less outer room, with the desk of the half-pretty, half-young lady stenographer, Miss Cantlebury—who was also the switchboard operator and reception clerk—with four chairs for improbable visitors, Miss Cantlebury's umbrella, and an extra-illustrated and specially bound nine-volume set of *The Chronicles of the Arctic and Sub-Arctic Expeditions of Explorers, Fur Dealers, and Missionaries of All Creeds, from the Earliest Times to A.D. 1799.*

Dr. Planish always felt that to read this tract would be of the greatest help in understanding Eskimos and teaching them to build Diesel engines, but he never seemed to have time to look into it.

The office was in a forgotten building down on Fourth Avenue, red brick and six stories, with an elevator that shook and protested as it swayed upward. It was handy to a saloon that through Prohibition kept on serving the best free lunch in Manhattan. On the same floor with the Eskimo office were the establishments of a chiropractor, an agent for rubber accessories, a publisher of New Testaments so efficient that he put up a good show even against the Bible Trust, an all-night stenographer who knew things about people, and the head offices, which were also the only offices, of the Swastika-Rhodesian Gold and Sapphire Mines, whose floor space and general moral purposes strikingly resembled those of the Association to Promote Eskimo Culture, Inc.

When he first took the job, Dr. Planish was fretted by his lack of knowledge about the Eskimos. All he had ever been told was that they lived in the North, in snow houses, and ate blubber. He planned to spend all his evenings in the public library, reading about snow houses and blubber.

At the end of the Doctor's second day in the office, which he had devoted to reading the letter files and making notes about prospects, especially rich widowers, Captain Gishorn rose from dictating letters to Miss Cantlebury, and piped, "Carry on, old chap. I'm off to cocktails at old Mrs. Piggott's."

He went off, very decorative with walking stick, white carnation, spats and black Homburg hat.

Dr. Planish looked at Miss Cantlebury and sighed. She seemed faded but companionable.

"Doctor, do you mind if I sit down and smoke a cigarette, now the Big Noise has gone?" she said.

"Why, no. I'll share one with you."

She sat at the Captain's desk, read one or two of his love letters, and murmured, "Look, Doctor. Let me know what I can do to get you started in this racket. From long experience, I'd say you were probably a good guy. Anything I can tip you off on?"

(He wondered whether once, as a young Rhetoric coach in a good line of business, he would have ruled out sentences ending in or on an "off on.")

"Yes, there is, Miss Cantlebury. Of course I know organizational work in general, but I don't happen to have worked much with Eskimos. What are the best books on the subject?"

"What would you want to read books for, in this joint?"

"Naturally, Captain Gishorn doesn't need to, but then he's studied the Northern peoples first hand——"

"Listen, Doctor, there isn't any Santa Claus, and you're getting a big boy now. Excuse me for getting tough, but I hate to see anybody taken for a ride unless he's one of the contributors. Fact is, ever since his boyhood in England, the only time Cap Gishorn ever spent in any country north of Bangor, Maine, was one day in Nova Scotia and one in Iceland and two days in Norway, on a Midnight Sun cruise in 1926. I guess he has done some real exploring in Persia and Africa—I dunno. But all he's got to tell the world about Eskimos is a great advertising slogan, 'If all the Americas are to stand together—that means All!' Get it? The Eskimos are our little cousins to the North, so we got to win 'em over to supporting all our own moral principles and civilized customs—which means Amos 'n'

Andy and Tom Thumb golf courses and Sweetheart Soap and flying two hundred miles an hour to places that the Eskimos got too much native sense to want to see."

"What do we actually do to help the Eskimos?"

"Do? Honest, Doc, the Seven Dwarfs are dead. Well, we send six hundred bucks a year to the First Day Antinomian Church Mission in Greenland, and they furnish all the photos and reading matter that we send out. They even sent us a full display kit—a kayak and a native harpoon and a whale vertebra and the cutest little stuffed baby seal you ever saw. It looks just like my nephew Irving. You'd be surprised the way the cynics and tightwads loosen up for enlightening the Eskies when they notice the pleading glass eyes in that baby seal. I damn near gave a quarter to it myself once!

"So we hand the Antinomians the six hundred—what they do with it I dunno—play rummy in the long Arctic nights, I guess. And that's all we do do—except, of course, the real purpose of any organization: pay your salary and mine and pay the rent, so you and I won't have to spend the snowy days in the Grand Central waiting-room. What's left over, say sixty-two per cent, goes to Captain Heth Gishorn for his carnation and his girls and his Napoleon brandy.

"You got to hand it to the Captain. He's the only organization owner that doesn't even pretend to do any good, except with the suckers. Most gangs do at least give the poor children one turkey a year, or show up one labor spy that the newspapers have already shown up, or give a hundred-dollar scholarship to one poor college student, or send out one house-broken lecturer. Not Cap Gishorn!

"There's just one other angle you got to know, so you'll quit worrying about doing any reading, Doc. That's John Littlefish. He's our prize exhibit. He's the native Eskimo that we civilized. I don't know what John Littlefish's name is—I don't think John does either. And I don't know whether he's a real Eskimo or maybe a Cree Indian. Some missionaries brought him down here from the North twenty years ago, when he was about five, and then they went broke and scrammed. Anyway, he looks like an Eskimo—I guess—and these grunts that he makes when you tickle him, I guess they sound like Eskimo, and so you have him sit on the platform when you're making a big drive, and the Captain has taught him an eighty-five-word speech about how he loves malted milk. The rest of the time, he plays professional billiards in a joint on Avenue A."

Thus guided, the Doctor found compensations which made him rather fond of the Eskimo Culture office. As Miss Cantlebury kept the books, he was able to have his salary adjusted to sixty dollars a week without bothering Captain Gishorn about it. He took a small new flat, far up in the Bronx, and sent for Peony and Carrie before Christmas. But they still left their furniture in Chicago.

One blessing of his Eskimo experiences was that among the contributors he met William T. Knife, one of the most strident laymen in that somewhat eccentric and quivering and fundamentalist sect, the Antinomian Church. Mr.

Knife was referred to in the denominational press as "the humble millionaire who has applied the principles of St. Paul to his private life and to the soft-drink business." He was also advertised as "a self-educated man who speaks with the eloquence of Cicero or Dwight Moody, and who writes with the power and beauty of Mary Baker Eddy or Mark Twain."

This was probably true, for Mr. Knife always had the Christian humility and business sense to hire the best press agents available as his ghost writers. He gave to oratory and to prose poetry the same zeal that he gave to the spread of temperance and of Okey-Dokey, which was next to the largest-selling soft drink in the country in 1930, according to statistics compiled, by the Enterprise Bureau of Industrial Comparisons, from 11,749 drug stores, 780 pool parlors, 61 church suppers, and 1,126 speakeasies.

Under the personal direction of the Lord God Almighty, Mr. Knife had, as a youth, weathered a cyclone of doubting. As he often told the Y.M.C.A., he had sometimes been tempted then to think that if you were traveling and missed church for just one Sunday, God would not necessarily condemn you to eternal roasting. But God pulled him up sharp, with a bad fit of rheumatics, and he got down on his knees—to extreme discomfort—in the waiting-room of the Highhack depot of the D.&R.G., and confessed what an atheist he had been. He had never missed a Sunday since.

By the same divine personal chaperonage, he had come through the 1929–1930 panic a richer man than ever, for millions found it cheaper to buy Okey-Dokey than soul-deadening whisky. And Okey-Dokey had just enough caffein in it to be profitably habit-forming without doing any provable harm.

Mr. Knife was, in 1930, one of the brightest contemporaries of the Spanish Inquisition.

The liberal churches were turning into lecture halls, but in 1930—as would later be true in 1940, and probably in 1960—the solid Fundamentalists, who knew that God created the world in six days and has spent His time since then in intensely disliking it, still held the true faith unshaken. No matter how red the Neon lights glow on Main Street, they cannot rival the horrid hellfire in the chapel of the Antinomians, or the True New Reformed Tabernacle of the Penitent Saints of the Assembly of God, or in most of the brick and gray stone Baptist and Methodist churches that resemble railroad depots of 1890, and he that knows not that encouraging fact has never been west or south of Blawenburg. Halfway on in the twentieth century, one-quarter of America knows all about splitting the atom, but the other three-quarters have not yet heard the news about Darwin.

For several years now, Mr. William T. Knife had left his six powerful sons to conduct his business while he skipped about the country, telling giant meetings that (1) he was self-educated, but a lot smarter than most Harvard graduates, (2) the superintendents always opened the workday at his several factories with prayer, (3) union labor was no good, simply no good at all, and (4) there wouldn't be all this bellyaching about shorter hours and longer wages if the workers could be coaxed to read the Bible—the one book that was inerrantly true from kiver to kiver—instead of selfishly thinking about temporal things like rent and the groceries.

The time had come, felt Mr. Knife, when the surprising miracle of his own life should be graven in permanent form. When he met Dr. Gideon Planish at an Eskimo Culture rally held by the Antinomians, he inquired whether the good Doctor was a believing Fundamentalist who had family prayers night and morning. When he discovered that that was just the sort of pious fellow the Doctor was, he offered five thousand dollars to have his first-person autobiography reverently ghosted.

Dr. Planish accepted, and moved his family to a boarding-house in Mt. Vernon, New York, to be near Mr. Knife and his sacred labors. He kissed Miss Cantlebury—for the first time—and resigned in a letter to Captain Gishorn, who was then gallantly exploring the tennis courts at the Arizona-Biltmore Hotel.

Mr. Knife was against all the vain luxuries of wine-bibbers and cocktail-bibbers. He said, "Why, I could buy and sell most of these unchristian cusses that show off their yacht boats and polo hosses, but Mrs. Knife and I believe in the Scriptural injunction to cleave to plain living and high-class thinking, so we are content with this hermit's hut. Oh, there's room here to exercise the sacred writ of hospitality, but for ourselves, we ask only a corner and a crumb. Yes, we ask but little. However! It's only sensible to have that little of the best."

The hermit's hut was a twenty-room Colonial manor house originally built as the rural residence of a motion-picture producer. It had a two-acre rose garden, and an eight-car garage—filled. Dr. Planish and Mr. Knife worked in the putative hermit's library, a forty-foot room adorned with sixteen feet from the library of the late Duke of Deephaven.

Before they started, Mr. Knife always said—always— "Doc, will you have a cigar? In principle, I'm entirely against smoking—it is unchristian and unnecessary—it makes me sick to see a gang of little punks puffing at coffin nails—I know for a fact that all labor agitators smoke cigarettes. But my doctor, a Christian man, advises me to take an occasional cigar for the sake of my throat, and I thought it would be healthiest to smoke Porcos y Toledos. I don't know anything about such things, but I understand they are a good brand—— By God, they ought to be! I pay six bits apiece for 'em, and show me one of these snobbish high-society heels over in Bronxville that pays half that much!"

Mr. Knife walked up and down, scratching his lumpy nose and spitting in any of the series of six cuspidors, each with a sparkling quotation from Dr. Frank Buchman painted on it, as he outlined the personal anecdotes and the theories of theology, metaphysics and soft-drink promotion on which Dr. Planish took notes for the book. His proud humility enabled him to be surprisingly frank.

"I'm like Oliver Cromwell. I want the portrait-painter, as I often tell the boys at evangelical tent rallies and the girls at Ladies Only meetings, to put in the warts as well as the unusual jaw and eyes.

"Yes, sir, this autobiography that I am writing is to be an humble offering to God, who will not be deceived, so put down all the errors and lusts I have committed—and have I committed some lusts in my time, oh boy, I'll say I have!—put 'em in along with the souls I've saved and the pile of dough I've made and the Antinomian chapels I've built—glory be to God, who has been my faithful partner in business, through the interposition of the Holy Ghost, and His be the praise and the profits!"

He shook out of the bag quite a few exemplary facts and tales. . . . His nine servants all had to take a Bible test and a Wassermann test before he hired them, and they had to attend family prayers. . . . He had once converted a labor-union organizer who up to that date had gone about like a raging left-wing lion seeing what innocent open-shop employers he could devour, and the fellow was now in the evangelical business in Oregon, with a nice little Christian wife and his home almost paid for. . . . Mr. Knife would furnish Okey-Dokey absolutely free, to be drunk at communion services, provided the church gave him a receipt, to be reproduced for his advertising in the religious press. . . . As a boy, he had first seen the value of religion in business when he had tattled on a friend who had stolen some candy, and the shopkeeper had rewarded him. . . . When he had been persecuted by an alleged health official on the silly grounds that Okey-Dokey was a drug, the Lord Himself had stepped in, and

[261]

enabled Mr. Knife to put the official away by means of that most righteous statute, the Mann Act.

Dr. Planish didn't really care for Mr. Knife, but he was valuable in enabling the Doctor to Make Contacts (as it is called in the uplift business). At the hermit's hut, the Doctor met one of the most earnest forces for co-operative good-doing that he was ever to know, in the person of the Honorable Ernest Wheyfish, an ex-congressman known in the trade as "The Deacon."

Honorable Wheyfish had realized, too late in life, that he should have been a clergyman instead of a politician, though indeed he had once been an undertaker, which had a nice ecclesiastical flavor. Moved by this pious perception, Mr. Wheyfish had renounced the glories of Congress—just as soon as he was defeated for re-election—and gone into the organizational world on the religious side. He was now president and working secretary of the National Christian Excelsior Crusade, whose purpose was to get the worker, the backbone of American industry, back into the church, instead of wasting his time and money on unions and Communist meetings.

Mr. Knife was a conspicuous giver to Honorable Wheyfish's crusade. They agreed ardently about the needs of labor, and said frequently that they were the best friends that the workers had, if they only knew it.

Dr. Planish noted that both of them, like Christian Stern, were undersized, meager, sandy men, but with energy like hurdle-racers, and preposterous bass voices, like thunder out of a graham cracker. He was wondering

[262]

whether he himself was of the right type to save Humanity when he was comforted by a pilgrimage to the hermit's hut of two quite different sorts of organizators: Constantine Kelly and H. Sanderson Sanderson-Smith, whom he had seen in Chicago.

Mr. Kelly looked like a bartender, perhaps because for several years he had been a bartender. He was now assistant and press agent to Mr. Wheyfish in the National Christian Excelsior Crusade.

Mr. Sanderson-Smith was a different kettle of goldfish altogether. He was a fine silky Bostonian—though some said Ontario, and others, South Frampus Center. When Dr. Planish had met him in Chicago, he had had a thin red beard, but he now showed up with his intellectual chin bare and with handsome red Spanish sideburns beside his ears. He was forming a less churchly and more political league than the National Excelsior Crusade, namely, the Citizens' Conference on Constitutional Crises in the Commonwealth, which was to have headquarters in Washington, D. C., and of which none other than United States Senator Felix Bultitude was to be chairman.

But its purpose was the same as that of the Crusade: to coax the workers out of this nonsense of thinking about more wages all the time. Mr. Knife and numerous other Christian industrialists contributed to both societies, as a form of spiritual and financial fire insurance.

There was really only one intolerable evil about working for Mr. William T. Knife: he talked so much about the evils of alcohol that Dr. Planish always got thirsty, and when he reached his boarding-house at night, he demanded so many highballs that it looked as if this life of diligent piety might land him in the sanitarium. And Peony, herself no especial enemy of wetness and cheering, always joined him.

They were at Pete's Café in Manhattan, on a Saturday evening, drinking away the week's cosmic dust, when they saw Hatch Hewitt, that lean tall devil who had stirred young Gid Planish's fancy and depressed his ambition all through Adelbert College.

He wasn't quite so lean now; he was, at forty, a little bald, and his face was worn. He looked at Dr. Planish in passing their table, did not recognize him and stalked on to the bar. He was expertly disposing of a straight rye when the Doctor poked his shoulder and murmured, "Hatch! Gid Planish!"

Hatch sat with them, and stared at Peony.

"Can you stand for the ole friend's wife?" she giggled.

Hatch solemnly nodded, turned to Dr. Planish, and solemnly said, "Nice woman."

Dr. Planish inquired, "I suppose you're a magazine editor by now, or a Washington correspondent, or a Sunday editor. You always had the most talent in our class."

"I always agreed with you about the talent, but New York doesn't. No, I'm just a plain reporter on the *Herald-Times*. Mostly do labor and politics. And how about you? I haven't heard a word since we graduated."

"You haven't?" Peony was indignant. "The Doctor has merely revolutionized rural education in the Middlewest and inaugurated education in Greenland and been dean of a college and refused the presidency of several other colleges, that's all!"

Hatch marveled, "My God, she believes in you, Gid! I didn't know there were any women left like that. Where did you find her? Have they got any left?"

"God broke the mold after he turned her out!" Dr. Planish looked at Peony as though, to his own surprise, he really believed it. Hatch sighed, and suddenly the Doctor knew that Hatch was possessed by a wife who was strident and opinionated.

The Doctor furnished a somewhat less laudatory sketch of his own triumphs, though he did not feel it necessary to inform Hatch that he had been discharged from the Heskett Foundation and that his associations with Captain Gishorn and Mr. William T. Knife differed from hijacking liquor trucks chiefly in being less useful. He sounded so doubtful of himself that Hatch cried to Peony, unsneeringly, "Seems as if your husband has learned not to take careering and butting into other people's affairs too seriously."

"But I want him to take them seriously!" flared Peony. "If you only knew what Colonel Charles B. Marduc said to him!"

As Colonel Marduc had never said anything to him beyond, "Ah, you come from Chicago—great city," she could not do much with it, and she had to sit back glorying in a wife's ancient privilege of disapproving of her husband's pre-conversion friends.

"Well, it's been swell running into you," said Hatch. "We must see each other again soon."

[265]

As this was New York, they did not see each other again for four years.

Speaking of crusades, Hatch had reported that the newest educational racket in town was a company called "The Modernistic Educational Bureau," which sold a new encyclopedia that—— No, the Bureau didn't *sell* anything. It just promoted culture.

It had set up the customary organization, with a publicity-loving board of directors, including the trusty Dr. Christian Stern, Professor George Riot and the learned Dr. Elmer Gantry. These directors were, it is pleasant to announce, laden with no duties aside from letting their names shine forth as guarantors, for which they each received fifty dollars.

George Riot nominated as suitable members of the Bureau all persons whose names were on Charity-Education Sucker List XM27E. The Bureau wrote to each of these prospects that he had been named by the distinguished professor and, as an almost inevitable consequence, elected as a "senior Governing Member of the M.E.B., annual dues $15.00, 5% discount for cash within one month, for which you will receive a handsome membership diploma suitable for framing, our own educational magazine, frequent and illuminating letters on official stationery and, as fast as each volume is issued, receive, Absolutely Free, the titanic new-from-cover-to-cover MODERNISTIC ENCYCLOPEDIA OF WORLD KNOWLEDGE, the FIRST cyclopedia to be prepared, by a staff of World Experts, on the NEW SCIENTIFIC

PRINCIPLES OF PHILOLOGY, BIOLOGY, PEDA-GOGY, AGRONOMICS AND MONEY-MAKING, and the most magnificently illustrated Book of Reference in the entire history of publishing."

The preparation of this encyclopedia was not really so difficult as the customer might have supposed. A small company of intellectual commandos, in a shaky old building on 23rd Street, in a loft once candidly devoted to the manufacture of gents' pants, went through the several older cyclopedias, lifted and combined and abbreviated the contents, and extensively illustrated this stew with photographs bought in job-lots of one hundred.

The staff also farmed out many of the articles, which involved Dr. Gideon Planish, and a number of college instructors of small prosperity. (After all, new college buildings are expensive, and you can't lavish *everything* on the faculty.)

When he had heard from Hatch of this cultural adventure, Dr. Planish sent for the Bureau's "literature," happily noted George Riot's prominence, had George recommend him to the "financial secretary" of the Bureau, who was also the sole owner of it and a fine fellow who had been graduated from one of the best grade schools in Jersey City, and obtained from him a little piecework. It was not well paid, but it padded out the Planish income without interfering with the Knife memoirs—and besides, Peony actually wrote all the articles that the Doctor signed.

So they were prosperous again. They brought on their furniture from Chicago, the Chippendale cabinet and the rug and the shiny bar, and in Mt. Vernon they rented a

"Cape Cod bungalow" not quite so comfortable as the house they had had in Kinnikinick at the beginning of their expedition to conquer power.

Carrie liked it and went wild in gardens, but Peony complained that out here in the suburbs, they were meeting as few notorious people ("interesting people" she called them) as back in Kinnikinick, and she fervently influenced the Doctor when Mr. H. Sanderson Sanderson-Smith invited him to join the CCCCC in Washington, D. C.

Peony yelled, "Oh, do it! Washington! We'll meet senators and generals and the President, and maybe it'll lead to your finally going into politics—— Saaaay! When did our plan to make you a senator get lost in the shuffle?"

Dr. Planish fretted that he didn't really like the purposes of Sanderson-Smith's gang, the "Citizens' Conference." Though it had on its board members of Congress and newspaper-owners and eloquent corporation lawyers and a lady author and an officer of the D.A.R., it was, almost frankly, an anti-labor-union lobby. He worried, "I know there are crooked labor leaders, but on the whole, I've always upheld the Rights of the Common Man, of the farmer and factory-worker——"

"Now don't give me that Number 28 Lecture!" said his wife, with tartness unusual to her. "Who knows but what you can do more good by getting this Citizens' Conference outfit to be kinder to the lil brothers than you can by staying out? Besides! I don't see any union organizer sweating over where *we* get a new radio and shoes for Carrie!"

"Well——" said Dr. Planish.

[268]

22

THE CITIZENS' CONFERENCE on Constitutional Crises in the Commonwealth was known in Washington as the "Cizkon."

It had none of the fuzziness of purpose that had bothered Dr. Gideon Planish, the new Assistant General Manager of the Cizkon, at the Heskett Foundation. Its offices filled two floors of an official-looking old red brick building. During the depression of the early 1930's, it was richer in funds than ever, because it was then that the large industrialists and merchants most feared revolution, and they were skillfully coached by Mr. Sanderson-Smith and Dr. Planish to believe that the Cizkon was insurance against their losing control of the country.

Any seedling notions about liberalizing the Cizkon that the good Doctor might have cultivated were frozen quickly in that icy competence.

On the surface, the Cizkon was so idealistic that it dripped, and this was the department to which Dr. Planish was particularly assigned. In lectures and pamphlets and newspaper stories which it manufactured or affectionately influenced, it shouted the best battle cries: "The traditional American right to work unhampered by labor racketeers," and "The menace to fundamental American institutions, by foreign atheism and Jewish international socialism," and "The Founding Fathers' ideals of Free Enterprise, an Economy of Abundance, and Free Competition unchecked by sumptuary laws, so that the Poorest Citizen may have his chance in the race for fame and fortune against the wealthiest corporation or the most aristocratic and highly educated individual," and "The Cross and the Stars and Stripes—or the Assassin's Dagger and the Crossed Hammer and Sickle—WHICH?"

And, in those days, "Mussolini makes the trains run on time."

All that Dr. Planish had to do was to take the slogans he had believed in and turn them inside out. He was still in the Ideals and Public Improvement business, even if he had gone over to a competing firm, and his salary was now a comfortable $4,500 a year. They had a thin tall house in Georgetown and they entertained senators—perhaps twice—and he and Peony and Carrie were happy—anyway, Peony was happy—anyway, Peony said she was happy.

The Cizkon's chief operative, Mr. H. Sanderson Sanderson-Smith, was an esthete. He had written a pamphlet on surrealism, he had been a theosophist, a nudist, a spiritualist, a Bahaist and a Douglas Planner; and he was enviously rumored to be a secret drunkard on benedictine spiced with pepper and maple sugar. But he was an excellent Organizational Engineer—his own phrase.

If the sort of beefy, Hamilton-Frisby, football-squad, Skull-and-Bones, Meadowbrook-Club millionaires who always intimidated Dr. Planish also despised Sanderson-

Smith, in revenge he knew how to make them tremble with his inside news about Jewish, Communist, and Scandinavian-Irish-farmer-labor conspiracies against them, and radicals now known to be manufacturing sub-machine guns in a cellar near St. Sebastian, North Dakota. He panicked them into giving him funds with which, as he caressingly put it, he would "put Bibles instead of tommy-guns into the horny hands of these sons of—well—of toil!"

The Cizkon issued a magazine called *Flag or Lag?* illustrated with pictures of strikers beating policemen, of Lenin and Stalin attending an orthodox synagogue, and of George Washington crossing the Delaware, with a caption hinting that if he did so today, it would be to spend a week-end with the du Ponts.

In fact the Cizkon magazine assaulted the Communists with all the accuracy and tender tolerance with which the Communists assaulted their opponents. It was well padded with the advertisements of banks, insurance companies and utility companies. The theory was that it circulated among the Common Workers, persuading them to leap out of their red cells and exchange their unions for the Union League. And at least it did reach the desks of all the fine old gentlemen in Massachusetts who owned textile mills.

The Cizkon also published, in pamphlet form, addresses which would certainly have been delivered on the floor of the House if any other congressmen could have been persuaded to stay and listen. These addresses stated that the author had had a good mother and a pretty fair father, and that all labor leaders were terrible.

Less directly, the Cizkon influenced many published writings. It encouraged local school boards to throw out text-books that alleged that Abraham Lincoln was an agnostic. It arranged with factory-owners to welcome journalists who wanted to do little pieces about the glories of modern machinery and the miracles of distribution. And it warned editors, by letters ostensibly from indignant subscribers, that Liberals were essentially more dangerous than Communists—which was probably true.

It assisted right-thinking professors to get lecture-engagements, and it got out clip-sheets with refrigerated editorials protesting that President Harding had been a great man, after all, that H. G. Wells had but rarely written anything about Bishop James Cannon, Jr., of the Southern Methodist Church, and that honest workers do not watch the clock.

But the Cizkon was not merely literary. In an emergency it would send expert lobbyists to State Legislatures, to choke the vile hydra of compulsory washrooms in factories. Once, Dr. Gideon Planish thus journeyed out West, to appear before a legislative committee as an economics expert and a disinterested tax-payer.

Beyond all other virtues of the Cizkon was its personal duty of collecting just as many contributions from the jittery captains of industry as it could cajole or frighten out of them. It annually got out a financial report which showed the gratified contributors "just where every red cent of your generous donations has gone," with lovely figures, down to the second decimal, about Office Expense, Salaries, Traveling Expenses, Postage, Publication and dozens of others. Still, Mr. Sanderson-Smith did live in the former residence of an ambassador, and did send three very charming and handsome young men through college.

He gracefully entertained here, and sometimes he invited the Planishes. So Peony met poets and actors and rather astonishing old men who tickled. She was in the pool of provincial hobohemia up to her neck, and so soaked with Celebrity that occasionally she wanted to go back to Kinnikinick for a rest.

But within the hour she would assure her husband that she didn't mean it; that she was as happy here as a Lark, as a Grig, as the day is long. She began to spend just a little too much for evening dresses, and she developed a way of confiding to newcomers in Washington, "I happened to be sitting next to a man who knows the Secretary of the Navy intimately, and he told me, but don't repeat it now——"

She admired the smoothness of Sanderson-Smith, even though she did refer to him privately as "Sneaky Sandy." She repeated often a dinner quip of Sanderson-Smith which soared right up to the heights of Oscar Wilde: "Last night Sandy told me—I made him repeat it—'I didn't mind it when oi polloi claimed that a live hog was better than a dead lion. That's arguable,' he said. 'But now,' he said, 'they're bellowing that a live hog is better than a live lion!' Now isn't that brilliant!"

Dr. Planish sighed, "Sometimes it seems to me that Sandy sacrifices true liberalism to a mere mot."

"Oh, stuff!" said Peony.

She still admired the Doctor as the fount of learning, but she was doing very well on her own.

She had learned that congressmen and even bureau chiefs were not hard to get for dinner. You just offered them free food and the best of illicit liquor. She became chummy with several congressmen's wives who, on cook's night off, had to scramble their own family dinners; who took Peony into their confidences and swapped servant stories, while their husbands fed her hunger for magnificence by grunting, even apropos of the President himself, "I saw Herb yesterday, and he told me we're coming out of the depression at last, yessir, that's just what he said."

She loved it. But the Doctor was ever more dubious as he toiled at labor-baiting; and as for Carrie, preposterous child, she kept whimpering that she wanted to see the suburban children with whom she had played in Mt. Vernon.

Their high triumph was in becoming charmingly acquainted with that great financial authority, Senator Felix Bultitude, who, as chairman of the board of the Cizkon, was something besides ornamental. He was even more celebrated for his honesty than for his intelligence—in fact, he wasn't really so highly thought of for intelligence—and when potential contributors to the Cizkon saw his name fronting on the board, they exulted, "Don't tell me that the CCCCC isn't on the level, with a man like Bultitude running it. You don't think *he's* the kind of grafter who'd stoop to padding his expense account ten dollars on his hotel bill, when he's out lecturing for them, do you—a man of his standing?" (Mr. Bultitude was always referred to as "a man of his standing," no matter what he stood on.)

They were right, too. The Senator never received a cent from the Cizkon. He merely let it interest a few prominent men outside his own State in his harmless, necessary campaign fund.

Senator Bultitude was always referred to by chairmen as "that great Liberal." He loved to dwell on the History of Labor, even though he did mix up Heywood Broun and Big Bill Haywood. As a young man, while he was studying law, he had worked as a farmhand for one entire vacation, so he could properly call himself "a real dirt farmer," and Sanderson-Smith regularly used him to put honey in the hair of farm blocs.

But when Sanderson-Smith wanted someone to come right out and tell club smokers that, in the opinion of the Cizkon, all workers, even the good or non-union workers, were dangerous to the peace of the state unless they were controlled by the Right People, then he used as prophet not Senator Bultitude but the Reverend Mr. Ezekiel Bittery, a former Fundamentalist preacher who really had been a farmhand. Mr. Bittery said, in Scriptural rhythms, "I've toiled with the toilers, I've preached to their stoniness, I know 'em—and they're all skunks!"

Mr. Bittery was trying to enlist a private army called "The Gospel Gentlemen" from among former Ku Kluxers, but he had too many rivals for the position of American Duce, and he was still glad to do Sanderson-Smith a sixty-one-minute exposure of the Jews and Radicals for

$65.00 cash—in advance—and a year later he would be throwing in two minutes of denouncing Eleanor Roosevelt.

The bad luck of the Planishes seemed over. The Doctor had been in the new job only a year when Franklin D. Roosevelt was elected President, and during the experimentation of the New Deal, so alarming to the Better People, who liked to have the objects of their charity grateful and transient, the Cizkon became important as a safeguard against loose spending and the horrid heresy of maintaining that Democracy also included people who did not live in your block.

Now, Sanderson-Smith was able to hurl gas bombs not just at anonymous Communists but even at the highly visible Administration itself. He was full of wit about the new Government bureaus and their names: SEC, PWA, FHRA. He said, "Our own little group, the CCCCC, has more C's in it than the CCC's but much less seize!"

"Isn't that just brilliant!" said Peony Planish.

One of the mysteries is the origin of dirty stories and political anecdotes. A tale will be repeated ten million times over ten years, and yet the original author, honest fellow, will be unknown, unhonored. But of the thousand anecdotes about Franklin D. Roosevelt and his family and aides, at least a dozen of the more popular were created by the patient artistry of H. Sanderson Sanderson-Smith, including the one about the psychiatrist being sent to God when He had the delusion that he was Roosevelt.

When Mrs. Roosevelt was friendly with coal miners, it was Sanderson-Smith who explained to the ecstatic mine-owners—and the even more ecstatic Young Communists, who were now beginning to exceed in nuisance value the young disciples of Proust and Joyce—that it had all been done by collusion with Moscow. He sowed the rumor that Miss Frances Perkins, the Secretary of Labor, was really Rebecca Prjzbska from Crakow, and originated the jest, attributed to several popular columnists, that "The Trouble with the New Dealers is that they're all small-town boys named Ray: Ray Moley, Ray Tugwell, Ray Frankfurter—and Ray Roosevelt."

It was one of the duties of Dr. Planish to see that these witticisms were spread properly. Mr. Sanderson-Smith was not always pleasant when he failed to do so.

When the New Deal started on wages and hours legislation, the Cizkon came out for the very factory improvements that it had abhorred.

All industries were threatened with having to recognize one union or another, and Sanderson-Smith hired an expert who had been a union organizer himself to go from factory to factory of the Cizkon's higher contributors and explain how to form reasonable company unions which would be nicer all round than the A.F. of L. or the C.I.O. This expert would also demonstrate how much cheaper it was to put in cafeterias and clean washrooms and free medical service than to have the workers think their bosses did not love them. He even went so far in a Southern State as to persuade an employer to hire one per cent of Negro labor, which clearly proved something or other, said Sanderson-Smith in an address "The New Liberalism vs the New Deal."

Years later, in the 1940's, even after America had entered World War II, Dr. Planish was interested to see that, though H. Sanderson Sanderson-Smith himself was in prison on the astounding charge that he was a Nazi agent, other bodies were carrying on the ameliorative work of the Cizkon, with the slogans "The American Way of Life" and "The Sacred Right to Work" and "The Founding Fathers who laid down the principle of Free Competition" still frequently meaning that employers did not care much for union wage scales.

Through all the Planishes' prosperity and social magnitude in Washington, the Doctor had spiritual trouble.

Whenever his former colleagues, Chris Stern and Dr. Kitto and Natalia Hochberg and Professor Buchwald and George Riot, all of them Reformers at whom the Cizkon had heaved a paragraph or two, came to Washington, the Doctor felt uncomfortably that they felt uncomfortably that he was no longer a Liberal. He tried to explain to them that, really, he was more of a Liberal than ever; he and Sanderson-Smith were all for Constructive and Enlightened Labor Leadership, and they opposed only the misleaders who made a living out of Labor. They seemed highly unconvinced by him or by the fervors of Sanderson-Smith, for whom they adopted Peony's name of "Sneaky Sandy."

Dr. Planish tried to be jovial about it: "All right—all

right! You get me as good a job with some liberal outfit in New York, and I'll leave Sneaky Sandy flat!"

He had, he felt proudly, "called their bluff." But he was still disquieted, and he tried to explain it all to Peony, when she came in from a cocktail party to celebrate the anniversary of the repeal of Prohibition.

"Now get this, Peony. To be realistic, I must admit that the first purpose of any uplift organization must be to support the executives who give their time and good hard work to it—like a doctor or a preacher. But I do feel that if I make my living out of a movement to strengthen the public morale, then it ought—well, it ought to try and do some strengthening, don't you see?"

"See what?" said Peony.

He went on, thinking aloud. "And I'm afraid Chris Stern is right. The Cizkon isn't really liberal. Chris is probably just as much of a fourflusher as Sneaky Sandy—just as crazy to get power and publicity—only he's a careerist on the right side, and Sandy is on the wrong side."

Peony sniffed, "So what? He's a Liberal, but he's practical."

"When was he ever liberal?"

"What's the diff? We get our salary, don't we? And do you mean to tell me that you don't believe in the American system of justice, as laid down by George Washington?"

"Now what——"

"Every man that's accused has a right to be represented in court by a lawyer, hasn't he? Well, Sneaky is the lawyer for the capitalists, and they need a smart one, don't they?"

"That's an interesting point of view. Very interesting. But there's another aspect of the matter. In the long run, I think that an executive does better if he's known as a Liberal. By 1940, I'll wager there'll be more money—or rather, I mean a more dignified social position—in being associated with anti-Fascism than with Fascism. Besides, I'm an oldtime Fighting Liberal, and a man with his battles behind me, I mean my battles behind me, he simply can't turn his back on the People, don't you see? . . . No, no, it isn't fly-by-night advocates of individualism like Sneaky Sandy that come out on top eventually; it's proponents of communal discipline, like Colonel Charles B. Marduc, the greatest promoter of widespread prosperity——"

"Want a drink?" said Peony.

"Of course I want a drink!" said Dr. Planish.

23

In the anteroom of Senator Bultitude's office, Dr. Planish fell to talking with a meager and gentle man of fifty-odd, with a thin flaxen mustache, baggy gray clothes, a bright blue tie, and a bright blue shirt—the uniform of a man who wanted to be different. His name was Carlyle Vesper. Something he said caused the Doctor to invite him to lunch at the Crayon Club.

The Doctor was fond of the Crayon, which was full of ex-congressmen turned lobbyists or Government clerks. The polite waiters called him "Doctor," and believed that he was a bureau chief at least.

It appeared that Mr. Vesper had an idea for a virtuous organization, and what was much more remarkable, he seemed to have the money, in the backing of Mrs. John James Piggott, intransigent old widow of the Silver Mine and International Railroad, and of Miss Ramona Tundra, who had started as a child star in the motion pictures and was ending as a child adult who patronized faith-healers. Without this cash behind it, Dr. Planish was too well trained an organizator to have been interested in the mere idea, though he did admit that it was possibly the noblest religious inspiration since St. Paul.

Carlyle Vesper was as simple as Cardinal Newman. During years as a commonplace bookkeeper he had dreamed of a Christian church in which the director would not be a pope or an archbishop or a stated secretary or any kind of paid minister, but Jesus Christ himself.

"I think we ought to believe that Jesus is perfectly capable of doing this without some Doctor of Sacred Theology helping him out," said Vesper, with the smile of a shy boy or a madman. "I think most churches started off all right, but then they had to support a lot of men who called themselves priests or ministers, and then these fellows wanted to put on fancy dress, and that cost money, and pretty soon they wanted to have churches that their voices would sound big in, and then the people didn't have a fellowship between Christ and men any longer, but just another salvation shop. I'd like our church to end all that."

Dr. Planish knew enough history to recall how many other Carlyle Vespers had started churches to end all churches. But the sweet simpleton had managed to interest Mrs. Piggott and Miss Tundra——

Vesper flowed on, "I guess what I want is just a gayer and more modern group of Quakers, without the old Pennsylvania and Ohio Quaker families acting a little like hereditary priests themselves. My organization, if it ever gets going right—and it will be a failure unless it destroys itself and quits, the minute it succeeds, like any good teacher!—it will do nothing but suggest to every man and woman and child that God really did make him a priest, as they understood so well among the early Christians, and that he can pray by himself or in company with others just as he is moved. I want to call it the Every Man a Priest Fraternity.

"Oh, yes, I've thought about this for twenty years, and I can keep books, but I'm not much of an executive. I can't bear bossing people! If we only had a man like you! Could I persuade you to take an interest—say, be our chief shepherd?"

"Uh—uh—how much would you plan to pay?"

"I hadn't thought about it. We have ten thousand dollars in the treasury now. Would half of that be enough for a year's salary?"

"I'm afraid I couldn't even think of it for less than six thousand a year. That's about what I'm getting now, and of course I have to consider my poor wife and child."

"Oh, I'm sure that as this world's goods go, six thousand would be very little for a man of your experience and your love for suffering humanity. Shall we agree on that and get to work, Brother Gideon?"

"Wow!" said Dr. Planish, to himself, but aloud he bumbled, "I'll think it over. Let's meet here tomorrow noon."

He telephoned to New York, to Chris Stern, who answered Yes, this preposterous outsider, Vesper, did seem to have coaxed a lot of money out of that tough old heathen, Mrs. Piggott.

The Doctor dared not hint to Peony, that evening, of his interest in the absurd charlatan.

Next morning, Sanderson-Smith called him in, and Sanderson-Smith had had an unpleasant dinner the evening before. He said, not so silkily as usual, "Planish, I want to talk to you about your next lecture tour among the colleges. I want you to quit all this pussyfooting and heavy Liberalism. Come right out and tell these simpletons of undergraduates that they can choose between bucking the unions and being enslaved by them. Understand?"

"I'll think it over," said Dr. Planish, not very belligerently.

At the luncheon table, Vesper smiled, handed over a lovely check for five hundred dollars, and said, "It's your first month's check, Brother Gideon—Gideon, the Sword of the Lord! Now will you come with us?"

"By God, I'll do it! Oh, sorry for cursing."

"I don't think we need worry too much about the ancient Jewish injunction against cursing and swearing. Don't you suppose God will take the spirit of the oath rather than the actual wording? I don't guess He is much deceived."

To himself, already beginning to resent the new employer as all that morning he had been resenting the old one, Dr. Planish groaned, "He's getting saintly on me! A careerist in holiness! I'll never be happy till I've got an organization where I'm sole boss—unless it's one run by a fellow like Colonel Marduc, who has real brains and power —and cash!—and not a lot of sappy sentimentality like Vesper or psychopathic malice like Sneaky Sandy—— Oh dear!"

But aloud he was beginning, "Now the first thing we want to do is to get the names of the top men, like Bishop Pindyck—no, that's so, no preachers for once, thank God.

[284]

Well, how about William T. Knife—a true Christian pioneer?"

It was hard to tell Peony that from now on his salary would be guaranteed only by St. Francis of Assisi. He remembered how game she had been in Chicago, when he had admitted that Hamilton Frisby had kicked him out, but he put off his confession till after they had come home from the movies that evening.

They were having a companionable drink at the scoured table in the dark Washington kitchen when he told her. Even as he spoke, the notion of anybody being a priest without being paid for it seemed as fantastic to him as riding the tail of a rocket.

Peony listened with horrified silence; then: "Have you gone completely bugs? To give up a settled job with Sandy, a racket that ought to be good for at least five more years, for this crazy religious maniac? As you know, I'm a true Christian and a church member, but—— Six thousand a year? You'll never get six hundred! It'll blow up in a month! You've got to get out of this insane picnic, right away. You've got to! Tell Vesper to go roll his holy hoop!"

"I'm afraid I can't. I've already spent half of the five hundred he paid me—we were two months behind on the rent—and this afternoon I finally told Sanderson-Smith that he was a high-class scab. I'm through there, I'm afraid."

"You're afraid!"

She shrieked it; she dashed out of the kitchen, and up-

[285]

stairs. He followed, and heard the key turning in the door of their bedroom. He hadn't even known that there was a key.

"Poor impetuous baby!" He smiled to himself. He knocked with playful lightness—no answer; then with marital firmness—no answer. He tried the knob.

After twelve years of married life, she had for the first time locked him out of their room.

He cried, in panic, "Peony! Sweetheart! Let me in! Let me explain!" To himself: "She's right. And suppose she divorced me? What could I do? I couldn't sleep alone nights!"

Peony was not answering, even with a sound of tip-toeing feet, as he called her name again and tried again to knock gaily, to show that he didn't really mind this little loving trick she was playing on him. Making his step as heavy and dignified and rebuking as he could, he thumped downstairs, and stood at the foot, waiting for her to rush out and call him back. She didn't. But she must—she had to! He went on waiting. He could not hear her at all.

"I've had enough of this nonsense. She's acting like a spoiled child. I'm just not going to pay any attention to her," he stated.

He went firmly into the small green-and-chintz living-room, and tried to do a cross-word puzzle—a form of escape still fashionable then. It would not come out. He threw the newspaper at the signed photograph of President T. Austin Bull, and sneaked softly to the foot of the stairs. He stood there in sick worry. Upstairs, he could hear her heavily sobbing. He dared not affront her, and he crept back to the living-room, to glare at the newspaper.

Where the devil was he supposed to sleep tonight? In Carrie's child-bed, maybe! And it was bedtime right now.

He pounded to the stairs, and yelled up, "Hey! Where do you think I'm going to sleep?"

After a noticeable pause, a mournful voice dribbled down, "In hell, I hope."

"Is that a nice way to answer me when I ask a civil question?" he put it. Yet it encouraged him to find that she was no longer so young and broken. He marched upstairs and tapped, commandingly. "Sweetheart! Let me in. Unlock the door."

She sobbed, "It's unlocked."

Mechanically patting her bare shoulder, he bumbled, "There, there, there! My own baby! Still such a little baby! And yet so wise. Oh, lambie, I'll never again make any organizational or occupational affiliation [he meant, take a job] without your advice."

"Oh, no, you mustn't, lover. You know it's only because I love you and have your best interests at heart. Of course you're stuck with the new mission now, but I just know you won't find this Carlyle Vesper fellow as smart as Sneaky Sandy."

Lying awake in darkness beside her, filled with the dark smell of her hair, he realized that he was her slave and told himself that he was very happy about it.

[287]

24

THE EVERY MAN a Priest Fraternity office, on 43rd Street in New York, was so much like the office of the Association to Promote Eskimo Culture that Dr. Planish was confused. The lone employee, a plump secretary named Miss Kremitz, so much resembled Miss Cantlebury of the Eskimo office that he felt like sitting down and finishing the letter that he had derisively left undone when he deserted to William T. Knife.

But when he went through the files, he found that this shop was notably different from that of Captain Gishorn, who was as methodical about the affairs of the Devil as Carlyle Vesper was slipshod about the service of the Lord. Here were unanswered letters—one, actually, a query from the wealthy chain-store man, Albert Jalenak, about the Fraternity's aims.

"Gosh all gracious!" winced the professional, "and Jalenak the very finest type of conscience-drugging philanthrobber! Why, he might have come through with five hundred! What kind of a way to promote the Lord is that —not answer feeler letters by return mail! Shocking!"

He found that Vesper hadn't even "elected," as organizations playfully call it, an impressive front of general officers and honorary directors. He fretted, "How right

Peony was! All Vesper really has here is his idea, which isn't new, and the support of Mrs. Piggott and Ramona Tundra, which isn't ironclad. I've got to go see those old girls and find out where we are."

He telephoned, inviting himself to meet them at tea at the old Piggott residence on lower Madison Avenue, not many squares from the J. P. Morgan blockhouse which still defends the last pioneer white settlers.

He arrived at Mrs. Piggott's without Vesper—and without Vesper's knowledge.

He felt at home in that ancient hallway, with a teak throne and a marble Psyche holding a gas-lighted torch. He felt that he natively belonged to this house with its resounding memory of past grandeur and of the epoch when a man's goodness could be exactly measured by the number of his millions. Nor was he embarrassed by the craggy old woman and the slim faded actress who awaited him on a worn satin couch behind a tea-table with a Georgian hot-water kettle resembling Mont-St.-Michel.

On the wall, in a shadow-box, was Mrs. Piggott's portrait by Sargent.

He accepted tea—yes, thanks, he would have just a wee drop of rum in it; he didn't ordinarily indulge, but it was raw today. Yes, it would be fine if everybody could feel Carlyle Vesper's high exaltation.

He mentioned his professorship, his deanhood, his installation of rustic education and Eskimos. Gently laughing at himself, he recalled saying, at the White House, "Mr. President, I trust you remember that *some* people didn't make their wealth by brigandage but by being exceptionally strong." (Maybe he really had said something like that, but maybe the President had not heard him properly, as there were fifteen hundred other people at that reception.) He touched on the characters and private ambitions of the Secretary of State, the presidents of Yale, Harvard and the University of Chicago, without feeling called upon to explain that his conversations with all of them had been limited to "How do."

All this presented modestly, with many little razor-blades of comment which showed that he understood the ladies' own great position. They listened with increasing trustfulness until his actor's instinct, so important to salesmen of philanthropy, told him that the time had come to play Old Family Doctor.

He gravely pushed the tea-table away, took both of Mrs. Piggott's aged hands, and started building his great second-act speech:

"Dear Mrs. Piggott, and you, dear girl" (Miss Tundra was, he calculated, at least thirty-five), "both of you, I have shockingly bad news. Let's take it in our stride and take it with a brave smile, and get it over. The Every Man Fraternity can't go on. It's finished."

"M?"

"It's a shame. I'd hoped, after my years of training, to find my lifework here. And I'd hoped that your two names would go down in history as the twin founders of a spiritual reform so powerful that it might be called a new religion, like Mrs. Eddy or Madame Blavatsky or St. Cecilia. But what do I discover when I get here and look over the books and files?

"Letters unanswered. Lists of names with the wrong addresses and even, believe it or not, the wrong titles—a high-class Methodist divine down as 'Mister' and not as 'Doctor'. Now perhaps I could correct all this but——

"We have at the moment only $9,044.37 in the treasury, and need I tell you two, who have handled weightier business affairs than most mere men ever thought of, that we couldn't even begin to spread this gospel of simplicity and unworldliness for less than thirty-five thousand dollars for a starter? So—but what a pity!—we'll have to let the whole thing go."

In the look that Mrs. Piggott and Miss Tundra exchanged his expert eye appraised a further twenty thousand. He hit again, quickly.

"And not only that, but a more spiritual matter. Carlyle Vesper is a seer and a saint—the most forgiving man I've ever encountered. Yet—well, I suppose he's one of these impractical souls that have to be managed. You *would* think that with his training in accountancy and office technique, he'd at least answer letters from poor, groping, soul-hungry seekers——"

He had not much farther to go before Mrs. Piggott nodded to Miss Tundra, who interrupted him, "Yes, we can see that, Doctor. It's like a heaven-sent cinema artist trying to produce and distribute. I think I may speak for Lady Piggott, as I always call her, when I say that we're already agreed *you* ought to be the boss—Director General would be a lovely title—and you can let Mr. Vesper go on dreaming his dear, lovely, lonely lotus dreams apart from all the hurly-burly, and isn't it fortunate that he's a

[291]

widower without children—I'm sure he'll be perfectly happy on thirty-five dollars a week, instead of the fifty that we have been temporarily allowing him."

Dr. Planish breathed hard; then he besought the two religion-founders, "But I'm not worthy to go to that noble spirit and tell him——"

"I'm worthy! I'm good at that!" announced Mrs. Piggott. "You let me tell him. I'll get him right down here. Poor Doctor, I know how hard it is on you!" He was suspicious, but he decided that she meant it. "Don't go back to the office this afternoon, and when you go in tomorrow, you'll find everything all okay and sublimated, or do I mean substantiated?"

He felt that for once he could afford the most delicate luxury he knew—having "the works" at the Gyro Building Barber Shop.

As he rode uptown by taxicab, he was only briefly bothered about Vesper's downfall. "After all, any other executive would have thrown him right out on his ear, and not even allowed him to stay on as a flunky. Besides! I hope I'm a just and humanitarian man, and for myself I don't want *anything,* but when people get in the way of Peony's rights, God help 'em!"

The Gyro Building was only the fourth highest in Manhattan, only seventy-nine stories, but it had more aluminum, more black glass, and more murals by Communist artists than any other building in the world, including Moscow.

[292]

The young Gid Planish, back in Adelbert College, had frequented the shop of an aged German barber, which smelled of bay rum and cigar-smoke and peace. The barber was one of the few people in town who took Gid seriously; he consulted Gid tolerantly about his preference in hair styles and his opinion of free silver. The place had been a refuge, a healing, and ever since then a barber shop had meant escape.

But his tastes in size and glossiness and gadgetry had grown.

The Gyro shop was on the forty-seventh floor, and he rode up in an elevator lined with marquetry depicting the chase of Diana. At the shop entrance, the manager, who tried to resemble Adolphe Menjou, said "Good afternoon, Doctor."

"Why, they know who I am!" rejoiced Dr. Planish.

It was quite a barber shop. While America might not as yet have developed a Sibelius, it could substitute for the shabby hairdressers' dens of Europe the combined genius of Edison, Frank Lloyd Wright, Steinmetz and Delilah.

There were forty barber chairs, upholstered in yellow leather, and twenty manicure tables, and ten bootblacks in Roumanian uniform, with the manager in his Easter-morning costume, and a cashier who had once been in a Follies chorus. The shrine was as filled with Beauty as it was with Service. The walls were of black marble with green veins, the washbowls of dark green porcelain, and the cupboard-doors were brass-bound mirrors. The composition floor was patterned in zodiac symbols of yellow and black, and the silvered ceiling was paneled, with inverted onyx bowls for the indirect lighting.

Here was the very sign and heart of the Metropolis which now, for the first time, Dr. Planish had conquered, and started to loot.

He did not encourage the barber's conversation, but sat in an ecstasy of silence, thinking how he could most dramatically tell Peony, waiting for him in their cheap hotel, the news that he now ranked with Chris Stern or Captain Gishorn.

He did have "the works": a manicure by a red-head who squeezed his soapy fingers; a hair-trim, a beard-trim, a shave, a face-massage, an oil shampoo, a shine, an electrical treatment with horrible little rubber tits, and a final Assyrian smearing with lilac ointment and violet lotion.

Yet after a time his dreams were so disturbed by the babble of his next-chair neighbor that virtue passed out of them, and he began to mutter to himself, through the scented foam, "Barber—barbarous; manicure—manicdepressive; electric massage—electric chair."

The neighbor was evidently an Important Man. He was having a quantity of expensive things done all at once: not only reveling in a massage and shine and manicure, but receiving telegrams from a Western Union boy and giving messages for a page to transmit by telephone. He was talking about the Spanish Republicans (he didn't care for them), the races at Hialeah, his new girl, who was in a floor show, and real-estate prices in La Jolla. He had, he informed the listening world, a yacht that would "sleep eight and eat twenty," and he had once lost thirty-five hundred dollars at roulette.

This magnificence so submerged the Doctor that suddenly he was no longer a conquering Hun of humanitarianism, but just Doc Planish, a Kinnikinick prof.

He went through the rest of his orgy as voluptuously as he could; powdered and pink and brushed and polished, he tipped spaciously, bought a large cigar, and went through the delicious nuisance of breaking the cellophane wrapper.

But as he tried to parade into their sordid side-street-hotel parlor like a Hialeah plunger, he gave way, ran to Peony, muttered, "I went and saw the Piggott woman and we got her for all the money we need, and I'm Vesper's boss now," then whimpered like a small boy. And his fat and pretty wife sobbed joyfully with him.

But young Carrie said, "The assistant manager of this hotel has a pet coon that eats Brussels sprouts."

An hour after this, a self-educated ex-bookkeeper named Vesper, who half an hour ago had been told by a high-spirited old lady what an unsystematic fool he was, walked quietly into his furnished room, in an old house that smelled of generations of death.

It was a small bedroom and, aside from a table, a chair, a bed, a bureau, a sink and a pile of books, mostly lives of the saints, there was not much in it but an old photograph of a lovely girl, a bundle of letters and a full bottle of strong sleeping tablets.

Vesper sat for some time on the bed, staring at the

wall where two evil blotches made the design of a gallows. He rose, looked at the photograph of the girl, took the bundle of her letters, and read them all. He carefully retied them. He hesitated for a while. Then he drew a half glass of water at the sink, and one by one he dropped the fifty sleeping tablets into it.

"It will be bitter," he said, aloud but without perceptible emotion.

He lay on the bed, the drugged glass at hand on the straight chair.

His head, on the pillow, was turned toward the girl's photograph. He looked at it for a long time.

"All right, Mary," he said aloud.

He rose hastily, threw the contents of the charged glass into the sink, and fell again upon the bed. He was sobbing, not as Peony had sobbed, but dryly and painfully and alone.

"I wish now I'd drunk it. It's the anti-climax that's so clownishly horrible," he choked. "But this too, O Lord, shall pass away. Grant me strength even to be ridiculous, for Thy sake. Amen."

All that evening, all that night, unfed but empty of hunger, he slept in spasms. In the morning he went to the Every Man a Priest Fraternity office and told Dr. Planish—after that worthy had got through his recitative of booming and manly and cordial lies—that he was ready to take orders. Perhaps he was one who could not work without orders. To himself he said that he had hoped it would be God who would give the orders, but perhaps

Brother Planish could hear them better and interpret them for him. . . . Not in our time, O Lord.

Within a week he was trotting out on office errands. Dr. Planish was not often impatient with his absent-minded pokiness—not very impatient—not very often.

From that time on, Carlyle Vesper was errand boy or typist or emergency accountant in one tender-hearted organization after another until he died. . . . Once, at Christmas, he got a ten-dollar bonus.

25

Dr. Gideon Planish was a man not slothful, not tardy, but forever going about his master's business—Peony being his master.

The office routine at the Every Man a Priest Fraternity was almost too easy for him. As automatically as a spider spits out thread, he wrote the suitable "literature," and it was sent to the old Eskimo Culture list of prospects, explaining that in this Desperate Crisis, unless they ran, not walked, to their desks and instantly made out checks to the Every Man Fraternity, it was doubtful if Christianity would last till mid-August.

He did not fret over the returns, for Mrs. Piggott and Miss Tundra were generous—so far. To his expert and cynical eye it was certain not only that some day these ladies would go gunning for something newer and sexier, for Communism or Anti-Communism or Glands or Vitamins or Surrealism, but that in his next incarnation as a messiah, he would have to take a drop from his present salary of six thousand to forty-five or six hundred.

But as he said merrily to his wife, "It's a swell racket while it lasts—and of course, baby, I don't mean 'racket' in any invidious sense—in fact, I'm fully conscious of my privilege in being able to pour new wine into a church that has become stultified by formalism and by the very grandeur of its imposing——"

"There's a swell movie at the Tetrarch-Plaza," said Peony.

He showed his industry and social value by writing and sending out free to interested friends a pamphlet on the need of introducing modern science and economic distribution into religion. The only time Carlyle Vesper made any trouble was when, after reading Dr. Planish's masterpiece, "More Horse-Power in the Chancel," he complained, "But, Brother, it seems to me that instead of breaking away from the church machine, you're trying to turn the professional preachers into sales engineers. Of course I'm not a man of much book education——"

"No, Carlyle; if you will pardon me, you're *not!*" Dr. Planish was as genial as a hangman. "Can't you see that just now, with an upset world, it isn't the time to start these revolutionary experiments that will disturb people's sense of confidence and alienate a lot of the best and most responsive top men? No, no. You really must trust the wider judgment and sharper sense of spiritual technique that I have acquired over so many years."

"I see. Well, excuse me, Brother. You told me to take some copy to the printer."

Vesper's peasant habit of calling him "Brother" was Dr. Planish's only mosquito on this outing.

Every national organization is afflicted by crank letters

and fanatic callers, but nowhere had they been such pests as at the Every Man a Priest Fraternity.

Nine-page mimeographed documents with shaky additions in pen, promising the solution of international enmity by using wooden money, or by having the world controlled by a board composed of the Pope, Josef Stalin and the author of the suggestion, who would work cheap. Pathetic letters from old ladies about ancestral first editions of Robert J. Ingersoll, which they were now forced to part with. Brusque letters from businessmen beginning, "What do you guys think you're up to?" Vasty telegrams from young preachers who would be very appreciative of ten thousand dollars, to be sent by return wire, with which they could go to Edinburgh and study. Callers with information about the Occult Inner Secrets of Subconscious All-Power as Revealed to a Scotch Geologist and Poet in an Ancient and Hidden Monastery in Tibet. The unemployed musician who came in and wept about his wife, and wouldn't quit weeping and go away for less than a dollar, cash.

At last Dr. Planish saw a way of making Vesper really earn his thirty-five a week. He turned all the crank letters and irritating callers over to Vesper, and he himself was left free to hold meetings in Miss Ramona Tundra's suite in the Ritz Towers, and to get better acquainted with "Deacon" Wheyfish.

The Hon. Ernest Wheyfish, ex-congressman, author of *Make Them Pay While They Pray*, was not a nice man, but he was an authority on Giving to Philanthropies, and an inspired diagnostician of Prospects. Let him take an ordinary sucker list and he could, by innate genius, by an inner and spiritual nose, smell out the fact that this name was useless, but that other marked a man who could be encouraged to double his annual contribution.

He stood four-square on the principle that, far from harvesting only the rich and middle class, we ought to look on the glorious majority of the poor as a philanthropic field yet unplowed, but so fertile that the pioneer fundraiser could only lift up his eyes in thanksgiving.

He peeped into every new organization to promote religion—and there were perhaps six new ones a week in New York City—because these bush-leaguers might have some new ideas, and new philanthrobbers to tap. Sometimes it was even worth while combining with them, and later dropping their original founders out of the window while keeping their typewriters, wastebaskets, pretty stenographers and lists of supporters.

Deacon Wheyfish had originally been proprietor of an organization called the National Christian Excelsior Crusade, which, even more piously than the Cizkon, promulgated the principle that if you can get your workers to attend prayer-meeting and to buy their own homes, on time, then you have them where you want them. But he had now divided this sacred assembly into two bodies: The Family Prayer Crusade, managed by Constantine Kelly, that unreconstructed Brooklyn Irishman who said he was a Baptist and in fact crossed himself every time he saw a Rockefeller; and the mammoth Blessed to Give

Brotherhood, of which the Deacon was president, executive secretary and, decidedly, the treasurer.

The Blessed to Give was the department store of philanthropic enterprises. It was interested in helping out fifty different charities. Often it worked through apparently rival associations, and it announced, "Whenever we see that somebody can do any given job better than we can, we do not hesitate to pass any contribution right on to them, with no charge for routing or bookkeeping."

In his first week at the Every Man Fraternity, Dr. Planish received an unsolicited check for five dollars from the Blessed to Give, with an explanation from Deacon Wheyfish that in return he wanted nothing but a kind smile— and some names of interesting new contributors.

There were scurrilous and uncharitable enemies who charged that quite a little of the money stuck to the Blessed to Give mail-chute in passing on, but the Deacon in answer published a budget showing that he, as the officers, couldn't have kept more than $942.00 a year out of contributions of $200,000.

Deacon the Honorable Wheyfish looked as a grasshopper would look if it had a rough complexion and wore a Biblical white tie and clocked blue socks.

There were friends of the Deacon who said that he should have gone on and become one of the professional money-raisers who do not spoil their pure art by fussing over where the money goes, but are engaged to put on campaigns for a college, a church or a Christian mission to China.

The best of the money-raisers will not waste time on

any objective under a hundred thousand dollars; they much prefer a million; and they get, as their fee, an amount which equals anywhere from five per cent to ninety-five per cent of the total blessed treasure. They represent such noble causes that they can command cabinet officers to preside at dinners, and permit bishops to introduce strip-teasers at spectacles attracting 25,000 persons at five dollars each. They efficiently make use of the "boiler-room," in which caramel-voiced young women sit all day long, telephoning to hundreds of strangers, "This is Judge Wallaby's secretary, and His Honor would like you to buy four ten-dollar tickets to the Fiduciaries' Fund Festival. If you'll have the check ready, I'll send right over for it." (Judge Wallaby? Is he that demon of the traffic court? You buy the tickets.)

Deacon Wheyfish might actually have become one of these higher money-raisers, even though most of them were Eastern university men with Phi Beta Kappa keys, who could placidly entertain their captives at the Brahmin Club; but he jeered that he'd rather run his own show, and not have to kiss the feet of a lot of old male hags. He remained supreme in his smaller world, revered even if he wasn't liked by his fellow organizators, and when he invited Dr. Planish to a lunch of executives and publicity counsels, the Doctor was delighted to go.

There were only a dozen men and four women at the luncheon, a simple repast of inedible food in a private room over an Italian restaurant, but those sixteen people had the strength of sixty in influencing the course of good works. Dr. Planish was there, and Chris Stern, *of course*, and Professor Goetz Buchwald, Commander Orris Gall of the Zero-Hour American National Committee for the Organization of Global Co-operation. Rabbi Lichtenselig, Professor Campion of the Children's Re-education Program, and rather unexpectedly, since he was a gay and charming man, the most intelligent in the room, Dr. Nahum Lloyd, graduate of Howard University and secretary of the Cultural League for the Colored Races.

Dr. Planish approved much less of Dr. Lloyd than of the distinguished Dr. Elmer Gantry, who was torridly also present. Dr. Gantry was pastor of the Spiritual Home Methodist Tabernacle on Morningside Heights, but he was better known as a radio pastor, with his weekly Torch Sermons and Swing Sermons and Blue Sermons and Vitamin Sermons, in which, with a splendid combination of modern slang and long hard words, he tried to show the younger generation that God is in the automobile just as much as He was in the oldtime hay-ride. Quite a number of lady society reporters and several male editorial writers had noted that "There is no better living exponent of a streamlined gospel than Dr. Gantry." But he did not appear at today's luncheon as a latter-day Henry Ward Beecher, but as the directive secretary of the Society for the Rehabilitation of Erring Young Women.

Deacon Wheyfish arose and spoke to them, earnestly:

"Our friend Dr. Gideon Planish, who has had such a rich and varied experience in the nation's capital, but who tells me that he is practically a stranger in New York, and whom we are glad to welcome to organizational circles here, is, as you can see, a sterling character, but I'm afraid he's a bit of a naughty fellow, too, because, with that sparkling wit of his, he refers to the gentry of our profession as 'organizators'.

"But what I think he is getting at is that all of us ought to have a much more hardboiled professional attitude, instead of the sentimental approach, and, say, he's dead-right—you bet he is. What we need today is to perceive that raising money, raising lots of money, not for one single second stopping in raising all the money we possibly can and then going beyond that and doing the impossible in money-raising—this is not, as some old-fashioned sentimentalists like to think, just a minor detail and bother in organizational work, but our first big duty, our very biggest one, first, last and all the time.

"We all talk too much about the supposed *purposes* of our organizations: how we feed so and so many children or help the victims of T.B. That work is glorious, that is near divine, and yet I'm going to venture a statement so radical that it will probably land me right in Moscow with the other reds, for I want to tell you right here and now that our primary mission isn't to *spend* the money we collect, but to train people, all the people, to give, to give generously, to keep on giving not only to accomplish charitable ends, but to expand their own miserable, narrow peanut souls by the divine *habit* of giving.

"If they come to me and squeal and carry on and say that if they give as I want 'em to, it's going to cramp their family lives and keep their children from having a lot of fool extras like music and endanger their savings accounts and so on and so forth, then I don't tell 'em I'm sorry—not me, not one bit of it. No, sir! I say, 'That's fine, Brother! Now you're learning to give in Jesus's way—to give till it hurts—yes, and hurts your family as well as yourself. That's fine,' I say. You bet!

"And when a lot of cranks and critics and mean-souled little carpers and cussers come around and say, 'Deacon, where's your financial report—where's your certified proof that you haven't wasted any money?'—why, then, I feel like saying to 'em, 'Damn it'—yessir, I get so mad I could curse—I feel like saying, 'Damn it, how do you cold-hearted and cold-faced carpers and critics know but what maybe the best training to expand the soul of man is to dig down for money that somebody *will* waste!' . . . Not, you understand, that we ever do waste one cent or even get any real salaries at the Blessed to Give Brotherhood, and our books are audited by the great firm of French, Saffron and Gubbey, C.P.A.'s, you understand, and show that every penny contributed to us, except for the items of overhead, postage, printing and rent, goes directly to some great body dealing with domestic or foreign relief, every last penny! You bet!

"As many of you know, philanthropy, in hard dollars and cents, already ranks eighth among the major industries of America. But it ought to rank first. What can a man purchase in the way of a motor car, a bathtub or a radio that will afford him such spiritual benefit, or for that matter such keen pride and pleasure and social prestige, as the knowledge that he is permitting the better organization executives the means and the leisure to go around doing good, and the reputation of being the best giver in his whole neighborhood? We may have to hypnotize him a little to make him realize that, but how satisfied he will be when he does! You bet!

"The philanthropic industry has been steadily increasing, but not because of any improving generosity or imagination among the great body of givers—not on your life—the sluggards—bless 'em! It's only because they've been scientifically coaxed to give—scientifically, mind you. The raising of funds must be a separate calling, with an infallible technique. And yet some of you, my friends, tend to forget this, and go around daydreaming about what good you'd do if you only had the cash, instead of tackling it the scientific way; first raising the cash, and *then* seeing if there's some good you can do with it. You all know, or ought to, that far beyond the fancy reasons that we spring in public addresses—like native virtue and friendliness and the responsibilities we're supposed to feel toward one another in a democracy—far beyond these are the two *real* factors: improved methods of obtaining gifts on our part, like using the radio and movie stars; and then, when we get folks into it, making them keep up the habit of giving.

"That's our job. Don't reason with folks—get them into the *habit* of filling out pledge cards just as regularly as they brush their teeth, and make 'em feel guilty as hell if they fail to do either one! You bet!

"You know that it's been determined that the habit of giving is on three stages. Highest of them is the passionate love of God—though I'm sorry to say that in the budget, the gifts from this class don't add up very big—there's too few of 'em. Then there's the class that gives from a kind of restless feeling that they ought to be useful. Lowest, but maybe most important of all to unprejudiced thinkers like ourselves, is the class that is pushed by fear, vanity and self-interest: the fellows that are afraid of revolution, the silly woman that gives us maybe one-tenth of what she spends on war-paint, *maybe,* so that she'll get praised as generous, and be invited on important committees.

"Now there we have the whole darn thing worked out, in perhaps the most profound psychological analysis since Freud invented birth-control, and yet what do we do? We go on circularizing and making personal appeals and getting our front, the top men, to telephone to all three of these classes of donors on exactly the same grounds, instead of laying our plans to attack each one separate, and with a different appeal. That's why philanthropy is only the eighth industry, that's why so many dollars go to the automobile tycoons that properly belong in our coffers, and it's all our fault.

"But what really gets my goat is the highly undemocratic belief that the mass of the people are so miserably shiftless and ornery that they don't even want to join their betters in giving. I tell you, I come from the commonest kind of common people, and I resent the imputation against the morale of this great class, and the unprofessional incompetence that fails to see that here is not a negligible but the very most important source of fundraising.

"It's the deepest and richest mine in the country, and yet it hasn't hardly been prospected. Don't the Scriptures say, 'As a man thinketh, so he is'? Well, if you'll get your *thinking* right, and on a higher plane, you'll realize that there's almost a hundred and thirty million people in this far-flung land, and that, at a mere dollar apiece, means one—hundred—and—thirty—million gold simoleons, and I guess that's worth the attention of even a highbrow like Dr. Planish or Professor Buchwald!

"Yes, sir, the fundamental principle of the art and profession of increasing the universal giving of money is that mighty few people do give much unless they're *asked* to give. And it's up to us, particularly in these necessitous days when the war clouds seem to be rolling up over Europe, to up and gird our loins and ask—and demand— and insist—that those hundred and thirty millions come through for the titanic moral and patriotic plans that we have so competently laid out, but in which we are checked for the lack of just a few pitiful millions of dollars. Now is the time! Don't forget that the menace of war, properly presented, will scare into giving even those people, rich or poor, who have been the most obdurate to our pitiful appeals for help.

"Come on, gentlemen and ladies, get out from under that bushel and, on behalf of the suffering and ignorant multitude, hit that line of potential lower-bracket contributors, and hit it hard! You bet your life!"

Dr. Planish was inspired by this Patrick Henry of philanthropy, and inspired further by attending a two-day Round Table Conference conducted by Commander Orris Gall, which presented a series of papers on geopolitics, the certainty that Hitler would some day go to war, the certainty that he wouldn't, and the use of graphs. It was like the contents of a very earnest and well-bred magazine that was, during the incarceration of the editorial staff, being conducted by several candidates for the Ph.D. degree.

Out of all this Dr. Planish was beginning to weave a plan. He would merge dozens of organizations—Whey-fish's, Kelly's, Gall's, Kitto's, Stern's—into one, and let these men in as vice-presidents, but he would be the supreme head, though at first he might work under Colonel Charles B. Marduc, the master as he was the publicizer of American speed and idealism. The time for his central powerhouse might not come for another year or two, but now he was ready to meet and really talk to the Colonel. His ambition was settled; his home was settled.

In Greenwich Village, on Charles Street, they had found an oldish house which pleased the Doctor by its cheapness, Peony by its tall drawing-room windows, Carrie by having a garden simply roaring with cats.

The gold and scarlet Chinese Chippendale cabinet, the blue Chinese rug, the jade Chinese lamp, the birch radio cabinet, and the portable bar could all rest now, happier than they had ever been, in the long drawing-room with its marble fireplace. There were four master bedrooms, which gave young Carrie a room of her own, and gave Dr. Planish a study, into which he fondly dragged the old splintered desk he had used as a college instructor.

They had a home now, and they were only a step or two from glory.

26

RICH OLD MRS. PIGGOTT had become bored with Every Man being a priest, and for two years now Dr. Planish had been with the Blessed to Give Brotherhood. His salary there had been reasonably adjusted at $4,800 a year.

He didn't very much like his commander, Deacon Ernest Wheyfish, to whom Peony referred as "Soapy Ernie," but with him the Doctor had taken profound graduate work in the professions of fund-raising and organization-executivity. He had learned that, against all the theories of the Reverend Dr. Christian Stern, the bounteous blessings of publicity had no value in collecting the temple money unless they were sharply followed up by solicitation.

As Deacon Wheyfish often said, "Don't wait for the widow to bring in her mite. Get right after her at the wash-tub."

This was not so merrily metaphorical as it sounded. The Deacon specialized on bequests from wealthy widows and, if he did not think the bequest was coming, in a dignified cat-burglar way he went right in to the death-bed and demanded it. . . . Did Mrs. Jones go off to Heaven without leaving a lot to the Brotherhood in her will, would she not look down o'er the golden bar and realize that solely as a result of her own carelessness there were evil and hunger in the world? And there was no excuse for her. Honorable Wheyfish had regular printed Forms of Bequest prepared for her use.

He once took Dr. Planish along when he prayed with an aged and affluent woman who, the Deacon calculated, was good for about one more week—just time to make a codicil to her will.

Embarrassed, a little itchy, Dr. Planish stood back in a corner of the stifling rich room while Deacon Wheyfish happily banged right down on his knees beside the bed, held the old woman's dry skeleton hand, and whooped, "O Lord God, Thou knowest that our sister here has been a good woman. It is none of our business to inquire to what charities she has bequeathed such a share of her earthly store as Thou, who didst say 'Give all thou hast to the poor' would approve of, but Thou knowest that her saintly heart and searching mind will have picked out and appointed for the dispensation of that gift some person or organization who will not take anything for himself, and with the expert knowledge to disburse it where it will do the most good."

When he had finished the prayer, the old lady asked timidly, "Could you tell me what is the surest way of making sure that my bequests will really accomplish what I want them to?"

"Well, I did have a date with an archbishop, but I am always at the service of suffering humanity," granted the Deacon, briskly drawing a chair up to the bed and taking out of his pocket Blessed to Give Folder #8A3—the engraved one.

Dr. Planish was just a little sick.

He reflected, "It's great technique, and I certainly don't look down on it, but I do wish I could be in some organization where the money rolled in just as fast but the aims were more refined."

Ernest Wheyfish was the first organizator to go right after the large corporations, which, to save their corporate souls and keep down income taxes, were now sending checks to philanthropies. As he himself gaily said, "No one else put so much punch into selling the fat boys on the idea that we who tote the grievous load of raising funds should be taken just as seriously in the financial line as any other merchant." So it came to pass that a corporation which employed two chemists, three industrial engineers, a Burmese explorer, an interpreter, and a press agent to reduce the cost of cable $00.0001 per yard, handed over large checks to Deacon Wheyfish for distribution as he pleased—merely with the prayer that this offering to the tribal priesthood might, by some pious magic, propitiate the dark diabolic powers of the New Deal and the Congress.

Wheyfish, a little later, was one of the first to note that when the Government permitted a fifteen per cent deduction from income taxes for charities, this really didn't mean that the tax-payer *could* give away fifteen per cent, but that he *had* to give it, and that Ernest Wheyfish was practically the Government official put there to receive it. His new "literature," prepared by Dr. Planish, was starred and shining with references to "15%—be generous without its costing anything," and hinted that if you didn't do this, the Government would merely take it in taxes anyway, and waste it on a lot of worthless loafers, so that a gift to Wheyfish was practically a social duty.

"Sometimes I wonder if I ought to write that stuff. It seems almost against true charitableness," Dr. Planish fretted to Peony.

"You're always so conscientious," she admired.

"I know what I *could* do—make Vesper write that junk for me."

"But would he? He's such a sanctimonious crank."

"He'll damn well do what I tell him to, after the loyalty I've shown him—almost risking my own job, getting the Deacon to take him over from the Every Man at thirty a week. Oh, yes, I think Mr. Saintly J. Vesper is beginning to realize that in *this* world, one should be sanctified in purpose but practical in methods. Well, Mrs. Planish, and what would you say to a bottle of Rhine wine?"

"Why, I think I would say, 'Thank you very much, Professor Planish, you sweet, saintly, and sanctified honeybee!'"

Wheyfish and Planish had the triumph of adding to their national board of directors no less a derivative power than Major Harold Homeward, the son-in-law of Colonel Charles B. Marduc and legal husband of Marduc's daughter, who was known to all Intellectuals as "Talking Winifred."

Peony demanded of the Doctor, "I hear this Major Homeward that you've got hold of is a regular polo-hound. You got to buy him for me. You meet all these big-money boys, but what about me?"

"Dearie, some day you'll be really meeting Colonel Marduc himself, right at his own home, maybe, if you'll be patient and give me time."

"Yes, that'd be wonderful, and I do believe you might pull it off."

"I'm not going to work for Soapy Ernie in that factory forever. I want an organization of my own."

"That's the dope," said Mrs. Planish.

"Somehow," said Dr. Planish, "I have a hunch about Marduc."

Colonel Charles B. Marduc was a military man as well as an advertising agent and an owner of magazines. He had been a fighting major in World War I, then a colonel in the New York National Guard. In 1937, he was fifty-five, and a fine, upstanding, silver-and-cherry buck, a biggish man, though with his ambitiousness you would have expected to find him a jittery terrier who went around barking "Notice me!"

He admired Napoleon and General Franco of Spain. Out of liquor, he talked about being liberal; but in it, he talked about being a Strong Man.

He was the legitimate son of an Upper New York State lawyer who became richly interested in manufacturing carpets and became a judge; he was graduated from Harvard, with no small fame for wenching and for remembering dates in history; he was a reporter, and then the owner of several small-town newspapers before he discovered the sociological principle, later worked out by professors in the Harvard School of Business Administration, that Advertising is a valuable economic factor because it is the cheapest way of selling goods, particularly if the goods are worthless. Thus it was really along the line of Social Service that his larger career began.

He was the president of Marduc, Syco & Sagg—formerly Marduc & Syco—who had been pioneers, more like military strategists, really, in both radio advertising and scientific research into retail markets—a Service given strictly free to customers. They had been the first to broadcast the song of the English skylark—sponsors, the King David Matzos Makers; and the first to let the radio world (far-flung) hear the cry of a just-born baby, in promotion of Vitaminized Vermont Flapjack Flour.

But the Colonel remained very Harvard through all of it, and at every annual football game, his Assyrian eyebrows came down on the quaking hosts of Bowdoin.

He was a publisher as well as an advertising man, and the chief owner of the *Zinc Trades Monitor*, the *Housewife's Monthly Budget*, the *Installment Plan Dealers' Trade Tips*, and of that popular journal *Lowdown*, which presented the confessions of highly seduced young women, as written by aged male hacks and illustrated with photographs of the most virtuous models in Manhattan.

He was also a vestryman of St. Cunegonde's Protestant

Episcopal Church, and for years he had longed and plotted to become President of the United States.

Illicit strangers were always running about with rumors that he wanted to be President, so naturally he denied the rumors with irritation: "These fellows apparently know more about my purposes than I do myself! Very kind of 'em to volunteer to represent me! But seriously, I've already got more than I can do, trying to grease the wheels of commerce. I tend strictly to my own business."

He did, too, and also to the business of quite a number of other people.

He honestly felt that he had to become President, to save the country from sliding down through New Deal Socialism into anarchy. Once, at lunch, he firmly told his brilliant daughter, Winifred Marduc Homeward, "Without any special pleasure in it, I can see that I have the best mind in the country." She, the dear loyal soul, agreed with him, and told the news to ever so many people.

There was only one thing that kept him from springing into a flaming sea of publicity, of dinners and tours and photographs and interviews, and thus swimming to the Presidency and saving democracy for the common people. That was the fact that he couldn't endure the touch of the common people. He felt that they were all fools and all noisy and all smelly. It had kept him out of any race for the State Legislature, the national Congress.

He had a large fame, but it was subterranean. Everyone in the world of printing and cafés knew of him and of his desire to sacrifice himself as President; everyone in the organizational world thought of him as young lovers think of Helen. All executive secretaries tried to get him to "write a little piece—just something off-hand that you can dictate to your secretary in five minutes—for our monthly bulletin." They coaxed him to preside at dinners and to stand at the microphone and say that agriculture is fine and brushing the teeth is fine, but most inspiring of all is the money-raising campaign of the Amalgamated Pan-national Interdenominational Committee for Study of and Union between the Kremlin and the Methodist Board of Public Morals.

One invitation out of one hundred Colonel Marduc accepted—preferably a dinner attended by the President's wife, by the University of Michigan football coach or by Professor Einstein. But he escaped the photographs and the eye-searing flashlights in the anteroom before the dinners, the handshaking and the "I don't know whether you'll remember me but I met you" afterward, by actually eating comfortably at home or at the club, not showing up at the dinner till nine-fifteen, and leaving always as soon as he had done his act.

Among the thousands of professional advertising men in America, only a few hundred were popularly known as literary, emotional and visionary; only six as positively scientific; and of this latter class, Colonel Marduc was the leader.

He made round-voiced speeches before church conventions, college assemblies and sociological conferences, proving that modern advertising was the cheapest way of selling goods, that it was a gallery of cooing prose and lifting pictures, and that it, single-handed, had provided what he called "Mr. Average American" with the silver-plated automatic electric toaster, the recorded works of Friml and Johann Sebastian Bach, the juke-boxes, two-ton trucks, two-tone summer shoes, tooth-paste which eliminated all dentists, radios which enabled the listener to hear the same jazz from Schenectady and then from Siam, mouth-wash that was equally useful for sweetening the breath, removing dandruff and as a cocktail in Prohibition territory, and all the other miracles that had made Mr. Average American the happiest and prettiest human being that had ever existed.

These facts Colonel Marduc proved with graphs, statistics and fury, and he became so esteemed as a man of science that he received two Litt.D. degrees, one M.Sc., four LL.D.'s, one L.H.D., and decorations from Germany, Italy and the D.A.R.

And yet his mistresses always said, sooner or later, that Colonel Marduc was not a man they cared to know.

These ladies were never Anglo-Saxon. The Colonel detested all American and English women, and his playmates were Italian, Greek, Russian-Jewish, French, or Chinese. They sharpened him up, and with them he could laugh—for a few weeks. His regular system for getting rid of them, as precise and tested as one of his firm's marketing reports, always started with a sudden and justifiable quarrel, and rarely cost him much money.

His wife must still have been alive in 1937, but nobody could quite remember. She was important only as having contributed to the dynasty the Colonel's daughter, Winifred, and she had been broken-hearted and sweetly mute for so long now that nobody noticed it any more.

But Winifred, Winifred Marduc Homeward, that was something else; that was a woman, *the* woman, the American woman careerist, and it is a reasonable bet that in 1955 she will be dictator of the United States and China.

Winifred Homeward the Talking Woman.

She was an automatic, self-starting talker. Any throng of more than two persons constituted a lecture audience for her, and at sight of them she mounted an imaginary platform, pushed aside an imaginary glass of ice water, and started a fervent address full of imaginary information about Conditions and Situations that lasted till the audience had sneaked out—or a little longer.

She was something new in the history of women, and whether she stemmed from Queen Catherine, Florence Nightingale, Lucrezia Borgia, Frances Willard, Victoria Woodhull, Nancy Astor, Carrie Nation or Aimée Semple McPherson, the holy woman of Los Angeles, has not been determined.

Winifred was as handsome as a horse, a portly young presence with a voice that smothered you under a blanket of molasses and brimstone. She was just under thirty in 1937, but she had the wisdom of Astarte and the punch of Joe Louis, and her eyelids were a little weary.

For a couple of years now she had emulated her father in having a mistress, who in her case was her legal husband, Major Harold Homeward, who had got his title by being a first lieutenant in the paymaster corps in

World War I. He was a handsome, high-colored man, a dancing man but a surprisingly good accountant, with an eye for interesting writing, and useful about the Marduc magazines. Even when he felt merely dutiful about it, he made love warmly, and Winifred used to come back from the office happily to the little man in the home.

They had no children.

Her one humility was toward her father, and it may have been due more to her demands than to his own that he was so often considered, in editorial offices and bars, as a possible President, who would look handsome at that starry and eagle-pinioned desk while Winifred merely ran the country.

She said, privately and publicly—though with her, the two states weren't always to be distinguished—that her father had taught her how to think incisively and boldly, how to write simply and distinctively, and how, at all embarrassing moments of being caught mentally naked, to duck into the refuge of that fine old word "Honor." With the Colonel himself, Honor was so developed that he wouldn't permit Marduc, Syco & Sagg to handle any patent medicine, liquor or contraceptive advertisements, but cared for them through a separate firm with which his name wasn't even connected.

When Winifred and the Colonel were together, she talked so much about his virtues that he had no chance to talk about them himself.

In all her dissertations occurred the face-saving phrases: "Oh, just a second. There's one other thing I wanted to bring up. I do hope I'm not talking too much tonight. Just let me speak of this, and then I'll shut up."

She wouldn't, though. Winifred Homeward the Talking Woman.

Besides being on the boards of twenty-seven different welfare organizations, serving as a Republican Committeewoman, and speaking publicly on an average of three times a week on all the Causes in which she believed—and they included every Cause that any active women's-college graduate possibly could believe in, during the years 1930–1950—Winifred Marduc Homeward was the editor of that feminist and liberal weekly *Attention!*, of which her father was the actual owner—or donor—and her husband the titular publisher.

The complicated and slightly hysterical ideology of *Attention!* may be formulated as a belief that the offices of President, editor of the New York *Herald-Times*, head of a united University of Columbia and California, and the official dismisser of all distasteful conclusions of the Gallup Poll, should be combined and held by a person whose description resembled that of Winifred Homeward.

Attention! had once been quoted in a sermon by the woman pastor of a Spiritualist Church in Oakland, California.

One other person besides the pastor quoted it, and that was Winifred, often and earnestly. It lacked nothing but circulation and the possibility of anyone's ever reading through an entire paragraph.

It was referred to—when it *was* referred to—as a feminist publication, but it is not certain that Mrs. Homeward was a "feminist," it was not certain that she liked women very much. She was more likely to be eloquent about males who praised her than about females who didn't, and far more likely to be seen with them. And though *Attention!* had been published, and Colonel Marduc had been highly public, during the year 1936, when Franco's revolution began in Spain and Zinovieff and Kameneff had been shot in Russia, neither Winifred nor the Colonel had taken a more belligerent stand on these matters than to say, with affecting earnestness, "One must not come to hasty conclusions on affairs so complicated and so uncandidly reported."

That was the reigning family—Colonel Marduc and Winifred and their illegitimate offspring, Major Homeward—to whose golden company the Planishes had long aspired.

Major Homeward appeared at a meeting of the directors of the Blessed to Give Brotherhood, handsome, graceful, his mustache like a lithe new-born thing, and his eye moist but lively. Ernest Wheyfish recognized him as royalty, but it was Dr. Planish who thought of whispering, "Pretty dull. Let's sneak out and have a quick one." The Major's eyes rounded like those of a cat beholding an injudicious robin; he seized the Doctor's arm, and they crept out behind Wheyfish's nervous eloquence.

They drank till seven. Dr. Planish privily telephoned to Peony, and brought a friendly Major home to dinner.

Now Peony was plump but biological. She had never stepped off Main Street, but her eyes could seduce even a traffic policeman, and to the Major she said, "This is so nice!" as competently as a woman press agent or an actress in her dressing-room. By ten o'clock the Major and the Doctor and Peony were such a trio of buddies that they telephoned, long-distance, to George Riot, and insisted on his flying down and joining them. (He didn't.) Before the Major was got into a complete state of liquid happiness, however, Dr. Planish had planted the seed of a Message:

"I know Colonel Marduc is a figurehead on a lot of organizations, but he never really has anything to do with 'em—lets 'em use his name and sends 'em a small check, but he never knows what they're up to. Well, if he really wants to be President of the United States——"

"He doesn't—he doesn't at all. I don't know how that rumor started," stated the Colonel's very own son-in-law. "He feels that he's just a plain seismograph of public opinion. He has no political ambitions."

"Well then, Secretary of State or Ambassador to England."

"Maybe he might consider those."

"He doesn't realize how an uplift organization that he really worked closely with could hook his name up with all these idealistic movements that get the votes. If he'd pay some attention, and maybe some cash, to a crack executive——"

"No, no, no! Thanks, Peony—that's plenty—whoa—that's better," observed the Major. "No, I'm afraid the Colonel wouldn't be interested in your Blessed to Give bunch. He thinks that having me there on the board as his stooge is enough."

[324]

"*That?* Oh, that damn racket! Of course not. I mean a more general idealistic association, more spiels about freedom and democracy. I'd like to talk to him, some time."

The Doctor did not belabor his message further, and not till after many more drinks did he probe the Major about the Colonel's mysterious relationship to Governor Thomas Blizzard.

(Peony was thinking how very pleasant and urbane and worth striving for this was: a parley in which the titles of Colonel and Major and Governor and Senator and Doctor and Professor and Haig & Haig were thrown about like beans.)

Tom Blizzard was one of the twenty men who, in 1937, had a chance to be Democratic nominee for President in 1944, possibly even in 1940.

In his own Midwestern State, he had been Speaker of the House and for two terms Governor, and the credulous readers of newspaper columns still believed that he spent nine-tenths of his time out in the little factory town of Waskeegan, and one-tenth in New York and Washington. It was actually the other way around. He kept up his millionaire manufacture of farm implements in Waskeegan, but most of the time he lived at his humble twelve-room log cabin on Park Avenue, in New York, and he knew every reporter, Communist editor, prize fighter, professor of economics and night-club bartender in town.

He was a large untidy man with a rolling and affable walk, a fetching youthful smile, and a core of hard shrewdness.

It was commonly reported that Governor Blizzard and Colonel Marduc had a political understanding, but which was to support which was not explained, nor, tonight, did Major Homeward explain it. Perhaps, concluded the Doctor, he didn't know.

The party moved into the kitchen, as all really intimate parties must.

That kitchen on Charles Street had become a very fine kitchen. Peony had concentrated on the once drab and wormy room and made it a splendor of stenciled walls, cupboards with little red oilcloth frills and unbreakable plastic dishes of red and green. They sat about the green-topped kitchen table, drinking highballs, and it was the joy of Major Homeward, son of the smartest tailor in West Virginia, as it was of the Midwestern Planishes, to express their communal affection in the tender strains of "Mandy, Mandy, sweet as the sugar cane," an American folk-song from the Deep South via Tin-Pan Alley.

During this recital, Carrie Planish, returning from some unexplained engagement, looked into the kitchen and sniffily withdrew.

Peony darted out after her, with "Come in and meet Major Homeward. Such a fine man, and important socially."

"He looks to me like an old silly," murmured Carrie.

"Old? He's not as old as your father!"

"Well?"

"Carrie!"

"Honestly, Mother, I don't want to be disagreeable, but he seems like an old tent-show actor."

"He's one of the very cleverest and most influential men in the whole world of welfare-promotion!"

"Honestly, Mother, I'm sorry, but I don't think I like influential people or welfare *or* promotion. I like sleeping better. Good night."

Peony stood bitterly in the hall. What had come over this new generation? She wasn't like that when *she* was sixteen! Why, she'd have been all eager and flattered if *her* mother had invited her in to help impress an important guest! But Carrie——

Insisting on leaving a good private school, where she met the daughters of prominent people, for that horrible, big, overgrown public school, all full of Micks and Jews and Wops! And so impertinent! When Peony had sighed, "But, baby, after your father and I have scraped and saved to send you to a fashionable school like Miss Clink's," up and answering so pertly, "Then you ought to be glad, Mother; you'll save money by my going to high school!" Trying to trap her own mother by saying things like that! And talking about biology and mechanical drawing and Ernest Hemingway and James Farrell and a lot of nonsense like that! And pretending to be so modest, and yet wearing those tight sweaters that showed everything——

Peony summed it all up, "I just can't make out these jazz babies. You can't get 'em to see the domestic point of view!" and she hastily rolled back into the kitchen and had a highball.

When, later, it seemed better for Dr. Planish to get the Major into a taxicab and accompany him safely as far as the Winifred Marduc Homeward residence on East 68th Street, Peony went along, and they sang quite a little more in the taxicab, and when the Major held her hand, she was proud to have such interest taken in her by one of those rare men who are liaison officers between rich society and the working intelligentsia—that combination that makes New York so fascinating and so very, very different from Kinnikinick, Iowa.

One of the most important activities of any liberal educational organization is an activity called Research.

Say, Research into the monkeyshines of the ex-Reverend Ezekiel Bittery.

You read forty or fifty complete biographies of him in the newspapers and then, under the name of your secretary, you send for Mr. Bittery's own pamphlets and read everything all over again. Then you craftily send out spies, with funny hats and their coat-collars turned up, to listen to his public speeches. So, by Research, you discover that Brother Bittery is a flannel-mouthed rabble-rouser who used to be charged not only with stealing the contents of the church poor-box, but of taking the box itself home to keep radishes in, and who at present, if he isn't on the pay-roll of all the Fascists, is a bad collector.

A couple of years later, a Congressional committee will summon a lot of witnesses to Washington and, after a lot of bullying and undercover work, will discover that Mr. Bittery used to be a hell-fire preacher and is now a hell-fire Fascist.

Two years after that, the more leftwing newspapers will send out all the Ph.D.'s among its reporters, and discover that Mr. Bittery used to favor lynching agnostics and now favors lynching socialists.

And during all this time, the Reverend Ezekiel himself will, as publicly as possible, to as many persons as he can persuade to attend his meetings, have admitted, insisted, bellowed, that he has always been a Ku Kluxer and a Fascist, that he has always hated Jews, colleges and good manners, and that the only thing he has ever disliked about Hitler is that he once tried to paint barns instead of leaving the barns the way God made them.

That is Research.

It was familiar to Dr. Planish, and he now tried to turn its fair light upon a more hidden topic: the inner purposes of the Marduc-Blizzard junta. That is to say, he went so far in investigation as to get hold of Hatch Hewitt, the reporter, for a drink, and asked him some questions—an example of Research Method not uncommon among organizators.

"Yeah," said Hatch—a man whom Dr. Planish fuzzily remembered having met some years ago. "Yeah, Tom Blizzard's hat is in the ring for President—any ring. In fact, if a bunch of kids on Eighth Avenue are playing marbles, they better watch their chalk circle pretty carefully, because if they turn their backs on it for ten seconds, they'll find his hat right in the center. He's just as likely to have a love affair with the Lake Erie Professional Hockey Club or the Aroostook Potato Growers'

Association as with the St. John's Sodality for the Study of St. Thomas Aquinas.

"He has the edge on Marduc, who'd like to do the same thing but he's afraid of getting his hat dusty.

"And Winifred Marduc Homeward—oh, it isn't that she's always giving her own version of the Sermon on the Mount, but that she always carries her own portable Mount right with her and sets it up even at a cocktail party. She's the first lady Messiah, and I'm afraid she's going to get the entire Messiah industry in wrong. After her third scream of righteousness whenever she attacks Hitler, Winifred almost makes me tolerate Hitler, and I don't like that. Her only trouble is that she read her Scriptures wrong. She thought they said 'If women learn anything, let them tell their husbands at home. It is a shame for women not to speak in the church.'

"I can't prove it, but I suspect that both her father and Governor Blizzard think that they're using her as a guide to the Presidency, but that she's using them, and when she decides which is the horsiest dark horse, she'll cut the other one's throat. Changed world, my boy. In the old days, you used to look for the *femme* only in love affairs; now, she's the hidden clue in political affairs.

"But what are you doing with these people, Gid? I thought you'd settled down with honest bootleggers like Deacon Wheyfish. Don't tell me you've gone over to the intellectual racket!"

Years of leadership and of oratory enabled Dr. Planish to throw everything into his annihilating retort:

"Honestly—you—make—me—tired!"

A week later, Dr. Planish was invited to accompany Major Homeward on a pilgrimage to the office of Colonel Marduc. (No Generals were involved as yet.)

The throne-room at Marduc, Syco & Sagg's was the masterpiece of Bobbysmith, who advertised himself as "the Gertrude Stein of Interior Designing." It was as plain and dignified as Rockefeller Center, but a little smaller. The only picture was a portrait of the Colonel, in which he resembled a full-blooded camel on a turquoise desert, and it hung against apricot walls, with fluorescent cornice-lighting. The curtains were ripples of champagne-colored silk, and the furniture was of polished white mahogany upholstered with coral leather. The ruddy marble fireplace was set in without a mantel, and by it was a case of books by Proust, Spengler and Zane Grey. On the plaza of the desk was one calla lily and a signed photograph of Lord Beaverbrook.

Colonel Marduc sat at the far end of the room and looked at you flatly as you made entrance, so that you already felt awkward before you had got within twenty feet of him. He had the trick from Mussolini, who had it from the Spanish Inquisition.

The conversation between the Colonel and Dr. Planish fell into that atmosphere of an Oriental court which always clung about the Marducs, even in a stratospheric advertising agency. The Doctor salaamed and said that he was honored; he said that of course the Colonel would never stoop to any political job, but if he desired to, he could be President of the United States by ten tomorrow morning.

He said that he himself was the humblest creature under Allah's beneficent sun, that he loved his present (well-paid) job, and was aboundingly loyal to Wheyfish Pasha, but if either Colonel Marduc or God, preferably the former, decided to start a real organization, one that would take the weak little ideology of Democracy by the hand and guide it tenderly, then he hoped he might be around to give advice. He said that such an organization might, incidentally, get its founder known around as the chief subsidizer of all Justice and Freedom.

And he said that now, as never before, was the time, with the war going on between Japan and China and with Hitler smirking at Czechoslovakia.

"Not going to be any European war!" snarled the Colonel.

"But it's possible."

"If there were, America would never get into it. We'll be so well prepared that we won't have to."

"But even in the matter of preparedness, we ought to have an association that would be the first big one that was keyed to war psychology," argued the Doctor. "If we started out now, and had speakers and hand-outs every week interpreting the news, then we'd get to be considered the final authority, no matter which way the war-cat jumped—win, lose, draw or stay out."

"Who do you think of as associated with us?"

"Well, your daughter, and Milo Samphire, the foreign correspondent——"

"Samphire? That fanatic? No! He's pro-English, and what's worse, he's eloquent, and what's still worse, he's honest. He wouldn't take my—suggestions," the Colonel grumbled.

"Well, we could get Senator Bultitude, and Christian Stern, and Walter Gilroy—he hasn't any ideas, but he has a kind of touching reverence for 'em—and maybe you could coax Governor Blizzard to come in. I wouldn't expect to decide which of the Big Names we'd get. My job is to know the technique of putting over an organization—for anything, or against anything—provided it's on the right side, I mean."

"And which do you regard as the right side?"

"I think that in any controversy, your side would probably be the right side, Colonel."

So he got the laugh that promised him spiritual victory and five thousand a year in salary.

"Are you doing anything for dinner next Thursday—you and your wife? Drop up to my place—eight o'clock, black tie." The Colonel said it casually enough, but to Dr. Planish it was the visitation of the Magi.

It happened that the Doctor had invited Hatch Hewitt and his wife for dinner the coming Thursday, but he wasted no time on anything so petty, particularly as Hatch had picked up a scraggly and unlaudatory wife.

He went home to inform Peony, "We're going to the Marducs' for dinner," in the tone of modest awe in which other men, in other places, have said, "I'm to receive a knighthood in the next Honors List," or "I have just made my first million dollars," or "I have at last devised a method of proving the existence of God by pure logic."

Peony answered with a yell of joy.

[333]

27

THE APARTMENT OF Colonel Charles B. Marduc, on Fifth Avenue beside Central Park, occupied one and a half floors of the building, and was served by its own elevator, with two shifts of elevator men especially trained not to mention the weather. It was famed throughout that whole world of *Household Decoration* and *Country Life* magazines, that little glazed empire, as showing the best taste in the country in having assembled the best examples of the worst Victorian furniture.

It displayed petunia-red satin sofas with frames of black walnut carved with grapes, rugs with hoydenish roses, a ruby and sapphire chandelier with electric candles, white satin draperies with rose-silk lambrequins, and a delicate old music-box cabinet containing cigars. It was so filled with reproductions of good needlepoint and good breeding that it would almost have fooled the connoisseurs.

Peony wandered blissfully, enjoying the bland flavor of wealth, and wondering whether she was expected to laugh or be awed at statuettes under glass and a tip-table painted with a Rhine castle seemingly constructed of taffy. The Doctor was too busy to notice, for besides the Marducs and the Homewards and Senator Felix Bultitude, here was the celebrated Mrs. Tucket, who had made a social career by being rude to everybody, and at last, here was Governor Thomas Blizzard himself, looking astonishingly like Governor Blizzard.

When you saw him, you knew that he was Somebody, though you were not sure whether he was a cultured ex-prizefighter or an athletic preacher. He had never been seen without his tie crooked. But he also was the first person to whom Dr. Planish had talked in days who smiled like a human being.

Though they came as strangers, the Planishes were immediately hoisted to eminence by the flattering screams of old friendship with which Senator Bultitude greeted them. He remembered that Dr. Planish must remember that once the Senator had been associated with H. Sanderson Sanderson-Smith in labor-scuttling, and he wanted all that brightly forgotten, for the Senator now called the labor unions by their first names. Some of his best friends were labor unions.

Dr. Planish believed that throughout dinner he would impressively be lecturing about organizations and their superiority to the Government at Washington. He sat down at table, he cleared his throat—and found that he was one second too late. Winifred Homeward had already started.

It was not that Winifred talked more than these celebrated men might have, for no one can talk more than one hundred per cent. But she could talk down talkers. She could put into her dinner offensives an assurance and a demand for attention that made forty minutes of her feel like the entire voyage of the Ark. She was so powerful that she could convince anyone at all of the exact opposite of whatever she maintained, including the man from whom she had lifted her ideas in the first place.

The moment now was some eight months after the Hitler-Chamberlain pact of Munich. Winifred held forth about Hitler's nastiness so ferociously that she had the same effect upon all present that she had on Hatch Hewitt, and they became stubbornly certain that Hitler was a fine, fat, jolly, drinking fellow, who loved girls and sausages and beer and stories about pandas; as she talked on, they longed to sit with Hitler in a couple of rocking chairs on the front porch at good old Berchtesgaden, and talk about fishing. There might have been a dangerous crop of Fascists grown that evening, except that presently, still hurdling over all interruptions, Winifred stated violently that all American young people were slatternly and impertinent, so that a considerable degree of trust in Young America was instantly restored around the table.

She also had a few pronouncements to make upon the movies, the immorality of symphony music, the coal business and how to decorate a twenty-dollar-a-month flat. She had a remarkable number of opinions, and she thought highly of all of them.

Colonel Marduc did not say seventy words during dinner, but Dr. Planish saw that he was watching. After it, the Colonel muttered to him, "Planish, you seem to be a good listener. You'll have to be, if we do start this new organization. Come see me tomorrow at three—sharp."

Dr. Planish was there at ten minutes to three

"We'll have to take a few months formulating the thing," said Colonel Marduc. "You'll have to resign from the Blessed to Give comedy, and devote all your attention to our show. Five thousand a year for a start? More later?"

"Okay," said Dr. Planish.

With these simple, brave words the new school of philosophy began.

There was a small commando squad of what were known in journalistic and welfare circles as "Marduc's young men." They were employed by his agency, but he frequently sent them off on detached duty all over the country, to raid or spy in every known political or ameliorative gathering. They numbered anywhere from four to ten at a time, and you could tell them apart only by the fact that some of them were graduates of Yale, some of Harvard or Princeton or Dartmouth or Williams, and some, for pioneer work in rough country, of the State universities.

All of them smoked pipes but preferred cigarettes; on week-ends, all of them wore tweed jackets with gray flannel bags and no hat; but in the New York office they appeared in modest and expensive gray or brown suits, with shirts and ties and handkerchiefs all in matching gray.

Each of them allowed himself daily exactly twenty-seven cigarettes—carried in a quiet silver case—with two highballs, two cocktails, three cups of coffee, one Bromo Seltzer, and fifteen minutes of sharp and detestable exercise. They averaged 1½ spirited minutes of love per week, one rather unsatisfactory adultery per year, and one wife —always from a Good Family, usually a dark pretty girl whom you could never quite remember. They averaged 1¾ children, and if it was not true that all of Marduc's young men had curly hair, still you thought they had, and they all read the *Atlantic Monthly* and the *New Masses*. They voted high-church Republican or middle-creek Socialist, or both, and all evening long, even when they were playing bridge, they listened to the radio and said how much they hated the radio.

They were all either born Congregationalists who had become Episcopalians, Episcopalians who had become atheists, or Christian Scientists who didn't talk about it.

Of them all, none was more average than Sherry Belden.

He was Yale, class of 1928, both Phi Beta Kappa and Skull and Bones. He had been a college tennis champion and cheer-leader, and now, at thirty-two, he was still a college tennis champion and a cheer-leader. But he felt very radical because he was a close friend of a man who praised Gandhi—usually for the wrong things.

Sherry had modest manners and a straight nose; he lived in Port Washington, in a brand-new, half-timbered Elizabethan cottage; he had the largest electric ice box in his block, the largest stock of strange liquors, including Strega and arrack, and the largest library of communist propaganda, erotica, technocracy and Sir Walter Scott.

It was Sherry Belden whom Colonel Marduc detached

from his fine job as an account executive to assist Dr.
Planish.

He said, "At least, Planish, Sherry will keep Winifred
off your neck. She's very useful to any Cause if you just
keep her gagged till you push her out onto the stage, or
if you keep some well-bred eunuch like Sherry for her
to talk to."

Dr. Planish found Sherry as shining and nimble and
useful as a new bicycle.

The Doctor's farewell to his recent boss, the Hon. Mr.
Ernest Wheyfish, was unexpected. He had pictured Soapy
Ernest denouncing him as a traitor and sneak, but Ernest
only caroled, "Going to be associated with Marduc, eh?
I envy you. Now, Gid, you mustn't forget the happy times
we've had here together, shoulder to shoulder to put over
the principle of Christian giving, just like a joyful old-
time prayer meeting, and let's see if we can't go on working together. Fix me up a lunch with old Marduc. God
bless you, my boy. I never did find a fellow that I liked
to work with better, and I hope your contributions will
come rolling in like salmon in spring."

There was, at first, no need of general contributions.
Colonel Marduc supported the preliminary survey, as it
was technically called, and if he did not seem displeased
by mysterious newspaper items mentioning him as a possible President, he never demanded them.

For months Dr. Planish held conferences with the leading thinkers and humanitarians and read their typed memos, which he called "highly suggestive," even if each one did contradict all the others.

Sherry Belden took for him, at first, a three-room suite in a hotel, with a small but distinctive bar in a closet. Here he worked with Sherry, Colonel Marduc, Winifred, Major Homeward, Natalia Hochberg, Senator Bultitude, Governor Blizzard, Bishop Pindyck, Rabbi Lichtenselig, Ramona Tundra the actress, and, naturally, the Reverend Dr. Christian Stern.

But there were a number of new intimates; for example, the Rt. Rev. Msgr. Nicodemus Lowell Fish. The Monsignor was one of the few Yankees who had ever become a Catholic dignitary, and it was his pride to be known as "the missionary to the intelligentsia." He called a Negro doctor, a New Deal economist, and a sports columnist by their first names, and he went backstage at all play openings. It was obligatory upon all atheist intellectuals to say that Msgr. Fish was a better Protestant than they were.

He had personally converted seven reporters and a Baptist minister to Roman Catholicism, and it was reported that he was arguing with Charles Coughlin.

Also, he would not have known a real "intellectual" if he had ever met one, and he believed that Hilaire Belloc was a profound historian.

And there was Professor Topelius, born on the Baltic, who had a plan to bring eternal peace by having Europe conducted as one federal state, governed by a committee of Americans—and Professor Topelius. There was Dr. Waldemar Kautz, a play producer from Vienna, who hated America because he believed that the entire population ate lunch at drug-store counters. The poor man was dying slowly of longing for his Stammtisch and the waiter calling him "Herr Doktor" or, with any luck, "Herr Baron."

There was Judge Vandewart, who was a tower of strength as a receiver for bankrupt utility companies. He liked to be chairman at all public dinners that had press tables.

Professor Campion, an almost new friend, was a surprising person to find in the Planish School of Economics, because Professor Campion actually knew something about economics, and was even licensed to teach it at a reputable school: Cornell University.

But Campion was a Signer.

Any group of rebels, Communist, Royalist, Argentine, Danish, S.P.C.A., Y.M.H.A., or O.G.P.U., who drew up a protest to be sent to the Congress or to a foreign ambassador, complaining because somebody was going to be shot at dawn, or wasn't going to be shot at all, could count on Professor Campion to sign. He often signed nine protests between 1 A.M. and bedtime, and his chief reading matter, outside of the works of Plato, was his breakfast-table pile of four-page telegrams from propaganda organizations asking for his immediate shirt.

Then, there was Ed Unicorn, a crusader in search of a crusade.

Till a year ago, Ed had been a simple-hearted American reporter, roving about Europe and filing to his string of newspapers whatever his local interpreter (for Ed knew no known language) told him was to be found in the native press that day. He had not realized that he was a "foreign correspondent" and he had denied that he was a "journalist." In bars in Budapest, Belgrade and Oslo, he was frequently heard to say, "I'm a plain newspaperman."

But he had come home and had given a public lecture, a very successful one, full of anecdotes about fooling the censors and the customs inspectors, rambling but diverting, for Ed was an extremely good fellow. The lone lecture had led to a lecture tour, and the tour to a magazine article, and the article to a book, and the book to broadcasting, and the broadcasting to a wide public belief that Ed was the original discoverer of geography and of a mysterious practice called Foreign Affairs. Ed was prosperous now; he knew the slickest girls in the Stork Club, and on the Linguaphone he had learned one hundred and fourteen words of Spanish; but he had exhausted every single anecdote about his adventures, and he was wistfully hoping that Colonel Marduc or Dr. Planish would hand him out a new set of gospels to broadcast about.

A very different foreign correspondent was Milo Samphire, and Dr. Planish found Samphire much less cooperative than Ed Unicorn.

Samphire had been stationed abroad for fifteen years; he was really a scholar, and he had manners and a manner. Even English journalists had sometimes been willing to call him a journalist. When he wanted an interview with a prime minister, he did not make inquiries of the American consul, the American Express Company, the barman at the Grand Ritz-Crillon-Superb-Schwartz, or the oldest son at Thos. Cook & Sons. He just telephoned to the prime minister.

He had been ousted from both Germany and Italy, and he had come home not to broadcast and be recognized at the Twenty-one Club, but, quite honestly and fierily, to persuade America that it was in danger from the Fascist fever. He was a fanatic, he had a single-track mind, he was as handsome as a Confederate Spy in the movies, and to him, Mister Marduc was just another advertising man.

Yet the skilled and professionally forgiving Dr. Planish solicited his advice, in the hope of using him at public dinners.

A comfort to the Doctor, however, were the familiar philanthrobber team of Henry Caslon Kevern and Walter Gilroy.

To the eye, they were opposites. Kevern was old and dry and refined and of a renowned family. Contrary to normal American eugenics, he had a great-grandfather. He collected first editions of William Blake; and his investment banking was so aloof, so disdainful of anything less than a million dollars, that it seemed less like money-making than like a further collection of rare editions.

Gilroy was a Westerner, youngish and burly and loud and very pleasant, an owner of oil wells. But these two were alike in feeling guilty at having so much money. They did not do anything about it so obvious as raising the wages of their employees; that would have been a little sordid, and lacking in any feeling of a mystic rite of expiation.

Another new friend was General Gong, U.S.A. (ret.), who had recently bought a new world atlas (in two volumes) and a history of maneuvers in which he himself had participated but which he had entirely forgotten, and who was certain, poor man, that if America ever did get into war, he would be recalled to command these inexperienced cubs of fifty and fifty-five.

The one man whom Colonel Marduc went to solicit, instead of sending the Doctor or Sherry Belden, was Leopold Altzeit, the international banker.

Altzeit finance was so vast and esoteric that, beside it, Henry Kevern's seemed like pawnbroking. He was tiny and frail and inconceivably old; in his private office, teakpaneled, there was only a desk, two chairs, a framed letter from Beethoven to Prince Lichnowsky, and an unquestioned Rembrandt.

Marduc did not need to tell him what Hitler was doing to the Jews. Altzeit's chief operative in Germany had already risked his life to become one of Hitler's staff.

Altzeit listened, still and impenetrable, then rang, and to an expressionless secretary, in a very little voice like a breeze among dry leaves in November, he whispered, "Lothar, will you please to bring me a check for ten thousand dollars made out to Mr. Charles B. Marduc, thank you."

It was Leopold Altzeit's third arrow that day at the Fascists. He did not think much of this bow, with the curious Oriental name of Marduc. But he would always go on shooting; he always had.

Between conferences, the Planishes proudly became intimates of Winifred Homeward and her little boy, the Major. Winifred lost so many friends, talked them to death so quickly or just forgot them into oblivion, that it was not hard for newcomers to step in and be friends—while it lasted.

Peony was a competent listener, and Winifred permitted her to come often to the red-brick Georgian chateau of the Homewards on East 68th Street, where Peony's position presently came to resemble that of a highly paid companion and maid—except that she did not get the pay. For a while, she was perhaps Winifred's only woman friend—Winifred complained that most women friends were selfish and jealous and were always interrupting her.

Peony was rapidly promoted, in this romantic chronicle of modern court life, from milkmaid to lady in waiting. She confided to the Doctor that she was at last enjoying to the full the social and intellectual advantages of New York, and, without paying one cent (except for taxi fare), she could always get a cup of tea (not very hot) at Winifred's.

Dr. Planish saw the great lady informally, too. Once, after a tense conference on the wickedness of dictators, Winifred said gaily to him, "Oh, let's go out and have a sandwich at a cafeteria. I love cafeterias! So jolly!"

In that vast white-tiled room shrieking with light, they took their trays and edged along the counter, inspecting cakes with marble icing, cakes crumbed with sugar, ingenious cakes like sections of a tree.

"Isn't this amusing!" Winifred screamed, so that a policeman on the corner outside nervously grasped his club. "I love an adventure! And don't you hate these people who come into a dump like this as though they were slumming? The whole pleasure of it is to feel that you're not really any better than the Common People."

Winifred set down her tray and looked at the tables about her. She sighed, "I must say, though, it worries me to think of loafers and lower-bracketeers like these actually having a vote, and deciding major issues. I keep trying to think of some way of combining absolute democracy—in which, of course, my father and I believe implicitly—with keeping the decision in really important national affairs in the hands of experts—like ourselves. I think I'll make that my next editorial in *Attention!*."

Pretty much everything was decided about the new organization except its name, and for what purpose it existed, if any.

Many suggested purposes were discussed in the months of conference. What were the purposes and the topics discussed may be ascertained by taking the following list of the words most frequently repeated during the meetings, and adding to them any nouns or verbs or flavoring that may suit the taste:

far-flung	category
founding father	keynote
global	dynamic
hail with enthusiasm	vital
decisive factor	implant

outstanding event
immediate need
brook no opposition
grave responsibility
white light of criticism
hot under the collar
hit the nail squarely on the head
get down to brass tacks
get over the message that
take with a grain of salt
take it on the chin
feet on the ground
lacking in solidarity
equal opportunity for all
resist the pressure
put pressure on
outcome of the crisis
to quickly sum up
in the final analysis
the sense of it is
what I want to say is
the point I'm making is
I want to say a word for
index of emotional state
democratically organized
to implement the policy
reaffirming the principle
keep away from political considerations
we surmise
another angle
not good enough
we agree in principle
basic principles
to get your reaction

indoctrinate
activist
suggestion
solution
resolution
stimulus
firm belief
turning-point
net result
memorandum
drive
tentatively
morale
organizational
policy
do the job
challenge
commonwealth
committee
community
conference
confidence
congress
constitutional
contributor
co-ordinate
crisis
the top men
sponsor
director
trustee
discussion
research
broadcast
union

[347]

complexity of the modern world
sickness in our civilization
along the lines of
break the bottlenecks
influence public opinion
refer the report back to
left to the discretion of
putting our shoulders to
duly made and seconded
venture to predict
bring up the point
remarkable progress
basic directive
definite objective
generosity in giving
neither the time nor the place to raise
the issue
one thousand dollars

grass roots
desire to serve
altruistic
make sacrifices for
willful minority
rallying point
pressing problem
immediate problem
face the problem
solve the problem
new set of problems
blue prints for
way of life
ideology
sense of security
courage to face it
I so move
ten thousand dollars

Winifred Homeward proposed that there should be a Federal police force—with her husband as chief. Governor Blizzard proposed that a job be found for his cousin, Al Jones, a fine young fellow. But, as the godlike eye of Colonel Marduc perceived, eventually it was Dr. Planish who settled on the purposes and title for their new organization.

The title was "Dynamos of Democratic Direction," though it was always known as the DDD. Winifred was to be the first president; Sherry Belden, treasurer; and the "directive secretary" was Gideon Planish, M.A., Ph.D.

The DDD was to have a chapter, called a "powerhouse," in every community in America. Each of these was, under instruction from New York about the latest

Conditions and Situations, to organize a Discussion Group, a Health Committee, a Gardening Unit, a History Class, an English Class for the Foreign-born, an Investigation Group to report on local Fascists, and a Committee to wangle free radio time. There was, of course, to be a national magazine, but it never did get started. The whole scheme, in fact—to supplant the Federal and State and Town Governments and the entire Christian Church by a new Soviet headed by Colonel Marduc—was beyond criticism, even carping criticism. Dr. Planish summed it up in a private memo to the Colonel: "All ordinary citizens, especially those west of Buffalo, need instruction and direction in becoming thoroughly democratic from trained thinkers like ourselves. When we have given our democracy to the entire nation, then America will enforce it on the rest of the world. That is our basic idea."

The basic ideas behind this basic idea were that Dr. Planish was to have a secure hundred-dollar-a-week job, which would some day become a two-hundred-a-week job, and Tom Blizzard and old Charley Marduc were to enjoy being known as great statesmen, and Charley's horsy-looking girl, Winifred, was to have an audience whenever she got hungry for one, and Peony and the United States of America were to enjoy one unending Christmas morning.

In the haven of the Dynamos of Democratic Direction, Dr. Planish passed three serene years, from late in 1938 until December 1941, while the rest of the world was not so serene.

28

DECEMBER 5, 1941, was a good normal day in the career of Dr. Gideon Planish, Directive Secretary of the DDD —the Dynamos of Democratic Direction.

He had returned late the evening before from a routine visit to Washington, where he had appeared as an expert on Eskimos before a Congressional committee.

He arose at eight o'clock, a pleasant, cherubic sight, with his gray short beard jutting out over his cherry-and-blue striped pajama jacket. He was fifty years old now, and his life of clean habits and thought, plus two hours a week in Pete Garfunkle's Gymnasium, had made him so sturdy a figure that it was evident that we shall be able to count on him for another twenty-five years of scholarship, philanthropy and political influence; and that, if we have any luck at all, he will still be molding public opinion for us in 1965.

He looked fondly at his wife, who was still asleep, her smooth face that of a plump and cheerful baby. He remembered that, for over a year now, they had not had so much as one word of quarreling, not even on the night when she had drunk three mint juleps with their friend George Riot, now worthily enthroned as president of Bonnibel College for Women, Indiana.

He looked fondly about their bedroom, on Charles Street, in the Greenwich Village section of New York. Peony had recently redecorated it with Swedish furniture. The refurnishing cost a little more than they had expected, but it was almost paid for, now, and they had, in solid cash, $172.37, to say nothing of seven shares of stock in the Artaxerxes Antimony Mine.

He could not quite live on his salary, but he was sure that, in 1942, he would be able to earn an extra $2,500 by lecturing.

The morning was chilly, but he took a shower with almost no shudders. In the past ten years, he had got as used to a daily bath as Winifred Homeward.

He hastily, for he was a man of affairs with an ignorant world awaiting his guidance, put on the short athletic underwear, pale blue, which, Peony often declared, "made him look as oomphy as the Great God Pan," and his newly tailored suit of pale-brown cheviot.

He bounced downstairs for breakfast of oatmeal and bacon and eggs and toast and four cups of coffee, with his daughter Carrie, aged almost twenty.

He supposed that he loved Carrie, and very much; he knew that he was irritably puzzled by her and by "whatever it is that she thinks she's up to."

She was a pert and pretty figure, in sweater and tweed skirt, but she did not seem to him richly and truly feminine, like her mother. And though her "Good morning, Daddy" was amiable enough, they didn't seem to have any of their good old-time intimate talks, such as those (he was sure he remembered them) in which she had told him that he was ever so much brainier than his bosses, Sanderson-Smith and Wheyfish. She never mentioned Colonel Marduc except when she snapped, "Do we have to take much time in defining a vestigial nineteenth-century stuffed shirt?"

(All out of books!)

She was a Junior in Hunter College, and devoted to such unglamorous subjects as physics, mechanical drawing and ethnology. She did not seem to be even normally soft toward any of the horde of boys who hung about her and about the house. The Doctor was fairly sure that he would not like to hear that she had been seduced, but he was just as uncomfortable in feeling that his own daughter was so superior to males like himself and to the entire idea of seduction.

Some of her boys were Wolves and Hell-Raisers, some were skinny and spectacled and superior, but none of them seemed to do anything but listen to the phonograph with Carrie, and talk with her about persons of whom the Doctor had never heard: Orson Welles, Bartok, Hindemith, Georg Grosz, Erskine Caldwell, Shostakovich. Some of the boys got mildly tight, as a young man should, but some of them were actually teetotalers—and, more embarrassing, so was Carrie.

He fretted that he certainly didn't want her to get soused, but still, it was disagreeable to have her look that way at Peony and him when they rejoiced in their evening cocktails and recalled the Good New Ones they had heard during the day. It was exasperating to have her, though ordinarily a civil young woman, calmly state that

[352]

they were old-fashioned survivals of a Flaming Youth era that to her was as antiquated and ridiculous as the Dutch Tulip Craze or Mr. Gladstone.

He had given up trying to be helpful to her young men by giving them valuable inside information regarding the International Situation of 1941 and the secret plans of fallen France. All of them, skinny and intellectual or stout and bawdy, expected to go to war some day as fighting soldiers, with no fuss about it; they disliked Hitlerism, and talked expertly about Spitfires and Stukas. Yet when he, the secretary of the DDD, tried to inspire them with his best explanations of what Winston Churchill was going to do year after next, they just didn't seem to listen, although paying audiences of the most expensively dressed women applauded him on an average of twice a week for bestowing exactly this same revelation.

"Sometimes," the Directive Secretary sighed, "I wish I were a plain college teacher again, instead of a leader of democratic thought."

This morning, he read the war headlines to Carrie, who had read them herself half an hour before, until Peony appeared, adorable and soft in a lace-trimmed peachblow negligee, gurgling, "Everybody here? I can't seem to get up mornings, any more. But, oh boy, did I dance with Hal Homeward and Sherry Belden last night, while you were gadding off to Washington! What, no strawberries?"

He rode to within a block of his office by subway, wishing that he could afford a limousine instead of having to be elbowed by these gum-chewing clerks. But he was restored to dignity as he walked up to the building of the Dynamos of Democratic Direction, which occupied all of a handsome old brownstone house in the Thirties.

The Blessed to Give Brotherhood headquarters had been like a warehouse, heaped everywhere with piles of pamphlets; the Heskett Foundation gloomy, the Every Man Fraternity and the Gishorn hideout like minute cells in a steel beehive. But the DDD offices were as proud and gay as that aristocratic scholar Dr. Planish himself.

Like a refined sultan entering his harem, he was greeted in the hall by the receptionist, Mrs. Ethel Hennessee, a flat lady with harlequin spectacles. Her desk was at the foot of the stairs, and it was her job to make inquiring visitors warmly unwelcome. The DDD did not want to see new faces unless the faces were backed by checks or by charters for new local Powerhouses. Particularly it did not want to see the cranks who brought in bulky schemes to save humanity by having the Government give $27.87½ to every person over forty-five at eleven o'clock each Thursday morning.

On this ground floor were the Lounge, and the Council Room and Library, once the drawing-room and the dining-room of the old house. In the Library were oil portraits of Colonel Marduc and Governor Blizzard, and also several books.

The basement, aside from the furnace room, was given over to the women employees and women friends of the DDD. It had the odor of a stenographers' school with a tea-room and a hairdresser's down the hall. It was cluttered—no man entered here to enforce domestic order—

[354]

with folding umbrellas, flowery gingham overalls, coffee machines, teapots and lipsticks.

Indeed the whole building was feminized. There were two and a half men in the place against fifty women.

Besides the Doctor, they kept a man named Carlyle Vesper, a thin and shabby and frightened clerk who was supposed to be office manager—he counted for half a man; Julius Magoon, the press agent, an enterprising wolf who was there only half the time; Dr. Tetley, the pale doer of Research; and Fritz Hendel, the Investigator—his job was to wriggle his way into secret seditious meetings, addressed by loud-mouthed Nazis on street corners in Yorkville and rarely attended by more than a dozen policemen, and come back with a report that he suspected the speakers of a tinge of anti-Semitism. Tetley and he were about the place not more than a quarter of the time. Average total male presence: two and a half.

Hovering about them, flattering them, listening to their jokes, filling their water carafes, taking down their letters, mothering them but wistfully hoping to be fathered by them, were the cloud of women: Mrs. Hennessee, the receptionist; Bonnie Popick, Dr. Planish's fat and adoring private secretary, who resembled a tawny Peony; and undistinguishable young ladies named Flaude Stansbury, Sue Maple and Adelle Klein, who were permanently employed at typing, filing letters, folding DDD circulars and thrusting them into envelopes, running the telephone switchboard and taking down numbers and handing on falsifications for Mrs. Hennessee when she was out at lunch, worshipping the Doctor, pitying Mr. Vesper, avoiding the fingers of Mr. Magoon, and going home to boast that they had seen Colonel Marduc or Governor Blizzard or Mrs. Winifred Homeward face to face.

They were about Dr. Planish all day, like a flutter of pigeons, and they never gave him reason to doubt that he was the wisest and pleasantest servant of humanity since Haroun-al-Rashid. And all evening, Peony and the billowingly female cook were about him, too, and the only louse among the pillows was Carrie.

Besides this permanent staff there were, addressing envelopes and inserting circulars, anywhere from six to sixty unpaid volunteer women workers—all prosperous women, for Dr. Planish just couldn't be bothered with poor ones. They came here with a shaky planless desire to do something for the world, and they were put to work, not because they were as good as girls hired by the week, but because if they worked here long enough and felt themselves part of the crusade, from 37 to 54% of them (figures by Dr. Tetley of the DDD) could be counted on to come through with cash contributions. So everyone was nice and helpful to them, very nice indeed.

As happily as a surgeon inspecting his hospital, Dr. Planish went up to the third floor, where, in a vast loft, worked all the women except Miss Popick and Mrs. Hennessee, where Magoon and Tetley and Hendel had their small disordered desks, and where Carlyle Vesper ineffectually watched the workers from a den seven feet square.

The Doctor was full of abounding joy and kindness.

"Good morning, good morning, my dears!" he shouted; and even to poor Vesper, who bored him, he threw a forgiving, "Splendid day for December, Carlyle."

Then he was free to go and sit in his fine Georgian office and be an Executive, while Bonnie Popick (of whom Mrs. Hennessee was agonizingly jealous) indicated that her day, her dawn, her golden sun had started—and please, would Dr. Planish try and get off that letter to the I.G.T.R.L.—he'd promised it yesterday—oh, she hated to bother him about it!

His office was a square, ruddy room, with a solid mahogany desk, a silver-framed picture of Peony, solid mahogany chairs, a portly fireplace, a case filled with autographed books about Conditions and Situations, and the Special File.

The whole building was banked with files of correspondence and of contributors' names, but the Special File contained only the names of philanthrobbers who might be good for a thousand a year or more, and all the cards had annotations by the Doctor himself: "pers letter—flatter on stamp collectn," and "gilded crook, likes to be taken for gent," and "honest, intel, don't send any bunk."

Before he settled down to his correspondence, the Doctor went to his private washroom for his regular morning session of quiet thinking.

He was glad that their office was so stately, but it was stimulating to see through the tiny hexagons of the washroom's wire-glass windows the strength and clashing angles of the new functional business buildings across the court: raw yellow brick walls, high-perched water tanks, roofs stepped back like ledges in an open-pit mine, fireproof windows with steel mullions. They were as harsh as factories, and as honest.

Dr. Planish felt that they represented modern power and speed, and from that thought it was easy to glide into a feeling that he had built them. He heard some unknown speaker, perhaps the suave Professor Campion, intoning:

"My high privilege to introduce Dr. Planish, than whom no man of his generation has more influenced not only political philosophy but the rebuilding of his native city, New York, from one of whose finest old Knickerbocker families he comes. Whether in such gracious palaces as that in which are housed the thousands of employees of the DDD, or in the streamlined efficiency of what is now universally known as the Planish or neo-Frank-Lloyd-Wright type of architecture——"

The Doctor happily finished his dream and returned to work and to the ministrations of Bonnie Popick, an active lady of twenty-eight who so appreciated his humor that sometimes she laughed when he hadn't meant to be funny. As he re-entered his office, she was brushing his hat and overcoat; then she adjusted the slanted glass ventilation-shield at the bottom of the farther window.

She snickered, "Our friend Mrs. Hennessee claims she's got a cold this morning."

In office ritual this meant, "I love you much more than that flat-chested old cat does, though I'd be ashamed to be jealous, as she is—always pretending to feel ill, just to draw your attention. And I know that you're true to your

[358]

stupid pigeon of a wife—men are such fools—but all day I'm closer to you than your wife or anybody else—especially that damn Hennessee woman!"

He read the mail that she had opened and arranged in a pile on his desk. He loved reading mail; it made him feel important to be denounced in the same batch as an English Tory, as a Russian Communist, as a Midwestern provincial; to be asked his opinions; to be invited to address clubs and colleges.

He dictated the answers as rapidly as a windmill. Only one letter bothered him: that from Mr. Johnson of Minneapolis, the unpaid local director of the DDD Powerhouse.

Mr. Johnson of Minneapolis was nobody and everybody. Sometimes Dr. Planish remembered him as a lawyer, sometimes as a newspaperman, sometimes as a farmer, sometimes as a small merchant, sometimes as a labor-union secretary, sometimes as a millionaire lumberman. He accepted intellectual manna from the professional manna-handlers, but he could never be depended upon. At any moment he was likely to complain that the manna had too much soda in it.

Mr. Johnson of Minneapolis wrote now: "I don't like the way our local Powerhouse of the DDD is going. We are supposed to be still in existence, and I notice in your bulletins that you say we are 'thriving and doing a fine work in acquainting the Scandinavian citizens with the ideals of Americanism.'

"I don't know. I haven't been able to get the committee together for a month now, and all our English for Foreigners and history classes, etc., etc., are just on paper, and anyway, I don't feel there is anything we can tell the Swedes & Norwegians & Danes about Democracy.

"I first joined the DDD because I had an uncomfortable feeling that in these days a fellow ought to do something more than just make a living. I'll admit I was a goat. I was impressed by all the titles and degrees that you fellows on the National Board have. But now I'm wondering.

"I guess maybe it would be pretty bad to never talk about Public Affairs, but I'm wondering if it isn't just as bad to make out that they are a special mystery that only the DDD can understand.

"A lot of this inside information that you send us and that we're supposed to hand on to the peasantry is pretty mildewed now. The ox-teams got across the Alleghenies with the news quite some time ago. You keep telling us that Zeke Bittery is a Fascist. Out here, we've known for twenty years that Zeke is nothing but a crackpot evangelist who would undercut Judas by eight pieces of silver. Why don't you give us something new? For instance. Are there any Fascists that contribute to the DDD so as to look patriotic?

"I'm bothered about all this chatter. Ever since Voltaire, and especially since old Marx, there's been such a clamor of authoritative voices. There's so many new branches of knowledge, from psychiatry to conchology, from wine vintages to aviation records, that any sensitive man keeps feeling guilty about his ignorance, no matter how hard he reads, and so he turns for clarification to the fellows that set up as authorities.

"Well, they better be good, or they're going to do a pretty terrible thing to the Common Man (like me). They're going to make him get disgusted with *all* authority, and turn to the comic strips or to anarchy."

Dr. Planish grunted to Bonnie Popick, "Regular crank. Mr. Johnson of Minneapolis? Yes, I remember his name now. He's always kicking about something he doesn't understand. Take this answer."

He wrote to Mr. Johnson that it had been a rare privilege to peruse his profound analysis of the present Confusion of Tongues, and might he please read his letter to the Board of Directors, and he was sure that so bright a man as Mr. Johnson would soon have the Minneapolis Powerhouse hitting on all eight again.

He was, actually, somewhat more disturbed by the letter than he admitted.

His circular letters asserted the busy existence of ninety-seven Powerhouses, as a reason for sending in larger and quicker donations. Actually, only sixteen of them were visibly operating, and if that fact got out, susceptible Generous Givers might think the DDD was a zombie organization, and quit giving.

But he did not let the recollection worry him long. After all, could a man be a leader of public thought if he was going to be disturbed by all the Mr. Johnsons of all the Minneapolises that, so many miles from the Directive Secretary of the Dynamos of Democratic Direction, were deep in provincial darkness?

"I'd like to see some of these fellows try to do my job!"

he said to Bonnie Popick, and looked at her as always for applause.

In his mail there was one most gratifying letter, from the Reverend Dr. Elmer Gantry, chairman of the DDD Insignia Committee.

Though he was a particularly stately man of God, who could use seven-syllable words just as easily as he could say Hell, Dr. Gantry was also an efficient man of affairs. With the consent of Colonel Marduc—since it did advertise the DDD, and cost him nothing—Dr. Gantry and Dr. Planish were permitted to control the sale of DDD buttons as a private venture. In the past six months, Dr. Planish had made enough out of this philanthropic enterprise to pay Peony's lingerie and shoe bills, and Dr. Gantry to engage, as an aide in his pious work, a new secretary who was an M.A. and very beautiful.

They had hired one of the most artistic button-designers to devise a DDD badge which, worn on the lapel, somehow gave the beholder an impression that the wearer had been an officer in World War I.

To list the telephone calls which incessantly disturbed the Doctor's high literary mood would be merely to give a depressing view of human selfishness. To consider how many persons wanted him to make speeches, without fee, how many rival dealers in oratory wanted to borrow from his stock of ideas about Abraham Lincoln, would be merely painful. But these annoyances he at last forgot in the pure ecstasy of composition.

Once a week he wrote a long Letter to the Editor, which

he sent to one of the New York newspapers and to a dozen strategically placed papers outside the True Jerusalem. Often they were printed, too, and even the expert Colonel Marduc admitted that they were good advertising.

Leaning back, scratching his beard, his eyes closed in ethereal bliss, he dictated to Bonnie:

The Editor.

Sir:

It was Thucydides who said to the Athenian people that, quote, In union there is not merely strength but a joy known ill to the striving hermit, unquote—no, wait, some bastard might know Greek, I think I better make up a name for whoever was supposed to have said that, make it—uh, let's see—make it Heresophos—H-E-R-E-S-O-P-H-O-S—I hope that sounds Greek. Put his name in, and then continue after the quote:

I have the honor of being a member of an organization called Dynamos of Democratic Direction, and in these days it has been a privilege to see how citizens of every shade of opinion have found inspiration in——

He went on until the bells of St. Timothy the Good struck twelve o'clock.

He reached the anteroom to the Gold Ballroom of the Grand Hosannah Hotel at 12:32, and was photographed with the officers of the Riverdale Ladies' Sociological Study Club; he lunched with the club till two; then, to that sea of upturned minks and Tecla pearls, he talked for twenty-five minutes about "Politics Needs Your Help."

[363]

He told them just what changes in the daily life of Paris had been made by the German occupation, and if he did not tell them that he had never been in Paris, neither did he say that he had.

He met Winifred Homeward in the Baboon Bar of the Hosannah, and they had a quick one and went together to a committee meeting of the new Call to Arms League, organized by Milo Samphire to advocate America's entering the war against the dictators.

Samphire and his organization happened to be entirely honest. Winifred and the Doctor were not very welcome there, but with smiles like the sun on an icy tree, they pretended to be, and rather nervously they made notes for Colonel Marduc.

The Colonel had been fidgety about Milo Samphire's demand that the American dislike for Fascism extend to war. Indeed, for a time, the Colonel had nearly slipped into the Isolationist faction. Secretly, he rather liked the way of Hitler and Mussolini in dealing briefly with anyone who opposed the Rule of the Strongest—the Colonel considering himself quite a good candidate for the Strongest in America. He had even spoken a few non-committal words at a Defense First anti-war meeting, a few months ago.

But when he saw the newspaper editorials about the meeting, he publicly explained that he hadn't said what he meant and, most decidedly, he hadn't meant what he said. He called up Dr. Planish and told him that from that moment on, the DDD would have nothing to do with the Isolationists.

The Doctor was relieved; but Milo Samphire did not seem to care what either Colonel Marduc or Dr. Planish thought, and as America tramped on to war, the Doctor felt a little scared and lonely. He did so much want to be a good man!

He rode the subway down to Pine Street, called on Walter Gilroy, looked tearful, and got a check for four hundred dollars.

He went back to the DDD office, signed his mail, and endured a little quiet torture with callers who were blessed with wealth but cursed with ideas.

At six, he was in a studio of the Brontosaurus Broadcasting Company, introducing Senator Bultitude on the radio. The time was bought and paid for by "a committee of Republican citizens." Oh, blessed age when Time can be bought and sold instead of being grudgingly bestowed by God; when the very aged, if they be also very rich, can buy Time on and on through eternity.

In swap for the Doctor's spirited introduction, the Senator mentioned the DDD—favorably.

At 6:20, the Doctor had another quick one, with the Senator, and at 6:40 still another, with Peony, at home.

Peony put on a new frock while he became beautiful in tails and white tie. They dined at a cafeteria, and Peony, in a crimson velvet evening cape and red roses in her hair, carried a tray with scrambled eggs, coffee, a chocolate eclair, a mocha layer cake and caramel ice cream.

At 8:15 they entered the Artists' Dressing Room of Village Green Hall, and embraced their friend George Riot, president of Bonnibel College for Women. At 8:24, Dr. Planish and President Riot began, before another set of furs and pearls and boiled eggs, a debate on "Resolved: in case of war, women should bear arms."

Dr. Planish took the affirmative, and many of the furs present believed that he was in earnest.

He spoke movingly of his wife and his learned daughter. Were those women, whose intelligence and energy alone had enabled him to do his modest work in Education for Democracy—were they mere toys to fondle in his idle hours, mere bric-a-brac to be laid aside if war should ever come? Were they? Never! He hoped and believed that it would never be necessary for them to be fighters, not so long as he himself could strike a blow. But should the occasion ever arise, he would be the first to applaud their putting on khaki and shouldering a gun.

President Riot said, at length, that Dr. Planish was a deep thinker, but all off on today's deep thought.

At 9:29, President Riot and the Planishes had a quick one at the Fanfare Folly Bar, and at 9:41 they sat down at the speakers' table at the dinner, in the Belle Poule Restaurant, of the Movement to Restore Christianity and Regular Church Attendance in Manhattan, just as Winifred Marduc Homeward arose and began defying the microphone.

Religion, said Winifred, would be restored only when True Democracy was instituted. Her father and she wished that there was some way of making every woman, man and child realize what Democracy was; that it opposed all pressure groups and held that the rights of man

[366]

and woman, rich and poor, were equal; that all honest labor, whether of the editor or the furnace man, the poet or banker or harvest-hand, was equally noble.

She didn't exactly say it, but she implied that if the poets, bankers and/or harvest-hands did not listen constantly to her and to her father, then civilization would smash.

Outside the Belle Poule Restaurant, which is expensive, Winifred's waiting chauffeur was talking with the doorman and a taxi-driver.

"What's this Democracy they're talking about? I don't mean the Democrat Party. It's some kind of theory," puzzled her chauffeur. "Me, I'd think Democracy meant you don't figure how good a guy a fellow is by how much money he's got or how much he shoots off his mouth. But if Windy Winnie is all for it, then it must mean something different."

The taxi-driver grumbled, "I guess it means rich guys ought to be polite to poor guys. And am I for it! Say, I wish you could hear the lip I have to take off my customers. 'Driver, I want you to go slow.' 'Driver, did you ever drive a cab before?' 'Driver, are you sure you know where the Grand Central is?' God! One after another."

"Troubles *you* got!" said Winifred's chauffeur. "You get rid of *your* headaches after a few blocks. You should drive private, where that hyena can not only bawl hell out of you for what she thinks is the wrong turning, but remember all the dumb plays she thinks you made yesterday and the day before, clear back to the Civil War. And does she bring 'em up? I'll say she does! And she's the one that's always yapping about this Democracy on the radio —so I hear—I wouldn't listen to it, not if you was to pay me for it."

The doorman, a monument in blue and silver, returned from bowing in a couple who made a point of entering the Belle Poule as though it were a soup kitchen, and snorted, "This Democracy is all nonsense. If you guys could work your way up to where you put on a uniform, like I do, instead of a chauffeur's suit, you wouldn't worry. These rich slobs are all right. See the tip I just got? Democracy! Think I'm no better than my brother Jake, that's still on a potato patch in Maine? And think Jake's no better than some hobo that comes asking for a hand-out? No, sir! This Democracy just can't work out."

Mrs. Homeward's chauffeur argued, "It's got to work, or we'll go bust, like Europe. Say! How the hell come we ever let porch-climbers like Mrs. Homeward and her dad —and their toadies, like you, Doorman—get control of this country?"

"I bet you wouldn't be very popular with your boss if she knew what you think of her!"

"I bet nobody wouldn't be very popular with their boss if he knew what they think!"

The chauffeur climbed into the Homeward car and went sulkily to sleep, just as Winifred Homeward was cascading, "It has always been my pride that the humblest truck-driver is just as free and easy with me, yes, and with that inspired sociologist, my father, as he is with any of his other pals!"

After the Movement dinner, the Planishes had the privilege of being taken, with the Marducs and the Homewards, to the flat of Governor Blizzard.

The Doctor rode with Winifred. She pointed to her chauffeur's back, and whispered—she thought she was whispering—"But look at my driver—the stupidest, stolidest man living. How can you persuade people like him to listen to the Voice of Democracy? He never thinks of anything but driving. I'm sure he's never even looked at me. He doesn't know whether I'm dull or clever. I don't believe he even knows whether I'm beautiful!"

In the other car, Peony patted the hands of Tom Blizzard, Charley Marduc and Hal Homeward, in turn, and told them that they looked tired but handsome after their gigantic labors, told them that she was *so* proud of knowing them.

All three of them smiled like appeased tom-cats.

The Governor's bachelor living-room was forty feet long, with a bar at each end and a fireplace on each side.

Dr. Planish interested them all by saying that either the Colonel or the Governor would be a much better President than Mr. Roosevelt. Winifred told them, but she had heard it confidentially and they must not repeat it, that a correspondent who had had a cocktail with a French diplomat, who had had a cup of tisane with Marshal Pétain, had said that France would rise up against Germany before the end of January, 1942.

So the Planishes were in bed by 2 A.M.

So Peony yawned, "What a wonderful evening."

Dr. Planish was awakened by her sighing, "Do you

know what that dress Winifred had on tonight probably cost?"

"R?"

"Probably three hundred and fifty dollars. And me paying $39.95 top!"

The ghastly thought awakened him fully, and he fretted, "This New York is an expensive town. I went in today to buy a necktie in a place on Fifth Avenue—I'd planned to spread myself; maybe pay two and a half. The clerk shows me a nice little number for five dollars, and when I asked for something cheaper, he shows a throwaway, at three dollars, and sneers at me. Jesus! I paid my three bucks, and sneaked out of there feeling as if I'd been caught picking up a cigar butt. For a necktie!"

"I know. To think that you make—I suppose this year it'll be about eight thousand, with salary and lectures and everything?"

"About."

"And yet we're poor people. Why is it? You're just as bright as Colonel Marduc, aren't you?"

"I'm not as much of a crook. I really do think it's worth while knocking out Hitler and Company for keeps, and I really do believe that people can live more co-operatively. And yet I do nothing but promote that double-crossing Marduc!"

"I won't have you say things like that! All the good you do, and the lovely ideas you put out about—well, about Democracy and so on. But to think of your making half again as much as President Bull at Kinnikinick, and yet we often have to eat at cafeterias!"

"Peony!"

"Uh-huh?"

"Do you sometimes think maybe you'd like to go back —go to some smaller town, or get into some good small religious organization, where we wouldn't have to train with millionaires like Marduc? I'll bet he pays *nine* dollars for a necktie!"

"No, no, never! Don't you ever let yourself get to thinking like that! That's how people degenerate—like in that play, *White Cargo*. You wouldn't expect me to associate with a lot of farmers, would you, not after all my years of struggle?"

"No, I guess not."

"There! You see?"

On Saturday morning, December 6, 1941, Dr. Planish flew with President George Riot out to Bonnibel College for Women. It might have been an extravagant journey, but the college paid his expenses, and he also charged them in full to Travel on his DDD account.

At one, there was a "banquet" at Bonnibel, with exactly the same committeewomen, flashlight photographs, handshakes, and ambitious high-school girl reporters, whose notion of interviewing him was to ask him how they could get New York newspaper jobs immediately, the same cold hot chicken and hot three-colored ice cream, that he had encountered at seven dinners in the past nineteen days. The only difference was that the girls' heads were a brighter vista than the dress-coats and sagging evening frocks he had seen at the others.

At 3 P.M., in the ceremony of Winter Convocation, he received from President Riot the honorary degree of Doctor of Letters. He now had almost as many stuffed heads and horns as Colonel Marduc: two LL.D.'s, three Litt.D.'s, one D.H., and even one real degree, a Ph.D. Thus invested, he had in his veins a different and more royal blood—maybe Type 5.

At 7:30 that evening, George Riot and he publicly repeated their debate of the evening before: "Resolved: in case of war, women should bear arms." But George had suggested that they change sides; it would be safer for him to tell his girl students, the darlings, that they might bear all the arms they wanted to.

That seemed a practical notion to Dr. Planish, since the newspapers had not reported their previous debate, so now he wailed:

"And so, as I say, of the equality of women and men, there is no longer any doubt, and no one, not a besotted fool, would any longer even in a spirit of mockery even so much as hint that it has not been a sovereign and healing blessing to have given, if indeed 'given' is the word, the vote to women, whether as a practical measure or as a symbol of that admitted equality, but still, nevertheless, gladly admitting all that, the question of whether their fine and delicate talents, so superior to men's in many tasks and, I haven't the slightest doubt, at the very least counterbalancing the larger gross muscular power of the male that, perhaps, is more suitable for certain other labors, should, I say, just for the interest of experimentation, be wasted in the more brutal tasks of actual soldiering—oh, my young friends, your great president, and, I am honored to say, my close and long-honored friend, Dr. Riot, may wish to play with this idea, as perhaps befits that sinuous intellect of his, but as for myself, I am a practical man of affairs, not unversed in military lore and training, and I tell you that for a woman, young or old, to be, even if she wished to, permitted to bear arms in the heat and toil of actual conflict, that, my young friends, and I implore you to put away all the vanities of sex antagonism, natural though these may be in view of the long and arduous and indeed properly prideful and in some sense, no doubt, belligerent struggle that women have had in conquering blind antagonism, witless prejudice, and the immobility of mere custom and habit and the cultural pattern of other civilizations that, though, to the unobservant, though possibly esthetic, eye, they may have seemed of the richest texture yet actually, in construction, they served but ill those basic necessities of the advance of human culture, among which the true and equal co-operation of men and women in all their relationships, whether of romance, war or the home is not the least, and yet the very historic force and intensity of that antagonism must, in the nature of the case, be a factor clouding the complete lucidity and severe brevity with which it is, I need scarcely tell you, necessary to consider a problem so complicated and far-flung——"

He caught a train at Indianapolis at 10:50; he flew from Buffalo to New York; he was home for breakfast on Sunday—Sunday, December 7, 1941.

29

DR. AND MRS. PLANISH attended church every Sunday, except when Peony slept late, which she did not do oftener than three Sundays a month. They usually favored the pastors who were patrons of the DDD, such as Chris Stern, Rabbi Lichtenselig, Msgr. Fish and the Reverend Dr. Elmer Gantry. This morning they sat under Dr. Gantry.

In his sermon, the Reverend said that Europe was at war because people, particularly in this section of New York, did not go to church more regularly. He and God were displeased.

"Handsome buck, Elmer. Wasn't he born in New York?" Peony speculated.

"I don't know. I've heard that he comes from a fine old Massachusetts family and went for some time to Harvard, but *Who's Who* gives him as graduating from a Western college. I believe that later he served in some of the most barren parts of Alaska, and refused a bishopric. You can see it in his bearing—fine upstanding type of manly leader."

"Was that his daughter in the front row—with the half-size hat?"

"No, I believe that's his new radio secretary. A wonderful new type of intellectual woman the radio is breeding, don't you think?"

"I do not," said Peony.

He had to leave her for luncheon, which he took with the National Directors, in the Council Room of the DDD Building. The food, brought in from an apartment-hotel restaurant down the block, was generously provided by Colonel Marduc, though the Colonel himself was in the country, and was represented by Sherry Belden and Winifred.

It was the regular quarterly meeting of the DDD directors. Present, besides the Doctor, Sherry, and Winifred, were Ed Unicorn, Professor Topelius, Chris Stern—who came late and would have to run away at three, for Sunday, as he said laughingly, "was his busy day"—Walter Gilroy, Henry Caslon Kevern, Judge Vandewart, Professor Campion, Albert Jalenak, president of the Spinning Wheel chain of stores for women, General Gong, Mrs. Natalia Hochberg, Otis Canary, the poet-orator, and a new friend, Mr. Johnson of Minneapolis.

They were gay and chatty during lunch, except for Mr. Johnson of Minneapolis, who listened so much that they were suspicious, for in that group, listening was only the price you had to pay for being the next to be listened to. However, he was just a provincial, not a crowned New Yorker.

They were a bunch of laughing boys and girls together till the waiter took out the last choked ash-tray. By magic then, they turned from friends into a stiff legislature, filled with stage-fright and pomposity. That was but natural, for was not the whole beclouded country waiting for this small and precious council to decide the fate of the next century?

Dr. Planish said, with the quietness of a veteran legislator, "In my official capacity as directive secretary, I declare this regular quarterly meeting of the board of directors in session, and as temporary chairmen pro tem, I call for nominations for chairman of the meeting, and with your kind permission and in order to save time, for important though our discussions will be today, and who knows, just possibly fraught with significance for future agenda not only of this but of all other enlightened organizations of the better class of Americans, yet I am also fully bearing in mind the fact that all of us have innumerable contacts, countless calls upon our time, and demands that we co-ordinate and develop the certainty that out of the chaos of our era, we seem slowly to be acquiring a nucleus, at least, and that a not merely dialectic and Utopian asseveration, and so, as I say, I will save time by, however irregularly, nominating one who, though the next to the youngest among you, for you are that, I guess, Winifred, but next to you, I mean, the youngest, although I don't suppose there is really any great span of difference between his age and yours, Mr. Canary, and you, Mrs. Hochberg, gallantry as well as a true admiration of your rare qualities as well as that ever-charming appearance which, and I would admit it to my dear wife just as readily as I would to you people, and so I would say that you certainly still *look* incomparably younger—and a lot handsomer!—than him, and I would say that if you and I had not for so long worked faithfully shoulder to shoulder for every cause that promises enlightenment and the rebuke of sloth and selfishness and windy talking and wordy demagoguery wherever found, in high places or low, for so many years, and so, as I say, I nominate Sherry Belden."

(He meant that he nominated Sherry Belden.)

After throwing this bomb, he went on, "And just to be regular, unless there are any further nominations, may I call for a second to my nomination?"

Mrs. Homeward screamed, "Second mosh. Look, Gid, in consideration of the news that the Japanese diplomatic representatives are to be at the State Department today, and will, I think, end all this nonsense about Japan being a menace——"

"Just a minute, please, Winnie!" The Doctor reflected inwardly, "By God, a meeting is one place where I can make that woman shut up, and do a little talking myself!"

He intoned, from the ritual by which a committee meeting is to be distinguished from a country-store argument, "Sbeen moved n seckd Mr. Belden servz chairm meet all fave sigfy sayn aye contrarmine no ayes zavit Mr. Belden take chair."

Winifred shouted, "Oh, Sherry, before you start, before I forget it, I want to express an idea I have—I have some very important inside information about the Japanese delegation, who are sincerely seeking for peace——"

Dr. Planish extinguished it.

"Just a minute, please, Winifred. There's one piece of formal business we ought to get through before we get down to work—just to keep the records straight. This is

Mr. Johnson, the director of the Minneapolis Powerhouse, a fine honest worker right after my own heart. He hasn't felt entirely satisfied with our progress, and so he has come on to New York to find out what we're actually doing to promote peace and Democracy. I'm sure that after he has sat in with us today, he'll understand better that our labors are not merely fundamental but, uh, well —pragmatic. So I move you, Mr. Chairman—hey, Sherry, listen, will you? I'm making a formal motion—I move you that Mr. Johnson of Minneapolis be temporarily elected a full member of this executive board for today."

"Arar sex that motion?" muttered Mr. Belden.

"Seckmosh," said Professor Campion, a great authority on Rules of Order.

"Muvseck Mist Johnss templeckt memboard tday aw fave sigfy raise riteand mosh namus carry," ordered Mr. Belden. "Now, boys and gals, we got to get down to brass tacks and get busier 'n a cat on a glass sidewalk. There's a hell of a lot of traffic on the trunk highway of international conflict; we got to jump the gun the second the green light shows, and jam the accelerator clear through the floor and drive like Billy-be-damned on to some clear delineation of the basic spiritual aspects of that monumental coming American Century, when we shall be called upon to fortify the global struggle."

All of Colonel Marduc's Bright Young Men, all of his private corps of trouble-shooters, felt that they had to curse and be metaphorical and folksy, just as they had to wear tweed jackets and gray bags, to show that, for all their college training and managerial talent, they had not become stuffy. They never said "No" when "Hell no" would do just as well, and of them all, none was more beautifully buttered over with the Common Touch than Sherry Belden. He had been reading Kipling's "If" since the age of ten.

Sherry continued, "You will all be glad to know that Colonel Charles B. Marduc approves of what we have been trying to do, and he has been pleased to make another generous contribution to our war chest of ten thousand dollars!"

Everybody applauded, except Mr. Johnson of Minneapolis, who said, "What for?"

General Gong snorted, "Hush!"

Sherry went on, "The first thing on our agenda today is the report of the Committee for the Determination of a Definition of the Word 'Democracy' for Propaganda, of which committee Otis Canary has been our invaluable chairman. Come on, Ote, let's hear your report."

In his time, Mr. Otis Canary had also been one of Marduc's Bright Young Men; he also had worn the gray bags and the hearty slang, but now he was a free-lance poet and essayist. His tall, clear, high face was still as open and friendly as Sherry Belden's, but his manner had become more pontifical.

"Mr. Chairman, ladies and gentlemen," said Mr. Canary, making it perfectly clear to whom he was speaking, "before I communicate this definition upon which we have agreed, I want to thank my colleagues on the committee: Mrs. Homeward and——"

Winifred shrieked, "Oh, I didn't really do a thing. You

see, I've been so busy with some reports I have from friends long resident in Japan and who really understand the Japanese aspirations, which are entirely peaceful and conciliatory——"

"PLEASE!" said Mr. Canary. (That meant "shut up.") "Just a minute, Mrs. Homeward. As I say, I want to thank my friends and co-workers, Mrs. Homeward and—PLEASE, JUST A MIN-IT, MRS. HOMEWARD!—and Professor Campion and Mr. Jalenak and Mr. Gilroy for their unceasing labors on this titanic task of accurately defining Democracy—a basic scientific determination that may in some degree be directional in all ideological activities for the next hundred years to come. We have all been working on it like demons, ten and twelve hours a day, meeting at five for cocktails and pounding right ahead, threshing this all out, till midnight or later. In its final form—and now at last we have it——"

"All right, let's!" said Mr. Johnson.

"In its final form, we have adopted this definition: 'Democracy is not a slavish and standardized mold in which all individuality and free enterprise will be lost in a compulsory absolute equality of wealth and social accomplishments. It is a mountain vista rather than a flat prairie. It is a way of life rather than a way of legislation. It is a religious aspiration rather than a presumptuous assertion that final wisdom inheres in man and not in the Divine, for it boldly asserts that whatever differences of race, creed and color the Almighty has been pleased to create shall also be recognized by us.' So!" Mr. Canary gave an

[380]

embarrassed but happy laugh. "There's your definition of Democracy."

"Where?" demanded Mr. Johnson.

Not exactly ignoring Mr. Johnson, but throwing at him a New Haven glare, Chairman Belden cried, "Jesus, Ote, that's the most magnificent piece of lyric prose, as well as the most tender and brave and profound job of straight thinking, that I've heard since the Gettysburg Address! Gentlemen and ladies, byes and gals, I want someone to put a motion trying to express our profound gratitude to Mr. Canary and his whole committee for formulating this stirring definition, to Colonel Marduc for financing the dinners during the conferences, and to Dr. Planish for his tireless checking and re-checking and re-re-checking of other definitions. Who will put this motion? Mr.—uh—Johnson, is it?"

"It is." Mr. Johnson was standing up, solid and placid. "Look, Belden. I honestly don't want to throw a monkey-wrench into this juke-box, but I came on East to find some group of people who weren't exhibitionists, who were really trying to organize all men of good will to back the Government and wake up the voters. I'd hoped to find a bunch at least as sensible as the average high-school football team."

In the hall, the telephone was ringing, and the bored Dr. Planish went out to answer it, as Mr. Johnson offensively blundered on:

"What do I find here? A bunch of congenital alumni and two very articulate women, all sitting around log-rolling, telling one another how smart you are, except

[381]

when you stop to thank your real boss, Charley Marduc, or to have a well-bred laugh at us innocents out in the Bible Belt——"

A mutter of resentment was rising, but it was stilled as Dr. Planish lumbered in, stammering, "That was my wife telephoning—news—the Japanese have just bombed our ships in Hawaii, and we are in the war."

They all babbled at once that they must rush out and take charge of the country, and they grabbed at briefcases if not at muskets.

Dr. Planish felt confused as he telephoned the news to Colonel Marduc, on his farm in Dutchess County, but the Colonel sounded jubilant:

"We'll wipe out all those little yellow devils in three months, and maybe I'll go back into the army and accept a major-generalship, and then make Tom Blizzard President—I've decided to let him have it. I want you and Winifred and Belden to meet me in my office tonight, eight sharp, and we'll make plans. Hooray!"

The Doctor walked painfully home. He was loyal to Marduc, but during all the years when he had been making a living out of shouting that he loved America, he really had loved his country, and it made him sick just now to go on peddling that love for profit. He was willing to quit the DDD and enlist. He was even willing to keep silent.

Yet when he came into the house and found his daughter Carrie talking with a young Columbia graduate student, the Doctor snapped back into his lifelong habit of being a professional wisdom-dealer—fact-softener—brain-picker — information-retailer — lay-high-priest — unofficial censor of all officials—critic so skilled in judgment that he did not need to know anything about anything in order to tell everybody everything about everything.

Carrie's young man was nervous of hands, widely spectacled, and probably scared, but his eyes were steady.

The Doctor roared, "Well, fella, I can't tell you how I envy you this hour of opportunity. I wish I were young enough to shoulder a musket!"

Carrie purred, "Now isn't that funny! I was just telling Stan how important you and Colonel Marduc and Mrs. Homeward are. He ought to study you and your influence instead of ancient Rome."

It sounded all right, but Dr. Planish was suspicious. He couldn't, however, waste this audience.

"Yes, it's a great chance you have, my boy. Perhaps you and your valiant generation will correct the errors that so many of the leaders of my generation have committed. It's up to you young folks—with such aid as I can continue to give you—to win the war and win the peace."

The graduate student remarked, "I've got to be getting back uptown," astounded the Doctor by kissing an unresistant Carrie, and walked out. Before the Doctor could get under way, it was Carrie who attacked:

"Daddy, listen. Please don't hand out any more slogans to my friends—not even 'win the war, win the peace.' That was a beautiful war-cry once, and it meant something to us, but all of us have had it thrown at us so many times in the last six months that it's just a sound."

"My God, to think that I could have a daughter who can be frivolous at a time like this, when men are fighting!"

"I won't stand your saying that! We're not frivolous! Maybe we know all the horrors, the creeping plague and the old churches smashed and the starving babies and the cynicism of men like Goebbels, better than you do, because our imaginations are younger. And we're going to do something. That boy who was just here—six months ago he was a pacifist, three months ago he was an isolationist, and tomorrow he'll enlist in the Marine Corps, if they'll have him. He used to use slogans, like you. Now he wants to use a machine-gun."

"But we have to have slogans! This is an ideological war—the first war in history that's entirely between two different sets of ideas. We got to have slogans—and trained leaders to coin them!"

"Didn't the French Revolutionists think they were fighting for a set of ideas, too, and didn't they have a slogan —Liberty, Equality, Fraternity? Maybe if they hadn't had so many perfectly swell songs and so many powerful orators and leaders, the Revolution would've had a better run."

"I told you you were frivolous—you and all your friends —shamefully frivolous in this dark hour of need."

"Well, most of them are going to be frivolous in khaki, in a few weeks. They'll fight—like the Civil War. But to people that try to get publicity for themselves out of telling the soldiers how noble they are, they'll just say, 'So what!' Can't you see that?"

"I see that my own daughter has become flippant to the point of blasphemy!" said Dr. Planish, and walked out of the house.

But he could not, as he sat in the Lafayette Café, go on hating her. She was too serious, and for once, this man who made a profession of preaching seriousness was actually serious himself.

In his hotel, Mr. Johnson of Minneapolis was writing to his son, who had been his junior partner but who was now a corporal in the United States Army:

Dear Son:

Am writing from NY. Have seen Life w Father, very funny show, father in the play not unlike me, when you're not around to kid me out of it. Your mother phones from Mpls that she is well, she is also a funny woman, sometimes funnier than she thinks. Well, it has come, with Pearl Harbor, you were wiser than I, getting into the army so early, tomorrow Monday morning I shall go out and see if I can enlist in some branch of the service, it would be fun if we could be together, hope however you are more careful with yr rifle than sometimes you were with shotgun when we hunted duck together, well I guess I jumped you for that sufficiently at that time.

I had hoped country could stay out, but I was wrong, and now shall think only of war. Have the business in shape so that Dave can wind it up. When you & I get back from the war we can start a new one. This town is full of stuffed shirts, do you know what is funny, son, they all bellyache here because the English come over and tell them what they ought to do about the war, and so they, the Easterners, tell us Middlewesterners what *we* ought to do abt war. A gassy uplifter here named Planish —I guess he was born in the Great Valley himself, but he's conveniently gone and forgot it, and this old windbag said to me, "I'm so sorry I haven't got time to go out and awaken the Middlewest to the realities and emergency of the international situation!" Have you still got that young Polish doctor from Winona for a lieutenant? Tell him what Planish said, will you, and write me his comment.

If I get into the service too, do not worry about yr mother and sisters, son, if anything happens—there is plenty insurance in their names, have found that place where we got such fine seafood that time, had a good dinner but sure did miss you, eating alone.

Yr father.

Dr. Planish had walked little, the past few years, but on this restless Sunday of December 7th, he walked all the way up to Colonel Marduc's office. He was wretchedly wondering if he always did know what was going to happen.

But he lost his indecision when he came into the buoyant presence of Colonel Marduc, who put a new rose in his buttonhole, lighted a gigantic cigar, pounded his desk and roared:

"Here's our chance. Germany will come in, and war must inevitably make a new political set-up, and Tom Blizzard and I are ready to step in. But I'm not so much

[386]

interested in office during the war—that's only temporary. What I want is influence after it. All right, call it *power*, if you want to!

"We must start right now identifying my name with post-war negotiations, and play it up so people will turn to me whether the war is lost or won. If we win, and I think we will, I have a new peace plan that nobody has hit on yet. We'd better get a lot of publicity on it, and get people referring to it as 'The Marduc Plan'. Realize you're the first person—except Winifred—that's ever heard those words, 'The Marduc Plan'? You won't be the last! And here it is:

"After the war, in order to make the Germans keep the peace permanently, we neither slaughter the whole lot of 'em—as a lot of sound people advocate, and there certainly is much to be said for that solution—nor do we let 'em into any new League of Nations, as the sentimentalists want. No. We just take their imperial government away from 'em, and reduce 'em to the small separate kingdoms and duchies that they were before 1870—a lot of small weak states. Doesn't that sound good? Doesn't it? And who can tell—the plan might even get adopted —why, it might even work!"

"But Colonel, mightn't those small states get to fighting one another, and just increase the chances of new wars?"

"Who the hell cares what they do? Besides, a little war now and then is good for business. Yessir! The idea of the Marduc Plan, then, ought to bring me a prominent seat at the final peace conference, and lead right to the post of Secretary of State . . . if not higher . . . but I'd be satisfied to let Tom Blizzard have the big job, if he'll get busy and move fast. I'm certainly not going to wait around while he backs and fills. Don't tell anybody this, but maybe the Japs did me a big service at Pearl Harbor!"

By just vigorously not hearing the last sentence, Dr. Planish was able to rouse to action, and forget the warnings of Carrie. "Fine! What do you think I better do now? God, I hope nothing will happen to the DDD!"

"It won't, my boy. I'll protect you. No, just carry on with the Powerhouses. Send 'em all a mimeographed bulletin tomorrow and remind 'em that we warned 'em about this Pearl Harbor danger months ago. Months!"

"But I don't think we did."

"Of course we didn't! What's that got to do with it? And begin to send out hints about the Marduc Plan—don't tell 'em what it is yet. Write some letters to the papers, under different names, demanding that Congress send for me to tell 'em what we're fighting for. I don't think they will, but they might have enough sense to. And phone Bultitude, if you can get him; tell him to start making hints about my Plan, or I'll expose him. Try him tonight—he'll be plenty worried. So!"

"I'll get busy right away, Colonel," said Dr. Planish.

30

Governor Blizzard's New York office, with its red carpet and weighty mahogany desk and steel engraving of John Quincy Adams, suggested a State capitol.

He had summoned Dr. Planish, who found a changed man. For years, in active State politics including biting and eye-gouging, Tom Blizzard had hidden the fact that he had been graduated from a university, *magna cum laude*. Of recent years, living in New York, he had played up the degree, and joined the National Arts Club. Today, in January, with the war five weeks old, Tom Blizzard had flopped back, and he was trying again to be the roughneck politician who loved silos, split infinitives and votes.

"Doc, I'm going to get out of this town and go back to the United States of America. This is the time for it. I think maybe I'm the guy to put up against FDR at the next Democratic National Convention, and till then I want to just set in Waskeegan and get the garlic and Chanel smells off me.

"I don't really savvy this Venusberg, and among other things I don't get is your organizations. Pressure groups. One half of you, all this past year, trying to make us stay to hell out of the war and the other half trying to get us in, and both sides forgetting we still have got a popular body called the Congress. What you're trying to do, all you uplifters and organizators, is to set up an Invisible Empire that'll be higher than the elected Government. You want to re-christen this country 'The Organized States of America, Inc.'!

"Now you, Doc, you're fairly sane, personally. I don't believe you believe your own spiels about what crooks and weather-vanes and foot-kissers we politicians are. You know damn well that politicians, at their worst, can be checked and thrown out by the popular vote, whereas you self-crucified Messiahs only have to keep on the right side of some philanthrobber and you're in for keeps. You are only a little cuckoo; you take care to hold down your job and play Charley Marduc's records.

"But have you ever noticed that nearly every one of the semi-honest uplifters and crusade-leaders and rousers of the masses, including the Communists and their brothers the evangelists, is anywhere from a neurotic with the hives up to a complete lunatic? Of course any man that deliberately sticks his neck out and goes into politics is a *little* crazy, but compared with all you self-appointed Galahads, Huey Long was a man of modesty and remarkable horse-sense.

"Yep, I'm reverting to Main Street with some of the fastest reversion you ever saw. Six weeks from now I'll have my feet up on the table with some honest ballot-box-stuffer, and forget all you unfrocked preachers and crayon-less professors and newspapermen that couldn't make the grade and women that made it too fast.

"But I might be able to use the lowdown on the virtuous shenanigans that Marduc and that bed-hopping daughter of his may pull from now on. My bank will be sending you—at your home address—a check for one hundred dollars, every month, and I'd like you to keep me informed on whatever that enlightened pair get away with."

Dr. Planish gasped, "You don't mean you want me to *spy* on Colonel Marduc?"

"Sure I do!"

"Oh! Oh, I see. Well——"

The publicizing of the Marduc Plan was interrupted by the most strategic idea Dr. Planish had had for a year. He saw a way in which, even during these troublous times, the DDD might be kept alive and useful no matter how wartime finances might go.

He felt that the citizenry were in a surprising and rather shocking mood; they were listening to the President and the Army and to airplane manufacturers, and not to the standard professional prophets, not even to those who were so inspired that they had been getting $1,250 for a lecture. The invitations to Colonel Marduc to attend public dinners had so diminished that he was accepting all of them.

The aureous life-blood of all organizations was, to Dr. Planish's public rejoicing and private worry, flowing into war bonds and Red Cross subscriptions, just when he had to pay the installments on Peony's new near-diamond and semi-sapphire bracelet. He knew that the other organizations must be suffering from the same anemia. Why not save expenses by combining all of them—with Dr. Gideon Planish as the executive secretary of the lot?

The idea was simple and brilliant, he felt, and Colonel Marduc approved it.

The word "co-operation" had long been one of the most valuable in the organizational treasure-house, but nobody had ever done much about it, because each organization had its paid secretary, and that secretary did not want to be co-operated out of his salary. But now, with the young secretaries being drafted and the old ones being starved, Dr. Planish felt that he could move in on them as easily as Hitler had moved into Poland—though, naturally, with an entirely different treatment of the office staffs.

He knew a good deal about the others. Using the names of Bonnie Popick and Flaude Stansbury and his other clerks, he had regularly sent for the "literature" of every new private circumlocution office as it was blithely set up. Now, with Bonnie, he began to list all the national welfare and educational organizations with headquarters in New York City.

He stopped when he had listed two thousand of them, mostly with titles containing the words American, National, Committee, Institution, Guild, Forum, League or Council. Even Dr. Planish had not realized that there were so many bands of light.

He arbitrarily picked out every hundredth league, called a taxicab, started out to co-operate the twenty he had chosen—and quit his crusade at 4:37 that afternoon.

He had started with "The Get Together Alliance,"

which had one pink and golden room in the Gyro Building, and proved to consist entirely in a Mrs. Willoughby Eck, who was a tailored fifty but enthusiastic. It was her notion that the cure for every world evil was for everybody to keep on shaking hands with everybody else all the time, falling on them whenever you could catch them off guard, in subways, at theaters, at bars and prayer-meeting. Mrs. Eck gushed, "The Rotarians have the right idea—good fellowship—but why should the Rotarians have all the fun? Why don't us moral leaders also recognize each other's humanity by the touch of hands? Let me give you my little leaflet, Reverend."

But the Doctor had fled, without even trying to co-operate with Mrs. Willoughby Eck.

By 4:37 P.M., the innocent Doctor had been shocked by the whole business of organizationality. He had found that the National American Eclectic Institute for the Advancement of the Popular Principle in Education was one large, gray old gentleman who had a small desk in a corner of a public stenographer's clattering office; that its rival, the Society for the Humanization of Higher Education, did have rooms and rooms and pamphlets and pamphlets, but was, all the while, just another league for attacking union labor; and that another rival, the Institute of Investigative Consideration of Education, was nothing at all but #3 Telephone in a row of twelve telephones upon the desk of a backroom real-estate dealer, which desk was equally the headquarters of the Mount Celestial Cemetery Corp., the Fig Leaf Publishing Co., and the League for the Protection of Home and Marriage.

He had also found that an association of poets headed by a lady who looked like Emily Dickinson, a drama league mothered by an insurance-man's wife, and a share-croppers' defense society, were all of them strangely like Communist fronts.

Dr. Planish returned to his office, and left the world to darkness and to philanthrobbing. He was so sunk that for a moment he thought of going back to work, of taking a school job so that some younger teacher might be released for enlistment.

But, he snorted, what percentage was there in being a professional Light to the Toilers if you merely became a toiler? That would be as silly as for a professional evangelist to go to somebody else's mission and get saved, with not even a look-in on the collection-box.

No, he would go on with his co-operation, but he would perform it with sound, reliable organizators, the ones he already knew personally.

Next morning, at 11, he was in the anteroom of the Anti-Racial Youth Committee for the Organization of Global Co-operation, waiting to see its managing secretary, Professor Goetz Buchwald.

He had to wait, for the Professor was "in conference" with another warm friend, Dr. Christian Stern. The waiting-room was comfortable enough; it even had a touch of splendor, with red-leather armchairs, rare volumes in Bantu, Hindustani and Hebrew, and handsome blown-up photographs of Youth Groups from sixteen different countries, all wearing shorts and horn-rimmed spectacles and all looking exactly alike, except that the Chinese and Palestinian groups looked more so.

Into this room militarily strode still another friend: Commander Orris Gall, executive director of the Zero-Hour American National Committee on Anti-Totalitarian Defense, which even since Pearl Harbor had gone right on in a surprised way telling the country that Adolf Hitler was no real friend of America.

"Well, well, well, Dr. Planish, this is swell finding you here. This will save me a trip to your office. I phoned you, but they said you'd just left," said the Commander. "I've got a perfectly revolutionary idea. Like this. I needn't tell you how the sources of philanthropy are threatening to dry up. So why don't a lot of us that have a common ideology join up and economize on expenses and efforts? Let's co-operate!"

The Doctor glowed, "Why, that's what I was going to suggest to you! I suppose you'll be going back into the Navy."

"No, not—exactly. The new people that are running it claim that because I belong to the old tradition, I haven't kept up to date. Imagine that! But I am going to take a key post with one of the most important manufacturers of naval equipment—in the public relations department. Right away."

"So that'll leave your ZANC without a director. I'll be glad to take it over——"

"That wasn't exactly my idea, Doctor. The fact is, my wife is going to continue my work—she's really a lot more

[395]

capable than I am—a very remarkable writer, too; you ought to see some of the fiction she dashes off—and what I was thinking was that since your DDD has always merely covered the same field as ours, like exposing scoundrels like Zeke Bittery—and after all, it was I who first showed him up!—why, Marduc and you might like to put the DDD under Mrs. Gall's supervision and you could—well, you could go on to something else, don't you see?"

Dr. Planish was staring at this insolence when out of Professor Buchwald's office glided Dr. Christian Stern. He bubbled as he saw them:

"Well, well, boys, this *is* a coincidence! I was going to call on you both this afternoon, but I guess this 'll save me some taxi-fares, ha, ha! What I want to talk to you about is—— You know how busy I always am, with my big institutional church, but somehow this crisis gives one superhuman energies, and I was thinking I might be able to combine your DDD and ZANC with Professor Buchwald's ARYC, and serve, or shall I say function, as executive secretary of the whole caboodle—and, practically speaking, at no extra salary, say just thirty-five hundred beyond what I'm getting now—and thus release you boys for war work. I regret to say that Buchwald can't see it my way. If there's any co-operating, he wants to do the *operating* and let us do the *co!* But you boys are more like practical men of affairs, and so—— Let's co-operate!"

31

Dr. Planish and the other directors of the DDD decided that, since they were kept from co-operation by a little group of willful men, they might as well help out the Government. When Washington announced to some millions of newspaper readers that it wanted scrap iron, the Doctor's bulletins hastily told several thousand members that the DDD was thinking of letting the Government have some scrap iron.

When the Government got tired of H. Sanderson Sanderson-Smith's taking too much German money without registering as an agent, and sent him to the Federal penitentiary, Dr. Planish rushed in to expose Mr. Sanderson-Smith; and who but he presided at the meeting where Dr. Elmer Gantry came right out and denounced his former buddy, Ezekiel Bittery, as a deceiver, a turncoat, a Fascist, a Fifth Columnist, a renegade, a snake in the grass, a Ratzi and an anti-Semite. (This was less than a fortnight after Mr. Bittery had joined Mr. Sanderson-Smith in his cell.)

With each of these courageous deeds, Dr. Planish felt justified in sending out a few letters suggesting an increase of contributions to the DDD.

In a general sort of way, at this time Dr. Planish and

the DDD also arranged a large public dinner, not because it had any value, not because anyone, except persons who like to be naked in public, could find it anything but agonizing, but because it was an American primitive tribal rite, astonishingly like the orgies of the Penitentes, except that the Penitentes do not have a busy paid secretary. In New York it is always possible to persuade from six hundred to fifteen hundred persons to put on evening clothes and pay from $3.50 to $7.50 each for a very bad dinner, at which very bad speakers, mostly throat-clearers, will arise and say nothing at all at preposterous length, with an "uh" between every adjective and noun. It is even possible to get these speakers, these non-private persons, not only to endure the horrors of oratorical vacuity, but also to put up with the torture of a reception before or after the dinner, when they will shake hands with strangers and smilingly listen to them without once protesting, "Everything you are saying to me is complete foolishness."

It is not Broadway that is the Main Street of New York, but the long, thin, prandial Speakers' Table, and every familiar—too, too familiar—face along it knows intimately and detests furiously all the other inevitable and self-opening faces there.

And one of the largest and dreariest of these rain dances was whipped up by the DDD.

So the Doctor was able to make a good report when a former acquaintance named Hatch Hewitt jeeringly asked, in a bar, what he had been doing about the war. This Hewitt was in uniform as a major of marines, and when Dr.

Planish took the trouble to ask him where he was going, the man merely growled "Abroad," and when, even more politely, the Doctor said that he felt like joining up, too, the Major observed, "————!"

Yet with all this effort driving the Doctor half-mad, Colonel Marduc incessantly asked that his name and his Marduc Plan for Permanent Peace be mentioned in more radio talks, more interviews, and in mid-spring, he was suddenly demanding publicity also for his daughter, Winifred Homeward the Talking Woman.

Colonel Marduc was on the loose that evening. He felt lonely and misunderstood; he felt his sixty years.

He had had words with his most recent mistress on the subject of telephoning to her at 3 A.M. If he found that she was then asleep, he was angry at her for neglecting him; if she was awake, he stated that she must have another lover with her; if she didn't answer at all, he called her at 6 A.M. to rebuke her for the sleep she had made him lose. His last attention to her had been a slap.

He scouted into his favorite stalking ground, the Vicugna Bar, where Park Avenue met Prospect Park and stage celebrities went to stare at the suave and beautiful visitors from Omaha. The Colonel walked up to the bar as if he owned it. He did.

Three drinks later, he felt healed enough to look around. One young woman, at a table with another girl, looked familiar: a slim redhead with a face as pert as a pearl button against black cloth. The Colonel, with an indifferent bend of his finger, brought the manager of the Vicugna on the run. "The redhead—what gives?" he grunted.

"I don't know, Colonel. I'll try and find out right away, Colonel," panted the manager, a less collegiate Sherry Belden, but more useful. While the hero stood erect and drank, always too dignified to squat on a stool at the bar, the manager scuttled through the café interviewing waiters, and came back to groan, "I'm terribly sorry, Colonel, but nobody seems to know who she is."

"Have I got to do my own seductions, at my age? Imperial power, intellectual panders on the court payroll, and still beneath the ermine the emperor is naked, *nicht wahr?*"

"That's so, sir," said the manager, who had understood only the words "payroll," "naked" and "*nicht wahr.*"

"Go to hell," said the Colonel.

The manager went.

The Colonel watched the redhead till her girl companion had gone off to what, in the infinite delicacy of modern American saloons, is known as "the powder room," then moved on her like a traditional grand duke, like a mighty bull of Bashan. He sat down at her table without invitation, and she stared at him, breathless, frightened and already conquered.

"I seem to know you, young lady."

"Oh, yes, Colonel. I guess you must a seen me. I'm a stenographer at the DDD."

"M?"

"Up on the third floor. Under Mr. Vesper. I've seen you when you've come into the Doctor's office."

"Doctor? Doctor? Which Doctor?"

"Why, Dr. Planish!"

"Oh. *Him!*" A huge silence. "Yes, yes, a Christian gentleman and a fine scholar. Undoubtedly. I'm sure that you girls enjoy working for him."

"He's awfully sweet and kind—you know, kind of jokey."

"I see. Jokey—— Look, dear, get rid of that piece of fluff that's with you, and we'll go drink some champagne at the Syrinx Den. Here she comes."

The redhead talked to her friend, aside. She came back to the Colonel and his bulbous stare as timidly as though it had been she who had started all this. She was amazed when, in the taxicab, he did not kiss her, but only patted her hand. At the Syrinx cabaret, where he didn't actually order champagne but a couple of innocent-tasting drinks called "zombies," he respectfully asked her opinion of Dr. Planish's latest pamphlet, *Defend Your Dollars*— which she had liked very much but which she had not read. Not till she had chattered herself into loving companionship did he ask her name.

"Flaude Stansbury. It's a kind of corny name, ain't it! My ma was romantic."

"No worse a name than Marduc, precious."

"Maybe I ought to use my married name."

"Nonsense! You can't be married! You'reyoungenough-tobemygranddaughter!" (But inwardly he was congratulating himself, "That'll save trouble!")

"Oh, I am so married, Colonel!" (He had not asked her to call him "Charley," and he never did. Seduction was to Colonel Marduc no ground for impertinence.)

[401]

"And who's the lucky boy, Flaude? I'll bet the dog is handsome."

"He isn't a boy. He's pretty old."

"Not as old as I am, I bet."

"He'd be twice as old as you are even if he was only half as old. Oh, I'm not kicking. Honestly I'm not! I hate these wives that whine and complain, don't you?"

"I certainly do!" said Colonel Marduc, with great sincerity.

"I thought it would be kind of different—he's such a student and idealist and all that junk, and he was so desperately in love with me—and God knows, I didn't want to always have to go on earning my living, and he was so in love and—— No soap. The poor thing does try so hard, but he's such a cold fish—and then he wants me to kneel down and pray with him! Figure that one!"

"Who is this egg?"

"He's my immediate boss—Mr. Carlyle Vesper."

"Vesper? Oh, that flunky at the DDD—excuse me, I mean clerk. But he's a million years older than you are!"

"I'll say!"

"And he's some kind of a Holy Roller preacher, isn't he?"

"God knows what he is, except that—— Oh, Colonel!"

He kissed her, so openly and so ignoring of all the drinkers packed in around them, that nobody paid any attention. And in the Colonel's kiss there was nothing of cold-fishness.

He took her to what she considered the most beautiful apartment she had ever seen, and he considered the most horrible burlesque in New York: a hotel suite choked with Spanish beams, escritoires in five kinds of wood and three kinds of carving, coffee tables shaped like drums, and armchairs that were also radios and smoking-stands and magazine racks. There was a bathroom with flimsy nightgowns and cosmetics for women, and in the kitchen, along with sound Bourbon, were crême de rose and Dantziger Goldwasser.

The young lady cried on his shoulder, but it was no cry of unhappiness.

He thought, as he met Flaude at the Vicugna for the third time, that the square-nosed man at the bar was shadowing him, but he forgot it in her young hand-clasp. Her husband, Flaude said, was out this evening, attending some dreary committee meeting. . . . The Colonel had seen to it that Carlyle Vesper should be attending a dreary committee meeting.

He wanted to see Flaude's home, particularly to look over her wardrobe, with a view to improvements.

As they entered that skimpy flat, a rear walk-up near the East River, he ached for his poor little friend. The place had none of the lip-stick flavor that he had expected; there wasn't so much as a tall gilt basket tied with a rosy ribbon. The living-room was hilly with old gray books, and between the two narrow and sooty windows, which faced the courtyard, was a *prie-Dieu*.

He growled, "What a dump! Come here and I'll give you something to make up for it."

Over her shoulder, as he kissed her, he could see, slowly

coming through the door of the bedroom, slow and silent and gray, a man who looked like a hill-billy preacher, a thin and sallow man, his mustache dribbling.

The man was Carlyle Vesper. He was carrying an old-fashioned razor, the blade clear and vicious even in that muggy light. His mouth was wide and trembling.

In a Harlem den, the Colonel had once seen a man sliced up with a razor, but he was interested to notice that he was not afraid. With no especial haste, he swung the girl round behind him. Then he laughed.

Solemnly, methodically, but with speed, a man who had been standing outside on the fire-escape was sliding up the half-open window, falling into the room, seizing Vesper from behind. He was the squat man who had been tailing the Colonel.

The Colonel gave Flaude three hundred dollars, which would more than take her back home to Stansbury Center —her great-grandfather had been the founder of the village, her grandfather a loafer and her father a drunk. He helped Flaude pack her two bags.

The detective was explaining to Carlyle Vesper that they just wanted him to understand that unless he kept his mouth shut, he would be killed. "I do mean killed—and I *do* mean *you!*" said the detective, cheerfully, and he bent Vesper's left middle finger back and back till the man screamed, "Don't—oh, please don't! I'll keep still. Anyway, can't you see I don't want to hurt her any more than I have?"

When they left him, the man was lying on his bed, sobbing.

The Colonel said, "Sniveling little bastard. By the way, flatfoot, how do you get a man killed?"

"Search me. I just read about it in detective stories, same as you. I'm very fond of a good detective story, though I don't know but what I like a Western better. How do you suppose these fellows think up all these ideas for stories?"

When they were seated in the back room of a saloon, the Colonel said blandly, "Come across. Who put you on me, and how much do you want?"

"Oh, well, Colonel, no use bluffing you. I won't ask you more 'n a couple hundred bucks, because it was only your daughter, Mrs. Homeward."

"Oh . . . Winifred . . . Sweet girl . . . Idealistic."

"That's a fact. But Jesus, how she talks! A check would be all right, Colonel. I don't think you'd stop payment on it."

"You mean, not twice I wouldn't."

"That's the idea!"

The two men of the world laughed together.

When someone—the voice was unfamiliar—telephoned to Dr. Planish that Mr. Carlyle Vesper would be unable to return to the office, and would they please send Vesper's things to this address, the Doctor was pretty indignant.

In Vesper's desk, Bonnie Popick and the Doctor found a small leather-bound copy of the *Imitatio Christi*.

The good Doctor protested gently, "Now isn't that just like a shiftless beggar like Carlyle to go and blow in his

[405]

money on such an expensive piece of junk! On *his* salary! Anyway, it was very inconsiderate of him to have married that Stansbury girl in the first place. If he'd asked my advice, I'd 've told him not to. I've always stood ready to give him anything—I mean, any advice—but do you think he appreciated that? Now, I suppose he and his wife will go batting all over the country, never thinking for one second how inconvenient it is for *me* to have 'em walk out and leave me flat this way, with all I've got to do. As I've always said, ingratitude and disloyalty and lack of imagination are worse crimes than—than—than——"

"Barratry," said Bonnie.

"What?" said Dr. Planish.

The Colonel had invited his daughter to come down to the office for a drink.

"I always do think you've got the nicest diggings here," she said.

"When the hell did an office become a 'diggings'?"

Her laughter tinkled lightly—anyway, she meant it to be lightly-tinkling, as in the newspaper items about her. "Of course. How silly of me!"

"What makes you so Park Avenue today? Or are you being English? You must have been bumming around with some new lover—maybe your husband!"

"Dear Father, what's all this rudeness a prelude to?"

"Why are you trying to get the goods on me?"

"Trying?"

"All right, getting 'em. Wouldn't it be cheaper to come

and ask me about my affairs? I can tell you much more than Operative Skink of the O'Pook Agency."

"Hm?" She looked glazed and impenetrable.

"He's now on my payroll. Just what is your game, my child? Are you trying to get something on me so you can step on my face and climb up over me, as you've been doing to other people all your life, starting with your classmates in Miss Mitch's School and continuing on up to your husband? Are you turning your fancy lightly to patricide?"

"Do you know that when you talk in that silly, self-dramatizing way, it's very hard for me to remember that you're my father—presumably? Of course I've been checking up on your little excursions. I have to protect you against yourself; I have to know just what exhibitions of puerility you've been up to, and decide whether to let your various associates know about them. My dear Father, if you had the slightest idea what I've gone through in my efforts to keep your old friends, even your own doctor, loyal to you——"

"You——"

"If you could hear the way they confide to me that they're just about fed up with your incessant drunkenness and whoring, and your badly informed talk-talk-talking about foreign affairs——"

"*Me* talk——"

"I've pled with them and I've begged them to remember that behind all your senile capers——"

"Senile!"

[407]

"——you do have a generous heart, and a pretty good brain, at least for business. Me climb? Me step on people's faces? Why, the only thing I've ever wanted from life was to go on being an adoring wife and daughter, stay home and sacrifice everything to help my husband and my father, and if I've ever stepped out and taken some poor, pitiful little interest in public affairs, it's only because I've been so sick at heart over the way you two men have made childish drunken spectacles of yourselves. I just couldn't endure sitting idle and helpless at home another hour. I've undoubtedly kept both of you out of jail, or out of the alcoholic ward, by my hourly and incessant struggle, and as for you—I warn you that from now on I'm going to take charge of your political career. Entire charge!"

On the Colonel's desk, the telephone that was connected only with his secretary was ringing. It was Winifred who answered it. She gurgled, "Oh, yes. Send him right up."

She turned on the Colonel in a sunburst of sweetness. "It's a reporter from *Events*. He wants your opinion on the psychology of the Japs."

The young man came in, nodded tolerantly to Winifred, and said to the Colonel, "The boss thinks your ideas about Japan ought to be valuable. He says you handled a lot of publicity for the Japanese Government a few years ago."

The Colonel sputtered, "Nonsense—nonsense! Just a few routine matters—some commercial promotion that happened to come into our office—carelessness on the part of an underling—fired him the moment I heard he'd accepted the vile stuff!"

Winifred Homeward, delicately gesturing with a cigarette, her bright voice soaring, caught the reporter's attention:

"But you're perfectly right to come to him. Even if he *is* my father, I must say there's no one who has more information about Japan and how to crush it than the Colonel, whether as a soldier or an administrator. Here's the way he and I feel about it. What's the shortest way from New York or Detroit or Pittsburgh or Washington or St. Paul, or for that matter, from Toronto, to Tokio or Kobe or Yokohama or, what really counts, to Korea where, we have inside information, the natives are ready to rise against their Japanese overlords——"

Colonel Marduc presently wandered out of the room, quite unnoticed, and did not return until after this spirited interview with him was over.

Winifred said to Peony, "These *men*—even the talented ones, like my father and your husband and mine—they do mean so well, but they have no sense of orderliness and human values, like us. I suppose we get it from housekeeping and from mothering them.

"We women have always controlled school-teaching in America, and conversation and manners, but now that so many of the men are away at war, here's our chance to have a much higher sphere of influence. When the time comes, I'm going to run for the city council in New York, and I don't see why I shouldn't be governor. I'm going to start an organization of my own, something like the DDD, but much more hooked up with practical politics. When peace comes, there's no reason why women shouldn't be in power, and dictate the terms. We're so much less emotional.

"You could save my life, Peony. I want you to start business school, right away, and learn typing and shorthand, and be ready to boss the corps of secretaries I'll have to have. I'll pay your tuition, and pay you twenty dollars a week while you're learning. How about it?"

"Swell!"

Peony had been bored. With shopping, movies, reproving Carrie, playing bridge with a gabby sister-in-law of Chris Stern, eating and a prodigious quantity of sleeping, she had put in twenty-four hours a day, but she had not met many of the powerful people whom the Doctor was always quoting. She had even been driven to taking courses in economics and history at Columbia, sometimes showing up as often as every other class.

Now, business college was the liveliest party she had known in months. She was thirty-nine, but she found herself of the same age with all the girls of twenty-two and the undrafted boys of eighteen in the school; with them, at the Palais de Hamburger, she gigglingly exchanged such conversational delights as "What's cooking in your filing class? Say, did you see the expression on that old bag's face when I *did* know the symbol for February? In the groove! That's cooking with gas!"

She was at home now; she had found that gay, urbane New York that she had known must exist; and when

George Riot slipped into town and on the telephone muttered that she must meet him again at the dreary Hex Hotel, she refused, because she was going to a party to be given by the clever Miss Teddy Klutz, aetat 24, the youngest and liveliest teacher at their Qwick-Shure Secretarial and Executive Commercial College, Positions Guaranteed.

Late every afternoon Peony was at Winifred Homeward's office, mixing Sazarac cocktails or confidentially helping the great woman in affairs too delicate for the routine hands at *Attention!;* working on the grand list of influential women all through America who were, know it or not, fated to be Winifred's future corps of Black Blouses.

Not Colonel Marduc nor the chirping Deacon Wheyfish and certainly not the anxious Dr. Planish had ever had so much fun in the invisible empire of propaganda as Peony Planish.

32

A DISTURBING LETTER had come in to Dr. Planish from Mr. Johnson of Minneapolis, written from the Great Lakes Naval Training Center:

"I have been asked to be a sponsor, whatever that means, for a Dinner Dedicated to the Plain People, to be held in your very fine Gladiola Hotel and to be conducted by three novelists, a portrait painter and an alderman, at $3.50 a plate, which is a good plain price. There are a lot of other names on the list of sponsors, but what bothers me is that they seem to have left out all the Plain People.

"Should I send some on? I can't come myself because I am now in the Navy, but I know quite a few of the Plain People in Minnesota—a dumb farmer who happens to be my uncle, and a surgeon who likes duck hunting, and my plumber, and a chemist who went to Yale, which I guess should make him a Plain Person as that college was founded to promote plain democratic learning. Or do you think they might resent the imputation that they are so Plain and so lowdown that they have to have dinners given to them by liberal novelists to bring them up to a level where Mrs. Homeward can notice them?"

Suddenly, a little heavily, he liked Mr. Johnson of

Minneapolis, and agreed with him against all the organizators and all the ethical raptures of his transmogrified Peony.

The next letter in the afternoon mail was from President T. Austin Bull of Kinnikinick, inviting him to be the speaker at Presentation Day, in early May.

"If you can possibly afford the time, stay on for a few days and get a real rest here in the quiet while the lilacs come out and the thin green lines of young oats look so pretty against the black earth."

A young Gid Planish was reborn, and he exulted, "I'm going, and maybe I'm never coming back!"

No, said Peony, Good Lord, no; she couldn't possibly leave her shorthand to go out to any Middlewest, and besides, she didn't think the Bulls and that Teckla Schaum, that Gid used to be so much in love with, cared so much for her; and now that Peony's father and mother were dead and she had lost track of all her dumb friends in that dumb Middlewest—— Besides! She wasn't going to waste all these lovely new clothes that she was (partly) paying for out of her new salary on a bunch of farmers, not *her!*

But she insisted on their having a Real Time, a typical happy evening in New York, before he went West, and they had it, to the full splendor.

In order to be at home on time, he called on five contributors in thirty-eight minutes, riding up and down in express elevators, past a total of 474 floors, with the shoulders of strangers unaffectionately thrust into his jaw; he took a taxicab home and got stuck in crosstown traffic; his

[413]

wife and he dressed in expensive special evening gar-
ments that were going to look pretty funny in the history-
book pictures in 1982; they took another taxi, endured
another traffic jam in the streets of the theatrical district,
smelly with carbon monoxide and Italian food; paid for
the unpleasant ride the ransom for a small prince; edged
past a doorman whose glance said "Tip!"; edged into a
restaurant; were insulted and kept waiting by a member
of the Fascist Party who was learning dictatorship as a
restaurant manager; waited for the pleasure of lending
the Doctor's hat to a girl who just didn't like customers;
squeezed in between a skinny table and the wall; looked
unhungrily through the varieties of chicken on the menu;
waited for the waiter; muttered their orders to the waiter,
who was German-Swiss and didn't like customers or anybody else; ate radishes and celery and olives and bread
and lumps of ice and the table bouquet till they didn't
really want their chicken, and then ate chicken till they
didn't want their profiterolles, and then ate the profiterolles;
listened to the shrieks of three business women, all in
tweeds and all drunk, at another table; waited for the
waiter with the bill; waited for their change; added a tip
to an amount sufficient to ransom a pretty big prince;
struggled out between tables; waited for the check-girl;
paid her fifteen cents for a ten-cent hat and got a vicious
look from her because it wasn't a quarter; waited for the
doorman to call another taxi; got a vicious look from the
doorman because they hadn't tipped him; tipped him;
sat in a taxi one-tenth filled with cigarette butts and the
corpses of paper matches during another jam in cross-

[414]

town traffic; discovered that it would have been six blocks shorter to have walked to the theater; lifted themselves out of the taxi at the theater; got a vicious, dirty, and awfully discriminating look from the theater doorman who, while the Doctor was paying another ransom to the taxi-driver, looked over their clothes and muttered "Yonkers"; produced the theater tickets for which the Doctor had paid the ransom for two princes and a king; crawled into the theater behind a line of paralytics until they reached their seats, where Dr. Planish fell into such a coma of exhaustion that not till the second act did he sit up and discover that he had seen the play before.

And so they went home, to be kept awake by the radio across the way, and the next morning he started for Kinnikinick, with enthusiasm.

The bluff by Lake Elizabeth had once been an hour and a half walk over a sandy trail. Now, it was an eight-minute drive from the campus by a new black-top road.

The Pridmore shack in which he had spent his first night with Peony had been replaced by a log-and-stone chalet, where Teckla and her father lived all year round; and next door, with a common plane of springy lawn, was the Virginia mansion of President Bull, where Dr. Planish was staying.

It was the morning of Presentation Day, and T. Austin Bull and he were already in doctoral robes, very gloomy and priestly and proper. But a catastrophe threw down all this majesty.

The small cat of the youngest Bull granddaughter

scrambled up a tree, and was too scared to come down. There was a domestic flurry. The President, with his robe flapping, tried with a bamboo fishing-pole to guide the kitten out on a branch that hung low. The four grand-children capered round and round the tree, screaming; the President's two daughters, and Teckla Schaum, from next door, stood watching, comfortable and amused, while Mrs. Bull leaned from one upstairs window, and the young colored maid from another, ironically cheering. Dr. Planish was excitedly giving advice to President Bull, who looked as much like a sleek, curly-headed leading man as ever, but an old actor now, old and kind and amused. The lake breeze was fresh, and wavelets ran up among the bright dry weeds on shore.

Suddenly Dr. Planish was homesick for precisely the place where he was; suddenly it was unendurable to think of going back to the city that was an hourly futility and a yearly defeat.

Teckla was shouting, "Here's a berry box! Put a piece of fish in it and tie it to the top of the pole and the kitten will crawl in to get the fish, and you'll have her!"

The children danced and clapped their hands as the box was raised to the kitten, who sniffed at it, scowled, and turned her head to the study of arboriculture.

"Now this is really important!" proclaimed Dr. Planish.

"Extremely important. Let the Presentation Day wait!" agreed the President.

There loomed up a farmer neighbor, bearing a lofty ladder and bawling, "You boys got great minds but no sense. It's a good thing I never went to college. Now let a real man get at that cat!"

"You're right," agreed the two doctors, as the farmer began to climb, the kitten to swear, and the children to sing, "At that cat—that fat cat—catch that cat!"

Then Teckla said to a young Gideon, "Now you're happy. It's the first time here that I've seen you relaxed. But I think your heart is still in our backwoods."

He looked uncomfortably at her, lonely for her even when he was actually with her. It seemed to him that Teckla, fifty-four and gray, was younger and more content than Peony at less than forty.

And not till then did he remember to ask for the Dr. Edith Minton who had been so admirably icy. He learned that she had been dead for seven years. Somewhere near by she lay in earth, alone.

He wanted to discard all of his careful Presentation Day speech. He had seen the men students in uniform, he had seen the girl students on the campus, smoking cigarettes, their legs bare with little rolled socks, and he felt that if this academic shrine was less decorous than in his day, it was shockingly more sensible. The Flaming Youth nonsense had been all pose; just the propriety of impropriety. It seemed to him that these young people now were too busy for posing—much posing.

He did not feel altogether safe in intoning to this audience, this sharp-eyed gang of intellectual pirates, that they ought to look into something new called Democracy.

[417]

In other colleges, he had had evidence that young people today were irreverent toward sloganeering, but he had not comprehended it till he had come home; and now, even this audience of over a thousand couldn't keep him contentedly bombasting for more than twenty minutes. All through his oration he heard, like a ringing in the ears, his own doubt, "Maybe I ought to be asking these young people about freedom and courage, not telling them."

He did not recover his front till, at evening at the President's house, he was surrounded by his old acquaintances, asking him respectfully—pretty respectfully—about the private scandals and phobias of the Great Leaders: Governor Blizzard and Senator Bultitude and Milo Samphire and, always, the dazzle-sounding, radiogenic Winifred Marduc Homeward.

"All noble souls, yet often I feel as if I wanted to give them all up and be back in this peaceful world of scholarship," he sighed.

"That's because you've been away a long time. You forget how many fakers *we* put out, in our modest way," said old Eakins, professor emeritus.

Dr. Planish was not even sure that Eakins was impressed by his inside news about what the British Army was planning in the way of future aircraft. "Some of these old devils out here are horribly on. They do read, and they know Europe—which is more than I do!" he worried.

But the chairman of the Kinnikinick trustees, Mr. Pridmore, sat admiring.

Dr. Planish rejoiced, "There's a man I can bank on. I'd like to have him for a neighbor again. And Teckla!"

[418]

He noted that since his time here, the Doctoring and Professoring of the faculty members had thinned out. Even that stickler Austin Bull preferred to be called just Mister. Dr. Planish was worried for a time. Was the whole country turning against its honorable titled leaders? Then it seemed to him that for a while it might be pleasant to quit going around Doctoring, and be plain Mr. Planish.

And just once say to the Colonel, "Hey you, Marduc!"

When the learned crew was gone, and Teckla had unexpectedly kissed him and bolted away, Austin Bull patted his shoulder and said gravely:

"Gid, a year from now I shall retire. How would you like to be president of Kinnikinick? I think when you left here, I said some very ill-advised things to you and about you. I realize now that I was jealous. I'm all for you as president, and I know some of the trustees are. It's a possibility at least. What do you say?"

"That's splendid of you. I'm very grateful. I'll—I'll have to think about it."

"You won't need to decide till next fall."

"I'll think quick and hard—Mr. Bull!"

And he did have to think hard, for he was seeing, all at once, a kitten up a maple tree, the amused face of a barelegged co-ed, the storm-clouds of Colonel Marduc's countenance, the pipe-smoke in President Bull's little study, twenty-five thousand admiring people at a rally in Madison Square Garden, and Peony's lips that could pout for kissing or square themselves in rage.

He stood on the porch and looked to the left, just a few

[419]

rods away, and saw the shack that had once stood there, saw the ghost of a girl who had come gaily to a young professor by night. She hadn't been renovated then by the world of fame and philanthrobbing. She had been so sweet! Now he was lonely. Oh, he would do *something*—

Once there was a man in a condemned cell and he got to thinking about all the places he'd like to see again, and he was a man who had already traveled a lot and knew about such things, and he was thinking and deciding between Capri and California, and he was picturing Point Lobos and Carmel, and he calculated that if he sold a few shares of stock, he could afford to drive out there, but then he remembered that there was gasoline rationing now, and, besides, he was going to be hanged at eight o'clock tomorrow morning.

He sat in his bedroom, thinking that if he became president of Kinnikinick, he would make less money than at the DDD; when he traveled, he would have only a lower berth, and not a Pullman compartment, where you had a private toilet, and could stand up when you undressed, as a man of years and dignity should, and where you could recover from the strain of lecturing by lighting a cigar and making nice smoke rings. And there was difficulty in that he had now forgotten whatever he might once have known about literature, history and every other branch of learning in which it was not enough to roll out, "We are called upon to bear the heat and fatigue of the struggle," and you had to mix some dates and figures with the oratory.

The president of a college was supposed to leave all these matters of study to the dean, and attend to the higher branch of getting money out of the alumni. Still, even the president couldn't always avoid meeting inquisitive undergraduates.

Then he snapped back at himself. All right! All right! It was a challenge. He'd meet the challenge. He'd read a book again. He'd look up his old text-books, and read them. He was only fifty. By the time he was fifty-five, he could again be as well-read as any of these undergraduates—almost.

Anyway, he had to. Wheyfish's titter and Sherry Belden's jitter and Marduc's totalitarianism and the swoop of express elevators filled with sharp and twitching elbows. Philanthrobbers, Organizators, midnight perpetual-motion discussions of Conditions and Situations, and Winifred Homeward the Talking Woman. Was that a life?

He walked through the village and saw the cottage where Peony and he had started married life. It was no longer white and shining. It belonged now to a professor, but he had five children and a crippled wife; it was as smeary and hopeless as something in factory slums.

Dr. Planish longed to paint it white again, but when he tried to coax a young Peony into the doorway, it remained mocking and empty.

He plodded to the campus and ventured into the office that he himself had once ruled, as dean. The present dean said, "Sorry I've got such a lot of engagements, Mr. Planish. If you can wait, I'll be right with you."

Mr. Planish could not wait for anyone, not in that room.

He returned to the lake, and lunched with Teckla, just they two, on the veranda by the blue water, by the silver birches.

"Gid darling, you trouble me. I know it's impertinent, but you always seem a little tired. There isn't anything that I can do for you again, but there's no one that loves you better and more lastingly."

"I'm sure of it."

"Or who doesn't care even if you *have* become a stuffed shirt."

"Me?"

"Daddy and I long to have you take the presidency and come back and be our neighbor again."

"If I'm a stuffed shirt——"

"Well, aren't you?"

"Don't be disgusting! Certainly not! Well—— What if I am?"

"Oh, it doesn't matter to me. Not any more than your having done a few murders. I still love you—God knows why."

She looked at him invitingly, but he was thinking that, aside from Carrie, he loved nobody at all save Peony, that he was devastatingly lonely for Peony this moment, and that Providence had used his loyalty to her—the one lone virtue he had ever had—to destroy him.

His good-bye to Teckla was a kiss so brotherly that even he was disgusted.

[422]

The young man across the table, in the diner on the train to New York, was in uniform as a seaman in the Navy, but to Dr. Planish he had a classroom air.

The Doctor hinted that it had been hot on the campus —oh, yes, he was a college teacher himself.

The young man said cheerfully, "I got my Ph.D in economics last February, and then I enlisted, to save my alleged Liberalism."

"Hm?"

"I had the job of making arrangements for outside lecturers at the university, and all these propaganda associations tried to sell me on lecturers that, they claimed, had the patent on Justice, Political Integrity and Love for the Chinese, and I set up *too* much sales-resistance. Then on the radio I heard a ballyhooer who calls himself Charles B. Marduc—and I bet I know what the B. stands for—and he attacked Fascism so hysterically, and with such a suggestion that he was the one lone anti-Hitler, that I almost found myself beginning to be pro-Fascist, anti-Semite, anti-Chinese, anti-feminist, anti-socialized-medicine, anti everything I had always believed in. So I thought I better get into uniform and get away from everything resembling organized virtue, and do it quick."

The Doctor protested, "Now, now, now! There may be some useless or even mercenary national organizations, as you suggest, but surely the majority of them awaken the public to immediate needs which the Government, however benevolent, is too slow-moving to tackle."

"Maybe. I decided that the rule was that if an organization was set up to achieve one definite social end, it was

[423]

virtuous, but if it was started by one busybody who just wanted a career and a salary, it was bad. But that's a simple-minded rule. Look at the Anti-Saloon League. I suppose it did have a lot of good intentions as well as an awful lot of millions, and look at the way it made the ideal of temperance ridiculous for another hundred years. In a republic like this, I'm scared of *any* private organization that can spend thousands on propaganda—that can persuade thousands of people to telegraph their congressman to do what the private organization demands. It's a little too much like a private army—like the Brown Shirts."

"All very interesting," said Dr. Planish. "I'm sure the heads of the great organizations would be very much worried if they knew you had decided not to okay them! Good night!"

But the fact that this young man *was* unknown to him made him, in his compartment, feel naked in a cold gale that blew from a million unknown icebergs.

He reflected, "Oh, I must go back to Kinnikinick. Maybe start all over again."

If he did that, could he win again the love, the confidence, of his own daughter?

No, she was gone from his tribe. However virtuous and lean-minded and strong that Modern Young Woman was, in her way she was just as dependent on clash and clatter and conversation as Peony. She had heard the new call: "Go East, young woman, and grow up with the steel and concrete and the electric waves."

If he could have kept Teckla's sympathy instead of Peony's florid ambition and Carrie's self-righteousness, might he not have been a man instead of an executive secretary?

"No, no, don't misunderstand me," he said to his other self. "I don't mean any more—oh—well—you know—love-making with her, but if I could have Teckla for a neighbor and friend again."

He would! He'd be bold and masculine and put his foot down and go home to Kinnikinick.

When he came into the house on Charles Street, Peony cried, "It's so sweet to see you back! I did miss you, even if I have been so busy. How're all the hicks in Kinnikinick? Did they bore you to death? Never mind—we'll have a Real Time, a real New York evening tonight."

He said nothing whatever about a college presidency, or about returning to Kinnikinick.

After he came back to New York, Dr. Planish made a lot of speeches, and there was a quiet man who heard one of them, and this quiet man got to thinking.

He thought that the one thing that might break down American Democracy was the hysterical efficiency with which these pressure groups crusaded to seize all the benefits of that Democracy for themselves: the farm bloc, the women's bloc, the manufacturers' associations, the consumers' associations, the bar associations, the medical associations, the Protestant ministerial associations, the labor unions, the anti-labor unions, the Communist Party and the Patriotic Flag Associations. Drug stores combining to force legislation forbidding the sale of aspirin on trains.

Irish Catholics voting not as Americans but as Irish *and* Catholics, Swedish Lutherans voting as Swedish Lutherans, Arkansas Baptists voting as Neanderthals.

Catholics forbidding the Episcopalians to advocate birth-control, and Methodists forbidding the Unitarians to drink their ancestral rum, and people who really believe in Christianity overwhelmingly outvoted by all these monopolies.

Gangs of Fascists damning the Jews—always the opening gambit in any mass insanity—until the Jews are forced to create their own alliances, and these become a new Sanhedrin that censors the Jews who won't submit to the new Mosaic Law.

The Friends of Russia, the Friends of Germany, the Friends of the British Empire, the Friends of the Slovenes and Croats, the Sons of the American Revolution, and the Sons of Dog Fanciers.

Each of these private armies led by devout fanatics—not always on salary—who believe that the way to ensure freedom for everybody is to shut up every one of their opponents in jail for life, and that this is a very fine, new solution.

God save poor America, this quiet man thought, from all the zealous and the professionally idealistic, from eloquent women and generous sponsors and administrative ex-preachers and natural-born Leaders and Napoleonic newspaper executives and all the people who like to make long telephone calls and write inspirational memoranda.

33

CARRIE CRIED, "I have my job! Draftsman in a Hartford airplane factory. I'm leaving this evening."

Peony fussed, "You'll never be able to stand it, away from New York."

"With all my young men in the service, I won't miss one thing in New York, except Stan MacGovern's Silly Milly cartoons, and the music on WQXR," said the modern young woman. There was a distinct period in her sentence before she added, "Oh, and you and Daddy, of course."

When Dr. Planish saw her off on the train, when it had slipped away in the mammoth cave of the Grand Central, he felt that it had been years ago that she had gone from him, and that he could not remember her face exactly.

A week later, Peony said, "It seems so strange not to have her around, turning to me for advice and help every minute, and I know you feel awfully blue, breakfast all by yourself. And yet, in a way, I'm relieved. Young people today have no discipline, like you and I were brought up to. They think the world's created to serve and please *them!* So they never can settle down to really serious work."

Peony herself was extremely settled down to serious

work, for Winifred Homeward, her boss, was now doing a bi-weekly Interpretation of the War News on the radio. Peony and she read the newspapers daily. As there was a lot of valuable news in the papers, so inevitably there was a lot of valuable news in Winifred's broadcasts, and after telling the far-flung what the far-flung had themselves already read in the papers several hours before, Winifred revealed pantingly that the Japanese were now going to invade India—or else they weren't—maybe they were going to invade Siberia.

So Peony received thirty-five dollars every Friday, and spent fifty of it every Saturday, and began to explain to Dr. Planish just what the Japanese and India and Siberia were.

The Doctor himself was also serious. With Sherry Belden and Otis Canary, he was preparing blue prints (that's what they called them) for a new Marduc organization to be entitled "The Citizens' Post-War Reconstruction Advisory Planning Unit, Inc.," and already he was sending things for Professor Campion to sign.

The Doctor suddenly had new burdens, for Sherry Belden came in, without warning, in uniform, and he was decidedly impertinent before he went off to take a train:

"Good luck to the Unit, Planish. I suppose you'll pussyfoot just as successfully on freedom for India, and freedom for the Negroes in America, as we did during the revolution in Spain. Good hedging, Brother. I'll write you from Iceland or Dakar."

Now was that nice? the Doctor asked himself.

He could have taken a month's vacation, two months, whatever he wanted, and apparently no one would have cared, but Peony was a busy and important person who could take only one week, and that in late August, and he nervously waited for her . . . and he still had not said one word about becoming president of Kinnikinick.

He told her on the Maine coast, on the sea-washed rocks, by moonlight.

"Gosh, this certainly is beautiful, Peony—the way the moonlight falls on that—the tide, I suppose you'd call it, I don't know much about oceans, all these waves and foam and so on coming back and forth, and so clear—you could almost read by this moonlight—don't you think it's beautiful, pet?"

"Yes, I love Nature. When you're on vacation, I mean. You're real happy here, aren't you, Gid."

"Yes, it's so nice and quiet. I don't somehow seem to sleep so well in the city. But I'm afraid it's been *too* quiet for you here. Hasn't it?"

"Well, God Almighty, figure it out for yourself! Whole tourist business shot to pieces by this gas rationing, and me with a new wardrobe that would knock your eye out, and nobody to impress with it—not even hardly any dancing, except with college-boy waiters! And the way I been working on the war effort—if anybody ever deserved a swell vacation, I do. And we can't even go see if the other resorts are better. I think it's an outrage you and I can't get more gas. If that isn't Government usurpation, I just don't know what Government usurpation is, that's what *I* think about this Government usurpation!"

"But we got to save gasoline for the army."

"Oh, stuff! That's all very well for the common ordinary people that where the hell have they got to go to if they *did* have any gas, but people like us, that have been sweating our souls out on behalf of Democracy and the common people, and that have got the qualifications to appreciate scenery and had ought to get around and look over the general feeling in various parts of the country and report on it, why, when *we* can't get enough gas, it's an outrage! And they expect us to not get any real vacation and go back to our long winter's work in New York, so tiring——"

"Peony! Sweet! Darling! Shut up and listen! *This* winter in New York, maybe, but after that—— Austin Bull and the trustees of Kinnikinick seem to want me for his successor when he retires in the spring of 1943."

"You're craaaaazy!" was his spouse's comment. Her further remarks occupied something over ten minutes, but they may be summed up in the statements that she did *not* think it would be agreeable to live in a house on Lake Elizabeth, that she did *not* wish to be refreshed by association with the young, and that she had *not*, in her experience, ever found one of the Kinnikinick male faculty members with whom it was pleasurable to dance. She did not mention Professor Planish as an exception.

He interrupted; he tried to sound like Colonel Marduc:

"Now wait—wait a minute! You've been doing all the talking. What you overlook is that I do want to take this job, and I fully intend to. You might just as well get ready to come along."

[430]

"And you might just as well get ready to take a tumble to yourself! For years and years and years I've done nothing but toil and sacrifice and stay home twenty-four hours a day, devoting myself to your comfort and welfare, but the day passed twenty years ago when women were nothing but slaves!"

"Why, Peony!"

"Oh, I know, you'd like to go on selfishly demanding that all my ability be devoted to you and your whims and comfort and your alleged important position in the world, but—you may not 've heard about it!—there just happens to be a certain Mrs. Winifred Homeward, who needs me in her ve-ry im-port-ant undertakings, and I do not intend to bury myself in that dusty hole of a tenement and sit back any longer and watch you showing off and making speeches and making a monkey of yourself all day long and every evening—to say nothing of your Teckla Schaum, the old hag—oh, I suppose you two old playfuls had a lovely time tickling, when I wasn't there to——"

"By God, I'll divorce you and marry Teckla and *be* president of Kinnikinick!"

"By God, you'll do nothing of the kind! A sanctimonious backwoods school like that—you think they'd stand for a divorced president—even if she was the daughter of the chief grafter? No, no, my boy, you better get wise to yourself. I'd hoped I'd never have to tell you, but you might just as well know that neither Winnie Homeward nor the Colonel thinks you're so hot, and they'd of muscled you out of the DDD long ago, if it hadn't been for me!"

So rigid he sat, so frozen in the moonlight, that she stopped, made a sound of regret, and poured herself all over him:

"Oh, I didn't mean that! I was just trying to get your goat! All I mean is, the Marducs think I'm pretty good, too. Oh, my little big, forgive your bad Pansy! It makes me mad when you even *think* of admitting that New York has licked you, and want to sneak back, without ever stopping to think and realize how wicked and horrible it is to expect me to live in a corncrib and not even be able to go to the Stork Club with Hal Homeward—oh, no, no, my precious, you wouldn't do that to me, when I've given my whole life to you!"

"Maybe you would find it kind of slow back there, but still——"

They went happily enough to bed; they said nothing more of Kinnikinick; and when they had returned to New York, he devoted himself to Gilroy, Kevern, Vandewart and all the other millionaires who, in the dread and misty future, might provide inspiration if Colonel Marduc should unfrock him.

Ex-Governor Thomas Blizzard, in September, back home in Waskeegan, was nominated for United States Senator.

Dr. Planish gloated, "I certainly am glad I haven't slipped up on keeping Tom informed about the organization racket here, all these months. His chances to be President look better and better and—— Peony! How'd you like to be wife of the Minister to Cuba or Sweden some day?"

"And how'd I like to be *Minister* to Cuba or Sweden!" she shrieked, and laughed a great deal.

Two days later, toward the close of his office day, Dr. Planish had a long-distance call from Kinnikinick:

"That you, Gideon? This is W. C. Pridmore. I've got some bad news. President Bull died suddenly this morning. . . . Yes, it was sort of terrible. It was the first meeting of the student assembly, I was there, and he started to address the students, and then suddenly he stopped and looked kind of shocked and he crumpled up on the floor and before I could reach him, I and Dr. Evarts, he had already passed away.

"I'm speaking from the bank. The trustees, there's a quorum of 'em here, and they all send you their regards, they think very highly of you, and we want to offer you the college presidency officially. How about it, son?"

Dr. Planish stammered, "I'll call you back tomorrow morning. Ten-thirty, at the bank? Fine. Oh, give Mrs. Bull my extreme regrets. Call you tomorrow. Oh, give my love to Teckla."

Dr. and Mrs. Planish actually had no engagement that evening. No one had telephoned to them; no one to whom they tried to telephone was at home. Naturally, that was pretty distressing to Peony, and she whimpered, "This is the coldest, most indifferent town. Nobody in New York cares about anybody else. Sometimes I almost think you were right last summer—that we might 've been happier in Kinnikinick. After all, I must admit that as the president's wife, I would have a secure position. I could even tell Winifred to go to hell!"

The Doctor was certain now that there would be a God-given moment, some time this evening, to tell her.

They took a Fifth Avenue bus to 34th Street and walked up the Avenue in the autumn evening. The whole city was dimmed out. With the shop windows dark, the traffic lights showing only as small red and green crosses, the avenue was like a country lane. But the softened light merely lured Peony's excellent imagination, which played tonight about furs and diamonds. War-savings did not seem to stand high in her fancy. She looked into the shadowy shop-windows, at the veiled glimmer of glass and silver and suave wood, and crowed, "You wait till I'm making as much money as you are—you know how I hate to waste it, but what a shopping bat I'm going to have, one of these days! Oh, I do love a city where you can make money in the first place and have somewhere to spend it in the second!"

They dined with elegance in the Plaza Oak Room. Peony seemed to be in a tender mood, whether because of the chicken casserole, or the fact that Caesar, the headwaiter, remembered their name, or just out of fondness for her loving man; and the Doctor took the chance. He addressed her as carefully as though she were an audience of willing philanthrobbers:

"Dear, listen to me now, and don't say anything till I've finished. I know what a wonderful, loyal heart you have. When I hear fellows like Homeward or Gantry kick about what grafters or conceited gabblers their wives are, I always think how very fortunate I've been, all these years, in having my own little steadfast Peony. Hey—hey—wait 'll I finish! I know sometimes you get a little impatient with the slowness of life—all of us ambitious people do—but I know that in the long run, you're as faithful as Ruth—you have the genius for love that so few people have—you'd follow your husband wherever he had to go, even amid the alien corn, hunh?"

Though affected unfavorably by the mention of corn or other crops indigenous to the Middlewest, Peony said Yes, she certainly was a Ruth.

"Then—listen now, and don't interrupt—poor old Austin Bull dropped dead this morning."

"Oh, I'm sorry!"

"Pridmore telephoned me—they want me to take the presidency right away. Remember that it would be a job for keeps, not dependent on Marduc, and with a pension. We could get away every summer, and come to New York or, after the war, go to Paris. Don't be one of these stubborn women that, just because you said no before—— And I'll fix up something so that you'll have a job of your own, and be just as important as I am—maybe I'll get the college to start a radio. Sweetheart, this is important, and it's immediate. Can't I count on you?"

"Oh, Gideon, I don't want to be unreasonable. I know. I suppose I would be sort of a queen in Kinnikinick—that would be a joke on all the people that highhatted me when I was just a squab there, and—— Do you solemnly promise we'll go to Paris if— My God, will you look who's here!"

By himself, lordly in a leather armchair at one of the small tables against the wall, was Thomas Blizzard, Senatorial Nominee Blizzard, who was supposed to be at home in Waskeegan.

Peony dashed to him—Dr. Planish rolled across the room more slowly.

Blizzard rumbled, "Just a little strategic surprise visit. Flew on here from home to address the big rally at the Imperial Temple tonight—fly back tomorrow. You two come and sit on the platform with me. Be some big guns from Washington there—the Chancellor General and the Secretary of Education and Arts. Doc, your reports have been fine, and you, young woman, I hear you're developing quite a knack of winning friends and influencing people. Maybe you'll be quite useful to the crass Blizzard machine, some day. You're going to bring your husband and sit up on the platform, like a crown princess, aren't you?"

"You bet your life I am—you bet we are!" said Peony.

They came through velvet curtains as tall as a political lie out on the mammoth platform. Rising four full stories to the top balcony, so vast that they ceased to be individual human beings and became a mass of white dots on a dark sloping tarpaulin, were an audience of fifteen thousand.

"Look at 'em!" exulted Peony.

Her husband bleated, "You know, we have quite big crowds at Kinnikinick College, too."

"Not a quarter this size, not even at a football game, and nothing like so many photographers, and lookit the flashlights! Now you got to admit it's pretty nice to be up here with all these famous people, and all those dubs down there staring and staring up and thinking what important somebodies *we* must be!"

"I don't take any interest in showing off to a crowd."

"Rats! You do so!"

"Anyway, not like I used to."

Well, I do!"

Peony sat on the platform between her husband and the Chancellor General of the United States of America. To the husband she whispered, "Think, prob'ly just this morning the Chancellor was at a cabinet meeting, talking to the President and getting the lowdown on Russia and the second front and the Solomon Islands and everything—just like in history! And me sitting here right next to him, with ten trillion women looking up and envying me! And you expect me to go back and give teas for all the old maids on the college faculty!"

"Oh, I know," sighed Dr. Planish, and after a long time, "I know."

Afterward, when the audience trailed up on the stage to get the Chancellor's autograph, several of them asked Peony for hers, and one of them took her for the Chancellor's wife. She giggled about that, on the bus home; then she spoke with high seriousness:

"Honeybird, don't you worry if old Marduc lands in the

alcoholic ward, and leaves you without a job. The way I'm beginning to stand with Winnie Homeward and Tom Blizzard, I can always support you, and you can stay home and have a nice, long, quiet rest."

The distant urgent whistle of a ferry, laden with freight cars from Winnemac and Iowa and the uplands of California, awoke him, and for an instant his square face moved with smiling as in half-dreams he was certain that some day he too would take a train, and in some still valley find honor and dignity.

But the whistle sounded again, so lost and lonely that Dr. Planish fell back into his habitual doubt of himself, and his face tightened with anxiety and compromise. He felt now, at fifty, that though he might follow the path of notoriety for another quarter century, he would never recover from his mountain-sickness.

"Are you awake? Will you get me a glass of water?" said his faithful wife.

"Yes," said Dr. Planish.

"Do you know what? Some day we're going to have a penthouse on East End Avenue!"

"Yes?" said Dr. Planish.